ANTONELLO'S LION

Steve Katz

Antonello's LION

GREEN INTEGER
KØBENHAVN & LOS ANGELES
2005

GREEN INTEGER BOOKS
Edited by Per Bregne
København / Los Angeles

Distributed in the United States by Consortium Book
Sales and Distribution, 1045 Westgate Drive, Suite 90
Saint Paul, Minnesota 55114-1065
Distributed in England and throughout Europe by
Turnaround Publisher Services
Unit 3, Olympia Trading Estate
Coburg Road, Wood Green, London N22 6TZ
44 (0)20 88293009

(323) 857-1115 / http://www.greeninteger.com

First published by Green Integer in 2005
Copyright ©2005 by Steve Katz
Back cover copy ©2005 by Green Integer
All rights reserved

Design: Per Bregne
Typography: Kim Silva
Cover photograph: Steve Katz with art
by Antonello

LIBRARY OF CONGRESS CATALOGING IN PUBLICATION DATA
Steve Katz [1935]
Antonello's Lion
ISBN: 1-931243-82-4
p. cm – Green Integer 142
I. Title II. Series

Green Integer books are published for Douglas Messerli
Printed in the United States on acid-free paper

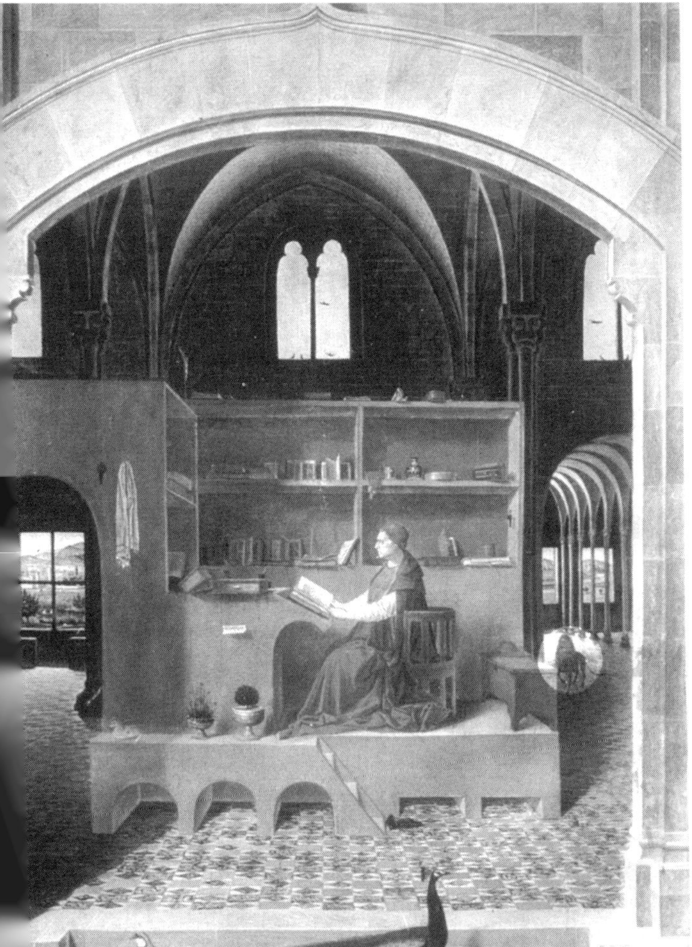

for
Primarosa Cesarini-Storzz
and
Francesco Tarquini

RED VENICE

RED VENICE : 1962

Isabel wore red sneakers, red socks, red coveralls over a red thermal. She had painted the walls of her studio red, and her large paintings leaned against them were almost entirely red, poppy red, bloodshot, stoplight red, blush, red as meat, though not meat exactly, but something drained from it, and not exactly blood red, but approaching. The surfaces looked not brushed but coagulated, clotted onto the canvases. Lately to talk to her at all, Solomon had to visit her in this studio. Since they had left the pensione in Venice, and rented a farmhouse outside Mestre, with its stone barn, she had turned into her studio, she spent all her time here, if not working, then inundated by this red flood, looking for all the great reds, she said, or else positioning red screens in front of the windows, or else napping under some red blankets.

The sculpture was a shock, some branching phallic forms she had done since the last time he was in the studio; and it was only two days since he'd been. It made him feel weird about his own art of doing nothing. Scads of work could suddenly appear, as if art exploded out of her, and now all at once these armatures, chicken wire, stuffed with rags dyed red and tied through the pentagonal openings, dangling like old bandages from wounds on gross twinned pricks.

"Oh, Sol." He knew she'd been aware of him from the moment he pushed the door open, but she played this harmless game of snapping out of trance, as if anything less transported would make her seem less an artist. Her drifting down to speak to him he took as the invitation, and he slid over to her and kissed her cheek. She turned to pick up a tray off her worktable.

"What do you think?"

"It makes me see red," he couldn't resist saying, though he knew his smart-ass mode risked little. She rarely heard his first remark.

"What?"

"I said I've never seen you do sculpture before." Solomon laid his words softly in front of her, and stepped back. This development in her stuff intimidated him. Why? The redness drilled deep into some drome where he skated on his fears, as if red was there to persuade him to enter her pulse, or some hostile corner of the womb.

"Look what Angelica brought." The tray she now held out to him was covered with small ceramic cups full of a milkwhite custard. "She's so sweet, and they're so nice to us. This is fresh ricotta, from sheep's milk. Mario makes it, you know. He's from Puglia, in the South. We can have some for lunch."

"I'm about to get us lunch. You never told me about this, that you were making sculpture."

"They're weird, huh? Nothing finished yet." She hugged one of the pieces. "I couldn't just stay with the paintings. I need something out in the middle, something confrontational."

Solomon sat down on the only yellow in the room, an old wicker settee she had painted to see how some lemon looked in all the tomato sauce. "They're like split male dicks."

"Well, thanks. I wouldn't know how to do a female dick. I call them my trees. See vein branchings. Blood trees."

"I meant whale dicks."

"Angelica told me the greatest thing, about what Mario said after the first time he saw all this red work. You know what?" She laid the tray of cheese in Solomon's lap. "He said it scares him, isn't that great?"

"Don't think it doesn't scare me, like it feels violent…"

"Not violent, but you know what he told her, that he said it felt too menstrual in here; at least that's what I thought she said, *mes…troo…ah…lay.* Isn't that so smart? He's a contadino, and works all the time with his crops, and a few animals, and he has such thoughts, such a direct response. I wish he'd write a review for Art News when I show the work. Do you think he knows how to write?"

"You want this to be called menstrual? Sometimes it looks a little garish, maybe." Solomon scooped a dollop of ricotta out of a cup with his middle finger, and laid it on his tongue.

"No. Not necessarily menstrual. Garish? Do you mean like vulgar, just because it's red? You find me vulgar? I think menstrual is good, though? No, but I'd like a response from some critic that was as visceral. Vulgar is not bad. I'd rather be vulgar than polite. That ricotta is really special, huh? I've never had ricotta so fresh before, not even from what's that place on Mulberry Street? D'Angelo's?"

"It tastes very white." He stood up, lifting the tray of cheese on his fingertips, to hold it above his head. "Come over in a few minutes, and lunch will be served."

Solomon laid the fresh ricotta on the table, and sliced some tomatoes and some pecorino and soft gorgonzola, arranged it all on a platter with slices of mortadella and some sheets of prosciutto carefully separated by butcher paper. He glanced out the window to the other side of the fence, where Mario was cutting the last of the artichokes.

"I hope we get a couple of those artichokes," Solomon said to Isabel, as she came through the door, wiping her hands on her coveralls. They looked more orange than red in the light of the kitchen.

"If he gives us some, we're going to pay for them this time," she said. "They deserve money like everyone else. I'd should give something back out of my Guggenheim year, like the Marshall Plan. Otherwise I'd feel like I was exploiting, living here so cheap with dollars."

She had wound her long brown braid into a bun. With her hair pulled tight back, Solomon noticed, her jaw seemed even more square, her blue eyes more metallic. He filled their glasses with a pale red wine. "This is that Bardolino we got in Vicenza." Isabel took a loaf of bread from a drawer next to the sink, cut some slices, spread ricotta on one, arranged slices of tomato on top of that, then peeled a translucent sheet of prosciutto off its paper. "This is precious," she said, holding it up to look through it into the light, then topping the sandwich with it. She sat down, and stared across the fence at Mario, who had been joined by Angelica, both working now.

"The way some people do some things, and others do others. Work is so interesting." Isabel remarked. "They have a hard life, and they're always cheerful. I couldn't live like that." She held her wine glass up to the light. "This northern wine is thin." She flicked the glass with her index finger. "Mario gave me a taste of wine his brother had sent up from the south. Really dark, almost black. They call it vino nero."

"Like your paintings. You should call some *studies in vino nero.*"

He didn't expect that to flatter her, but her smile flashed like a blade across the table. She bit the end of her sandwich, and shut her eyes. "Hmmmm, so good." She followed it with a swallow of wine. "Who would have thought I would ever be doing this red work." Her gaze lay blankly on Solomon. "I hope there are no Guggenheim police that come around, because this isn't anything like the work I showed when I applied. That was all Edward Hoppery figures in cityscape geometries. You know that stuff, my academic. This happened, I think, after we visited Dachau. Reality didn't hit me when I was there looking, but then I had these thoughts, that there were all those deaths, millions of deaths, and so little blood. That's why vulgar is okay for this. The neatness was horrible, that famous German efficiency."

It was the first time she had mentioned Dachau figuring in her paintings. It sounded like a rationalization; but he couldn't talk about it yet, not till he'd thought more. "I like these early green tomatoes," he shifted subjects. "Especially with the ricotta. I think they're grown to be green like this, but they're super tasty too."

"I felt something, like I had to work with that missing blood, memorialize it." She peeled another translucent slice of prosciutto off its paper, folded it onto the remaining sandwich, her eyes closed as she tasted the salts and acids. "It would be great," she said after some moments. "To be able to show this work at Dachau, or Buchenwald…hmmmm. Who could I talk to about that, Elliot Moorhead?" She paused to pull another morsel off the sandwich. "If the art world was in the whole world, and not just on 57th Street or Madison Avenue, I'd be able to arrange a show like that. It would be a revelation of blood. Could you imagine fishtanks full of blood by the windows and the doors of Buchenwald or Dachau or Teresienstadt?" She took another nibble. "Though I have to say, I don't think blood is the only way to look at my new work. It's just one layer. There's many ways to see it."

"Like everything you do."

That pleased her too. She winked at him, a thin piece of prosciutto fat caught in a corner of her mouth.

"Your new work, the red, and now Dachau," Solomon said. "I had a strong reaction to Dachau, of course, it made me sick—I'm half Jewish. You don't have any Jewish in you, but your work is affected by it. And my obsession is a Catholic painter."

"Yeah. What was his name?"

"Antonello, from that scrap of paper that turned up in the British Museum. I haven't been able to forget about it."

"Far be it from me. I don't get it. What's the deal about a dead painter? This is now." She raised her arm to indicate the door of her studio. "Art always happens now." She enjoyed hearing herself formulate such aphorisms. "It happens now, and it happens here." She swung her tongue to the corner of her mouth and pulled in the stray prosciutto. "But tell me that British Museum story again. What's the painter's name?"

"It's Antonello da Messina. You know, Saint Jerome In His Study is one of the greatest paintings of all time? And now maybe there's a St. Francis somewhere, hidden away for centuries, like his annunciation in…in…" It was in Sicily, he'd forgotten where. "St. Francis talks to the birds, or whatever, Antonellus Messaneus pinxit…"

"That's his name, Antonellus, right?"

"Antonello. Antonello da Messina."

"Well, he wasn't big in any of my art history classes, anyway. So tell me. You were in the British Museum, and then…"

"Yeah, I went to see a drawing that was attributed to Antonello, or one of his followers, you can't be sure. I told you this. They actually put the drawings into your hands. You hold it. A drawing by Rembrandt, whoever. It's a great experience."

She picked up an orange, and smiled at it. "So…"

"So they led me into this enormous room crowded with cabinets and stacks, lit by skylights, smelled like centuries of dust, and they sat me down at a long table, and brought out the folder of drawings, and they warned me not to use a pen. Across from me was this guy squinting into an old book of etchings on a bookstand, one of those gaunt-faced Brits in a tired old tweed jacket, you know, the kind that wears a bowtie, and always looks around with a disapproving scowl. The British academic gaze of scorn. His skinny neck was white as toothpaste, rising from the collar of a white shirt that was grey at the collar, threads hanging off. The bowtie was bright lime paisley, incandescent. When he met my eyes, he frowned. Six furrows, I mean deep grooves, formed on his forehead, that exactly paralleled the scowl on his mouth, as if seeing me multiplied his general disdain for everything. But something about him stunned me."

"Shit," Isabel exclaimed, as her knife slipped, sending a flake of peel flying at him across the table. She picked up another orange. "Then?"

"Then it happened. As if it was jarred loose by the reaction in my hands to the way the guy looked at me, a scrap, a curl of paper, that had been embedded maybe for centuries in the drawing, wafted down to the floor. Anyway, this came off the drawing."

"This was in your imagination."

"Bullshit. Listen to what I say. I saw this. I picked it up. It felt weird to be the first person ever to look at it, and there it was: …*issimus*…*t. Franciscus Antonellus Pinxit*. It was a shock, because what could that mean except that there was an Antonello painting or paintings even, of St. Francis. No record of this anywhere else."

"All this could be in your head, knowing your head. Where's this painter from?"

"Not in my head. It was inscribed on that paper scrap."

"Come on, Solly. You were having a psychotic flash,

an hallucination. Show me the scrap of paper."

"I wasn't going to steal that? I pressed it back against the drawing, and it was like sucked back into the paper. I tried to get it loose again, but it was stuck."

"That wouldn't be like stealing. I don't want to tell my child that his father is chicken, has no adventure in his heart. Where is this painter from?"

"Messina, from Sicily, and that's strange enough too, because most of them were from Tuscany, or from the North. I had to think, what if there is such a painting, and it's been lost? A painting by Antonello of St. Francis talking to the birds. It would be like finding a great undiscovered Massaccio, or Giotto. He did St. Francis, but Antonello…Antonello…" Sometimes Solomon's enthusiasm stole his voice.

"So that's what this is, some kind of nostalgia, speculative nostalgia?"

"No…no. I can't… That's not nostalgia, Iz. Nostalgia is for the recent past, for something within your lifetime. But there are so few paintings of his at all that have survived the earthquakes and general indifference, and he was the greatest painter, I think… I was just commenting, that's all, your interest in Dachau, and me, I'm obsessed with this Christian…although I think his greatness is beyond religion."

"St. Francis isn't even a Christian, Solly." Isabel progressed slowly with a spiral cut on the peel of her blood orange. "He's like an alien, an outer space guy, who landed on this planet and looked around and didn't see any reason to privilege humans. Why talk only to humans, don't you think? In fact, why talk to humans at all? If he'd been an underwater guy he'd talk to whales. They're more impressive. Anything imbued with life, and particularly with feathers. Of all the saints, he's the most likely from some outer space place."

Solomon sighed deeply. As hopeless as it usually seemed, every once in a while he needed to explain himself to Isabel, like her output made him want to justify his own inertia. "This stuff is important, Izzy. You know you're an artist, but I'm not an artist myself."

"That's right. What am I doing with someone who isn't an artist, who's just a…I don't know. What are you?"

"No, I don't know, I love to see the way you work." Sometimes he had to hold back because he sounded too obsequious. But she was all confidence, chutzpah, and that kept him off balance. "And I have a passion for all this, especially the Italian painting. It was like in the Renaissance artists began to turn their genius, like a communal spotlight, onto an understanding of the human being. The truth of what a person was in the space he or she occupies, physical and spiritual space, and psychological with Antonello. Just to figure out what it is; I mean, what do all these people…? That's unique in the history of world art. Most of the rest is narrative illustration, religious instructions, decoration, not discoveries about people, and how they fit into the world. And how did that get started in the goddamed Catholic church? Giotto, Massaccio, Piero, all broke through, and pushed way beyond the religious story. Antonello is at the peak of that genius, and so little work of his remains, and he is the most subtle, the most revealing psychologically. He's like Shakespeare, looking into the souls of men… It's like we've lost a whole language somewhere."

"Oh," Isabel exclaimed, as the curling peel snapped before she got all the way down the orange.

He had been reaching for a moment when he could explain his thoughts, that the art she participated in was a kind of personal rhetoric attempting to deal with the unthinkable situations of the twentieth century, that the renaissance was long over, but its human vectors that focus on people, is still important, and needs always to be remembered and reinvented, to maintain a humane polity, but he was glad he never got there. It would have been painful to finesse around her defenses an explanation of what he meant about her painting.

"I did this once, that's all," she whined, waving the broken curl of the peel in the air. "That waiter at that Ezra Pound restaurant in Verona, what was it? Dodici Apostoli? He could just spin the orange, or apple, or whatever, and it was voilá, perfect, a perfect spiral."

"I'm sure it's the knife." Solomon consoled her. "He always has a sharper knife."

"What color was that guy's bowtie? The guy in the museum.."

Solomon could never depend on her to listen to what he was saying, but only to grab a few details out of the flow.

"It was green, paisley."

"This is red," she waved towards her studio with the coil of peel.

"What are you saying?"

"Red is go."

Once lunch was finished, they settled for some moments into separate digestive reveries, watching Angelica help Mario strap a huge basket full of artichokes onto his back. Isabel looked at Solomon, everything mellow and sweet. Her eyes were moist with affection; at least, Solomon saw affection in her look, some tenderness for him, that had been so scarce since she'd got the new studio and plunged into her work; no more strolls arm in arm onto Piazza San Marco to explode the pigeons, or stop for a campari and watch people wander in the space, or cross the Rialto bridge to check out the fish market. She slid her chair closer, and leaned over to kiss him. He shifted to take it on the cheek and she gripped his hair, and turned his face, his lips to hers.

"I've been working so much, we've done very little of this." She kissed him again.

"Well, I've been busy too. You didn't even notice I

was gone all day Wednesday, in Padova."g

"I thought you might have gone somewhere."

"They have a portrait, by my guy; at least, half the scholars say it's by Antonello. He looks just like your friend, Hendrickson, even to the five o'clock shadow. The museum says its by Alvise Vivarini, but I don't think. It's too subtle. There's just a prejudice in the North against Sicilians."

"Did you bring me a postcard? I'd like to see Freddie in Renaissance drag."

"I was sure you'd want to go back with me, to the Scrovegni to see the Giotto. It's amazing the Scrovegni chapel survived in the war. Everything around it was flattened."

Isabel pushed closer to him. "I'd love to go to Scrovegni with Solly, see Giotto." She said this holding her sexiest pucker, then kissed him again right away. He swayed into her sexual thrall. She was always the one who had to start it. If he went after her now himself, she usually turned him back, and that made him stop trying. In these moments when she offered herself now, he felt he needed to get some when he could. He had chosen to be here with her, so he didn't complain. It wasn't like that in the beginning. At first she had enjoyed being rampaged by his juggernaut lust, but since Venice she wanted it all to be her idea. He loved her for whatever. Anything was okay with him, as long as it happened enough. He couldn't force himself on her. That wasn't his style. He'd like something maybe more mutual. He'd fail as a rapist.

"It's been a while, since we moved out here to Mestre, practically," she said. "We're always such busy busy peoples."

"Well, you look forever so distracted, and you're always in the studio. It's okay."

"I'm not tired now." She screwed up her face like a little kid.

"Well," he said, a little tentative. "Let's give it a try?"

"Try? Ohhhh. I think success is guaranteed." She pulled him out of his seat as she stood up. He turned for the bedroom, and she tugged on his belt.

"In there?"

"Yes. I want to do it there, all in the red."

"I...so much. I don't know..."

"What, you worry? Don't worry. Be sexy."

He entered her studio with his eyes narrowed almost to dark, looking through a slice of redness below his brows. She stepped behind a screen and he loosened his belt and unbuttoned his shirt and sat on the red blanket on the edge of her cot. He wished he was a smoker. Like she always took to a cigarette after sex as if turning away from an antagonist to greet an old friend. He would enjoy something like that to breathe in, even the stench of it, that he hated, just to smother all this redness. Then she stepped from behind the screen, in a lace chemise, a sheer black flimsy thing, and his anxiety fled. He immediately rose to know he would have no problem with this. She looked so pale under the black, and vulnerable with all that redness vibrating around her. He'd almost forgotten his lust for her, how much he wanted her body, her breasts pressing against the lace, the dark fur wedging her slim round thighs apart. In clothes, perhaps because of what she'd been choosing to wear, she lately had looked unappealing, plain and boyish; but when she came on like this, cheeks flushed, lips ripe, he was still overwhelmed. As he stood up, his pants dropped, and he pulled her to his body.

He could feel her sigh, and when she said, "Whoops!" It was like a small explosion against his belly. "Sometimes I…" Isabel touched his cock with the tips of the three fingers she slipped inside his skivvies, then she stretched the elastic out and down so his erection sprang into the room. She let it lie in her hand, and kissed it, then lightly slid it on her palm, and tipped his balls with her other fingers. "I almost forgot how I love your hands, Izzy." She closed her fist around him, and he pulled a breath between his teeth. "It's such a pink peony," she said, and grabbed some lipstick off the crate next to the cot, and stroked his erection with ruby grease. "Now it's more like something…more for me." Solomon looked down to catch a glimpse of himself like a stick of xmas candy, filling her cheek. He closed his eyes and felt her mouth, always just a little too much teeth. He never found the moment right to tell her that. He grabbed her hair, and a shoulder. Whenever he opened his eyes just a squint the redness hammered through. She slipped him out of her mouth, and smooched up his belly. "I think I'm so wet," she said, moving her thighs to press against his, to squeeze him. The narrow cot barely held their bodies, and he had to slip to his knees on the floor to caress her breasts. "I've missed these sweet wobbles," he said. He put his lips to her nipples, and pulled back just for a moment at a bitter taste that lingered as he tongued the aureole, and even when she pulled him back on top of herself, and straightened him into her wetness.

"Is it in?" he asked, meaning her diaphragm. He knew there was no jelly; he would smell that. She didn't answer, but just moved under him, in the way that made him crazy to do this only with her, a disconnect that happened below the waist, so she clung around his neck, in a fierce moaning as her pelvis moved out of her control, to its own small animal brain, and he slugged away abstracted as well into a rapture as they deepened into each other, fury of breath and sweat; and she rolled on top of him, still in the disconnect and they both screamed as if they were victims above of the plunder below, as she came, and came again, and he blew out inside her.

"Was worth the wait." He barely had breath for the words.

"Now I'll have your baby." She was grinning as she turned to him.

"My baby? I don't have a baby," he said, disingenuous.

"Now you do. I could feel it right away. I want your baby. I wanted to make this baby here in the red room."

He looked at her, her lips red, bubbles of saliva red. "Is your mouth bleeding?"

Isabel grabbed a hand mirror off the crate, and looked at herself. "Ohhh! Yes. I forgot." She showed him his own mouth.

"God," he said, when he saw the red bubbling off his lips. "Did I bite your tongue, or something. I don't even know what happened."

"It's nothing," she said. "I put some henna on my nipples, to make them rosy for you. And it worked. I have your baby."

"How can you be so sure?"

"I know. I always knew I'd know."

Solomon leaned away from her. He had to challenge the way she could make him feel helpless. "So what now? Do we get married now, now that it's a baby?"

"Don't be silly. I don't want to marry. I want to be a mommy. I don't want to be a wife."

"Isn't this my child too?"

"Yes, yours. I've wanted yours. I always wanted to have your child."

He felt flattered. He felt betrayed. "Shouldn't I have had a say in this? "

Isabel shrugged, grinning at him dumbly.

Solomon looked again in the hand mirror, at his hennaed mouth. "Then why not marriage?" He didn't know even if he wanted to be her husband, or anybody's. He just needed to make a move that might relieve his sense of helplessness. The smugness in her smile, like when she was too pleased with her work, twisted his pride. He felt distant and lonely, and didn't want to seethe into anger. "You shouldn't have done this. I hope you're wrong, you have to be wrong, because if you're pregnant…But it's stupid. It's just speculation, anyway. You're not even pregnant."

"Don't get pissed, please. I'm almost certain I am. Ninety-nine percent. I was sooo ready. And it's okay, not your problem." She pulled a red blanket across their bodies.

"I don't get why you didn't even say. You didn't even ask me."

"It's not…It's a gift, take it as a gift. You should see it that way. There will be a beautiful little girl child, and she will call you dad. Conceived in red."

As he opened his eyes, the redness punched into his brain. He moved her body, so he could slip from under her, off the cot to the floor, where he rested on his knees a moment, his head leaned on the mattress at her feet.

"Are you mad at me?" she asked, coyly.

He stood up, and looked down at her, in a deceptively vulnerable sprawl across the cot, pale flesh rusty in the tinges of light, red blanket bunched in a heap below her knees. Her mouth, hennaed from his kissing, looked like a gash, and the nipples were a pair of wounds.

"Mad at me?" She made her voice very small.

"No." He squeezed shut his eyes and saw a green reversal at the backs of his eyelids. "Yes."

"Why, Solly? This is good."

"I think I'll go. I need…I'm going to go into Venice, take a gondola ride, or something, or maybe I'll go out to Murano and watch them blow glass."

"Do you want me to come?"

He knew she wouldn't come with him, and hated these little tricks in the game of the heart. "Sure, if you want to." He matched her move.

"No. I think I'll stay today. I've hardly done any work today."

"You've accomplished plenty."

She smiled, taking that as an affirmation. "Thanks, Solly. I love you a lot."

That last phrase was the red dragon he rode mutely out of the room.

He walked slowly to the train station, where he could catch a vaporetto to the Accademia, to take another look at Christ at a column, or that portrait of a young man. Or he'd go to the Correr museum, if he could catch it open, for the Pietá with three angels again. He needed to see something. Fuck the women. Down with the women that twisted his mind. His happiness was to look for this St. Francis, to do this for all the people in the world. That was how he had chosen to spend his trust, his small income, just enough to live frugally in New York, a little better in Italy. An income that made him feel just uncomfortably outside the world of working people. This was why he had come with Isabel, not to get tangled in her red web. Let her suck up the whole red world into her womb. He would find this painting. He would not indulge himself, as his brother did, in mere danger and adventure. Yet it gave him an heroic premonition—a feature in the New York Times, himself and the St. Francis of Antonello.

But no loneliness was ever as painful for him as this intimacy betrayed. The beauty of Venice was a sudden cruelty. The reflections off the canal, and the tinkling of small waves against the walls, washes of light across architectural fretworks, gondolas gliding on the luminous chop, lovely girls whispering in the shadows, all seemed an inundation of torture, beauty so intractable and distant. Snared in his own revolting sensitivity, unable to say, "O, did you see that?" to anyone, particularly not to Isabel who now seemed to have disappeared for him, at least in the way he had ever hoped to be with her here in Venice; so that the place became unbearable now, reduced to the stench of sewage off the water. He had a moment of nostalgia for New York City, where there was no conflict between the way things looked, and how they could stink.

For some holiday's sake, his museums were closed, so he went to San Marco, the piazza, to sit down with an expensive aperitivo, watch the dreadful pigeons fly through the light slanted from the clouds, and try to think of Antonello, Antonello his friend, arriving from Sicily, in Bruges, alone, his first trip so far to the North.

UPP

UPP : 2001

Nathan watched the Fiat Uno wedge back into traffic and disappear. He felt very stupid. "God, when someone pulls his car up next to you, and says 'Psssst!' you ignore it, you just don't answer, not in Rome, not New York, not anywhere." He held up the jacket he had just bought, a smooth black suede folded into a clear plastic sack. "I can't believe I did that. I've got to change my life. Stupid. I was just stupid."

"Sweetheart, it's not a big deal. Don't beat yourself up. This could happen to anyone." Miriam peered through the trees lining the Lungotevere. "What is that ahead there?" They'd arrived in Rome that morning so she was still disoriented.

"Come on, your basic Vatican, Mims. Michelangelo's cupola, pietà in there, Bernini altar in there, museum, Raphael frescoes, restored Sistine Chapel. Your basic Pope."

"Sorry, I just never saw it between the trees, from this angle, before."

Nathan slapped at the package in his hand. *"Please, I am lost. You look like a nice man."* That's how he started."

"He's right." She leaned over to plant a kiss on his cheek. "You do look like a nice man."

He shrugged away from her affection. "That's what's got to change, among other things. I'm not a nice man, Mims. Not that kind of nice. *"I am not from here, please. How do I get to the Vatican?"* I should have told him he was in the wrong city, that he should go to Naples. Then he pulls that, *"I'm a fashion designer"* stuff, *"here for a conference. You're such a nice man,"* and he hands me a jacket, because he says I was a nice man. *"I have one of these left over."* Then he says he just wants a little money for gas. If I'd been here a few more days, and had my Italian oiled, he couldn't have done that to me. I talked to him in the first place because I wanted to practice my Italian."

"It's okay. Be happy. Don't obsess about it. You're in Italy, and now you have a new jacket. It's a nice jacket. You're so lucky, and I'm happy for you."

"That's not the point. Weren't we warned to watch out for gypsies? He wasn't even a gypsy."

"It only cost you exactly sixty-some dollars, a hundred thousand lire."

"He knew immediately how much I had in my wallet. He was so slick."

"You can't blame him for that. It's the way he survives." Nathan prided himself on being an old Italy hand, and not your average tourist. Miriam knew he wanted some reassurance from her to cool down the humiliation of the con, but she wasn't going to coddle him. "You make your living managing other people's money, Nathan. So does he."

Nathan's roll of his eyes and exaggerated sigh of exasperation at her irony and unwillingness to sympathise seemed just silly to her. She slapped the plastic sack draped over his arm, *PERVIN, alta moda, made in Italy,* printed in gold across it. "So now you have a jacket. I've been here just as long as you, and I don't have anything yet."

Nathan turned away from her, and swung the package as if to fling this jacket over the wall, into the river. A sleeve slipped from the package *"Pssst!"* Nathan repeated, as if talking to the river. "Rid of all of it. The whole…everything." He held a sleeve out to Miriam. "He stole this jacket." Now he looked squarely at the jacket. "This is a stolen jacket," he said to Miriam.

Miriam felt the sleeve. "It feels nice."

They continued walking in silence.

"What a dreary walk," Miriam finally said.

"Mims, this is the Tiber River, the emperor Tiberius Gracchus etcetera etcetera."

"I think it's just because I'm hungry. Everything gets dreary when I need food. Maybe I'm hypoglycemic."

"When we get to Trastevere, we'll eat something there. I remember the world's greatest pizzeria."

"Save me from pizza, not my first day in Italy. Unless you absolutely need to have a pizza, my handsome man of jackets and pizzas." She kissed him again on the cheek, and this time he leaned his cheek towards the kiss.

They wound up in a small restaurant on a side street, La Cucina di Maria, specialità Abbruzzese. Miriam gripped her knife and fork in separate fists on the table as the waiter brought the pasta course. "I'm so excited now about eating lamb, and I used to be such a vegetarian," Miriam said.

"When was that? That was before I knew you."

"That was when I was serious about diving. Maybe if I'd eaten meat then, I could have gone to the Olympics."

"You mean, with the team?"

"I was good. I don't talk about it anymore, I guess."

"You mean as a competitor? Diving?"

"Now I'd eat anybody. I'd eat Bambi."

Miriam shrugged, a little annoyed that she'd brought this up at all. She lifted a tortellini out of her soup, and examined it on the end of her fork. "Everything is meat, anyway. These look like little anuses."

"Assholes."

"Anuses. Asshole refers to character. You're always an asshole, you're never an anus."

"How many assholes have you looked at, present company excluded?"

"I was working for Dr. Storm, remember? He was a proctologist, remember? That's where we met. One of my first memories of you is your winking little tortellini, or do you say tortellino?"

"I thought…you looked at me?"

"I looked at it. I looked at all of them. I never told you? Not a big deal. Eat your clam sauce before the spaghetti gets cold."

After lunch they strolled around the old quarter, paused for coffee in the piazza of Santa Maria in Trastevere. "This is all changed," Nathan mused. "This used to be a workingman's, revolutionary, bohemian, artist neighborhood. Now all these old facades, and narrow streets, the creaking shutters, the flaking balconies, it's all just a patina over the disgusting gentrification, modern renovation, expensive apartments. It's sad. It's a ruse. It's bourgeois sentimentality."

Two grey-suited men crossed the piazza in opposite directions, gesturing broadly with their free arms, as they talked into cell phones.

"At least it's being preserved. I mean, but where would you live, if you lived in Rome? This would be a good place. I'll bet those two suits are talking to each other?"

"Yeah, but it's sad. It's not like real."

"That's just the times we live in, Natto. Everything has to be made up. Everybody's busy and anxious, but nothing's really strenuous or physical any more where we work, so we invent difficulty, tests of strength and endurance, phony reality shows. Extreme sports. We have to prove we're alive. Work is easy so play hard. If it's not fake, it's not now. Like this place. It's all restored, propped up with sentiment. I don't understand why it bothers you so much. Why isn't that good? It's just Italy. I can't take Italy seriously, anyway. It's a big museum. O, sweetie." She stroked his cheek. "Don't cry. You look like you're about to cry."

Nathan rubbed his eyes, didn't know where this rush of emotion came from. "I'm…I don't know."

"What is it?"

"I just thought about my father. He disappeared into Italy, somewhere."

She kissed his cheek.

"I never even knew him, but secretly I'm obsessed with who he might have been."

"You never talk about that. You never told me anything about your father before."

"I never met him. I know I was conceived there in Venice, and whoops, he goes south without Brightwatch, because she's painting, and he's doing some research, mom tells me, and then he's gone, disappeared."

"I didn't know your mom was a painter too. I thought she was always a performance artist."

"She never told me about him till I was a teenager, and I came here with her for the first time. Now when I come to Italy, I feel like I'm coming to my father, if that makes any sense. I feel like he's here, somewhere in the stones, in the paintings, in all the people. He wasn't even an Italian."

"Like you even see him in a jacket someone conned you to buy." Miriam needed to change the mood. She wasn't used to Nathan vulnerable, and was uncomfortable dealing with real emotions.

"Okay, now you call me a tortellino for buying that jacket. A guy pulls up and asks me how do I get to the vatican. That's like you're in New York, and someone sells you the Brooklyn Bridge."

"A little jacket is not the Brooklyn Bridge," she said, cupping his face in her hands, and kissing him this time on the lips. "But you are my tortellino. It was love at first sight."

They crossed the Tiber by the Garibaldi Bridge, headed towards the Ghetto, first stopping by the steps of the synagogue. The little church of San Nicola in Carcere, where the Jews were required to attend mass once a year, on a certain day, to apologize for being Jews, sat facing them like a small vault.

"I'm Jewish," said Miriam. "But I never thought about any Jews in Rome. Is that why you brought me here?"

"My father was Jewish too." They walked down a narrow street, past some shops with signs in Hebrew. "They still make the best rugalach here, and macaroons you wouldn't believe." He looked at the jacket again.

"Nice man. I'm a fashion designer," he mumbled through clenched teeth.

"Drop it, Natto. That's enough. Where do we meet Holly and Max?"

"At Campo De' Fiori, but that's not till five." He pulled the jacket out of its sack, and held it up. "Antelope suede. If this is antelope suede, I'm the abominable snowjew. It's naugasuede." He held it up in front of the Fontana delle Tartarughe, the tortoise fountain.

"You are the abominable snowman," said Miriam. "And this was the abominable snowjob, Okay?"

"I gave him a hundred thousand lire, for gas, he said he needed money for gas."

"Nathan, that's maybe sixty-five dollars, and it's a nice jacket. If it were New York City he would have hit you over the head, taken all your money, even stolen whatever jacket you were wearing."

"Do you really think it's nice?"

"Yes. It's elegant. It's Italian fashion, it's Alta Moda."

"They probably stole a whole truckload of these fashions."

"It's a very spiffy jacket, Natto. You'll enjoy wearing it. How many times can you wear something that has a story like this? Wherever you wear it, you can tell this story. It's going to be a social asset, so stop obsessing. You get on my nerves. Let me enjoy this fountain. How come I've never seen anything about this fountain before? It's so sweet." Water flowed into the grey basin below from beside the four bronze boys, each resting a foot on a dolphin. The stone tortoises clambered up the sides of the upper basin.

"This is the first fountain built in Rome," said Nathan, not knowing if he was right.

Except for someone occasionally hurrying across the small piazza, they were the only ones paying attention to the fountain.

"I think this is my favorite," Miriam said. "Because we are alone with it, and because unlike all the other fountains, this one is in the ghetto."

"Helps also that it's so beautiful; beauty counts for something, Mims." A trick of the clouds levered a swath of sunlight just then across the piazza, sparkling the water, illuminating the bronze.

"Yes it does."

"It's the grace of those youths, against the struggle of the tortoises clambering into the bowl forever at the top," said Nathan, happy to have someone snug with him on one of his light transports of insight.

"That's nice," Miriam said. "Do we learn that from the Eyewitness guidebook?" She scrunched up her cheeks when she saw how her sarcasm annoyed him. "I'm sorry, baby, baby. I didn't even know you ever liked art, sweety."

Later they crossed Via Arenula, onto Via degli Specchi, and then onto Via Giubbonari, mosying towards the

Campo de' Fiori. It was after five, light moving towards the gilded hours, the magical time of strolling and shopping.

"Holly seems really good for Max. I'd call them a success. And they're good with the kids, even Kevin in these difficult years. Holly puts up with a lot from him." Miriam looked at herself in the window of a Salumeria.

"He likes lanky women," Nathan said.

"I'm not lanky."

"That's why you're not with him any more, and Holly is. You're compact, and athletic, and you're with me."

"It isn't because I'm not lanky that we stopped seeing each other, Nathan."

Nathan followed her into the store.

"On our next trip we'll go to Rio. I've read that they're good at lipo, and I'm sure if they can take out they can easily put in, even bone, so you'll be lanky enough to get back with Max, no problem." He winked to try to neutralize the discomfort the subject created.

"That's not what I mean; I said it wasn't because I wasn't lanky. That's one of those words that sounds ridiculous if you repeat it too much. Lanky lanky lanky. And they've had a kid already. Look at that, a whole big jar of rabbit sauce." She picked it up and turned it in her hands. "What makes you think I want to get back with him? Besides, Holly is good at it. I wouldn't be good at raising kids. I didn't get along too well with his Kevin."

"Kevin's a good kid."

She tried to smell the sauce through the jar. "Do you think this is lucky sauce, like a rabbit's foot?"

"And Tanya, she's the Lolita of the house. One of the precociously sexy eleven year olds."

"Shame on you, Nathan."

"Anyway, tell me I'm not someone you settled for after Max. A compromise." He knew he shouldn't be in this territory. He shifted subject. "I think we'll buy that rabbit sauce, give it to Steve and Vicki, see how the vegans deal with a kilo of gourmet rabbit?"

"I don't…you're being silly. I don't compromise. That's cruel." she said, as they waited by the counter to be served. "You are definitely my upgrade, my very big improvement. Max drove me crazy. You know what he is. A pumped ego without a pressure valve. I'm sure I did him bad too." She shifted to look in the case at the cheeses, and the Parma prosciutto, and the pancetta, and the soppresatto, and the mortadella with pistachios. "It smells like heaven in here."

"Italy is definitely for the nose."

"What else did you get?" She snooped into the bag.

"Olio Santo." He lifted out the bottle, shaped into an S. "It's olive oil flavored with hot pepper. I don't know why they call it holy oil. Nice bottle, huh?"

The light of the street they stepped into as they left the salumeria had changed palpably, as if little angels from all the Caravaggios and Berninis in the city had decided to rise into the actual air to sprinkle well being over the old streets. Stones glowed as if from within to reflect beatitude on all the human faces. Everything slowed, slow as the light, movement of everyone, everything that moved, like streamers in a fading wind, and the Romans, strolling in their elegance, were buoyed upwards by their shopping bags which they held in front of themselves like lanterns. Some dispersed across the stones of the Campo de' Fiori, and some elevated above in an effortless levitation. How did they do it? Nathan and Miriam shrugged, and pressed their shoulders together, delighted to be in this agreeable other culture, to feel so much of its loft, so leavened in the evening. Much earlier the flower markets had shut down on the Campo dei Fiori, but the fragrance of lilac and hyacinth lingered, crosshatched by spiciness. A cacophony of silverware bruised the silence as restaurants prepared to open for the evening meal. Shoppers and strollers moved through the space like clouds, some out over the pavement, some along the walls and entrances, and some up into the atmosphere along the eaves of buildings, their callings to each other like a conversation among whales. — Did you see Elisabetta with Piergiorgio and the princess? — Where can you afford those shoes, you didn't buy them at Principe? — It's the fascists, the fascists again eating our pants.

Holly and Max showed up, drifting in luxury above all pedestrians, in their exorbitant luxury tour. "Natto, Mims." Max's voice came down on them like the voice of God, except they'd heard the voice of God before, and that sounded more like Charlton Heston, not these tones of Max's Brooklyn. They looked up to see Max, himself. Holly swooped and dived like a swallow, giggling loudly as if she'd never flown before.

"Come down. Come down, Max. I want to show you something."

"Can't," Max shouted down. "Not till the tour ends. There's a finale."

Nathan made a megaphone with his hands, "I got a new jacket you'll like."

"Yes. That's good." Max swooped away.

"Holly looks pretty buoyant, for a lanky woman," Miriam said, cattily.

"Those upper level tours are good; expensive, but they get some of the crowd off the street."

As if to a certain music calling them to dance, waiters suddenly bounded out of all the restaurants, spinning plump, fresh, porcini mushrooms into the air, that if they weren't snatched by members of the tour group, kept rising like frisbees above the roofs into the Roman sky, where they became dark matters of the night. In the brochure, Nathan remembered, they promised porcini for everyone, at least, and perhaps truffles, but the truffles were unlikely. Miriam landed lightly on Nathan's shoulders, a meaty bolete in each hand. Max landed with overflowing armfuls, and twisted his ankle slightly, so he stumbled around till Nathan grabbed him and propped him up.

"How did that feel?" Miriam asked. "How did they get you up there in the first place, and what was it like?"

"It was good. It felt like Italy used to feel, once upon a time."

"How do you know how Italy used to feel once upon a time? Do you mean before or after Mussolini? Or during?" Nathan asked. "When were you ever here once upon a time?"

"No, but you know, like I heard about it, like Fellini, like you never touched the ground, like you were always in a movie or a dream. Life was more or less Felliniesque if you came here. Parties, affairs. Life was gay, in the old sense of the word. You've seen those early Antonioni films. Monica Vitti. And when I was up there I felt like peeing on all the little people walking around down below."

Holly waved to their tour group as it started lifting away for Castel Sant'Angelo. "We should go with them, just to get our money's worth, but I've been to that castle plenty, and they're supposed to be coming back over here anyway. We're going someplace after dark, where you can see the lit-up dome of the Vatican through a big keyhole."

"Didn't you feel like peeing on everybody when we were up there, Holly? It was almost irresistible. Would just feel like a drizzle down below."

"It's easier for a man."

"Like the putti peeing out of the clouds in a big mural I remember in Venice. Is that by, uh, Tish…Tiepeelee? We should go to Venice."

"What a fun idea," Holly said, and kissed Max on the cheek. "You're so full of them."

"Of them? Of what?"

"Good ideas, Max. So many fun ideas. What'll we do about Kevin and Tanya?"

"They're happy as clams in Switzerland. Another couple of weeks would be great for them. Mmmm. Venice." Kissing Holly, he threw an arm over Nathan's shoulder. "I had one great business idea while we were bopping around, and I'm going to run it by Nate, see what he thinks. It's a virtual reality thing, could fold right into some stuff we're developing now."

"Venice could be such a great idea, because you know what I just learned about Nathan? He was conceived in Venice," Miriam said, too much enthusiasm making Nathan cringe. "And his father disappeared in Italy."

"Amazing," Max winked. "I never knew he had a

father at all."

Nathan forced a grin into his cheeks. He needed to separate from them, and started walking away. "Good idea," he heard Holly say behind him. "Let's go to Piazza Navona, sit down with some ice cream and coffee. My feet are killing."

Nathan reached Corso Vittorio Emanuele just as the semaphore was changing, and he crossed over, leaving Miriam and the rest stranded on the other side. He lingered in Piazza di San Pantaleo, feeling the embrace of the Museum of Rome, until the light changed again, and his friends started to move. Miriam waved at him to wait, but he didn't. He set out alone into the narrow feeder street, then stood there at the mouth of Piazza Navona, peering into the space as if looking for someone, till finally everyone caught up with him.

"Why didn't you wait for us?" Miriam scolded.

"I am waiting," he said, darkly.

In the mingling of sunset and pale electric lights the sky above Piazza Navona arced like a long honey-hued lozenge. The piazza was packed in the mild evening, large chunks of Japanese tourists loitered here and there waving cameras. Holly got waylayed by a quintet of Japanese girls who wanted their pictures taken, on each of their cameras, with the obelisk and Bernini's River Ganges as background.

"Look at this," Nathan's humor improved as they settled at a table. He unfolded the jacket, stood up and put it on, strutted in front of the table.

"How much did you pay for it?" Max heaped the porcini on the table. "We'll find some restaurant, and they'll cook these up for us. They're supposed to be delicious."

"I hope they're not some poisonous…"

"Don't be silly," Max interrupted Holly.

"Do you want it? What will you give me for it?"

"You mean that sweater…I mean that jacket? I like it a lot. I'll give you a hundred dollars. I don't even need a jacket." He touched the sleeve. "It's suede."

"Antelope suede." Nathan winked at Miriam, who rolled her eyes. She dropped the porcini into the jacket bag.

"Poor antelopes," Max made a sad face. "Aren't there some animal rights people around here with buckets of blood? I'll give you a hundred and twenty."

"Don't worry. I think it's fake. It's naugalope."

"And definitely a popular jacket," Max said. "Look around."

Throughout their caffe, and across the piazza, at almost every table someone was showing off this very same jacket, smooth black suede, or some in grey—flat, simple elegant Italian styling.

"Aren't you appalled?" Miriam said.

"I don't know. I don't think so," Nathan smiled. "I've never been swept by a wave of fashion before. They must have stolen a semi full of these. I wonder if

49

all these other tourists are nice men too."

"I see some women."

"Okay, nice people."

"It's definitely alta moda. It's high fashion," Miriam said to Max.

"Look, if you really don't want it I'll give you a hundred and fifty. You just don't find a jacket like that at home."

"I think we ought to march somewhere, all the jackets. To Piazza Del Populo. All the nice people in the nice suede, marching down the Spanish Steps."

"Hamachi unagi saba toro uni domo arigato." Holly finally found the table after completing her snapshot chore with the Japanese girls. "If I didn't go to eat sushi a lot, I would never know any Japanese at all, except banzai, and hara kiri." The Japanese shuffled off in thick squadrons, leaving a much greater concentration of suede jackets among the tourists.

"It's interesting they didn't sell any of these to the Japs," Nathan noted.

"They've probably got one of them, and that's all they need. They'll make their own, better ones," Max said. "I'll give you a hundred and sixty, my last offer."

"It's a deal. You own a jacket."

"Why do you want that jacket, anyway?" Holly asked.

"Because he's going to take it back to one of his

sweatshops, and make copies of it, put his own labels on it, and make his next million." Miriam said, "I remember from when I used to sleep with him. He never slept." She turned a nasty smile towards Holly.

"Oh," Holly responded. "He sleeps well now."

"Yeah, but I'm never asleep. Listen to this, Nate. I've got this idea for a virtual Italy, I thought. It could be a whole tour of Italy in virtual reality. No muss, no fuss, in the comfort of wherever. You got all the monuments, all the statues and paintings. We hook you up for automatic delivery, from pizza to ossobucco, as soon as you log on. Or pasta of your choice. You won't have to put up with taxi rip-offs, over-priced hotels, funky bathrooms, weird food. We could do all of Europe. It would be great for Asia, because who really wants to go there; I mean, you might want to go there, but once you're there do you really want to be there, and the diseases? Who wants the health risks? What do you think, Nate?"

"Max, please. We all know about your golden touch, but virtual Italy…"

"Don't be negative. Can't be negative. First you get the idea. It doesn't come from nowhere. It's a good idea. It's an inspiration. It'll benefit a lot of people. This is a money idea. You can take my word for it. Then you apply the attitude of get it done, go for it straight ahead, and don't deviate. No negativity. Then you go to work on it. Virtual Italy. Virtual France. Virtual Pittsburgh.

Virtual Mongolia."

"I'm not sure I'll want to go there, Nate. Anywhere virtual."

"I'll go there," Holly said.

"I never saw any virtual reality," Miriam said.

"Max'll show it to you one day, if you ask." Holly smiled.

"See, I've had a team working on these dildonics for sixteen months. It's two guys, and a woman. Very bright. They've got us really close to presenting a product that will change the world. This virtual Italy would be another powerful line for them to follow. The woman, her name is Toni Gruber, she's an MIT grad. She's a genius, especially quick, and she's got an imagination the size of Las Vegas."

"What do you mean by dildonics?" Miriam shrugged.

"It's virtual sex, but way beyond," Holly explained. "Now they can wire you up so you actually feel like it's happening to you. Max's system will make it easy, like opening the door into the most sophisticated house of ill repute."

"Good repute," Max corrected.

"It's clean, it's dry. And no STD risk, what a boon in this day and age."

A singer dressed in a grey satin Oakland Raiders team jacket and a black mini, with torn black net pantyhose, stopped by their row of tables to sing some tunes in her native Slovenian, Bulgarian, Serbo-Rumanian, Latvo-Hungaric—none of them recognized the language.

"Have you and Max ever had virtual sex?" Miriam was locked on the subject.

"Not yet," said Holly. "It sounds so…so…I want to say spiritual, but that's not what I mean. It's more specific, more like on demand."

"Yeah," Nathan said. "I bet Max could arrange us a whole virtual life."

"A virtual father, at least. You could have a virtual father, Nate. We'll get Toni Gruber to work on it. Toni Gruber can do this."

Nathan closed his eyes as if to squeeze Max's words away. Any conversational drift towards his phantom father felt like an assault. Something was wrong. He would have to change his life, he told himself again. His heart constricted in his chest, like he was having a virtual heart attack. What a relief when the waiter set down the gelato and the coffee, to give something else to occupy everyone's mouths. The singer explained in fractured English that her songs were about the sufferings of her people, then she sang in English a few sour choruses of "You Light Up My Life," and passed the hat.

"Omigod, now I get it," Nathan slapped his forehead.

"What do you get?" Miriam asked. "What language was that?"

"Now you don't want to sell me the jacket?" Max said.

"Now I know. I thought I'd seen the guy who sold me the jacket before, and now I know."

"We had a deal. You don't back out on a deal. I wouldn't."

"Here, you can have it." He draped the jacket around Max's shoulders.

"It was a deal. I'll pay you for it. You don't have to give it to me."

"Mims, remember the last time we were here, when we went to the Villa Borghese?"

"You mean the place with all the Roman statues, the one on the hill?"

"No, no. You had to make a reservation for this museum, because it was being restored for so long. It's in that beautiful park, and it was raining, and we were walking through and that guy had stepped out of the car, and was pissing by the door of his car. You said oooh because his cock was so long."

"Is this for free? I don't like to take anything without paying," Max said. "Then I feel like I owe you."

"You have to learn to accept gifts," Holly told him.

"Credit is one thing. That's doing business. But I don't like to owe personally."

"Long cock?"

"Yeah, you remember. It was where all those beautiful statues, by Bernini. I have to go back there. And you remember I stopped for a long time to look at that portrait, remember…"

"No. not at all. Why should I?"

"It was by Antonello Da Messina, you remember. I told you he was the painter my father was obsessed with."

"The one who disappeared?"

"I had only one father. And that was the painter…"

"It can't be, because this is the first time I've ever heard about your father. I used to ask you about your father, but you never would answer, so I gave up."

"Come on, Mims. It was that picture. You just didn't listen. We stood in front of it for a long time, because I was so obsessed with it, and you said it was spooky because it looked so much like Kevin Spacey."

"Okay. Yes. Vaguely, but I don't remember about your father. We went to see my father, but you never said anything about yours. As if you didn't have one."

"You did take me to meet your father. That was very sad."

"Why do you say sad? He's happy enough."

"He's demented. He's always obsessing about fire. He never leaves the house."

"When my dad leaves the house now, he always disappears," Holly said. "He gets lost."

"Wait. Isn't he a mapmaker, a world class cartographer? He's famous."

"Yes. Ellis Prefontaine. That's my daddy. He wanders now. Though Tanya usually can find him."

"Trouble with being our age," said Miriam. "Is that on the one side you remember clearly what it's like when you're young, and you realize you're not any more; and you watch your parents, and know too much about getting older. You see all that pain, the troubles your parents are having. Who wants it." Miriam, peculiarly agitated, got up to chase the singer, who was already at other tables, and drop some coins in her hat. "You never even mentioned your dad to me," she said when she came back. "It was always Brightwatch, your mom."

"Brightwatch doesn't have troubles, she makes trouble," Nathan said, and realized it didn't sound like a joke.

"Mid-sixties is not so old any more." Max said. "I expect to be just hitting my stride. I'm going to have my people write a program that will allow you to age only virtually, while you remain young physically." He leaned over to smooch Holly.

"Tomorrow I go back to the Borghese," Nathan said.

"Natto," she moaned. "There are so many other places I haven't been yet, sweety."

"Look, up in the sky." Max pointed to the rooftops, where the upper level tour group was drifting in, to

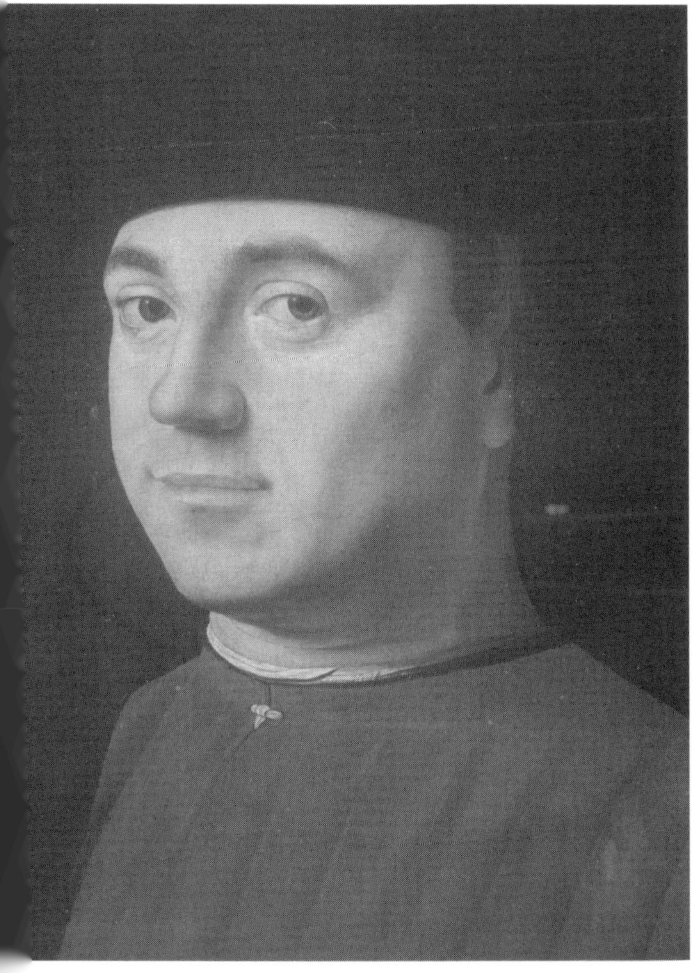

view Piazza Navona at twilight.

"I have to go back," said Nathan. "The face in that picture is exactly the face of the guy in the car who conned me into the jacket, I think. Don't you think so? It's like I've seen Hamlet's ghost."

"Hamlet, huh? Aren't we special," Miriam mocked as if to spite him, and then she regretted it. "But if it's important to you."

"Don't think for a minute I'm not going to pay for the jacket," Max insisted, but was distracted by his incoming tourist colleagues.

"I'll take Hamlet's word for it," Miriam said. "But I'm going to go somewhere else, that I haven't seen before."

"Whatever you want, but I'd like you to come with me, to look at that portrait again, that face; besides, it doesn't hurt to see those Berninis twice. Maybe it doesn't seem important to you, but Antonello da Messina… my father…How my father disappeared is important to me. Sometimes, like now, the most important."

Each of the tourists drifting through the piazza atmosphere was equipped with one of the same jackets. "Let's get out of here before they see us," Holly said.

"No," said Max. "Of course not." He stood up, and to what sounded like a distant blare of Lamborghini tailpipes, he lifted away from the table to join his fellows still aloft, leaving the jacket on the back of the chair. Holly watched him rise into the nicely spaced and uniformly jacketed drifting of tourists, her eyes moistening.

"I didn't come to Italy just to float around everywhere with rich people," Holly brushed her eyes with the back of her hand. "Even though I'm a rich person, but I'm just not like that." She grabbed the jacket to carry it up to Max.

"Now the jacket's gone," Miriam smiled. "And they left us the tab," She lifted the bag full of porcini. "And now we have these mushrooms to worry about."

"I'm going to the Borghese tomorrow, definitely." Nathan repeated to himself.

"And I don't get it. How do they do that?"

"What?"

"Go up in the air like that."

"They're rich. They've got the chip." Nathan smoothed his moustache.

"Chip? What do you mean, the chip?"

"You know, when a person is born rich they implant this chip. Most of the population doesn't know about this. And that allows them to do stuff like Holly and Max are doing."

"Why don't we get that chip?"

"You have to be born rich. It's like circumcision, although for a long time Jews were denied the chip. And also if you make enough money at a certain point. They knock on your door and ask if you want the installation. It's all hush-hush. All for the rich."

She looked into the bag of mushrooms. "What are we going to do with these?" She pushed on Nathan's arm.

"It's very painful, the chip installation. And it changes you in certain ways you can't even imagine. See, if you were lanky enough…"

"Stop it, Nathan, no more lanky. We're on vacation. We should be able to do what they're doing. It's not justice." She pulled out one of the porcini and sniffed it. "They leave us their mushrooms. Can we get chipped too?"

"Whatever you want, Mims. As soon as you get rich enough." He reached into the bag for a porcini, and put it on his head. He felt himself entering a zone of melancholy giddiness and got up to find himself a mirror back in the caffe. What he saw made him sad and nervous. A face getting older, under an edible mushroom. He returned to Miriam. She had tears on her cheek, that he swiped at with the back of his hand. Was it the darkness encroaching, the lights slowly coming on, the people leaving Piazza Navona, that made so melancholy an evening all of a sudden?

"Tomorrow I'm going to the Borghese. I owe it to myself, and to my father, whoever…." He sat back down.

"We can get this chip when we're rich, right?"

The thought of getting rich made him feel slightly queasy. "I'm sure it's possible, Mims; but it's painful, and like I said, it changes you; I mean, it's not just the money that's the price you pay. The rich become different. Look at Max." He found trying to explain this nauseating. He didn't blame her for wanting money. They had a lot of rich friends, because it was his job to make people rich. He just never had the need, the drive to grow his own wealth. "Tomorrow I'm going back to see that painting, no matter what else we plan."

Miriam wasn't used to it, found it difficult to enjoy Nathan while he was obsessive and emotional. She watched the faintly illuminated tour group disappear across the rooftops. How high they got, she thought. How far they could go. "In the movie it was laughter, wasn't it? Didn't they laugh, and then they floated up to the ceiling. What is it here, just money?"

"I have to see it, because I have to…" He had no way to finish the sentence.

Everything should have been lovely, but Miriam's mood darkened too with the slow encroachment of night. She couldn't explain her doldrums. O, Mary Poppins, she thought. Perhaps it had been the mean talk about fathers. And his father, what was that about? "Holly and Max weren't even laughing, Natto. And they go so easy upp." She rested a hand on Nathan's shoulder. "Life is so sad, sometimes. And we don't even know why."

KRISTIN

KRISTIN

Solomon Briggs imagined that Antonello's *St. Francis Talks to The Birds* was painted on wood, perhaps as part of several panels for the predella of an altarpiece commissioned for who knows where. Perhaps he'd stumble somewhere onto a record of the transaction, as had happened with the painter's *Annunciation* now in the regional museum in Siracusa. That one had been forgotten for centuries, against a damp wall in the Church of the Annunciation in Palazzolo Acreide, and wasn't rescued for restoration until 1925. Depending on where this St. Francis painting or paintings had been put away, it might be in decent condition for him to find. That's what he hoped. The idea of finding it made him tremble like a little kid anticipating Christmas presents. According to Vasari, Antonello was the first Italian painter to learn the varnishing techniques of the Flemish master, John of Bruges, his secret a preparation that didn't need the sun to dry it, but could cure slowly in the shade so there would be no cracking. While in Naples on business, Antonello saw a painting done by this master from Bruges, and thought to himself that this was something he needed to know; so he determined to go to Flanders and try to eke the secret of this wonderful technique out of the venerable Master of Bruges, reputedly so secretive.

Solomon enjoyed imagining what it was like for Antonello to go to Flanders, a man with dark southern passions, venturing into the cool, cerebral North, though from his paintings Solomon took Antonello to be one of the most rational of the Italian masters. Passionate and lucid, was that possible? He went north from Rome, stopping first to wait in Venice till the weather got better, and visit with his beloved friend, Giovanni, to tell him about his plan. This young Bellini, later the teacher of Titian and Giorgione, told him to go back to Rome, and continue his studies there. This would be a futile quest, and a waste of time. John of Bruges was not approachable. "Probably true," said Antonello. "But I have something that will open his cabinets for me." "What is that?" asked the young Bellini. "I will show him some paintings, and my sketches for the St. Francis altarpiece." "Not even that." Bellini threw an arm across his shoulder. Bellini's admonitions only tweaked Antonello's Sicilian stubborness, and hardened his will to get what he wanted. Besides, he had never been so far north, and he was curious to know the qualities of light that made the few Northerners he'd met appear so sallow, so stern and circumspect, as if they had never, and would never, go outside into the grove to lower their pants and squat, awash in the yellow and red of dandelion and poppy, to relieve themselves by an olive tree. A great northern shit in the clear southern air.

It was three weeks to Genoa by a private coach from Venice that the Bellini family arranged through their good offices with the Doges. They were held up twice by brigands however, stripped of everything save two small paintings and a sheaf of drawings, and a letter of introduction to Orazio Vivarini, commendatore, head of a merchant family with offices in Bruges, where Clemenzio, a brother, and his family managed six ships that plied the route from Genoa to Bruges. They transferred parchments, salt, spices, aromatics, wine, ceramics, camel's wool, and etc. from North African ports, and brought back fabrics, lace, and beer. This letter survived with a letter of credit that he kept strapped to his thigh in a thin leather pouch. Through the Vivarinis he hoped to find pigment and canvas once he got there, and perhaps get an introduction to the workshops of the painters of Bruges. From Genoa the ship sailed a regular trade route through Gibraltar, around the Iberian peninsula, along the northern coasts of Spain and France, through the English channel to Bruges, a journey of several months, with the many stops along the way.

He found most people polite enough once he was established in quarters the Vivarinis found for him, though in general the Flemish were suspicious of his swarthy complexion, and those he talked to about it were reluctant to help him with an introduction to the workshop of the master of Bruges. The old painter was notoriously suspicious, and careful with his secrets. Antonello's dark looks made people reluctant to be associated with such an introduction. Had he wanted to visit Hans Memling's studios, some of them said, it would have been easier, the garrulous German painter much more amicable and open to strangers. It was for the master himself, however, that Antonello had come all this way, and in his stubborness he believed that the more difficult path produced the richer results. He was determined to find the workshops and introduce himself, whatever the cost. He had confidence in his own charm, and was willing to humble himself, become the lowest drudge of an assistant.

An uncharacteristic self-consciousness overtook Antonello as he searched for the workshop in the rain, through the narrow streets of the artists' quarter behind the Gruuthuuse. A Sicilian in Flanders was as conspicuous as an ox grazing with the sheep. His dark complexion among this fair race made him shy, careful to hide his face, as he tried to do within the hood of his cape. No one he spoke to on the street trusted this man with his alien looks, his peculiar language, and they wouldn't help him to the door of the artist. There was no sign to indicate the workshop, but the Vivarinis told him they'd heard it could be identified by a unique brass door clapper in the form of what might have been a walrus, or a narwhale, with a horn as its handle, protruding from the center of the forehead, as in the designs he'd seen in Venice of the fabulous unicorn. After winding most of the day through the rain, and probably passing the door many times, he found it set in the shadows at an angle. When he lifted the clapper, he was startled by a harmony of bells struck within. This was as ingenious, Antonello thought, as some of the devices produced in Palermo at the workshop of Tito Panormita.

Someone peered through the peephole, and then there was a pause and Antonello narrowed the opening of his hood so his complexion would not alarm anyone within; then a throwing back of the bolts, and a young woman boldly pulled the door open. Not even in Venice would a young woman answer the door like this; and certainly not in Messina or Palermo, where the girls of the merchant families were kept deep inside the house, in a room within a room, and allowed onto the streets only escorted and veiled. Her startling hair, like spun gold, came half undone as she looked into Antonello's hood, and when he pulled the hood back to reveal his face, she exclaimed, "Oh!" and took a small jump away, blushing, her bosom swelling, as she tried to get her hair back into the comb. She shrugged when he mentioned the name of the Master, and as he spoke it repeatedly in variations of the accent, and mimed the act of painting, she started to giggle, covering her mouth in embarrassment. Their lack of a common language gave them an immediate intimacy, as she began to understand through an exchange of gestures why he was there. She led him by the arm to a bench in a small waiting room. She smelled of sandalwood, and something more hidden, more acrid. He let his hand touch hers as she settled him onto the bench with a slight pressure from her palm. Her name was Kristin. From the sounds of what she said, Antonello guessed she was the grandaughter of the painter. He had difficulty taking his eyes from the blue veins swelling with her bosom, and she stared at him as if she'd never seen his like before, a young man so dark, and yet so handsome, with grey eyes that seemed to look all the way through her. She let her hand dally on his shoulder, and removed it only when her grandfather entered. She felt herself blush as she stepped back from the stranger, and Antonello suspected he could follow that blush into the most guarded secrets of her grandfather's workshop.

From the freshness and vibrancy of the painting he had seen, Antonello had imagined John of Bruges to be a much younger man, and from his reputation he expected someone unfriendly, even hostile; but the old man was almost welcoming, though playful, cantankerous when he claimed never to have heard of the Kingdom of Sicily, and insisted there was no such city as Messina, certainly no Palermo, though he allowed there might be a place called Napoli. Antonello thought he saw the old man wink at his granddaughter, who was watching the negotiation of this introduction with great interest. She was gratified that her Popo, which was what she called him, seemed to take a liking to the dark young man, as she had immediately, his charm and intelligence, his looks, his humble but self-assured demeanour.

The whole nature of the conversation changed, however, when Antonello pulled from beneath his cape a small painting to show the master, and a sheaf of drawings, folding them aside one at a time, displaying his powerful secure movement of line and shading, and clarity of design, and beyond that a psychological subtlety in even the slightest penciled portraits. Antonello made him a gift of one of the drawings, and when he asked if he could stay as an assistant in the workshop, the old man explained, as best he could between languages, that he already had his assistant, Roger, who was conscientious, though without a grain of this talent; but Antonello was welcome to stay with them for a few weeks, and work at his side. It did not escape the old man that his granddaughter was taken with the young Sicilian, and that Antonello treated her quite sweetly.

Kristin showed Antonello to the largest room in the attic above the studio, with two small dormers facing north, where the young painter could set up an easel, and there was a small table where he could draw in charcoal and pencil. He ground and mixed his pigments in John's workshop below, and there he could watch the old master work, and learn from Roger how to mix the linseed oil with oil pressed from walnuts and filberts, and how to formulate this varnish. This invention thrilled Antonello as he saw it did dry in the shade without cracking on the canvas, or checking and cracking the wood of a panel. The Master worked only in the mornings, so Antonello would stay in his room in the afternoons and draw, or work on a panel, with the pigments he had mixed in the morning.

One day he caught reflected in the window glass a glimpse of Kristin watching him from the shadows of the doorway. He was working on the portrait of a face he remembered from his childhood in Messina. Recollecting such a face pushed back the homesickness, and the ache of yearning for the sun, that sometimes weighed down on him in the general greyness of the world of Flanders. He motioned for Kristin to enter his room, and she did, moving close to the easel.

"Who is this?," she asked, leaning a shoulder towards the panel.

"This will be St. Francis. Our gentle St. Francis of Assisi."

"Yes," she said, lifting her hand. "But who is he?"

He didn't know what to make of the intensity with which she stared at the unfinished panel, as if she were painting it herself.

"It's someone I know, from childhood."

"Yes. Yes, but who?"

By now Antonello had a bit more of the Flemish language, but he still didn't know sometimes if such questions were a result of the depth of her curiosity, or a failure to understand. He looked at Kristin in the light of the dormer and saw her now for the first time, understood her face, could feel the pale luminosity of her skin, the dimples when she smiled, her brow, clear and broad, the exquisite curve of her nose, and the mole above her lips, those full lips that seemed agitated constantly, brushed by a private wind. This was a face of innocence and intelligence, a kind, northern face. And something smoldered within her, her youth, her need, an infatuation with Antonello that he could, if he wanted, explore for both their pleasures.

"He's a memory," Antonello said.

"Remember whom?"

"From my childhood. Someone. A face I know. Michelino, the boatwright."

"Why will he be your St. Francis?"

"He is. I don't know why. I never question this. I suppose because he was from the Abbruzzo, and he came to Messina to be near the water, and to work with wood, and he loved the wood, and he carved the rudders and the keels and the oars, and he would carve birds into everything. He loved all the creatures, and would always tell us about the birds of Abbruzzo. When I was a boy, I looked at his face a lot, because I liked to be down with the fishermen, and I loved his stories, and I watched his face when I listened to him. He looked really old to me then, but now I understand this face, not much older than mine is now. It takes time. First you see a face with your eyes, and then your mind starts to understand it, and you feel it enter your fingers, your hand, your arm, but you can't start yet; then if you are blessed, your heart penetrates the heart of this subject, and your spirits intermingle, and only then you can start. Many fishermen would not go out into the straits without Michelino's oars, his rudder, and they believed that a boat built around his keel would never get lost, and would never sink."

"So you use him as the face of St. Francis? Because he had the gift of manifesting the protection of God. I don't believe in your God, not as we are expected to believe it, and please tell no one that; but I do believe in art. Your Michelino yoked the earth, the water, and heaven. And you knew him, of course, as one close to heaven, beatified in your own childhood perception, as you were closer to heaven as a child. But why the face, only the head?"

That she confided her belief, or lack of it, to him, startled Antonello; as did the intensity of her thought. "You ask so many good questions."

"I'm sorry. Not so many." She held her hands out towards him, as if she were going to bring them together in prayer. "Because when I think of your St. Francis, who thrills me more than many of your other saints, I think of a whole physical body in the world, not just a face, but a body relating to the body of the world, and the physicality of all the creatures in God's kingdom. St. Francis isn't just a face in ecstasy or pain. He's an embrace, a total enfolding." She touched Antonello's face. "Why just the face? I don't…" Her voice tapered off, as if suddenly embarrassed by its own boldness. She withdrew her hand.

If a young woman of Messina, or Naples, had such intelligence, she would be afraid to show it; not that he would ever find himself alone in his own room with someone so young and attractive. And this was a challenging question that couldn't be answered simply no, yes. He'd done some sketches for his St. Francis predella, imagining him in his shack, in a cave, on a mountaintop, looking down on Assisi, all quickly done, not to be shown to anyone. But first he had to get to the face. Even when he did his Annunciation, he wanted to see the message received in the face of the woman he knew to be Mary, then the rest follows. Faces first, the virgin, the angel as it is appearing. Even for the crucifixion he needed first to do the face of Christ. All action is resolved in the face, all that really interests him. Could he say that? To anyone?

"I enter every action through the eyes." He felt peculiar, as if he'd slipped up and told some secret he never intended to let out.

Kristin touched Antonello's furrowed brow, embarrassed herself by the strain in his expression. "I'm sorry. I didn't mean to…I am just curious…I am, myself… If you like, I can pose for you. I would like to pose for you."

This startled Antonello, that she could dare to offer herself to pose. To draw from life in Naples he had to hire women off the streets.

In the few months that Antonello remained in Bruges, Kristin came to his room every afternoon, and he sketched her over and over, in different poses—as the virgin receiving the annunciation, as the virgin revealing to Joseph, the virgin in the adoration, the virgin with the child suckling, for which Kristin undid her bodice, let down her hair, bared herself for him. The aureoles of her pink nipples faded imperceptibly into her white flesh, and the veins spread like flashes of soft blue lightning. Antonello came around from his easel. It excited her just for him to come closer. What would happen if…She shuddered as she thought she felt him touch her breasts.

"You are so lovely, Kristin. What can anyone say…She is you, the holy virgin is yourself." He wanted to explain something, but didn't know what it was.

"That's not who I want to be," Kristin said, then blushed. She wanted to be, O, Cleopatra; any great courtesan, rather than the virgin. She wanted to be a mistress to the greatest painter. No. She wanted to be the greatest painter, with handsome, admiring paramours. "I want to be the greatest lover, the greatest painter." To say this swelled tears into her eyes, and then all her breath escaped when Antonello leaned forward put his lips to her breast. She gripped the hair at the back of his head, and pulled his face into herself.

"There," said Antonello, smiling as he drew back. "It felt like that when you nursed our saviour. Although I am not…"

He returned to his easel, hoping to catch something of the transport in her look.

She continued to unlace herself. She had to make him understand something different about herself, because Antonello didn't get who she was. If she turned out as he seemed to understand her, she would end up in the beguinage, where all the virtuous women with nimble fingers produced in their lives nothing but lace. "Do me now as Mary Magdalene," she pleaded.

Antonello was amazed to see herself so much undone. As Mary Magdalene? Why would she want to be seen that way? He stepped towards her again, brush in hand, and when he felt her sigh draw him closer he embraced her fully, leaving a circumflex of umber across her cheek.

While he remained in Bruges after that he made many sketches of her posed nude on the windowseat, or on his bed, or in front of a mirror. Did he make paintings from those sketches? It would have been revolutionary, beyond what any of his patrons could imagine.

How fun, Solomon thought, to search for those masterpieces, throughout Bruges, and the low countries, turning one up, perhaps, in a small monastery outside Copenhagen, or in Estonia. A full nude by Antonello would have amazing qualities, every passage of its flesh informed with his passion, perception, and intelligence, and the gorgeous landscape behind, and her face so aware of its audience.

"That's a sweet story, Sol, my Solly." Isabel kissed his cheek. The blanket lay on the sand of The Lido, themselves looking out at a grey Adriatic reflecting the hazy winter sky. It was a rare day he could drag her out of her studio, and into the world. He'd written some of this Antonello story into a notebook, the pages of which wanted to curl as he turned them open in the damp air. "Such a romantic story you tell about your painter. I don't think I like him much."

"You think it's romantic?"

"It's sexy, full of flesh, and weighty ideas about painting."

"You have weighty ideas. About painting."

"Of course. But I'm an artist, and I've paid my dues."

"Which dues?"

"Art world dues. So tell me, Solly, I still don't get all this obsesson with an ancient painter?"

"He's not an ancient. I think it's important. We lost track…if not for this humane experiment in painting, there would be no modern art. You'd be decorating, I don't know…bigger and better altars…" He felt a drizzle coming down on his words.

"That's nonsense. My work has nothing to do with…anything of that."

He wiped the moisture off his face with a t-shirt. "We've got to look at all that again. I've always looked to art for a kind of redemption."

"Lordy, lordy, Solomon. Redemption?" She said the word slowly, as if she'd never pronounced it before. "When you get serious, you really start to smell corny. Redemption from what, Solly?"

"We live in brutal times. Yourself, you visited Dachau. This is a stupid age to live in, like a dark age. Redemption from how we live in so many lies about ourselves. I can't say it right. I want an alternative to this gross materialism, our lack of culture. I think a painter like Antonello pointed the way to a secular spirituality. In our time the artist mediates between the material and the spiritual, more significantly, less compromised than any religion."

"You're so earnest, Solly. I feel like I'm back in the dorm."

"Listen to me, Isabel."

"If you were a character in a novel, the author

would have to kill you off."

"What? Why?"

"I don't know, just so she could keep the story moving."

He pulled her hand across his belly, to lay it on his crotch. "Let's make it a dirty novel."

"You know what I mean."

"I don't."

She jerked her hand away. "Anyway, you've got a trust fund. What's so brutal in your scene? You're Mr. materialism. You're the only person I know in New York who owns a car."

"Big trust fund. The best it does is give me some time to think." He never solved the problem of getting around her bullying sarcasm.

"Too much thinking. You should try some time to survive as an artist, and stay out of the academic trap, and stay out of the Madison avenue trap. All the traps."

"That's exactly what I mean, Izz. That's why I loved to look at Antonello's portrait of the young man at the Met. Or have him look at me. That's what Antonello's portraits do. They look at you, and make you acknowledge the exchange with the anonymous subject of the painting. His smile is as loaded, as mysterious as the Mona Lisa smile. It pulls you right into the spirit of that youth. But you're not looking at him through a window. It's not a story about him you look at, but what seems to be his acknowledgement of your presence there. Every one of his portraits, the way they look back at you makes for such a rich negotiation. You're not just looking at a picture of someone, you're in a silent dialogue, a humane dialogue, that makes you have to admit that you're there too, and not just a voyeur looking in on the interpretation of someone's life. This is a powerful interaction, and I think it's been lost. This is more exciting than anything on the art scene now, present company excluded? You are there, and I am here, and what is 'we'? What is the human being? That's the question that we have to keep asking. The artist mediates between spirit and matter. That's a high calling. It's your calling. More juice to this than to any papacy." He wiped some sweat off his face. "That's what I'm looking at."

"It's all way before yesterday, Solly, and boring, kind of academic, you know."

"Come on. I'm not talking peanuts. Who says what I say? And even…"

"All right. Great ideas, Solly, but it has nothing to do with what I do. I'm a worker in red. I see how far I can go with these reds. Cheating in red, and I hope no one figures it out. Cross your fingers for me, Solly."

"Why now do you numskull yourself? It's convenient, right?"

"Besides, you're making too much of the pose. Every self-portrait is painted three-quarter view, the painter looking in the mirror. Half the portraits in the world look out at you."

"Not like these. These aren't self portraits, Isabel." She always worked to dismiss his thoughts as glibly as she could.

"So what do you get out of this that you don't get out of others."

"Clarity, Isabel. Absolute humane clarity."

She shrugged. One thing she suddenly realized was that she'd have to change her name. She didn't like the ring of Isabel in an argument. "I'm saying I pay my dues at the back door, and hope they don't catch me," she stretched and yawned. "It's business dues, Solly. The art business dues. I've stained my spirit a little to get where I need to be, to do what I need to do." She pulled the blanket across her body. "Redemption. Woof woof."

"What did you do to stain your spirit, Isabel?"

She shuddered at his saying the name again. "How did your boy, what's his name…?"

"Antonello?"

"Yes. How did he get the money to go to Bruges, and survive there? Did he go to the parties? Did he suck up to the critics? Did he elaborate a little bit the ambition of what he could accomplish? Was there an aging Contessa he had to service?" Isabel stood up and started to walk. A light mist blew in off the water smacking of fuel oil. Sandpipers angled across in front of her at the fringe of the waves. Solomon stretched upright, shook out the blanket, and followed.

"There's no evidence he ever went to Bruges, anyway," he said. "One theory is that he learned the techniques in Rome, from Petrus Christus, a Flemish painter who was visiting. Or some think in Milano. John of Bruges is Jan Van Eyk, you know, referred to in some of the stuff I've read as Giovanni di Bruggia, Gianes de Burges, Janes di Bruggia, and it's improbable that he ever went to study anything with Van Eyk, because he was eleven when Van Eyk died."

"So what's the point?"

"Point is my story is just an invention, a flurry of my imagination."

She waited through a moment of silence, then put an arm around him, and drew him to herself affectionately, the air heavy with whiffs of tidal decay. "Hooray for imagination! That's what I meant. A romantic invention, so sweet of you to get your Antonello laid, and with a young, flaxen-haired beauty. You've got a best seller going."

"Stop."

"Ohhhh," Isabel looked at him, her face in what she knew was his favorite pout. "Don't you love me anymore?"

"He might have been queer, anyway. The only flesh he ever exposes in any painting is male. Not even a nursing madonna to show a little holy tit. I totally made up that stuff about painting Kristin nude."

"Ooooh. A queer. Queer queer quack quack queen. I'm queer."

He embraced her, if only to quiet things down, and they remained folded together like that for a long time. "Do you want to do it?" he asked.

"Do what? You mean here?" She looked around the beach. "On the sand? That would be very queer.'"

"Yes. Here on the blanket in the mist."

"They'll see us from those hotels."

"When did that ever bother you before?" The first time they made love they were at a party, on the floor of a bedroom where everyone had thrown his overcoat, and people apologized for intruding as they grabbed coats to leave.

"That was then, Solly. Besides, it's wet here."

"Wet is good, Izzy. And you know, this is the beach of desire. This is the *Death In Venice* beach. This is Aschenbach's beach."

"Solly," she separated herself from him. "Don't tell me you found a gorgeous youth out here to love? You Gustav Von Aschenbach you. I didn't even know you went there. You and Antonello. Queer and queer. Is that the secret reason for Antonello?" She pinched his chin.

"Don't be silly. Give me a break. You know me."

"Well you never know anyone, totally. But I know." She reached down to cup his groin. "You're the straightest guy on Tenth Street." She squeezed lightly. "And it's too soon for you to need to recover your youth, anyway. Isn't that a big thing for Gustav? You're still young."

The moment for lust had passed, and just some trivial confusion persisted as they started to fold the blanket.

"I think I'll leave tomorrow," he said.

Isabel looked at him, disarmed and startled, one of her rare moments of insecurity. "Leave? Why?"

Solomon touched her arm, feeling some tenderness. "Well, I have to begin some time to hunt for the St. Francis picture. I'll be back."

She smiled, recovered. "Aren't you even going to wait to see if I'm pregnant?"

He had finally resolved in his mind that it would be okay either way, part of the crapshoot of life. "Are you?"

"It's not time for my period, yet. That'll be soon."

"I'll be back, Izzy. Plenty soon." The vulnerability in her voice was unexpected, for him a rare thrill.

"I know, sweety. I'll have a ton of work done when you get back."

He smiled. This moment filled with tenderness. How nice, how rare, how unusual for them, he thought.

They boarded the half empty traghetto that would haul them back to Venice.

"So once you find this painting, what will you do?

Sell it?"

"No. Of course not. I'll look at it. The whole world will look at it. I'm not doing this for profit. The odds are too much against to do this for profit, anyway."

"Well, you know for sure that someone will come around to be selling it at some point. Why not you?"

Solomon sniffed the air, and twisted his nose. "Let's go over there." They crossed to a seat free from the diesel fumes blowing back over the deck.

GIRL CRAZY

GIRL CRAZY

Once they spotted the whatever it was glowing in the sky, Nathan knew this conversation with Miriam was over. He knew he could drive almost anyone off when he obsessed, now particularly about his father. At least he was aware of what a bore he was about this, but he'd hoped Miriam would have more patience, more sympathy. She was, for all intents and purposes, his fiancée. Fee (fo) on (off) say (shutup). What a word.

"So explain to me again why we came here," Miriam blew on her nails, as if she had painted them.

"Weren't you curious? Max and Holly in Colorado! Who would ever have thunk, Mighty Max of the endless Bronx. How far from the Yankees would you ever expect Max to go? The Colorado Rockies? Give us a break."

"He can fly back to any kind of game he wants. He'll be back in New York all the time. But why did we have to come out here now?…Wait a second. What is that?"

"I'm saying, if Max is making a change, and I have the same feeling, that I have to change my life now, and figuring my father makes a big part, so that's why going back to find him is so important, to me I mean. I'm sorry, it's not…"

"No no no no no no…Look up there, will you, at

that shiny…That's…What is it?" She was desperate to deflect conversation from the wearisome target he had set up as soon as they got into the car.

"That's the Malaveaux," he chuckled nervously. "Famous hologram."

"A little young yet for the mid-life thing…" She reined that one in, didn't want to push talk back into that morass. He had just told her, in the midst of this missing father mishmash, that he wanted to drop everything, postpone their wedding, get back to Italy as soon as possible. Actually, postponing their nuptials seemed more of a relief than a problem for her, particularly now that he was being so annoying and needy. Some time to reassess was certainly in order, see if this passes. Every engagement, she told herself, should provide a period of reassessment.

In himself the old story festered like an untreated wound. A father (hardly a father, really. He'd never met the ejaculator, and knew very little about him) had disappeared somewhere into the Italian boot almost as soon as he conceived Nathan. As far as he understood, for Brightwatch it had been a relationship, not a one night stand, though it had played out that way; at least, in its affect on Nathan. He had suppressed his curiosity for most of his life, but suddenly it was different, and he didn't know why. A sudden obsession. In his younger fantasies the father had been an occasional drifter, hugging to the secondary roads. Then when he began to understand those things, he became merely a Brightwatch boffer, at a period in her life when she still did it with guys. Thus Nathan had been conceived, and thus Solomon disappeared. He knew the name—Solomon Briggs! She had given him the Briggs name. Why? Because she wanted an exclusive on Brightwatch. Maybe a boy child embarrassed her. Solomon Briggs was the vacancy sign in the wisdom folder of Nathan's life.

Brightwatch liked to call it just another case of a father shirking the responsibilities. What Nathan couldn't figure was why no trace of him ever showed up. Never a letter, never a message through a friend. Never even a slight, oblique inquiry, curiosity about the flavor of his progeny. Nathan would have been curious, at least, if he ever fathered ever; in fact, he would never father, unless he was ready to take on the whole job description, ready to be a dad, corny as it sounded. But this Solomon was like Atlantis, gone with all its knowledge. Why even assume he's alive? Perhaps he could put together at least some faint idea of the father, assembled out of the places he'd been, and those paintings Brightwatch had told him were once his father's obsession. He was now close to the age at which Solomon Briggs had disappeared, and with Miriam he felt pressed to start a family, and it seemed maybe important to know some more about his own father, in order to get the proverbial grip on himself.

They'd never been to the Rockies before. Max had talked about his new mini-ranch as if it was a preview of heaven. Nathan had relished the idea of flying with Miriam, but she slept almost the whole trip from La-Guardia to Denver International Airport, and so he chatted with the old guy across the aisle, one of those long, craggy cowboy faces, above a bolo tie, and a western shirt with mother of pearl snaps. He was an "oil-land" man, and he explained what that was in tedious detail, gesturing with flips of his large, scarred hands, once roughened from work. He reached across occasionally to pat Nathan's hand, his now became soft as mouse fur. Because of the damned solar people, and the wind-farm people, the son-of-a-bitch ecologizers, his knowledge and experience had become practically obsolete. "Or maybe it's just because I'm getting old," he grinned, squeezing Nathan's forearm, with a grip that left ridges, and red marks that remained till evening.

"That looks like a great giant meringue," Miriam giggled as they drove from the Hertz lot towards the interstate, and glanced back at the tented Denver terminal.

"You're in a good mood," Nathan said, touching her hand.

She let out the twin chimes of laughter he had once fallen in love with when he met her eight years back, she just out of NYU business school with an MBA, he at that time running a small start-up investment company that failed, learning the ropes of on-line trading before it became as easy as the one armed bandit. He hadn't heard for a while that two note laugh, like a flatted fifth, coming from a freer part of herself than she was able to access lately.

"I took a long nap," she said. "I forget how to sleep in Manhattan." She leaned over to kiss his cheek, and chimed again, "We're not in Brooklyn anymore, Toto," she sang, as they drove towards the Rockies, that bulked up mysteriously against the horizon.

The kiss, the laugh, the Wizard of Oz, all combined with the spaciousness of the landscape to give him the courage to explain how excellent it would be to have her company and support on this trip he was going to make towards his father, an old fashioned *stand by your man* kind of indulgence. He already knew she had judged this an exercise in futility, though her interest was piqued by the idea there was a wayward uncle in the mix. He wasn't even disappointed when in perfectly good cheer she said, "My support one hundred percent, Natesy, but I'm afraid not my company. This is the worst possible time. You know what I'm saying; I mean, a wedding can wait. For my folks it would be a relief, because they keep telling me they don't even know you and sister Sarah keeps dropping poison in their ears about you, because she's so jealous; after all, who has she got, generic Bob Whitestone. And you know how much I loved being in Italy with you before, and chasing daddy even sounds exciting, but we're supposed to be ready to ship product in six months, or we lose the rest of our Microsoft support, and I'm the nerd in charge of recruiting a whole geek squad to write the rest of the codes. You understand what it's like, trying to launch a silicon valley kind of a thing in old slow Westchester County." Her laugh chimed out again. "And you do know how much I want you to find your daddy. Maybe after the wedding we can go look for the grandparents." The "d" word used twice seemed sarcastic. He didn't know how to measure that. Grandparents was an idea that couldn't interest him until he knew what the parent had been. Miriam's bottom line, however, was "no."

Max and Holly's place sat deep enough in the hills that only the very peaks of the purple mountains' majesty appeared behind the foothills. On the way they had passed several other holdings on the huge ranch that was being subdivided into thirty-five acre "estates" and "miniranches." Bulldozers, backhoes, semis hauling gravel and building materials moved around on the hillsides as once the cattle had, and before that the deer, the bear, the elk, the lion.

"Just look for the Malaveaux. We'll be right underneath," Max's phone message had said, and certainly this ghost in the sky was the only Malaveaux hologram hovering above the road. Nathan knew he had seen the image before, that glowed as an apparition above them, but it took Miriam to place it; the cute little bear in pee-jays and nightcap, his weighted eyelids, sleepwalking towards the trees.

"It's the little Travelodge bear," Miriam exclaimed, excited by her moment of recognition. "Snoozy, I used to call it. My mom always insisted on Travelodge when we went on vacation. During Vietnam she said it would keep us safe from protestors. I don't know why."

"At least Max is consistently tacky—trophy house on overpriced acreage, and steal an ancient commercial logo as if it was high art, to fly above?"

"Relax and enjoy, Natesey. You're too young to be a curmudgeon yet; besides, there's no high art, remember. Andy Warhol? He erased all that in the 60's. We went to that lecture together at the museum, remember?""

"By high art I guess I mean whatever costs the big bucks."

Miriam looked at him, but didn't tell him how dreary he was being on this trip; definitely not someone with whom she would choose to be festive.

The gate hadn't yet been installed, though a gatehouse was in place, moved and restored from another part of the property, a red shale lean-to once used by ranch-hands at some remote corral, for branding and castrating. The driveway, freshly graveled, curved in a long halfmoon opposite to the shallow curve of the building. Building material was stacked around under tarps. They squeezed their rental Mazda Protege between a Lexus SUV and a Humvee painted dayglow camouflage. They were directly below the hologram now, that wisped in and out of its cutesy bearness. In the center of the turnaround, a small group of helpers gathered around a man fussing with the projectors.

"I think that's Malaveaux himself," Miriam started towards him. "Let's go meet him."

Nathan grabbed her arm. "Later," he said, not understanding himself why he was impatient. "We can meet him at dinner or something. I didn't realize they were going to invite so many other people. Let's find Max and Holly first. We're already late." Miriam went along with him as he tugged her by the arm towards the light and noise on the other side of the passageway. Sometimes he could be contrary, just to be in control. She would work on that after they were married.

The shallow arc of the motel-like complex of rooms cuddled a long oval swimming pool, its water illuminated and in it several young women splashed around in thong bikinis, and some swam laps through pastel tints of light, in their black tank suits. Others wandered the hard-scrabble grounds, craning their necks for a better view of the hologram, and yet others gathered at a bar set up on the south end of the pool, and toted drinks to their companions relaxing at tables. Max and Holly's new west overflowed with youth, mostly shapely young women, wholesome and healthy. Why so many? Had Max's Hugh Hefner ambitions come out of the closet? Below the pool, a long acre of scrub descended into the trees where a trio of new guest cottages sat like outlying units of a resort motel, their eaves dimly lit in the twilight. Beyond the trees what looked like a thirty-two foot catamaran swayed in the shadows, a red and a yellow light rocking at the tip of the mast. Nathan saw now how true the architect had been to his "vision" of motel architecture, all these separate but attached units unified by a long balcony; popular American road culture built better, with materials to make it last, and flares of luxury, like the retro nouveau wrought iron on the balcony designed by Ellington Reuter. The whole project made Nathan slightly queasy, settling the drek of contemporary wealth on the American West. When Max had mentioned hiring the architect who had convinced him to do this, Nathan thought he was kidding, a moment of trendiness for his friend, but now here it was come true, a motel built personal for Max and Holly.

"This is a little bizarre," Miriam said.

"What is?"

"The whole scene. Girls. Motel house design. Mountains. Max. Where's Holly?"

Nathan was glad they saw this the same way. "Maybe this is what he meant when he told me we'd meet his network. Bikini bimbos. Are these his dot-com millionaires?"

"Too young these girls to have jumped on the dot-com trolley. They're like, college students." Miriam looked around. "I don't see Holly."

"Maybe it's his neighbors? No. Too young to be neighbors." He pulled Miriam closer with an arm around her shoulder.

"What's with that catamaran, anyway?" she laughed. "Maybe I could see Max living like this by the shore, but a mountain man, Max? Holly makes sense. She's got a bit of the cowboy…girl about her."

"Could be a hologram, a virtual boat. Max is fixing to become king of the virtual." He turned to kiss her. "Virtual kiss."

Miriam covered her mouth and sighed, then yawned. "You think when we get married we'll ever have all this?"

"What?" The question irritated him.

""Stuff. All this stuff."

"Do you want all of this?" He never envied anything his clients had, especially not Max's accumulation.

"No. Not want…It's just…I think it's wonderful that we have friends who can afford this, at our age. Do you recognize anyone else here?"

"Max is forty, Mims. Besides, I don't want any of this."

"Whatever. We're not that far from forty. Do you recognize anyone else here?"

"So it bothers you that I can't afford all this?"

"We know you can afford everything, if you ever wanted to take your own investment advice. Where's Holly, anyway? And if you can't, I will. When we get married, look out. And when I'm vested…" She didn't often talk about cashing in her stock options, but just enough so it was clear they were on her mind. They weren't worth anything yet, but a kind of dream value.

"You're right, sweety. I can't afford it, not yet."

She kissed his cheek. "You sell advice to the rich, and make them richer. Like the girl who's always the bridesmaid. It's not like it would be an effort for you to become a rich man."

Holly rushed across from the pool to intercept them as they headed for the bar.

"Arrivoderci, you two, buon gusto," she said when she got close. "I'm glad you got here. Finally someone for me to talk to." She waved her arm in an arc that took in the rest of the guests. "These are all Max's supernerd friends. And all the young women he's hired to put together the dildonics prototypes. Students, mostly. Gorgeous, aren't they? He calls them his databiabes. And these programmer types talk only in code. Maybe I'm just paranoid."

Miriam rolled her eyes. "That's the language I talk every day."

"I don't get a word of it. I have to get Kevin, if he's taking his meds, to turn on my computer. Then I had a horrible conversation with that one over there in the white suit. That guy."

"You mean the tall one?" Miriam asked. "He's cute. Among all these nubiles, he's a relief. And ooooh look! He's got a cane. You should carry a cane, Natesie."

"Fake cane. It's really a James Bond thing. He showed me. It shoots. It stabs. It squirts pepper. He's been a mercenary, and he's probably still an arms merchant. He publishes that magazine, *Shoot First*. And how do you think he knows Max? I don't know. You think it's just because he's a neighbor? Next time Max and I will have a long discussion about who gets invited. Ooooh!" She embraced Miriam. "I'm so glad you came." She kissed Nathan. "Time passes since Italy. Max told you, you can stay the night. We'll put you up, of course." She swept her arm towards the house. "Lots of units. It's so fun. You can have your own, like, motel room. Do something kinky is the only requirement. Can you imagine how nice this will be once we put in the lawn? And when we can crank up the dildonics too. You wont believe how much fun that is. It's a great time to be alive?"

"Where's Max?" Nathan asked.

"He went up to Kevin's unit." She shook her head. "Both kids have had some trouble dealing with this move. Kevin especially, so temperamental."

"What's the catamaran all about?" Miriam asked

"Ask Max," Holly laughed. "It's one of his silly notions. Some day, he figures, California will crack off, and this will be shorefront property. No. I'm joking. He just wasn't ready to give up the idea of the ocean. Neither am I. And the Chembo Brothers from Panama City owed him a favor, so they sent up a crew to build it for him. We can take it to Lake Powell, or to Florida. It's seaworthy. We can learn to sail. Be good for the kids. Meanwhile it makes a fun guest house."

They continued walking towards the bar.

"Is your dad here?" Nathan asked. "I've wanted to meet him."

"Not here yet. He won't go anywhere since that snowmobile accident in Vermont. He's afraid."

"Why? What's he afraid of?"

"His brains got rattled up. He goes out and keeps getting lost."

"The world's most famous cartographer, for god's sake? He probably has every detail of the planet in his head. Anyone who knows mapmaking…."

Holly rolled her eyes. "Well, you know, it's been a long lifetime. He's pushing eighty now. If you come to the official housewarming, in October, he'll be here. That's a promise. Because we're going to dedicate a whole room to those freehand maps he did in the fifties, and those beautiful fantasy renderings he did for me when I was six. Like a little Prefontaine gallery. I still have them. And I think he's giving us one of his mighty globes."

"Was that Rencide Malaveaux when we came in?"

Miriam asked.

"Yes, of course. He was the architect's idea. I'm glad he got it up there a little bit for this." She pointed to the sky, where the drowsy bear had been, now a green wisp. "It's the architect's idea. Still being installed, you know. I want it to be just the Travelodge guy, that's enough bear for me, but they're supposed to put Smoky the Bear, Yogi Bear, Pooh bear, then an enormous terrifying Kodiak. I don't know what bears have to do with anything that's really us, except this is a Travelodge idea, and I don't know what they're doing about copyrights. Do you think we should buy the piece? Just to rent it for a night is like the price of a Picasso etching. You wont believe how much it costs to own it. From my perspective the nicest thing is that you don't have to turn it on if you don't want to look at it; it's only at night, anyway, and you can reduce it and move it inside, in the fireplace or wherever. The bedroom, ha. You know, his name isn't really Rencide Malaveaux." She paused to wave at some people calling her name from the pool. "Max's dad, and his girl friend. They make me crazy. No, what was I saying, o yeah, Malaveaux, his name is Jack Grossman. They're Bronx boys. Both went to DeWitt Clinton. Pallad's real name is Mike Clancy, I'm told. That's Pallad, the architect. He's a one name artist type, like Christo or Marisol." They arrived at the bar. "You know how Max is with the single malts. Now he's got them all."

A line of single malt scotches stood at attention across the table. Holly grabbed one dark bottle with a simple white label. "I think this is the one Max usually drinks, Clapgiddick. Don't know if I pronounce it right," Holly said. "It's older than any of us, sixty-five years."

The age caught Nathan's fancy. He lifted the bottle and held it to the light. "There has to be a ritual, at least a special invocation for drinking a scotch so much older than yourself." He poured a couple of fingers neat, and lifted the glass to Miriam and Holly. "Here's to the grandfathers, and all the grandfathers before them, who couldn't have had Max in mind when they filled the barrel." He sniffed it. "Not this rocky mountain party, anyway."

"I don't like the taste of Scotch. Maybe a kir," Miriam said.

Nathan sipped and tasted. "Unflusterably smooth, like wiping your tongue across a baby's tush. Gentle aftertaste of haggis, sconescuzz, and peat. Finishes like a toboggan. Geribibing the greythirst." He peered through the amber potion into the haze from the barbecue that lay above the pool.

"You're in a sweet mood," Miriam said.

"Yes, a sweet one. And here's to the architects, who bring us…" He swung his arm across the length of the house, unable to find an inoffensive term for what seemed to him this cheat of a design. "…bring us…balconies…and units…" He saw someone come out of a room and lean his elbows on the balcony railing.

"That must be Max up there." Could he talk to Max? He felt an urge, several urges twisting in many directions. He wanted most of all to talk about his father with someone, talk about him as if he could will him palpable with words—but talk to Max?

"Did you guys bring some swimsuits? Yeah, that's Max."

Miriam slapped her forehead. "Didn't think of it."

"Come on down to the bath house. I'm sure we have something that'll fit."

"Do I have to get into a bathing suit now, with all these flagrant nubiles on display?"

"O, Mims. You have a flawless body," Nathan said. "You're an indisputable ten…uh…nine and a half."

"Thanks." His sarcasm lay so thick in his voice since they arrived, she couldn't tell if this was a real compliment, or an ironic dig. "Where did I lose the half point?"

"Yes. I think I'll go see Max," Nathan said.

"He's up there, but I'd stay away just now. Take a swim first."

Miriam picked up a glass of kir. "Where's Tanya?" Tanya was the child of Holly and Max, Kevin's half sister.

"In her unit, thank god, with her friend, watching cartoons, I hope." Holly started for the bath house.

Miriam, glass in hand, followed after Holly.

"If you're going up," Miriam warned, once she saw Nathan was staying behind. "Careful when you get there. Kevin's in a state."

Nathan savored the scotch for a moment, then started towards the house. He'd known Max a long time, and would love to be able to talk to him, his most successful, luckiest friend, at least in the material world, at least financially, a world in which his own success was mostly vicarious, and that was by choice. It was easy for him to help other people make their fortunes, and for himself he did make what most people would call a decent six figures, but something in himself resisted taking the step from well off to rich. Money was an interesting enough form of energy but repugnant as an obsession, and he could be involved in it only if he was free to be contemptuous of the people he served.

He found the outer stairway to the balcony, and climbed to where Max leaned against the railing. His dark, semitic face was tinged acqua from pool reflections, so his new western gear—the big stetson in his hand, grey ostrich leather boots, pearl snaps on blue western cut shirt, Zuni slide on string tie, sandcast Navajo buckle on belt of new jeans—made him seem the complete embodiment of "greenhorn." He sucked on a filter cigarette through a girl's body whittled into a short bone holder. The moment he saw him there he realized Max was not one to talk to about his own situation.

Max looked back nervously at the door to Kevin's room. "Glad you got here, Nate." His words rose with the cigarette smoke. "Did you talk to Henry at all? He's in heaven. Look at him." Max's father was stretched out on a lounger under an umbrella, with a drink on the table at his side. "He'll be glad to see you. He always says, where's that Nathan, I got to buy some of his advice. Look. He thinks he's in Miami Beach." He rolled over, and a young woman leaned over to rub his back. "Hustled his whole life selling used office furniture, now his son becomes a millionaire for doing what looks to him like a half hour's work." He pulled Nathan close, and hugged him. "I owe all this to you. I tell him that whenever I can. That's why he loves to see you, but today I've hardly talked to him, because of that." He pointed his thumb back at his son's door, then drew hard on the cigarette.

Nathan felt a pang of envy at Max's concern for his father. He watched the old man lift his drink to toast his girl friend, as she fussed around his lounger. "He looks like he's at Miami Beach. It's late in the day for that suntan oil she rubs on him."

"It's not about the protection. Henry just wants the rubbing. I think this one even likes him."

"What do you mean, this one?"

"Well, she's payroll. A few years back she did some

soft core, maybe a couple of fuckfests too, but she enjoys this more, I think. He doesn't like them too smart, and she fills the bill. Needs someone who'll rub him with sunblock at night, if he says so. Ask no questions." He put his head into the Stetson, then tapped a cigarette from the pack and pulled it out with his lips, though he already had one lit in his hand.

Nathan pushed at Max's cigarette arm. "Looks like you're going have to quit again." He stepped back. "And this new fashion statement. You're like a fugitive from Christopher Street."

"Western. I really got into it. It's stylish. And I like the silver." He fingered the Zuni slide on his string tie, "And the craftsmanship here." He realized he had a cigarette in each hand. "As far as these go, I'm not a quitter, Nate."

"So what's up with Kevin?"

"Nothing. He's got himself a thing in there, and I want to talk to him about it. Truflesh something. He bought it with this money his grandma gave him, my mother. She's too busy to come out here."

"What's a truflesh thing?"

"One of those life-size woman dolls. A sex toy thing."

"Good for him. How old is he?"

"He'll be fifteen. I can't wait till these years are over. We should have put that money in a trust. He spent more than five grand on the thing."

"Stop calling her a thing. She's not a thing." Kevin threw his door open.

"Then what else is it? It's some big rubber thing. Where'd you learn about it? Howard Stern?"

"She's latex, not rubber. And she's not a thing." Kevin stepped up to speak into his father's face, then recognized Nathan. "Oh, hi, uncle Nate. Sorry for all this…this…you know."

"Can I see her?" Nathan took a step towards the boy.

"No. Nobody. Especially not my dad's grubby mongrel friends could understand. Oh." He covered his mouth. "I don't mean you, uncle Nate. Maybe I'll let you." He let Nathan peer into the room. "She's my real imaginary friend."

The first time, a year ago, that Kevin had called him uncle, Nathan was flattered by this signal of intimacy and trust. Now the intimacy felt a little uneasy. "I promise I'll respect whatever rules you set, Kevin."

"Next I'm getting a gun, a really cool M16 or something, like an Ouzi. I like that word, the way it sounds, Oooozzeeee."

"I don't want you bringing guns into this house," Max said.

"It fires sixty rounds in thirty seconds," Kevin obviously relished irritating his father.

"Why would you want such a vicious weapon?" Nathan asked.

"No more of this, Kevin," the father said.

"It's easy to get one. If you've got the cash. I don't even need to go into the city."

"But why?"

"To protect her."

"Protect her?" He looked over at Max. "Who is he protecting?"

"You know," Max said. "It's nuts. He thinks he has to defend the thing in there. The Truflesh."

"Stop calling her a thing."

"If I could take back the sperm that produced this aberration."

"Max, take it easy. It's your kid. Relax. You've got a party going here."

"Should have chosen abortion, like his mother wanted."

"Max!!! Calm down. Don't say things you don't want to say." Nathan laid an arm across Kevin's shoulder. "Let's go in and you can introduce me to her, okay?"

"I should have been an abortion." Nathan put a hand in Kevin's back to urge him towards his room. He was a big kid, but he was soft. "Then I wouldn't ever have had to listen to you," he threw back at his father, just before he closed the door. "You can't touch her, though," he told Nathan, when they were alone together.

The doll lay under the covers on the double bed furthest from the door. She seemed almost to be breathing, as he thought he saw the bedclothes rise and fall, and she seemed to meet his eyes, so he had to turn away. "Does she have a name?"

The boy whispered in Nathan's ear. "Esther."

"Esther. Like the bible Esther?"

"She's an orphan, and an alien, like Esther who was raised by her cousin, Mordecai, and he was sworn enemy of Haman, who hated any Jews, and wanted to kill them all, and her name, you know, means star, and king Ahasuerus, and he was really Xerxes in reality, practically snatched her up, away from her people when he didn't want his wife, Vashti, any more, because she was disobedient, but Esther was beautiful, a fair young virgin, and now he needed a new wife; but my Esther is not like a real alien, because she's a friend. My real imaginary friend." He lifted her head, and tenderly fluffed her pillow. "I've never touched her, not in that way. I never will. That's not why I bought her."

"Why did you buy her?"

"Esther. The real Esther's real name was Hadassah, which is a tree, a myrtle tree. But this is Esther, and I want to have her and protect her. She is a fair young virgin. I want to practice respect."

The noise from the gathering below swelled and ebbed and swelled. Out the window, beyond the horizon, occasionally some few lumens of lightning, and the thunder almost a whisper. "That's very, ummm, chivalrous, very noble." Kevin smiled at the compliment. Nathan would rather have said that this was really nuts.

Nathan looked around at the room, furnished with the standard high end Travelodge commercial package. Kevin had made it somewhat his own with pictures of insects of the Amazon taped to the wall across from the beds, a Metallica poster and a bouquet of swastikas on another wall, Britney Spears and Jennifer Lopez hung over each of the two beds, mostly naked, violent tattoos of an air battle carefully drawn on each of their bodies. The two queen size beds took most of the space. His computer and Nintendo control center filled one corner. One of the beds was heaped with women's clothes. She "slept" in the other bed, dressed demurely in a lace trimmed flannel nightgown fastened at the neck. Nathan couldn't figure out which bed Kevin slept in.

"She looks light, but she's not," Kevin said. "With the crate and all she was over a hundred and fifty pounds shipping weight. They sent her in a wood crate, sitting on that little stool, with nothing on but a miniskirt and one of those tube tops the girls wear in the summer."

"She looks very real in your bed."

"Well she's not real, Uncle Nate, but she's here. That's her bed." Kevin gently brushed her hair with his fingers, and stroked her cheek. "Her hair feels so nice. It's so silky." He grabbed Nathan's arm. "But don't you touch her, Uncle Nate." The boy became thoughtful. "I thought the crate was, you know, like insulting, and the miniskirt, and that crappy little stool she was sitting on when she got here. It was demeaning."

Kevin always surrounded his fantasies and obsessions with information. It was almost admirable, and the only way to deal with it was to play along. "Well it's nice they let her sit down. Imagine if she had to stand up all the way here, and then find her way to your room, even if she had the address and directions; it's a hike, all the way from Louisiana or L.A. or Chicago,…"

"She came from Minneapolis."

"Wherever she's from, imagine she gets to your door, knocks, 'It's Esther,' she says. Her long cigarette holder…"

"She doesn't smoke. My dad smokes too much."

The way he had her dressed, the doll looked more dowdy than erotic. Underneath the flannel nightgown there was a tanned effect, intended to look healthy, though the color was like coffee spilled across a white countertop, and the expression on the face was slightly startled, slightly stupefied, as of someone surprised to find herself there, cheeks rouged, an annoying smile that might have looked sexy if she had been dressed in her lingerie, eyes greenish, lips glossed apricot.

"Do you pick the eye color, and lips, Kevin?"

"Yeah. I didn't even care what color, but they give you lots of options, like I chose "tanned" for the body color, and I got the five foot six option and the medium

112

blonde with apricot lipstick and rose eye shadow, and liner, all light. Do you like the eyes? I chose the oval head shape, and the French manicure on the nails. She comes automatically with two entries, but I got the three entry option, though I never…why do they have to call them "entries"? But she's odorless and flavorless, and nothing on her is toxic. She can withstand over three hundred degrees of heat, and she's waterproof."

Nathan looked over the array of jars and vials on the nightstand.

"That's her accessories," Kevin said. "There's a sponge-stick, for whatever that does. Do you know what it's for, Uncle Nate? And there's liquid soap, some water based lubricant, perfume, other stuff. A lot to learn. You must know about it."

"Where did you get the idea for this, Kevin? You spent a lot of your money?"

"What good does money do, unless you turn it into something? All those weird loser friends of my dad turn plenty of money into sex. Who turns it into love? I don't see much love. I've hardly touched her, except to put her in some decent clothes. There's nothing says I have to touch her. Her breasts are supposed to feel like real breasts. They're real silicone implants, with special silicone in them, but I don't think…I don't touch them. Does a person have to touch breasts just because they're breasts? All her, you know, 'entrances,' are made with some special slippery stuff. She's special everywhere."

The smug cosmo pout on the doll's face seemed to mock Kevin's earnestness. That Kevin never touched it was somewhat bizarre. Nathan wanted stick something in the mouth, pull her tongue.

"You can put her in hot water, like a bathtub, like soak her warm and she keeps the heat for a long time." He looked at Nathan as if he knew his thoughts. "Please don't get too close to her."

"Kevin, get real. It's really a doll." Nathan moved closer to the bed, but held back when the boy interfered, his fists clenched.

"I know she's a doll, really. This is why I have to get a gun."

Max opened the door, and looked in. "That's it, Kevin. Your uncle Nate is here for the grownups party, not to talk about your toys."

"She's no toy, either."

"Okay, all right. So do you want to come and meet some people?"

"I'll stay in my room," Kevin said.

"Pretty girls down there, real ones," Nathan tried to entice him. Kevin slammed the door.

Max sat down on the balcony steps, and lit a cigarette. Nathan settled next to him. They looked out over the pool and bar. "Kevin looks like he's got a few problems. Maybe it's the move, a new place, no friends," Nathan said.

"He's a kid," Max replied impatiently. "All I can do

is wait him out. I hope that he'll…Maybe when the ski season comes he'll take to skiing…snowboarding I guess is what they do. His kind of kid."

"Maybe you should get him some help. He's basically a great kid."

"He goes to therapy twice a week. Once a month I go with him. Holly won't go. He's not really her kid. You should try raising a teenager yourself these days."

"This is a rubber doll, for chrissake. It's no big moral dilemma. He hardly even touches it."

"Abstaining is trendy, Nate. Virginity is really in, believe it or not." He threw his arm over Nathan's shoulder. "Let's forget Kevin for now." He waved his cigarette towards the darkened landscape. "What do you think about this place? Don't you love it. It was the right idea, this go west young man thing. All this spaciousness, all this land. I feel like I've always been part of the west. Maybe it was those movies on TV when I was a kid. *High Noon. Shane.* Roy Rogers. And anything you want is here—skiing, climbing, hiking, hot springs…It's like back East, in New York, there was no outdoors, and here, look at it, we've got our own piece of the outdoors." Max sucked in a chestful of air. "Later on I've got a surprise for you, I'll show you something. It'll blow your mind. And speaking of that, have you met Toni Gruber?"

"Who's he?"

"She. She's…I think I mentioned her before. She's

the web architect who's going to build your father program, like your virtual father. She probably wants to ask you a bunch of questions."

"My father is already virtual enough, I mean…." He didn't know what he meant. Virtual father didn't fit. "Anyway, I don't need a father, I just want to find out what happened to the one that once contributed to make me. That's why I want to go back to Italy. I'm way past needing someone to be my father."

"But that's what I'm telling you Toni Gruber's doing, and you won't have to waste time looking in Italy, because whenever you want to, you insert the program, and your father boots."

He looked at Max's dark face, tough to crack, like a brazil nut. He knew he couldn't get his real feelings through that shell. Not that he was after sympathy, but this was one of his oldest friends, whom he wanted to understand what he was doing.

"All these girls blow my mind." Nathan changed the subject. "How did you get all these girls to come here?"

"Plenty of colleges around here. You put out the word. The girls need some cash. It's better even than titty bars. You just advertise in the school paper, and you get more than you need."

"Why do you need any at all? What's the deal?"

"It's not what it looks like, although I don't know what it looks like. We're building the dildonics prototypes, and the girls are data. Photo data. We're almost finished. We grab some parts from each of them, mix and match. No one's perfect. A pity it'll be over soon. I'm going to miss the girls when this is over."

"So that's why all the cameras around?"

"Yeah, around the pool. And some we take into the studio. It's all very innocent. Very programmable. No hands on."

"The older you go, Max, the more your devil rises."

"One rule is no silicone. We don't want that porn look. A little sag is good. Everything natural, is our motto. Prototypes from real flesh. And no MadAv anorexia either. For instance, check out the dark-haired sweety just coming out of the pool. I think that's a Stacy, lots of Stacies here, and a ton of Tiffanies, enough Courtneys to make you crazy." He blew a kiss towards the pool. "Great shape, huh; but look at the nose, that gentle promontory, and the lips like two pillows. I'm waxing, but girls have always made me poetic." Max ground his heel onto his half-smoked cigarette, and stood up.

"What do you think about Miriam?" Nathan asked, as they slowly descended the steps.

"Why? What do you mean? Miriam?"

"You know her real well. We're thinking to get married."

"O, I thought you meant for data…Marry Miriam, why not?"

"I've never, and this is your second, and since you

know her…"

"My third."

"I never got married yet because I never thought I could deal with monogamy, even as much as I care about Miriam. It has never seemed natural to me, being with one person, all the time."

"You and Mims having problems?"

"No. I mean, what I'm saying is I am maybe, but…"

"Don't worry about it. I know Miriam for years, you remember. She's a good woman. You work around it. You work it out. Like, see that guy down there in the white suit, the one with the cane, chatting up those two bikinis? He's a neighbor. Holly's got an interest there, and I don't pay any attention to it. I can always tell when she has a strong attraction to someone. Particularly when she objects. Loyalty does not have to include being faithful. As long as…"

Max always confused him, particularly about women. "But seeing all these young women here. What does Holly…"

"I know what you're going to ask, but this is not about exploitation, Nate. She wouldn't put up with it for a minute if she thought…" He swallowed the smoke from a big pull on the cigarette he had just lit. "She's a hundred percent behind this."

"Even though the girls are all young? Her guy, if that's what he is, the one in the white suit…"

"Let's face it. I'm not doing an anthropological investigation or anything heavy. This is entertainment technology. It's about what's physically attractive, and what's most attractive, I think you'll agree, is always what's coming ripe. Maybe we'll find a reason for thirty something or forty something eventually, but for now…"

"No boys, either? Wouldn't Holly…?"

"It's my project, Nate, so we start with my interests. One thing at a time. And my money, too. I say it's entertainment, but I wont say I haven't learned something about women."

"I hope so."

"I'll tell you about that later, first let's go have a swim. You'll meet Toni. The virtual father project will blow your mind."

Nathan followed Max to the pool house, glancing back at the door to Kevin's room. Max wasn't really interested in Nathan's father, but the project was just another way to tweak his own ambitions in the virtual reality market; and meanwhile seem to help a friend, why not? That didn't interest Nathan any more than did the silly dildonics. At best virtual sex would be an embarassing titillation, maybe a moneymaker for Max. Another upscale porn adventure. He watched porn sometimes, with an easily exhausted sense of pleasure. As a vice it was minor league. Max's involvement with it frustrated Nathan; he wanted to construct a Max he could talk to easily. He was an old friend, and had a comfortably bizarre mentality, and Max had been there with him in Italy when the idea first swamped him that he should look for his disappeared father. Unfortunately, a sympathetic ear wasn't one of Max's attributes

When they arrived at the pool, Nate thought he'd try to broach it anyway. "My mother's going to be in Venice again," he said. "I thought I'd go back there to pick her brain about my father again." Max didn't respond. "She'll be with her little girlfriend, for the Venice Biennale."

"One thing they've got here in Colorado, is they've got a lot of different kinds of therapists, therapies from A to Z. I don't know the names, but you can talk to Toni Gruber. She's up to speed on therapies too," Max responded. "Some of the therapists are good looking, and they give massages. Find yourself one of them, and talk about this, it'll help you straighten this out. That's my advice, Nate."

This was as much as he'd ever get out of Max.

They looked out from the bathhouse at the water of the pool. It was fed by a hot spring so steam rose off the surface, water quiet as jello, with people wobbling in it. Miriam was about to dive.

"Look at our Miriam," Nathan exclaimed with some pride. "Sometimes I forget she was competitive in college."

"Beautiful," said Max, as she did a clean, splashless swan into the deep end. "We'll get our data to move like that, eventually. Maybe we can use Miriam, come to think of it." Max laid an arm on his shoulder. "Be good to her. You've got a real woman there." He swung around to look Nathan in the eye. "But, you know, your father aside, Italy doesn't interest me much any more, especially since we've almost got it in the virtual; I mean, not perfect, but close with a bottle of Chianti. I'm ready to go to Thailand. Northern Thailand has some interest. Chungmai. And if we could get something in Burma. And Angkor Wat. Borobudor. Virtual holy places is an idea I'm cooking. But Europe is over, especially Italy. It's been too overdone."

"Right," That was Max. Europe is over. Italy overdone!? It was just opening for him. The place itself was like his own father.

His gut hung over the waistband of the swimsuit Max had given him. "That must be Kevin's," Max said.

"Don't you have one that won't embarrass me?"

Max slapped his big belly. "I've been a little too prosperous to fit you."

As soon they stepped out of the bathhouse Miriam and Holly rushed towards them, followed by a pair of young beauties in string bikinis.

"Those were some nice dives. You've still got the form."

"O God, I've really lost it, Natesy. I feel like the famous splashing cow. I'm getting old."

"These girls want to meet you," Holly said, grabbing Nathan's arm and pulling him to the corner of the pool where they waited, shifting shyly from leg to leg. Max winked at him just before he jumped into the swim of girls. "They all want to meet you, because they heard how you were the analyst who made it possible for Max to make all the money, Mr. Financial Adviser."

Nathan greeted them, feeling uncomfortable, pudgy and older in the undersized swimsuit.

"I heard a lot about you," one said. "I'm a graduate business major, Asian commerce and finance, at Holyoke." She jerked her head, as if flipping hair back from her face, though her scalp was Sinead O'Connor cropped. "And I came to visit Nevada, that's my friend. She's getting her Master's at DU." The serious one with the name of the gambling state looked out at him from inside her long black hair.

"Do you have any tips for us?" Her demeanor coy, her voice deep. She almost smiled.

Her breasts, he noticed, were slung deliciously in their tiny hammocks. Had they been captured for the database? He glanced at Miriam to see if she noticed him noticing. "Tips of what?" he asked.

"Something etrade advice. Something to watch." She moved close enough for him to smell the chlorine on her skin.

"Stay away from money," he said. "It's deadly."

The girls laughed.

"O come, Mr. Briggs" said the hairless kitten, with

the ring through her protruding bellybutton. "You must have something to tell us."

"Follow the dildonics," Nathan fished that out of nowhere. "It's clean, it's risk free, it's virtual. Watch for Max's IPO on the NASDAQ."

"Dil…don…ics." The dark one pronounced it slowly, sensually. "Thank you. We will be forever in your debt," she said, sweeping into a precarious bow, that ended with her flopping into the pool.

The other girl turned and jumped, and they swam away. Nathan took Miriam's arm. "You think they know what dildonics is?" They headed for the buffet table. "I didn't, till Max told us."

"O, come on, Natesie. Girls know everything."

"By the next time we invite, we'll be ready to crank you up into the virtual," Holly said. "Don't you just love out here in the west? Why did it take us so long to find it? In the East, we were all bunched together in New York. Now there's all this space," she waved her arms around. "For the mind to expand, for creativity. I have to get to work on some guy prototypes. Yummy. I can do that."

Kevin had got to the breakfast table before any of the overnight guests, and arranged all the bagels into a swastika on the blue tablecloth. Near the foot of the table he stared sullenly into his freshly squeezed grapefruit juice. Holly in her housecoat stepped in from the kitchen, waved at Nathan and Miriam who had just arrived, sleepily arm in arm. "Good morning, you two. Sleep well?" She was about to say something about the bagels to Kevin, but decided not to, and turned back to the kitchen.

"Sieg Heil, Uncle Nate," Kevin raised a hand in fascist salute, as Nathan and Miriam sat down. Max arrived, his green paisley silk boxers showing under the mauve smoking jacket. He sighed in tired exasperation at his son's display. "Kevin, if you only knew how evil that was, what you're playing with," he said, and with stainless steel tongs lifted each bagel back into the basket.

"He's not my son," Holly shouted from the kitchen.

"That's good news," Kevin sang out.

"And they're delivered fresh, and are usually still warm, but you ruined it."

"Bagels suck," Kevin hissed.

Another couple arrived, Toni Gruber and her partner, Elizabeth Dickson. Max introduced them. "You two should talk later, and brainstorm the father project."

"O, this is that Nathan. Great." Toni said, a slight, boyish woman, with shortcropped black hair, and a dragonfly tattooed on her left shoulder. She shook Nathan's hand firmly, then sat down next to her friend at the table, a larger blonde woman with a bad complexion, and an expression locked somewhere between shyness and hostility.

"If anyone can put a man together, it's Toni," Max said.

"Lezzies," Kevin growled under his breath, for only Nathan to hear.

"Look at this feast," Miriam said, as Holly backed in through the swinging kitchen door, a platter packed with smoked fish in each hand, —"salty and nova lox," she announced. "Smoked sable, shad, mackerel both hot and cold cured, whitefish, sturgeon, smoked chubs, trout, pike, caviar, flying fish eggs, and etcetera. All gets flown in." The other platter was full of sliced onion and tomato, radish flowers, celery, carrot curlicues, fluted cucumber, capers, grapefruit sections, clementines, kiwi slices, strawberries, passion fruit, mangoes, carambola in starshaped slices, etcetera etcetera.

"Just another Sunday brunch at the Milsteins," Max said. "And we do eggs if anyone feels the urge."

"What do you call this?" Miriam asked, lifting a translucent slice of something from the fish tray.

"Here comes dad," Max sang out, as Henry and the girlfriend entered arm in arm, both yawning, the old man in blue striped flannel peejays and terry-cloth bathrobe, the younger woman in red spike-heeled sandals and a short embroidered silk housecoat that covered little of her great bosom.

"One of the greatest pleasures in the world," Henry proclaimed as he entered. "Is when the whole loaf comes out in a single squeeze, one long perfect salami.

I'm talking natural functions." The girlfriend took his arm, and pressed against him. "I think you're good medicine for my systems." He planted a kiss.

"That's smoked abalone," Holly told Miriam, as she set a tray of cheeses on the table. "Isn't it great. It flies in from California every weekend. There's the most wonderful store, run by these Russians, a miracle, like an old time lower east side appetizing. Except I think there's something Russian mafia going on there too."

Another thirty-something couple, dressed in matching royal blue shorts, she with a yellow tube-top, he in a starched yellow short sleeve shirt, came to the table.

"Did you all meet our neighbors, the Elliots?" Holly asked. "Bob and Francine Elliot, meet everybody. Nathan Briggs, Miriam Shuchter, etcetera. Introduce yourselves. Bob and Fran are mom and dad of Nancy, Tanya's little friend. Where are the girls?"

"Playing stinky with each other upstairs," Kevin injected. The Elliots looked at each other.

"Kevin, don't be so…"

"Sieg Heil." Kevin grabbed a bagel, and got up to leave the table.

"Ask to be excused," Holly whispered.

"Watch," said Max. "The art of cutting the bagel."

"Max is so compulsive about cutting bagels," Holly leaned over to kiss him. "As about everything else."

"Last time he cut himself," Kevin said. "Didn't he, Holly?"

"I've never cut myself slicing a bagel."

"Then where did the blood come from that was on my bagel that time?"

"You know that was ketchup. You put it there."

"Was not. I know the difference between ketchup and blood."

Max dismissed his son with a wave of his knife. "A serrated is best. You can cut carefully towards the hand about two thirds of the way through, then turn it over and finish cutting away from the hand and body. Voilà!" Max displayed the two yellow halves of an egg bagel.

Kevin leaned across the table to grab another bagel, then turned to leave.

"Ask to be excused," Holly repeated in a whisper.

"You're not even my mother," Kevin whispered back. "Will you please do me the kindness and allow me to be excused?" he said slowly, exaggerating the formality. He held the bagel up for Nathan to see. "This one's for Esther," he winked. "Blueberry."

"What'll we do with him?" Max asked, after Kevin left the room.

"Don't do anything. He's young. He'll get over it," said the grandfather.

"But this swastika stuff. It's as if he doesn't know from evil."

"He just wants to get your goat. Nazi'll do it every time. Just wait till he discovers girls. It's all testosterone. He'll learn to ski out here. He'll figure out where to point his pupik."

Toni and Elizabeth looked at each other, and rolled their eyes.

"Lots of Henry's relatives died in concentration camps," Henry's girlfriend said, soberly. "That's why I'm converting to Jewish. I want to make up a difference."

"It's testosterone, and it's money. His grandmother gives him too much money," the grandfather said. He lifted half a bagel layered with fish, onion, cheese, and tomato, and was about to put it in his mouth, but transferred it to his girlfriend's, just as she was about to speak again.

"Jewish breakfast is the best," she said, through her full mouth.

"Well, he seems to like Nathan a lot. Just like I do. That says something for him," Miriam advocated.

"Look who's here for breakfast," Holly singsong. Tanya and Nancy arrived at the table, rubbing their eyes. "Hi, sweeties. You shouldn't come barefoot to breakfast. You both have slippers."

"My slipper bunnies are still asleep," Tanya pouted, trusting her cuteness. She winked at Nathan. "Hi, Uncle Nate." Four of the seven powers of seduction were already in place, her dark hair, green eyes, complexion of a Sienese madonna, all unnerving to Nathan. How had a couple as basically plain as Max and Holly produced a daughter so astonishing as Tanya, the most precociously sultry eleven year old?

Holly led the girls to seats at the table. "Just have some juice, and I'll make you eggs, unless you want the fish."

"I don't eat fish, it stinks," Nancy whispered to Tanya.

"Yukky fish." Tanya looked at her mother, and the girls giggled.

Breakfast mostly over, Toni Gruber brought her coffee cup around to sit down with Nathan. "What do you want to tell me about your father?" The expression on Nathan's face caught her off guard. "He did tell you about the father project? You are Nathan Briggs?"

It crossed Nathan's mind that maybe he could get out of this by denying to be himself.

"I need a little something to go on; for instance, we know he painted something."

Nathan shrugged. "I don't know anything to tell you. He wasn't a painter, though. That was my mother."

"Well that's a little something, at least. Max said he was a painter."

"I'm glad to see you finally cornered him," Max shouted across the table through his cupped hands. "After you're through with him, Nate and I have something to do."

"My mother is still an artist, Brightwatch. She's pretty famous. My father was obsessed with an Italian painter, Renaissance." Nathan volunteered this, despite his disinclination to talk about it with this stranger.

"That's a sweet place to start. At least I can look that up. I know this must be a difficult subject for you to approach. But I think…I know we can help." She placed a hand on his shoulder.

It's no subject at all, Nathan thought. Not for you. He wondered if someone less unctuous might make him more inclined to cooperate.

"Who's we?"

"Me, and my staff. We're professional, and compassion is a big thing for us."

The woman lightly squeezed his shoulder, and stared through her dark moist eyes.

Nathan pulled his shoulder back, and almost blurted out, "His name is Antonello da Messina."

"Who? Your father?"

"No, the painter."

"I thought you said your father wasn't a painter."

Nathan saw this turning into an Abbott and Costello routine, so he didn't respond.

Toni pulled a small camera from her pocket. "Well, this is a start, anyway. Anything else?"

"I'm trying to find out anything else, myself." Nathan said, brusquely.

"Well, you have to start with something. You don't even have to leave your computer to access the resources. We have many archives for finding out about anyone. And of course, there's family resemblance." She moved the camera close in to his face, and Nathan lifted a hand to protect his eyes from the flash.

"And wasn't there a brother somewhere? His brother, your uncle?"

"I never met an uncle. Maybe I heard about one once, but how did you find out about that?"

"That's not a problem."

After breakfast Max led Nathan and Miriam on a walk back through the sparse woods, on an old cowpath trail, over some rusted barbed wire fence, past the remains of a hollowed log watering trough. Green lizards skittered through a heap of rocks that at one time marked something. As they descended the slight downhill slope, the snowcaps, visible from the house, slowly disappeared behind the foothills. An occasional crescendo of dozers and chainsaws rode up the valley on warm breezes. Miriam picked up half a rusted horseshoe, sniffed it, turned it over in her hand, let it drop. "Horses once," she said.

"I'm going to bring the horses back," Max said, lifting his chin with pride.

"Come on, Max. You've never seen a horse," Nathan pushed his shoulder.

"I'd love to be around horses again," Miriam said. "When my family had some money we kept a horse, Winks, it was a retired pacer. My father would get seasick when he rode it. We kept it in a stable near Prospect Park, and I took lessons. It was the best two years I ever had as a kid, my time at the stables."

"I want Tanya to ride," Max said, again lifting his chin as if practicing his snob.

He offered a long Cohimbe panatela to Nathan, and lit one himself. "White man speak with forked tongue." He puffed the non-sequitur out with the first mouthful of smoke.

"You can say that again," Miriam laughed.

"A man with forked tongue speak double. Forked tongue pokes twice…" Max waved his arms at random at the hills, as they skirted some low lying cactus, and continued down through a stand of juniper.

"I can't imagine," Miriam said.

Nathan clasped the cigar in his fist. He'd lost the thread of this conversation, and the purpose of this walk. He paused on the trail to look down at some scat. "What is this, is this bear?"

Max came over to check it out. "Looks like shit to me," he said.

"I looked at this wildlife book, to identify by prints and by droppings, like this."

"That's next week for me, this week I do women. Forked tongue pokes what?" He gestured at Miriam as if she should have an answer ready. She shrugged.

"Pokes the plush treasure, the jewel box, treasure cache. Secrets hidden there, the sequesterings of the woman's essence." His nose once again lifted to congratulate himself.

Miriam looked up to try to see what Max found above his head. She saw a lot of sky. "God, I need a cigarette. Why did I stop smoking?" She sat down on a large rock, then stood up again, then sat back down when Max started to wave his hand at Nathan.

"Look at the average guy," Max said. "He's all plumage."

"Nathan?" Miriam wrinkled her nose.

"A man is all show. His musculature is advertisement of who he is. Beer belly as well. And for instance, look at the much maligned dick…"

"Come on, Max," Nathan chuffed. "If you can't say something nice, don't malign."

"Wait. Yeah. It is a persecution, because it hangs out there on display, to suffer slings and arrows etcetera. Tattoos for instance are part of a man's presentation of himself, if he isn't his tattoos he wants to be; whereas on a woman, tattoos are just another layer of cover to wrap her essence, her jewels, the secrets, her undiscovered…Even the clitoris lies under a little hood…"

"Max," Miriam shouted at him. "You're so full of it." She threw a clod of dirt at him. "This is the great outdoors. Why are you talking indoors talk?"

"No. I mean it. I've put in some serious thought here. Exhibitionism, for instance. I can tell you why it's so easy for a woman to be an exhibitionist."

"No. Just shut up, Max." Miriam hit him on the arm.

"Wait. The joke is on the guys. Can't you see? And

you know why, because she isn't really giving anything away. Everything essentially her is hidden under that soft cover. Her flesh is like armament. The whole body is a concealment, even the labia when they close, but not quite, just a little pink tempty…"

"Shut up, Max. Now I feel sorry for Holly." Miriam turned her back on him and settled on her stone to watch a black beetle, with long, crooked legs, stumble across a mound of twigs and pine needles.

"So then the cock, dick, penis, a little quixotic, goes on its exploratory expedition, its penetration like research."

"Max," said Nathan. "An expedition? You should email that to Masters and Johnson. What's the orgasm, then? Shangri-la, Valhalla."

Max's voice rose with the screech of excavators working on the other end of the valley. "It's a ruse, Nathan. I'm here to tell you this. The orgasm prevents his ever getting there, to that lore, that lowdown, the real dope, the secret he wants to know so passionately."

"You know how to have fun, Max." She prodded her beetle with a stick.

"Wait, wait. That's why men don't scream so much, because they are listening. They have to, in case something is revealed. Something they need to hear."

"Nate, we'd better get Holly the world's most passionate vibrating dildo."

"Holly already has all the dildoes, believe me." Pillars of light tilted from between the clouds and bore down into the valley though the constructon dust. "All I'm saying is that a woman's screams are nothing but a diversionary tactic."

"What about having fun?" Miriam and Nathan said, almost in unison, and they high-fived as Nathan sat down next to her.

"We're looking in all the wrong places," Max said, sitting on a rock across from them. "Someone told me those were stink-bugs." He pointed at the tortured beetle.

"No. We're not," Nathan said, sounding more impassioned than he felt about this. "Pussy is a great place to look."

"And cock," Miriam added. "What is more mysterious than cock?"

"Well, maybe it's like string theory. My own string theory. Dark matter hidden in a dimension we can't access." Max flipped a hand towards the treetops. "On the other hand…"

"People get horny, Max. End of research," Miriam interrupted.

"…maybe fucking is just fucking." Max sucked hard on his cigar, to rekindle the dimming ember, and looked at them with his most self-satisfied grin. Then he rose and took a few steps further down the slope, and swung his arm in a wide arc. "What do you think of all this land here?"

Nathan watched as Max gazed over the tops of the junipers with a blind, visionary stare. He looked like the rabbi of some as yet unnamed religion. Dotcommoners, Cyberians, Pyritists, Dildonians. Maybe, Kinkish.

"Well? What do you think?" He flicked his lighter, and pushed the flame in Nathan's face.

Nathan nudged Max's hand away. "Nice land, Max. Very nice land."

"Light your cigar, Nate. Smoke it," Max said, flicking the flame again.

"It's so dry here, and empty," Miriam said. "I like more green around me."

Nathan looked into the small flame and remembered the panatela in his fist. He peeled off the cellophane, nipped a bit off the end, and sucked at the fire.

"You get used to it, Miriam. You get to love the dry air." He picked up a clod of dirt, and crumbled it in his hand. "So Nate, what do you think?"

"About what?"

"Your land. I'm giving you this piece of land. It's the least I can do." He squeezed both Nathan's shoulders. "Your piece starts here, and goes down to a dry stream bed down there."

"What do you mean, giving it to me? How can you give it to me? Why?"

"To both of you. I mean, I'm grateful. I wouldn't have what I have today if it wasn't for you."

Nathan and Miriam looked at each other, both puzzled.

"I'm not forcing it on you. Only if you want it. It's just a little parcel that's left in the subdivision, just eighteen acres, so here it's zoned that you can't buy it and build on it, but if you own a contiguous piece and build on that, you can do a secondary building. So I bought it for you." He brought the flame to Nathan's face again. His cigar had gone out. "This is out west, man. This is the Rockies. This is where it's at for the twenty-first century."

"So you bought this for us?"

"Yeah. I can't deed it over to you, because you wouldn't be allowed to build on it if you owned it, but I can give you a letter of intent, and you have my word that it's yours, and you can do what you want, and it's yours forever. I mean, the zoning will change eventually. I'll give you a letter."

A shift of light caught something Nathan hadn't seen before in the distance below them. "Is that a boxcar?"

"We can remove it. At one time the Santa Fe Rairoad was selling them off just for the price of delivery. There are several around here. We'll get rid of it."

"Isn't that someone?" Miriam asked.

Nathan too saw someone moving around the boxcar, stooping as if to tend a garden. What kind of life, he wondered, could someone live in a boxcar? From this distance he couldn't exactly tell what was going on.

"Someone lives there?"

"Yeah, I think someone does. He's a squatter in a boxcar. I haven't been down to speak to him, but he must know he has to leave."

"You can't just kick him out," Miriam said.

Max lit another cigarette. "Why would he want to live here anyway, with all this new development going on."

"What are you going to tell him?" she asked.

"We'll work that out. That's not a problem. So how about it, Nate? Nice spot, or what? We'll be neighbors."

"I have to think about it, Max. Thank you, anyway. First I'm going back to New York. You know I'm moving my office out of the damned World Trade Center, up to the Lehigh-Starrett, that huge renovation. And then to Italy…"

"To look for a phantom father." Max said, disparagingly.

"I've got to do that, Max. I've got to get out from under this father thing."

"What a waste."

"And I'd have nightmares about evicting the guy living in that boxcar," Miriam said.

"By the time you get back, he'll be gone."

The honking of two small V's of geese made them

look to the sky, one V headed North, the other pointed West. Nathan put an arm around Miriam, and pulled her to himself. Down there the boxcar dweller seemed to have stopped to look at them, as if he had smelled them on the wind.

"So?…You like?"

"I don't know. I have to think. It's…first I'm going back to Italy, then…"

"Once we get Italy into the virtual, and your father program up to speed…What do you think, Miriam?"

Miriam felt suddenly trapped, as if the wide open spaces threatened to clamp shut on her. Max looked like someone from far away elsewhere, a demon from some underground, risen from his own private subway into this confusing clarity of a place, a blinded demon that couldn't really see where he was, but pretended to own wherever. "I can't if we have to move that guy."

"That's automatic. You don't have to worry about it."

Nathan didn't know what to say, didn't even know what he thought. Mentioning Italy brought him back to his father again. Now this was all he wanted to think about. "So if we say yes, do any of those girls come with it?" he said, because he knew it would neutralize Max. Miriam pulled away from his arm, and looked at him, pretending to be offended.

"Now we seem to be getting somewhere," Max said.

Something barked in the distance. It could have been a dog. Or it could have been a coyote. Does a golden eagle bark? If a bear barks is it a bear? A small dog in the distance barks.

ISLAND

ISLAND

She had abandoned Solomon in front of *The Triumph Of Death,* a potent anonymous fresco in the Palazzo Sclafani. He had come to Sicily to get the feel of the island where Antonello had lived and worked. He hadn't ever heard of this Death but had come to look at the Antonello masterpieces here that still pulsed with life. This fifteenth century work looked earlier, but was contemporary with his Antonello. It once had "decorated" the wall of a convent hospital, the gift to Palermo from a mysterious artist some say might have been Pisanello, because there was a vague stylistic echo, though it could as well have been Simone Martini, or an admirer of Giotto, or perhaps it was some itinerant Spanish master who worked this job in during an extended sojourn. It looked almost Mexican with its passion for the skeleton. For Solomon this was some visual static on the line, not necessary to his mission; but before Violeta would let him in to see what he had come for, she insisted on making him check in at several points of death; these morbid representations that Palermo served up. Here in Palermo he wanted to see Antonello's *Vergine Annunziata*, an annunciation focussed totally on Mary's face and hands, on her state of mind. He found out it was in storage, unavailable, and Violeta Nizzi was his only chance, because she was a curator with a key. He had been introduced to her by a friendly young man who rode the train with him from Naples. She promised to be helpful, though she seemed a little morose and reserved. The sombre mood was caused, probably, by her father's grave illness. She had even dragged Solomon with her to have a look at her father dying, in the old city, of pancreatic cancer.

Now he stood alone in front of this immense death fresco, while his "guide" returned to her father's bedside. She promised to be back within the hour, at a better time to visit the Antonello. He'd seen this triumphant death theme before, painted by the elder Brueghel, in the galleries of the Prado in Madrid. That one was a deep smoldering landscape across which the armies of death marched, and the painter illustrated there a terrifying array of punishment for sinners and blasphemers. But the images of this fresco were in your face, no "window" onto a vanishing point, to distance the viewer from the figures. The skeletal figure of death so delicate, rode a horse stretched out into a corrugation of ribs, a baleful, jeering icon of pain, of loss, of grief. Picasso must have known this horse, before he painted his *Guernica.*

All through the morning Violeta Nizzi had shown him death. First she took him to the necropolis in the catacombs of the Cappucine Monastery, then to her father's death bed, and now to this great fresco. "You have to enjoy the taste of death," she said. "Appreciate the mortal comedy, to appreciate Sicily."

He didn't want to swallow this idea. It would be enough to see the painting he had come to see, and to move on.

The most beloved holiday, she explained later, was I Morti, the dead, All Souls Day. Children loved it because it was a chance to romp in the cemeteries, and there was a wild feast of sweets, particularly the marzipan, formed into apples, bananas, peaches, nespoli, fichi d'India, grapes, even peas and corn and beans, even spaghetti, lasagna, all the shapes and colors of all the foods transformed into an almond confection. Death in Sicily was a sugary celebration, as it was in Mexico on "The Day Of The Dead."

Violeta's strangest move was to take him to her father's house. He'd always heard that Sicilians didn't easily open their homes to strangers. Maybe Violeta felt this was part of her duty, to teach him about Sicily. Or maybe she brought him to distract other people in the room, so she could manage some intimate moments with her dying father. The smell of the deathwatch filled the narrow street below, herbs smoldering, camphor, incense. Death coated his tongue like rancid oil. Two people stood next to the bed, one who Violeta said was a brother, her uncle, a man prematurely old, in a threadbare brown suit, a greasy ageless Borsalino that perhaps before his hair had thinned and turned grey sat on top, but now was held up only by his ears. The Sicilian sun had permanently scorched his face, burnt as the Sicilian hills. He stared at Solomon through dark, sunken eyes, and worked his toothless gums. Solomon saw the question of who was he in the dying man's eyes, but neither of them said a word. The other one was the dying man's mistress, a wraith of a woman, sobbing a relentless pulse of grief in a corner. She moved restlessly under the black cape she wore, that came straight down stiffly from her shoulders, like a bell over its tongue. The wife, her mother, was dead already six years, Violeta told him, and a good thing, because seeing the mistress would have caused too much pain. Solomon stood next to a third person in the room, a cheerful plump older woman who tended the burning of herbs, and incanted a verse in her Sicilian dialect, occasionally interrupting to speak to Violeta and even to Solomon, who didn't understand a word. Occasionally she'd laugh at something she herself had said, and the brother on that cue would expel a painfully gasped ha-ha, coming from that place in his belly where laughter had once originated.

"This is Ciccina," Violeta introduced them. "She comes from Menfi. My uncle Pino brought her with him. It's near our family's land, accursed land. It's worthless, now that the mafia keeps all the water for itself, and sells it, sells water that comes from the heavens, at prices no *contadino* can afford. Uncle Pino's been working the salt in Selinunte. That's what has made him look so old."

Her father lay beneath a new plastic crucifix colored poorly, so the lips bled onto the cheek, and the eyes slipped out of their sockets. His color because of the liver failure was murky and brownish green, as if mold was growing under his skin. His jaundiced eyes strained upwards through the ceiling. In time with Ciccina's voice, he started to moan, then suddenly sat up in his bed, and screeched with her some notes of the incantation. Solomon didn't think he could have that much strength in his voice. Violeta rushed over to settle him, then filled a hypodermic with morphine, and shot him up.

"I just want to make him comfortable. He takes some comfort in the dialect, you understand. Italian is the language of the corrupt government that ruined his life. It's television language, the language of hallucination, of northern prosperity. And at this stage he prefers his Ciccina to all the doctors, all the specialists, who haven't done him any good anyway. One comes later today to visit. That will be trouble. It has to be the malocchio, he explains it now, somewhere someone who works the lemon groves he manages gave him the evil eye, and that was how he got this condition. He's an educated man but this is how he prefers to make sense of it now, rather than call it cancer. Cancer is a corporate word, too impersonal, universal. Cancer does not take him to his roots. Maybe you call this superstition, but this is the way he understands what has happened to him. That is so important, Mr. Briggs."

Ciccina spoke to Solomon, and Violeta translated some of it. "She tells you about the worms, how the worms have deserted his sack, I guess she means his stomach, because he can't keep any food down, and it's the worms that help you digest, that keep the food down for you. She says she is waiting for three worms to come out of him, because there were three nails put into the lord." Ciccina held up three fingers to illustrate.

A wounded cry rose from the bed to remind everyone in the room of the source of the grief. The dying man had thrown off his covers, and wrapped a hand around his penis and feebly tried to masturbate. The brother sank to the floor against the wall, and Violeta rushed back to the bedside. "Miraluccia, basta," she implored, and reached for the skeletal woman, who had undone her dark cape at the neck, and let it fall to the tiles. She was bare underneath, skin white as if it had been bleached, the hair over her mound swollen bigger than her poor belly, and pitch black as the entrance to a pyramid. Before Violeta could stop her, she twisted onto the bed, a whimpering, skeletal thing, and then thrashed onto the dying man, who threw his jaundiced head back, wheezing.

"I'm sorry. Please go downstairs, wait there for me."

Violeta pushed him towards the door. Exiting the melodrama so suddenly tripped Solomon into a void. There was nothing familiar on these streets. The women who leaned from windows or stood in the doorways, with black scarves around their heads, their arms around a child, were not from his world. A Vespa sputtered slowly up the street, carrying a young man with a green umbrella. Here creeped a bent old man who pushed a two wheeled cart of metal scraps past Solomon. He stopped to rest. He turned back and stared. All of this from a different planet. This was more than he had bargained for. He had come to see a painting, not to visit this poor comedy of life and death. The heat of an ancient sun sent chill into his bones.

After a while Violeta rejoined him to lead him away to this crumbling palace, to dump him in front of *The Triumph Of Death,* saying nothing more about what had just happened in her father's room, her distance and reserve reassumed, so he was reluctant to ask any questions. He could have left her and this whole embroilment, and forgotten about all this, except that she was his only chance to see the painting. Wasn't it stupid that he should need to see this painting?

Here he waited while the skeleton on its grey horse gathered indiscriminately the wealthy and the poor, the weak with the strong. Here the horse he called inevitability, all ribs and bones, mocked the haughty as it mocked the meek.

When he first hooked up with Violeta, they had met near where the Antonello was housed, at the Palazzo Abatellis. Many of the streets of old Palermo were mysteriously empty, abandoned to decay. To meet someone in this almost negated place piqued his fantasy. He had anticipated her as his adventure with a dark-eyed Sicilian beauty, mysterious. charming, someone voluptuous, a temptation he would have to resist, but felt a twinge of disappointment when he first saw her. Her eyes were dark as he had hoped, with creases of disillusionment and sadness radiating from the corners. She looked as if she had been neglecting herself, and had recently put on a lot of weight, had perhaps given up her last grip on youth, and had abandoned whatever battles she fought to keep herself attractive. The nicely tailored grey suit she wore was uncomfortably tight, and as they walked together into the Abatellis courtyard he caught glimpses of her bra where her rayon blouse pulled open against the buttons. She called him Mr. Briggs, even after he offered her Solomon or Sol, and all her responses were formal, which made him apologize for the imposition, but she said, "Figuravi, mister Briggs. I am here to help. I enjoy this." When the workers told her the afternoon would be a better time to take him in to see the Antonello, she suggested they go over to the Cappucine Monastery. It was appropriate anyway, she told him, that he experience the necropolis first. He'd hardly had a thought about what it was, a necropolis, a catacomb.

At the monastery door she left him on his own. She'd spent enough time, she said, in there with the dead. "Better to visit this place by yourself."

According to the pamphlet he picked up at the door, this was the largest collection of mummified bodies in the world. Shelves of skulls stretched down the long corridor, and vanished into the dusty light. A smell like tanning leather and the air dimly overripe intensified as he moved deeper down under the vaults of the gallery. Bodies hung from hooks like life-size marionettes. That they still wore their clothes, their monks' robes, made it seem that for them death had been unanticipated, had given them no time to dress properly, out of their clothes and into their shrouds. Their heads were bowed, as if in homage to himself, to Solomon Briggs still among the living. Maybe it was nerves that started him giggling, way in his belly. Many of the mouths stretched taut into grins, and he was electing to join that jollier company, rather than taking on the grimace of those for whom death had been a painful arrest.

"What's that laugh about?" One thing asked.

He shouted into the snickering that surrounded. "You guys are all dead," and then a prideful. "I am alive." His robust laughter this time shocked everything else into silence. I am talking to them, he told himself. Crazy to do this, but who knows about it? And it's my choice. "I'm alive to choose," he said aloud, and moved deeper into the various pungencies of the displays, down the corridors of many dead.

"So are they treating you well in this place," he asked aloud, because he felt more comfortable hearing at least his own voice.

"Si," responded the bassoonlike chorus of the dead, stirring not the slightest plume of dust. "No!"

No caretaker was evident. He was the only visitor. Speech was his best recourse.

"What difference does it make? I am a visitor. All of you are dead."

"You are dead," echoed the dead.

He was in an alcove now, with the smallest mummies of children, cute mummies, and excellent ladies mummified in their fineries. With them he took a few turns of a dance, a hesitation kind of boogie, and the music he danced to seemed to sift through the walls with the dust on a wind from Africa. This was a jolly and a horrible celebration.

"Ha ha, sweetheart, you are dead," he said to one small girl, arrested just before puberty, brittle pink bows fading in her lusterless hair. She was hanging from a hook, under the protecting skeleton hand of a matron in a nightdress. "You two will never get out of here. Dead before the maidenhead decapitates. When did you last get laid, lady? And you, little girl, did you ever swim naked in a river? Now you'll never get out of here."

"Never get out of here," replied the oboe of her ancient voice.

Solomon spun on his heel when he heard a laugh behind himself. There was a monk, a long one hanging almost from the apex of the double vault. "Sorry, signore, but I might never get out of here either. Don't think I don't know it." Solomon apologized. "Better here, I guess, than in a plane crash." This was one of those grinners, lips stretched back against his teeth. "How did you get yourself into this condition, mister?" Solomon stepped closer. "When you were a kid, didn't you play with hoops? Didn't you catch scorpions in the dry gullies? Didn't your father take you to work in the vendemmia? And your mother brought you bread, salami, goat cheese? Didn't you drink the vino nero? Didn't you play the flute?"

Solomon heard the yellow growl of the bassoon again from somewhere deep within another corridor. "Soon you," said the sober tones. "Soon you."

"I know. I know. Life is the masquerade. Death is a snap shut."

Being there was to mingle with the members of a club that he hadn't yet joined, and though he felt not unwelcome, he was for the time being excluded from their initiations, and the information that they shared in their private cliques. Easy to join. Death is not an exclusive club. No one is ever more than six inches from his own cadaver, and Palermo is organized to make you aware of that. Before long he would make his own contribution to the exhibition.

Though he feared he had gone too deep, and maybe was lost, he found his way out easily. Violeta waited for him in her small Lancia. "You were in there a long time," she said. "I thought maybe you had joined the monks."

"Alive or dead?"

She smiled at him as if she didn't want to say what she could have said.

"Were you waiting here long?"

"No, I went to see my father. I'm going right back there. You can come along with me now, and meet him. Just a few blocks away."

"And the Antonello?"

"In time. So you enjoyed?"

"I had some interesting conversations." Solomon resented her pushing him through this. He hardly knew her, but she acted as if she was his weird sister, as if she knew what he needed.

"Not everyone appreciates to talk to the dead." She smiled, the first smile he'd seen on her face, and it made her look less cheerful than her neutral expression. It was the smile, Solomon realized, of one of Antonello's portraits, a very Sicilian face, like the guarded innocence of the blonde youth at the Met, or the cunning of the unknown sailor in Cefalù, or the ancient sleazy grin of the portrait in Torino. Each so mirthless.

And here in the fresco of triumphant death, they all

were falling, the youths and the maidens, the lutanist falling on the lady, the warden with his hounds, the smug nobles at their fountain, those deluded spectators dropping down with those already gone. Was the apprehension he had felt on crossing to Sicily related to the feeling he got from this fresco? Was it that he wanted to resist the whole comedy of death played too easily in the burning footlights of this island?

When the train arrived at Villa San Giovanni to wait for the ferry he got off and looked across the Straits of Messina at the island of his Antonello. Big bellied clouds gathered above the mountains. The prospect of crossing made him uneasy. Wouldn't it be better with someone, to play with Isabel for instance, and they could indulge in the beaches of Taormina, or Agrigento, or Cefalù, or Catania? They could perfect their tans. This was the wrong season. Maybe no season would come when Sicily could be comfortable, because what he knew already about them was that they were a sad people, unlike the friendly, demonstrative, outgoing Romans, or the Neapolitans who would immediately enfold you in their embrace, as if you were a friend, and sing a song into your ear as they picked your pockets, stole your shoes, sold you your own watch, offered you a trip to Venus. The Sicilians were a taciturn, dour people, courteous and always formal, and they took little or no interest in your business, unless you transgressed their cryptic boundaries, in which case the consequences could be grim. There was the look of their Arab ancestry in their faces, tinged with fatalism. Inch'Allah. You could see this in some of Antonello's portraits, cunning eyes that gazed on you with knowing circumspection, and enigmatic smiles that made the Mona Lisa's expression seem banal.

He knew from the outset that he would never find the St. Francis on the island itself. Why expose even slightly the thin fabrics of his obsession, to the risk of disintegrating them with the truth? His search depended on its location outside logic, somewhere on the cusp of dreams? There was something he needed on this road he traveled, but as yet he didn't know what. Perhaps he was taking everything too seriously. Too earnest, Isabel had said. Relax, Briggs. But what was this, if not serious? Could he ever reconcile the cliches of violence, the oppression, the corruption, all those women in black, walls built of corpses, tapestries woven of sheer blood, the unmentionable Cosa Nostra of everything, with these sublime paintings he loved, and the transcendant humanity of his painter. Did Antonello come from the Sicily they approached? And Allesandro Scarlatti, and Luigi Pirandello? Elio Vittorini? Some of those kids he'd grown up with near the George Washington bridge were from Sicilian roots — Mike Petruzzi, Nick Bennardo, two tough kids, angry, brave, attractive; and then there was Vincent Falconieri, unique amongst the kids he grew up with, practicing hard every day to be a concert pianist, till he died young.

Sicily. He jumped back onto the train just as it was being fed into the hold of the ferry. Thunder pounded the straits, and roared through the dim emptiness inside the ship. Each peal dropped against Solomon's back like a lead shawl. Then there was a jolt, and release, as the ferry pushed back, and let loose of the last threads of mainland Europe, making a sudden vertigo, himself so tiny, adrift, light as insects to be carried up into thunder on transparent wings.

He sat in the compartment, looking blindly through his window at the dim, yellowed atmosphere of the hold. Two men in dark suits, and a young student dressed casually had traveled in the compartment with him all the way from Naples. They had exchanged not a word. The suited men sat across from each other near the corridor. They were as if in uniform, traveling together on business, one with a briefcase on his lap, from which he occasionally pulled a sheaf of papers that he passed across to the other, and they discussed the pages in guarded whispers. The young man sat in the middle seat across from Solomon. He wore grey twill pants, and a blue angora sweater over a pale pink shirt. He clung to a pack of Marlboros in his left hand, as if to steady himself on a difficult ride. Occasionally he moved the hand holding the cigarettes to slip them into the shirt pocket under his sweater, but the pack always emerged again, stuck to his palm. He tapped a smoke out of the pack, then put it back after just touching it to his lips.

Solomon felt the ferry swing around. The two men got up and left the compartment. He watched as they entered a stairwell marked by a small red light. It hadn't occurred to him before that he could go up on deck, and that was a happy idea. Once the other two were gone, the young man glanced at him furtively, as if he wanted to speak, but then he looked away.

"Are you going to Palermo?" Solomon ventured to speak first.

"I go to Partinico." His response was like a gasp, and he looked at Solomon as if that was supposed to register something, some signal in the name of the place.

"But this car does go to Palermo?"

"Yes. Palermo, it stops." He pulled a cigarette from the pack. "I think so." He fumbled the cigarette, so it dropped to the floor, and rolled under Solomon's seat. Solomon retrieved it, and handed it to the young man, who made an attempt to clean it off, then crushed it into the ash tray. "I like to stop. I don't want to smoke."

"I guess I'll go up on deck," Solomon said, mostly to himself.

"Yes," said the young man. "My name is Annelino," he offered, as Solomon stepped into the corridor, and he felt the eyes watching as he entered the stairwell.

In the cafeteria he bought a paper cup of espresso, and an arancine, the fried rice croquette official Sicilian snack, which he munched as he walked along the rail to the bow where passengers huddled to watch the great island approach. Where was Scylla, which Charybdis? Except for a couple of young nordics embraced against a bulwark he found nothing in this company to leaven his mood. Messina itself looked from this distance like a whisper of white chalk, fragile under the slate grey thunderheads flexed over Sicily. This city had been ravaged by earthquakes, and reconstructed, and ravaged again, rebuilt again and again, buildings leveled, monuments, paintings erased. So could he say the city he now approached was the same as Antonello's birthplace? He tried to find the hill on which the painter had set his Messina crucifixion, a work that Solomon had seen before, on a dreary trip to Bucharest, in the dark rooms of the Rumanian national museum. He looked for the church, the wall, the castle at least which Antonello had used as the setting for the crucifixion drama, Christ tragic and calm, the two thieves, so excruciated, above the figures of women below dispersed in a choreography of isolation and grief. Messina was no Calvary. That was Antonello's joke, an homage to his home town. The curve of the shoreline resembled somewhat the picture, and the hook of the small peninsula, along which now the buff facades of dull government buildings crowded, and nondescript hotels, and apartment houses that rose precariously up the hillside, hanging on there in anticipation of the next catastrophe. It was as if planners didn't want Messina to call attention to itself. Compared to the grace and strength of other Italian cities, set like jewels in his mind—Firenze, Siena, Pavia, Napoli, Roma, Parma, Padova, Venezia—this place looked like nowhere, as it waited for the fierce island to quake again.

What was left of Antonello's Madonna on her throne, with the powerful infant on her lap, was housed here, and he would have to plow through the distractions, the pollution, the noise, all the crud of modern Messina to get at it. This was his pilgrimage, after all. He would start at Palermo, and make his way around the north coast, to the great portrait of the unknown mariner in the museum in Cefalù, and back to Messina, and down to Siracusa where the ruined *Annunciation* rested. He assigned himself to see all the paintings left in Sicily, to prepare for when he finally came on the lost St. Francis, wherever he found it.

The others were already in their seats, when he returned and settled back down, as the ferry pushed into the Messina terminal. The idea of a pilgrimage, the pretense of it, plastered a grin onto his face, that disappeared when he noticed one of the suits seated across from him staring at him through the semi-dark. When the hold opened and the train jerked back to life, and pulled in to the Messina station, the man kept staring.

The sneer on his face made Solomon sure he'd offended someone, violated some protocol. This was his unwelcome to Sicily. The young man near him sat holding on to his cigarettes with both hands, gazing into the empty seat across from himself. Solomon looked out the window. Perhaps he should change compartments. Strange there was no one in the station. This discomfort could be a sign of what he was in for. Was he going to be reminded again and again that he didn't belong here? Rain came down hard, streaming through holes in the canopies. He looked back into the compartment, and noticed the man's chin settled into his chest. He was asleep. He'd probably not been staring at all, but had been falling asleep all along. "Briggs, you're a paranoid jerk," he thought, the paranoia from exhaustion, from traveling alone.

The two businessmen got off at Termini Imerese. Turning in the doorway before they left, one of them spoke with great formality, his voice higher than Solomon might have guessed. "Buon proseguimento, carissimi signori, e buona fortuna," and they both bowed, and disappeared.

"I didn't want to talk while they were here," said the young man, shifting seats so he was directly across from Solomon. "You never know about them." He leaned very close.

"About them? About whom?"

"Cosa Nostra. The mafia. They don't travel on

trains, usually, especially not second class. But I have to be careful."

He was close enough so Solomon could feel warmth coming off the young man's body, his breath of fried fish and garlic.

"I have been at the center in Partinico, with Danilo Dolce. You know who is Danilo Dolce? They say the mafia knows well who we are. O, excuse me. Did I say my name is Annelino, Annelino Ballatore. I was living in Trieste, where Danilo comes from, but I was born near Siracusa. And you are from America?" He put the cigarettes down at his side to take Solomon's hand.

"Solomon Briggs. Yes. I'm from New York City." The young man's sweating hands encased both his own.

"New York City. Yes. Little Italy. Chinese Town. Brooklyn Bridge. Staten Island Ferry. Statue of Libertà. Magnificent. I been there, not for long visit, but I been."

"There are plenty of Italians in New York City." Solomon pulled his hand away, and wiped it on the seat.

"Plenty, yes, but bad Italian restaurants there." The young man looked out the window and toyed with a cigarette, then held the pack out to Solomon. "I'm sorry. I didn't think. Maybe you want a cigarette? American Marlboro cigarette." When Solomon refused he leaned closer. "I am trying to stop, myself. Danilo says it would be good for me to stop, a good sign for me. So why do you come to Sicily? You are a tourist?"

"Yes, and…not exactly."

"Well, you should come to Partinico, and see the work we are doing at the center. If you come, you will stay and work with us."

Solomon shifted to move his face away from the young man's, who then leaned back against his seat. "So many poor people, and so much misery, and the Cosa Nostra, call themselves men of honor, but men of murder is what they are. This is a beast that impoverishes the contadini, and the government allows that beast to feed off poor people. Only Danilo tries to help, and to tell the truth about it." He leaned close to whisper in Solomon's ear. The young man's breath was moist. "You understand what I'm saying."

Solomon pulled back, "Yes." After a few uncomfortable moments of silence, and feeling too close to Annelino, Solomon leaned away and said, "I have come to see the paintings of Antonello da Messina." Solomon felt like he was professing his virtue, to ward off what he took to be the young man's advances, and as if he had to justify his presence in Sicily.

"Ahhh. Antonello da Messina. What a marvel. I can help you." He leaned close again. "But I think the painting is in storage now, while they do the restoration on Palazzo Abatellis, to be the museum." Their noses were practically touching, as if the next move had to be a kiss. Solomon had spent plenty of time warding off come-ons in the queer world around Isabel, and her friends in the arts. Those doors swung open several times, and he felt some curiosity, but he had enough to deal with in the passions of what he took to be his normal life. He moved away from the young man, who pulled out a pad and scribbled down some names and numbers as if nothing had been intended. "This is Violeta Nizzi. She is a curator, and she'll help you, and this other is a pensione in the Vucciria. Vucciria is in the middle of old Palermo, the market they call "the dream of the starving man." We stay there sometimes at this Pensione Svevi, when we come down from the center in Partinico. Very cheap. Very clean. Very nice people. And an optimum restaurant."

Solomon took the scribbled paper and thanked him.

"And Violeta, I'll tell her, will show you the Catacombs of the Capuchines, and *The Triumph Of Death*, great fresco. Palermo is the city of death, yes, and this Sicily the island of death. You could say that life here is only an intrusion, an interruption." Annelino was so matter of fact about this, that Solomon listened to him as if he was being invited to a party. "You will look at the art for a while, then remember you have to come to Partinico and work with us. I started out to study some buildings. I am architect like was Danilo, and he came down here too to study buildings, ruins, but couldn't keep it up when people all around me suffered, and the government held hands with the mafia? You will see."

Solomon looked out the window at the slow passing

of the outskirts of Palermo, the shabby, makeshift cinderblock buildings, that looked like they'd been thrown up in an afternoon, and a strong gust of the scirocco could take them down. Clotheslines stretched from house to house, a bright fluttering of laundry as the passing train stirred the air. Women dressed in black stepped through strings of beads that hung in the entryways to watch the train, and check on their children. Kids jumped from puddle to puddle of wastewater on the unpaved streets, their feet stained rusty brown. They too stopped to watch. The train slowed down, and at his window a boy held up a tray of peeled cactus pears, violet, green, orange, yellow. He kissed the fingers of his right hand, screwed his thumb against his cheek, delicious, only fifty lire. He ran along beside the train as it started to move again. Forty.

"Before I came here, after was in school in Trieste, I went to study architecture in Pavia, so these slums cause me a lot of pain. It's the mafia that profits from this criminal shabbiness, these murderous buildings. They build them so cheap. A wall just like that collapsed, just a month ago, killed a baby and paralyzed the mother. The building was two years old." Annelino laid a hand lightly on Solomon's shoulder. "Danilo himself was an architect. That's how I knew of him. I'd heard of him in Trieste, but didn't pay attention. I didn't come back here to meet him. I wanted to look again at the great Norman churches, and also I was in Puglia for the folk architecture, the masserie that Corbusier loved, these big stone-walled enclosures, with beautifully arched stalls built in for the animals, and the houses also built into the wall. See, I still love them. People maybe were poor, but they had a sense of beauty and proportion. There is a genius grows in poverty. But then you have to have at least something to eat. Now there is so much misery here, and I spoke with people, and learned their problems, and I couldn't look at the buildings any more. To be an architect seemed a trivial thing without some benefit for these people. So I went to Partinico." Annelino gathered his bags, and moved them to the corridor. Solomon stood up to grab his own off the rack, and he stumbled as the train lurched. The young man steadied him with an arm, then put a kiss on Solomon's cheek, close to his lips. "You will come too. I see you are a kind man. Look at your paintings, Solomon Briggs. Spend some time in that dry world, without people, then you will come to Partinico and help us. I will welcome you there, and Danilo will embrace you as a brother, a comrade."

The word, "comrade," came to mind again as he stood before *The Triumph of Death*. This great word carried such a burden of stupid politics for his American ear, this once rich assertion of friendship and loyalty. After years of McCarthy horror, it was impossible to use it innocently, a word driven out of the vocabulary as if it was a curse. And where was his "comrade" Violeta now, who had promised to sneak him in to see the painting he had come to see in the first place? Everything always gets complicated. He'd wanted to come through, be invisible, see the Annunciation Virgin, leave. No obligations. He watched a family linger for a few minutes in front of the fresco, the children pointing, asking for explanation of the bony horse, of death itself that looked so delicate holding its axe aloft. "Poor death," said a little boy. The family didn't linger. Enough of death for them. He'd had enough too. And why was death so delicate? And where was Violeta, his comrade? Was she delayed because delicate death had just taken her father, or playful death had just released her father from pain?

After he had settled himself into the pensione he had taken a long walk before dinner, ending up at a telephone office in the Politeama Square, where he first called Violeta to arrange their meeting. He decided then to call Isabel in Venice. It took over an hour to get a line through. Finally Angelica answered the phone, then it took another five minutes to pry Isabel away to speak. Mario was helping her build a kiln.

"You're making ceramics now?" After the wait he didn't have much control of his tone. It sounded more disparaging than he intended.

"I'm not stopping anything else, don't worry. It's just a simple low fire oven kiln. You can make pizza in it when you come back. There's just really this gushy red glaze that Hastings wrote me about, that I have to make something with it. How about you? Is everything okay for you down there?"

"It's a little different. The people are really different here; I mean, I've met nice enough people, but it's like different. A little depressing alone. I wish you were here, and we could have a great dinner together, Izzy. Do you miss me?" A long silence made him wish he hadn't gone fishing for that. He could almost see the pained expression on her face, but unable to hold back, he exacerbated the moment. "Don't you miss me at all?"

"Solomon," came a whine. "No, not really…" Another pause. "I don't mean that exactly as it sounds, like I don't mean no, absolutely not, because I do have the little moments of missing you; I mean, you know, sometimes, when I'm feeling really good, and I get into bed…But I don't have time to miss you, if you know what I mean. I'm so busy, Solomon. I don't have enough time as it is to do what I need to do every day. I've got to get this work done. And in the mornings I'm useless, because I feel so lousy."

"Well I wish you were here, to go to these catacombs with me tomorrow. Take a look at corridors full of mummified people, they tell me, monks hanging on hooks from the walls. I'm not sure I'm looking forward to seeing this alone."

"Sounds like an opening at the Modern. What are you doing there, Solomon? Just to see a painting?"

"You know. Izzy, there has to be some consolation."
"What?"
"You know, some consolation for living."
"A painting? You're easy to please. When did you get so, I don't know, so morbid, Solly."
"I sound morbid, you think?"
"I think you'd better get out of there, Solly. You're taking yourself too seriously. Have a few laughs."

He fell silent. He'd been telling himself the same thing. Too serious. This silence was uncomfortably familiar, a lightless cul-de-sac. He couldn't figure which way to move, until he finally managed, "Did you say you felt lousy in the mornings? Is this what it sounds like?"

"It's the second month I've missed, and I'm always so regular. My body feels a little weird, really like someone else is setting herself up inside me. But maybe I'm just imagining something."

As she spoke Solomon was unprepared for the surge of jubilation on which his spirits rose. It was like a total reversal. This was what made everything meaningful. He looked out into the dim Palermo dusk, such an exalting lavender light. The old theater glowed like a golden temple in the reflections. "O God, this is so great."

"Do you really think so?"
"I can't wait to see you, great big belly."
"Not so big yet, Solly. You can't see anything yet. So

you're having a good time?" She asked as if they hadn't already discussed anything.

"I...yes. I guess so. Someone here I hope is going to get me in to see the *Annunziata.* I get here and it's, wouldn't you know, in restoration, and not open to the public. And then I have to go to Cefalù, and I'll go to Catania where there's paintings by his followers, and then Syracuse, and then I'll come back to you two. O, first to Puglia, and I promised Mario to go to his family, and there's supposed to be this great fresco here, an anonymous thing, and the horse is like Guernica. Picasso must have known it. I'll send a postcard if I find..."

"Don't Picasso me, please."

"It's called *The Triumph of Death.* Do you know about it?"

"That's enough about death, Solomon. I'm not into it right now, please."

"O. Yeah. God. I'm sorry. You must be so full of life; I mean, literally full of amazing life."

"Well, it's a little while before she starts moving."

"I definitely want to be there when it kicks first. I definitely want to feel it move."

"She's not an it..."

Some static hit the line, and then it went dead. They tried several times to reconnect him, but no luck.

"It's okay," he said to the telephone clerk. "I'm going to be a father."

The dining room of his pensione's restaurant was

just off the street, lit up to attract extra business. The harsh fluorescent light, and the large black and whites of the *mattanza,* the tuna slaughter, the *tonnara,* would more likely chase tourists away. Men in the photos bashed the brains of the great fish that had trapped themselves in the nets, the men up to their elbows in blood. One of the owners of the pensione held a part interest in a tuna boat, and the pictures of the slaughter, the tons of huge fish, were like a promise of abundance. Though nine p.m. was early to eat in Palermo, several of the tables were already occupied by men, workers from the quarter. No women. Nothing fancy at these tables— clean tablecloths, simple heavy white plates. Solomon sat down on a bench at one end of a long table; at the other end two stone masons, still covered with dust, wiped their plates of *pasta e fagioli* with thick hunks of bread. The dark-eyed woman with the long black braid, who Solomon had noted cleaning rooms during the day, immediately delivered a basket of *panelle* and bread, the *panelle* a delicious crisp made of fried chickpea flour, and then a bowl of glistening *caponata,* the sweet, sour, slippery blend of eggplant, olives, celery heart, tuna roe, capers, onion, garlic, tomatoes, each sauted to its own perfection in the most virgin olive oil. She brought a half liter of their heavy black wine, and a small plate of *datteri,* sea dates, like razorback clams, steamed open with butter, garlic, wild oregano. Then came a large bowl of *pasta alle sarde,* fettucine with a piquante sauce of sardines. Isabel would love this meal, thought Solomon. "I'm going to be a father," he said to the woman who brought the pasta. "Si," she responded, and took the bowl back, thinking he'd said he didn't want it. He grabbed her arm and retrieved the pasta. "I'm becoming a father," he said again, though he realized she didn't understand him, probably spoke only dialect. "Si. Si," she said again, not touching the pasta this time.

When she came back, she brought the chef with her, carrying his *frittura* of tiny fish and squid, lightly battered, fried golden and crisp, sending up a perfume of hot olive oil, garlic, and herbs. "Tell me what you want," the chef said. "I don't want anything," Solomon replied, raising his carafe of wine and offering some to the chef. "This is wonderful. Everything is wonderful. I just was trying to tell her that I'm going to be a father soon." The chef translated for the waitress, who looked at Solomon for several moments, without smiling. "Eat. Eat everything you can now," she finally told him through the chef. "Because children are a gift from God, but you'd better eat now, because as they grow up, some days they won't let you eat. When you are poor your children eat your bones." He was flattered that she took him for a poor one, like herself, an acceptance as one of her own, if that's what it was. What else could he be, eating in this restaurant at night, where the only other customers were workers from the market, street-cleaners, ragpickers, stone-masons, house-painters, even though for Solomon the food they served was an ambrosial experience. This was the place where only occasionally these workers could afford themselves a meal. Otherwise their dinner was a bit of *panelle,* or some bread drizzled with oil and wild greens. The waitress shouted away the children who had gathered to gawk in through the doorway at people eating big plates of food.

In the early morning he took a walk through the narrow streets, down an alley packed with herb sellers, to the Vucciria marketplace, hollowed out of the dense neighborhood like an open pit mine of food. It teemed like a hive of paper wasps, stalls packed one on the other, under grey umbrellas and awnings that kept the sun off the fresh slices of fish, the slabs of tuna and swordfish, the bright-eyed merluzzo and triglie, gills still purpling with blood. In a clay tub shining eels knotted and unknotted their lengths, and squid so recently caught, the squid-monger said he'd show Solomon how fresh it was, and with his teeth tore off a bite of tentacles. A small mountain of sea urchin creaked next to buckets of vongole and quohogs. Ropes of mussels hung on a line, and special tiny oysters in a cup, and some edible barnacles shipped all the way from Portugal. A great manta ray hung against a wall, like a coat of arms. This was quieter than the markets in Rome, or Naples, no shouting of wares, nor loud cajoling of customers. Boys in rubber aprons and boots wielded straw whisks to shoo the flies off the fresh meat, the hearts and brains and sweetmeats and kidneys and livers, the tiny lambs and kids split open on hooks, the opalescent entrails, and offal, the pink hoofs, the hairy ears, the spiral penises of pigs, the peeled heads of sheep and goats, grey, blue veined testicles gleaming in a basket. And then the sausages, and salamis, the soppresato and mortadella, the blocks of coagulated blood, and great hanging cheeses, wheels of parmigiano from the north, and peppato from Enna, pecorinos hard and soft, and cups of ricotta white as cotton, and mozzarella in its bath, fresh that morning. And such heaps of fruit and vegetables, lemons and oranges, freckled apricots, nespoli, cactus pears in all their hues, honeydew melons, and watermelons cut open, and peaches, figs black as the eyes of the women that sell them, and green figs too, eggplant both ebony and pale, zucchini in a spectrum of greens, and zucchini flowers like a bin of daffodils, and great yellow gourds, and a rainbow of peppers, and tomatoes from green to pink to damask to ruby, and garlands of garlic, and leeks, and shallots in a box; and all this gave off such a complicated perfume of plenitude, such an illusion of opulence, that it was difficult to believe anyone back on the streets in this neighborhood could actually be going hungry. But who could afford to buy some shares of this? Few of the people living in the crumbling apartments of the old city. For them money was unattainable, a dim abstraction; but the grand signori could send their servants to shop for the freshest, the nobility not yet impoverished could order their share delivered, and the government bureaucrats, and the mafiosi, the politicians, the lawyers and doctors and undertakers, and Solomon could afford it, like any tourist, even the ones with backpacks, who slept by the side of the road. Food was a privilege for the privileged, and this market opened only as a dream for the hungry man sleepwalking into it.

"Hello, Mr. Briggs. Please forgive me. I'm so sorry you had to wait for me," Violeta arrived finally, to relieve him from *The Triumph of Death.* She waved her purse at the fresco. "You see. Even the archbishop has taken one of the arrows through his throat." She could feel that Solomon was annoyed, and restless. "I kept you waiting so long. I apologize again."

"I'll avoid ever becoming the archbishop." Solomon struggled to lighten up the mood. "Maybe a shepherd. Maybe a fisherman. Maybe a worm in his fish."

"I had to stay for the visit from the doctor, and then Miraluccia needed more comforting. Sometimes she's good to take care of my father, believe it or not, except when she gets crazy."

"I thank you very much for showing this to me, but can we get out of here? I'm tired of it now; I mean, death can wear you out." A feeble joke.

"Yes, you have to have patience. Art can be a burden. Now I will take you to see the Antonello."

Solomon could have backed out right then. He'd already seen more than he could absorb. No more paintings, no more death stuff. His mind felt thick and useless. Only that he reminded himself that this would be his one chance to see this picture now made him follow her into the street. At this point he could have said he didn't care what this painting looked like. He'd seen it in books, in photographic reproduction. Enough of Palermo, he thought. Enough Sicily and its grim attitudes, its Cosa Nostra, its misery. Enough of the joys of death. Enough of the rich sweets and the bitter histories. An easy Roman orgy would be nice now, some flashes of the Etruscan love for life. This pilgrimage was just a tangent to, not central to his hunt. He could have rushed back to be with Isabel, a hand on her belly. He followed Violeta anyway through the crumbling streets, back to the Palazzo Abatellis, a plain facade, but inside a beautiful courtyard half covered with scaffolds and piles of stone for the restoration. She did have the key, and took him inside, up a wide stairway, and around through rooms with floors torn up, and walls covered with tarps. Occasionally she'd stop at a work that interested her, of some saints, or some moment in the Christian story, and lecture him enthusiastically about its place in the church, and the story of Jesus. Finally they came to a room that was finished and clean. Standing on the terra-cotta tiles, in the center of the room, was a heavy easel, a white sheet tented over it.

"Here it is," said Violeta, and she removed the sheet. "Here is your famous painting, Antonello da Messina." He detected a tinge of sarcasm in her voice, but let it pass.

At first from his angle, he couldn't see through the reflection off the glass. There was a simple mahogany frame, with a golden inner border. He rubbed his eyes, as if to wipe away some blindness.

"I'll leave you alone with this, Mister Briggs. I can trust you, no? Please don't touch anything. I can lose my job for this. But I'll be in my office downstairs, and when you're done you can come down, and perhaps we'll go have some coffee if you want. Annelino would like to meet with you again."

"Annelino?"

"Yes. He is here in Palermo today. I will arrange with him."

It seemed a century ago he had been on the train with Annelino, though it had been only a few days. He had already spent a lifetime in Palermo. He watched Violeta walk out. That she was always disheveled, her blouse hanging half out of her skirt, was an endearing counter to her formality. He turned back to look at the painting. As if in his mind a breeze had come up to dissipate the fog, clarity blew across his perceptions. This is the human clarity we need, he thought. Whispers of "glory" and "sublime" he rejected as wan approximations of what he saw. This was why he had come through all the confusion and misery of slums, the dreary mummies, the death cookies, skeletal horse, skeletal reaper—to experience this jewel, a pulse of human strength grown in a culture of the humane, a culture that now seemed all but disappeared, this truth painted by an artist whose psychological insight, and capacity for expressing it, was as wide as the continuing creation of the world, an affirmation of life impossible to subdue, even on the island of death.

Mary, (though it could be any young woman), her face of sublime Sicilian beauty, is framed in her robe of shimmering blue, more heavenly than the brightest Byzantine gold. She seems to absorb and ponder her news even as you watch her, news delivered by archangel Gabriel that she is chosen to bear the son of God, and you see her dealing with it within herself, even a light skepticism, as she extends her right hand, perhaps to ward off the archangel, or maybe to begin to offer this gift to everyone for whom she was bearing this consequence. You can see the whole human package, the yes/no passing through her mind, as well as the enduring faith, in her expression, on the edge of serenity, just a hint of panic in the balance, and that makes her human for us with her attention directed inwards, her gesture an attempt to reach us out of her private mystery.

Violeta didn't look up at him when he got back to

her office. "So you saw your painting, yes." She tucked in some strands that always escaped from her tight bun of brown hair.

He sat on a wooden chair as she started to rise. "Why don't you seem to like that painting very much," he said.

"She is so beautiful, Mr. Briggs. It's a nice painting, but beside the point." She fussed with the button that kept coming undone around her bosom. "Beautiful, an ideal beauty comes from Ancient Greek influence."

Solomon disliked the game of attributing influence. It was the scholar's trick, to trivialize genius.

"This is the study of her state of mind, of a woman to be told that she…It's so subtle and clear, and ambivalent…"

"Why do we need such a study? We don't need it."

"You're wrong. We do need all…Antonello is…"

"He is irrelevant, an aberration."

"You had so much enthusiasm for those crappy minor paintings, petty works, boring repetitions of…"

"Better a minor painting that reminds us of the greatness of the church, the glory of God. Better that than the masterpiece, so called. A painting of confusion. Faith is not psychology."

"The human story is the whole story. What does it feel like to be told by an angel that you have been chosen…We have to understand and love each other as human beings first, and then we…We have created god in our own image." Solomon didn't know if she even heard him. He felt the impasse growing like a cataract over their eyes. He saw her father dying under a cheap plastic cross, in a flow of pagan incantation.

"Your painter has given us his slut, from the brothels of Messina." She threw her overcoat across her arm. "You been to Messina? Famous for its whores. You like her?" They started for the door. "And Mr. Briggs, La Vergine Annunziata, this virgin, is the patron saint of the Cosa Nostra."

"No," said Solomon. He felt this as a sharp pain between his shoulder blades.

She looked at him, with a tight grin, shaking her head.

"No. That's not…that can't be. I don't believe it."

"It's not a question of your belief. It probably is not her choice, either," Violeta said, wryly. "But that's what they claim. They have chosen her."

In the caffe Solomon took a glass of marsala, and they each had a *granita di limone.* He inquired about her father, who was still hanging on, and asked about the rest of her family. It surprised him that she volunteered a bit of their history. They came from the southwest of Sicily, and had been given some worthless land in the late nineteenth century in payment for a large accumulated debt of unpaid salary by the impoverished household of nobles her family had served for many years. They managed to survive minimally on those arid acres, and even to send Violeta through the university. She studied to do curatorial work, and managed by a process of luck and attrition to get this job at the museum in Palermo, which payed little, but took her as far from home as she ever wanted to go. The mafia, she explained, choked off their lemon production and vineyard by withholding irrigation water, a fight that still went on, but she thought it inevitable they would lose the land.

She inquired why Solomon had wandered so far from his home just to see these paintings. He told her about the fragment he had found in the British Museum, and his hunch that there was a lost St. Francis by Antonello, hidden somewhere, and he wanted to find it.

"It is impossible, Mr. Briggs. There is no such painting. Such a painting does not get lost."

Sadness sputtered through as the exhaust of a Vespa running up the street. "I expect to find it," he tried to assert.

She laughed. What she saw as his folly seemed to relax her. "You will find nothing. A painting that important, never."

Solomon sipped his marsala, and nibbled on a crumb from the dish of *pannele* that came with it. Why this pressure, under this double-vaulted ceiling, at this table, in this old caffe? He told himself, I am just a visitor. I am just a visitor.

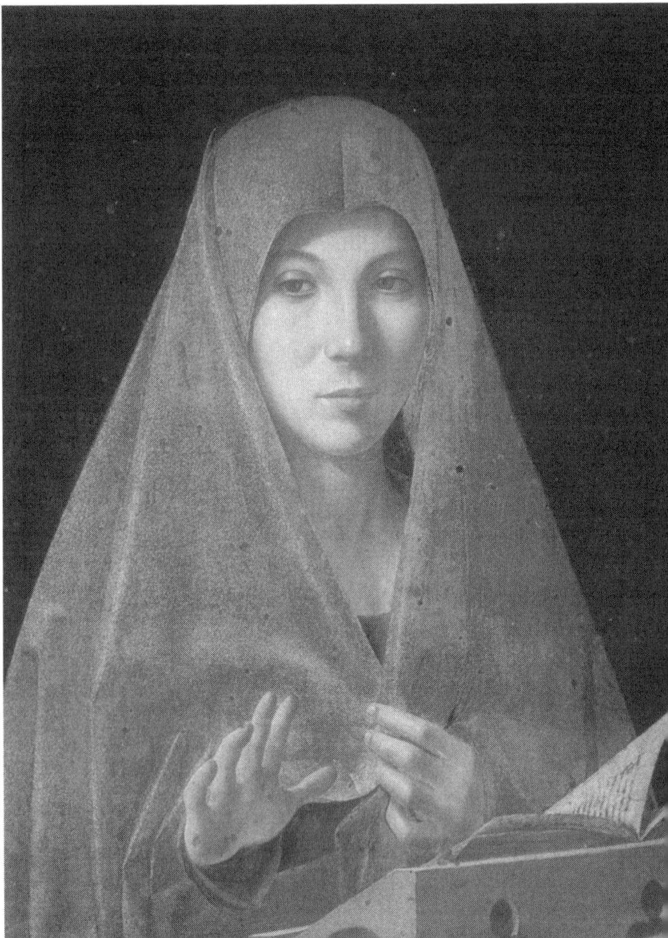

"St. Francis was the first who ever received the stigmata," Violeta said. "But no." She laughed. "There is no such Antonello painting. Giovanni Bellini, yes. That is in New York City, but Antonello…"

"They were friends."

"Maybe, as far as we know, if Antonello ever stayed in Venice, if he ever did."

"Then they both did the St. Francis. I can feel that Antonello did one too."

"Why is this so important to you?"

Words had become painful for Solomon. "He shows us the way to a secular spirituality."

"What?"

"A totally humane spirituality, outside the overarching imposition of religious narrative. That's where the trouble has always been, the rigidity, the insistence on the stories of god we each hold. Enough to think you can justify murder in the name of your god." He sipped. The marsala tasted so sweet, and the words tasted bitter.

"You are in trouble, Mr. Briggs. If you want to see the stigmata why don't you go to the Gargano, and visit Padre Pio?"

"I don't want to see the stigmata, I want to find the painting."

"You can't invent a painting by Antonello, and expect to find it somewhere. If you come here to Sicily, you have to take what Sicily offers, for better or worse, not what you imagine for it, Mr. Briggs."

"Call me Solomon, please." He felt difficulty breathing. Superimposed on her face, so he had to blink it away, he saw that dusty character from the British Museum, that scornful face, that green bowtie, furrowed brow like the treble clef that bore the discordant melody of his futility.

"Solomon, you can go to the Gargano, and there you can meet an actual saint, and real stigmata. Why do you want a painting?"

Of course it was futile. So what. Life. In general human life had little meaning except that most were desperate not to give it up. Just look at the fresco, look into the catacombs. Anyway, he went on. "A painting is the human expression. I want to see how Antonello gives us the face of someone who receives these stigmata. Stigmata is a belief. I'm more interested in how Antonello, the most humane genius, penetrates that belief in the psychology, in the human face and gesture. I don't understand stigmata, not even sure I believe in it, whatever it is."

"Are you a Catholic, Solomon Briggs?" It was as if she'd had a startling revelation.

Solomon knew that how he answered that question could change everything between them. He waited a moment, then chose the most honest response. "I have no particular faith nor belief."

"What do you mean?"

"My mother and father are Jewish, though not religious."

Confusion landed on her face like a grey shroud. He didn't know what Jewish meant for her, nor what he might have to explain. She leaned back in her seat and looked away, and at that moment, as if to rescue them, Annelino walked through the door. "Ahhh, here he is, our Annelino." She stood up, met and embraced him half way between the door and the table. She took a cigarette from him, and went to the bar for a light, and was smoking as both of them sat back down with Solomon.

"So you have seen your painting," Annelino said, leaning forward to kiss him on the lips. "And now you can come back with me to Partinico, and do something, really do something for your soul."

It wasn't just the kiss. That was a light enough touch. For good or ill, Sicilian men kissed each other. Maybe it was the dusk, and the people outside, the Palermitani who had begun their *passegiata*—so many centuries of walking in the dusk—a something that somehow made him feel that around himself this box was closing. The fear slipped over him that he would never be able to leave, that he had never really arrived, in fact, but had always been here. It was this box constructed of nothing, the dimmest box of history, in which present moments disappear, in which there is no elsewhere, only the island, its distant volcano, and the recession of time descending in a pitiless whorl. He could count so few days here, and he felt so much already holding him. As if he had always known these people and always felt the strain of obligation. He had never experienced this pressure before, not certainly in New York City, where he was born, where his parents were hard working business people, wholesaling buttons and ribbons. That city could shed its natives like old skin. And no place else in Italy that he'd been had this grip, not Venice certainly, not Rome. What reassured him was only that everyone walking the street was meticulously dressed, so careful of shoes and ties, and they were making such precise estimations of each other, and that Solomon had no such clothes, and was in no way estimable by them. By that he guessed, he hoped, he was sure that he would be able to leave; in fact, by whatever means he tried, he could never be one of them. Yet looking into the faces of these two new friends, Annelino, whose expectations were so great and threatening, and Violeta who still pitied his confusion, he knew he would have to try to explain all of it, himself, what he didn't yet understand, at least out of courtesy for their kindnesses. Explain himself, that was at best a joke. He had gotten to see the painting. Now he feared he had been settled, at least for this while, into a maze from which there was no easy exit. Only the rail lines that lay in his mind like Ariadne's thread reassured him there was a possible way out.

ACQUA ALTA

ACQUA ALTA

He finally managed to eke her phone number out of the offices of the Biennale. "She never mentioned a son," said the angular, elegant curatorial assistant, as she reluctantly handed him a sticky with the number. "I hope that here I'm doing the right thing." Her haughty, disparaging look, gilded with an Oxford Italian accent was painful for him, but getting to his mother always involved a dose of discomfort and pain. In her position as a hero of her gender, he thought, it must have embarrassed her to have borne as her only child, himself, a male. He never felt ready to see her, always could find some excuse to put it off forever; except, this time he was determined to probe just once more for information about his father. It had been more than a year since he'd even talked to her on the phone. She never made the effort to keep in touch, though he was part of her email network, including him when she let people know where she was headed next. At least she kept him in her network; that was motherly. This mother relationship was better, he guessed, than with some overweaning, guilt provoking mom, like the one Max always described. Whatever residue of affection or sentiment she had kept in her dim role as his mother was buried deep in the closet of foregone ambitions. She was even more energetic now, at least for her art, than she had been when she was raising him, supporting them then by following teaching opportunities from state to state, to Canada, even to New Zealand. These times probably were happier for herself, he thought, living almost exclusively on the income her art generated. And she had a portfolio of investments now that Nathan watched over for her, another reason for them to keep remotely in touch, though in that regard they communicated mostly through her accountant.

For this visit he had made an appointment, around four in the afternoon, because he didn't dare just walk into her studio, surprising herself and Lolly, her new young companion and art buddy. She probably secretly dreaded that he could arrive on the scene with some filial demands, while she was being cozy and impressive there with her fresh young girl artist protégé, and blow her ancient virgin youthful crone image, however she now preferred to be seen. He would embarrass her by calling her mom or mother or ma. Mommy, he had taken perversely to call her since they separated more than fifteen years earlier, him to university, herself into the public swim of her growing notoriety. When they lived together, mother and son, she had insisted he call her Isabel. In his teen years he'd called her by her family name, Ms. Brightwatch, as if she was his teacher. There was too a nasty period, when he called her Officer Isabel. With friends, when he talked about her, he always felt a measure of pride in her accomplishments, her idiosyncrasies, her position as a minor icon. Someone was always curious, interested. Notoriety gave one rank in these times, even when the fame came second hand. Only when he was about to deal with her himself did he have any misgivings.

Maybe to avoid getting there too early, he lingered at the Correr Museum, in the room set aside for Antonello's *Pietà With Three Angels*. Whenever he had the chance, whenever he thought of it, he would take a look at the works of the painter so much admired by his alleged father, finding a portrait of a young man once in Philadelphia, and a saint in Baltimore, home of two of his favorite film directors. Himself, he was never much interested in art, maybe because it was too much embedded in his mother's life, but he'd look at these as if he might find something of his father there. Art seemed to him like some lint on the surface of the economy, at best a tricky investment, at worst a superfluous human indulgence. If it weren't for the business of his father, he would have no reason to look at paintings, and didn't, but for occasional curiosity about what Picasso was, or why Van Gogh, or which is Matisse. The whole kaboodle seemed to him overvalued, though he'd grant it its charms. Then there was the double coincidence of his attention being grabbed on an otherwise perfunctory visit to the Borghese gallery in Rome by a portrait that resembled the guy who had conned him while he and Mims walked by the Tiber river, selling him the very jacket he was wearing now. And that portrait was by this Antonello da Messina, as if his father had organized the swindle, to say, "wake up and find me." The ghost of Hamlet's dad, for instance.

This was his only patrimony, after all, these paintings by an Italian master he would never have heard of otherwise. It was all of his father Ms. Brightwatch allowed him as a child, though he always suspected she had more to tell. These paintings his father adored were like part of the battle he liked to imagine had taken his father's life, or the plane crash in which he perished, or the disease that took him so young, or the paradise to which he had escaped, abandoning all vestiges. How seriously he had taken it when Brightwatch's sister, his wonderful buddy, the boozy Hilda, had told him on a trip to the Everglades that his father was an alligator. Why not? Certainly Brightwatch wouldn't have hesitated to wrestle an alligator, if she could do it nude, as part of a performance. Hilda, his buddy, was dead now, her liver collapsed. What Nathan didn't get was the Christianity. The father was a Jew, after all. So many of these were depictions of the story of Christ, this one a pietà, Christ lowered from the cross in the arms of three angels. Nathan had never cared much for crucifixions; in fact, he avoided them when he found himself in church or museum. This icon of Christianity was repugnant to him, a grim story point in the Christian legend projected as the dominant glory of its spirituality. For him it suffered by comparison with the tranquil, compassionate Buddha, or Krishna at play, or Ganesh always amusing, or the neutral iconographic void of both Islam and Judaism. Crucifixion seemed designed deliberately to create tethers of guilt and obsequious pity to control the flock.

Still, the longer he stood in front of this half ruined painting, the more he felt drawn into it. Perhaps his father had a point about Antonello da Messina, something compelling in these pictures. Not the crucifixion idea, the body being taken down into the arms of these sweetly adoring angels. That was interesting, okay, some suffering that seems only the most modest tweak compared to the twentieth century's parade of high end massacres—Native Americans, the advent of the machine gun, King Leopold in his Congo, the holocaust, the actual use of nuclear weapons, Turks on the Armenians, slaughter in Vietnam, etc. etc., ad nauseum. You'd need more than a crucifixion to resurrect conscience in this past century. But he found this Christ depiction compelling, himself shown as supple and frail, no body hair, so vulnerable in the belly. And the landscape background, a serpentine road, a solid church, trees and shrubs aptly distributed, and further away, the sea. What were those buildings at the edge?

"Why such a weensy wiener?" The voice of a young woman surprised him from behind. "Don't you think it's small; I mean, for the son of God?"

Nathan turned to see her, hair cropped short and dyed chrome yellow, iridescent acquamarine eyeshadow, fine tattoo lines radiating from her lips, a gold ring through the pierced lower lip. She wore a t-shirt with the word SKUNK printed across the chest, a blue suede miniskirt over black net stockings, thick soled black clomper boots with heavy three inch heels.

"Look at him. There's hardly anything under the cloth. You'd think the son of God would rate a bigger package. Like if God were making a son, say you were God, and who knows, you might be, in which case stop me right now because I don't even know what blasphemy is, and I would like to avoid lightning or the big voice or anything; but if you were making a son, and as God you can do whatever you want, you'd give your son a sizeable kit, wouldn't you? I'm not saying that size matters, but if you have a choice between small and large, which do you choose? God. You gave him hardly anything in the grabowski category: I mean, nothing there under the cloth to wrap your fist around."

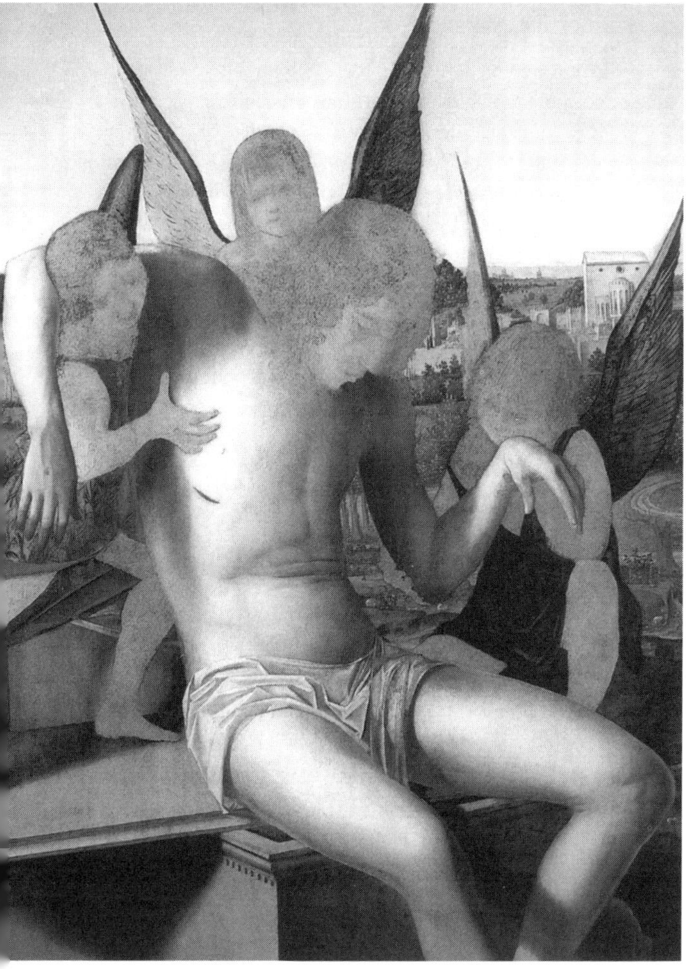

"That's…I didn't think about that…" Nathan smoothed back his hair, feeling somewhere between uncomfortable and flattered that this young woman chose him to receive her wisdom.

"Oh, I'll bet you understand English. How embarrassing." She covered her mouth with her hand, in mock shyness, then reached out to shake his hand. "I'm Saffron, Saffron Denes."

"Nathan Briggs," Nathan said, thinking he could have said Brightwatch, since he was going to see her. It was also his name. Why not? On the original birth certificate she had used her own name, though for some reason, after her sister died, she got him to change it to Briggs.

"I just had to get away from that instructor. I don't know where the program finds them. She looks like she wears tweed underwear. She doesn't know anything, and she's all dried up. I think she barely escaped from the nuns. Wherever we go we get these people, and some of them are so stupid. So what do you think? About that boy's thingy?"

Even though Nathan didn't understand why they were having this conversation, or whether the girl was coming on to him or what, he went along with it. "I don't know, but I think you're looking generally in the right place." He wasn't sure why he said that.

"O my, an American. Or else you've got a very good accent. Up till now I always ran into Germans. I feel like a holocaust survivor; which I am, being from LA, conceived by the coupling of a civil rights lawyer mom and an activist union organizer dad, during the Watts riots. I guess they were Jewish. How do you tell? No, I'm kidding. Like now my dad sells real estate, big time. Sniffle sniffle. The glory of the world, how it passes. What do you mean, I'm looking in the right place?"

"…well…I think…the hands…the hands too…but the belly and the groin are the most expressive parts, especially since the faces are obliterated."

"Obliterated is such a great word. Like, do you think it's damaged or just never, like, finished? I appreciate this no face kind of a thing. It's like South Park, almost, not quite." She moved closer, for a better look. "You're so right. Excellent. The folds of his belly are such sadness, so collapsed or something, and the dark bellybutton echoes the dumb grin that wound makes in his side, and the guts is like so tender, and slim hips, the legs so vulnerable. Look how his death is a kind of surrender. His arms gone all abandoned. He's so feminine. Don't you think? You think he was bi? Christ must have been bi. Amazing he's got a bellybutton. Hard to imagine Christ keeping his bellybutton clean. And have you ever imagined the Virgin Mary, shlooping out the afterbirth? Do you think there was a virgin afterbirth? You don't hear anything about that. Francis Bacon should have painted that. Can you imagine what a little bit of the placenta would be worth today, if they kept it, to sell little packets of it frozen or dried, in Westwood or somewhere? A million bucks a gram. A whole church could be built around a few ounces. And the skulls at his feet are so cool. I was into skulls once when I was a kid, and I was totally, like, goth."

"You're really good, you really look at the painting. Most people don't see anything."

"O, thank you, mister man. It's so fun to talk about it, and the other women just don't like to. It's all the MTVness of their lives. The internettitude. Hector says I'm insightful. He was my studio TA last semester. He was just a graduate student, but like I wanted to fuck him so bad, and when I did, everyone was like, how did Saffron get Hector so fast? He's really a talented artist. I used to hate my name, but now I like it. Hey, look at his hands."

"What?"

"How come they don't have any wounds, from where the nails went in?"

"I didn't even notice that."

"I notice all these kinds of things. That's why I'm famous for being insightful." She looked at her palms. "I almost put some, what do you call them, stig somethings, on my palms, when I did my lips, Hector was like, 'Get serious, you can't do that in a tattoo parlor.' He thought it was blasphemy. He's afraid of blasphemy. That's what happens to a catholic. See my lips? Each of those lines is a different rune. Hector says I'll be sorry some day, when my mouth starts to wrinkle. I hope that's my biggest worry, when my mouth starts to wrinkle." She pointed to the painting again. "All the architecture is so cool, like towers and fortifications, the opposite of flesh. And the little angels' wings look heavy with sadness. So businesslike, they look, and mournful, even if you can't see their faces." She leaned intimately into Nathan, as if she'd forgot that they didn't yet know each other. "Hey. There's something interesting… ummm…what did you say your name was?"

"Nathan…Briggs."

"Briggs," she repeated, and pulled away from him as if she had suddenly noticed they were touching. "You're an accountant. Nathan's an accountant's name."

"Wrong."

"Well you have something to do with money, anyway."

"Right."

"Some day money will be important," she said, then clapped her hands as if applauding the idea of money. "I don't think you probably know the answer to this, but I want to ask you. When a man is hanged (you say hanged, not hung, right? Hung is, like, endowed) he's supposed to get a stiff one right away, an erection, pop a woody in junior high school lingo. I read about that in William Burroughs. Stretch the neck, and up pops little Albert wank wank. Did you ever see that weird Japanese movie, *In The Realm Of The Senses?* It was half required by Candy Lutz, my Film and Eros teacher. She's gay. Anyway, I recommend it now, and now the question is, do you think the same thing happens with a crucifixion? I mean, when you get crucified, does that bump up an erection? I hope I'm not embarassing you. Sometimes I tend to embarrass."

"I'm not the one to ask. I haven't been crucified yet."

"Cool. Great answer, Nathan Briggs. Let me think. We can arrange that. That would be drastic. We can do it on the island of Murano tomorrow. We're supposed to go to the glass factories. Glass-blowing and crucifying Nathan. Twenty-two horny college women would love to crucify you, Mr. Briggs. No extra charge. Uh oh." She slipped behind him when she heard a crowd coming from the adjacent gallery. "Protect me, Mr. Briggs. Here they come."

Her sensible shoes squeaking only a little, the small, intense Italian guide led her group of college girls past Nathan. Saffron stepped out, patted Nathan's shoulder, then tagged on to the end of the line, caught up with a friend, and blew a kiss his way as they turned the corner.

Back with her peers, the girl seemed even younger than at first, nonetheless he felt a pull to follow her. This exchange that had been so intense turned to a vacuum around himself as soon as she vacated. He felt the void fill with loneliness, and looked back at the painting that now seemed to be hers more than his father's, and for the first time found it curious that there was no woman in it. There was always Mary in a pietá to help the crucified down from the cross, to lay her son across her lap, and her expression to give you permission for your own feelings. He'd seen the Michelangelo ones in Florence and at the Vatican, Mary at least equal in importance and power. Saffron had noticed how businesslike, yet compassionate the angels seemed. Did she say "compassionate"? Did she note how gentle they were as they lowered this slim Christ? And where was the cross? He might have discussed that with her. Was it perhaps somewhere to the left, out of the picture? And no wounds on the hands. She had mentioned that. They hadn't really finished their conversation about the stigmata. It had been so much easier to think about this painting, with her to talk to, this girl who had accosted him, and now disappeared; a girl who was not as flaky and frivolous as at first she seemed, and then she had moved him enough so that now it was sad for him to endure her absence.

Nathan descended the steps leaving the museum, and turned left towards Piazza San Marco, a space that always astonished him. Out of the human proportions, such grandeur. A brightness of pigeons unfurled like an embroidered banner into the sunlight. The tide was in and the elevated plank walkways let pedestrian crowds shuffle dry above the high water. A few of the hipper tourists had brought rubber boots, and seemed almost gleeful as they cut through the Adriatic tidal surge. At least the weather was mild on the day he was meeting with Isabel Brightwatch, just an occasional sprinkle from the putti leaning out of their cottony lairs, peeing into the blue. He missed Miriam, having her there to feel this Venice with him, and to be a foil for his Isabel encounter. Miriam the practical, Miriam the wise.

He stepped onto one of the board walkways, and shuffled with the rest of the tourist cattle towards the San Marco stop of the vaporetto. Tourism to Nathan, even as a participant, seemed always such a sad and crowded endgame. Slow slow going, amidst the crowd of first world youth, that carried their packs on their bellies to thwart theft from behind, as if the opulence promised in their futures was a pregnancy they were forced to display on their walkabouts; amidst cliches of Japanese who turned together like the pigeons, a phalanx of cameras pointed in every direction. Germans with guidebooks and checklists, ticked off every stone, every window, every step. And wherever were some warring Serbs as well, some muslim Croats, some Albanians six to a donkey clopping on the boards, draped in blood overcoats, over an elegance of smashed bone? Close by. Just a few miles down the Adriatic they were, the Dalmatian coast, beautiful coast, that's all. Children abandoned, lost into refugee camps. Why not set them up in the piazzettas of Venice? And a vacancy there on the boards full of the pale ghosts of Hutus. A killing field clacks through in a chaos of skulls, looking back on the end of this cruelest millenium. In the glory of Venice, Nathan felt a tease of rambling phantasms skimming high water. Shrapneled limbs, scarred families, chopped babies all together asserting their rights to visit this enchanted city, this Venice, its elegance and luminosity. Venetian grace, light wines of the Veneto, carnival yummies. It was everyone's right as a human being to taste of this beauty. And here come some Aussies, surfing the high waters, sounding for beer. Chechens huddle in the shallows of a gallery corner. Could all the architects of Melbourne or Seattle have thought up such a place? Could Frank Gehry, Philip Johnson, I.M. Pei put their heads together and design this city? Could this be the Titicaca of their dreams? And where now are the cultured Venetians, so haughty and aloof, so greedy, so cunning? Do such Venetians remain in the world? Do they live now in their submarines, their periscopes crowding the small canals? These subs are fitted out with walls of velveteen, with silk settees, soft velour recliners, wide canopied beds, submarines slow and supple as manatees, jostling for position sottocanale. Random notes from chamber orchestras squeak up through the periscopes. Sink not Venice with your light and grace. First bright city, redeem the world.

A tug on Nathan's pants, pulled him almost off the

platform, and seeing her pulled also a shock of relief and laughter from his belly.

"Like you're happy to see me. When you meet someone, especially someone you like, then I always want to finish the circle I begin with that person, especially someone like you, Briggs."

Nathan must have looked confused, puzzled to see her again, because she explained, "I'm Saffron, remember? We met in Venice. Early June, 2001. We looked at a painting together, by that painter. Come on down here."

Nathan didn't say anything. She tugged on his pants again.

"Come on down here," she insisted.

Once again he said nothing. He was almost too glad to see her, though for some reason it was a bigger surprise than if it had been some random friend shown up. And he felt a twinge of guilt, because he'd been having thoughts about Miriam, and here he inadvertently had a whole complex of feelings, so glad to see someone he'd just met, and someone who not only was young, but looked young, dressed aggressively young, made him feel superannuated in his mid thirties.

"If you don't want to see me again, that's okay."

This all was much thicker than their casual encounter warranted.

"I can't come down there, it's all water."

"I'm down here."

"You've got rubber boots on." She had slipped some

yellow thigh-highs over her clodhoppers.

"Briggs, don't you think it's time you got your feet wet?" She tugged on his pants leg again, and this time he let himself stumble off the boards, into water halfway to his knees.

"Here you are. That's better." She slipped her arm under his. "And here I thought maybe you weren't attracted to me, and I'm so attracted to you. Even though you're old. How old are you?"

"How old are you?"

"I'm twenty-one. Well, almost. You?"

"I'm in my thirties."

"Upper, or lower?"

"Thirty-three." He lied a little.

"That's old, Briggs. But you're not the oldest dude I've ever been with."

He enjoyed that she called him a dude. "This water is cold." Nathan moved towards a high spot in the center of the Piazza.

"Where are you going now?" Saffron followed him.

"I'm going to meet with my mother."

"Mother? Briggs, you're here with your mother? Where?"

"I'm not here with her. She's here, and I came to see her."

"Very nice of you. Like, what does she do?"

"She's an artist. She's here with her protégé. They gave them a little studio in the biennale park."

"Cool. Like your mom's a real artist. What's her name?"

"She's Isabel Brightwatch." Nathan swallowed the name, reluctant to field the response it often evoked, particularly in young women.

"Did you say Brightwatch?"

"Yes."

"Omigod. Your mother is Brightwatch? She was like almost my total hero for a whole semester. She's a great artist. She's like totally important. How come your name isn't Brightwatch?"

"Briggs is my father's name."

"Is your father an artist?"

"I don't know my father. He disappeared."

"How'd he disappear?"

"That's why I came here, to look for him and find out. He vanished when he and Brightwatch were in Venice years ago. They did it, conceived me, then poof. I want to ask her some more questions about it, then maybe look for him."

"God, you would never know she had a kid, no less like a son. There's no kids in her art. When you look at her work, or the films of her performances, you can't imagine she was ever like with a man. Brightwatch. You're kidding me."

Nathan shrugged. His feet were soaked and cold, and he wondered if the cheap running shoes he was wearing would come unglued with the salt water.

"Of course, I can go with you to see her, can't I. When are you going?"

"Right now."

"I can go with you, can't I, Briggs? You should probably change your pants and shoes if you're going to see your mom. You have to let me meet Brightwatch. I can't believe this has happened." She kissed Nathan on the cheek. Her lips felt big and wet, even though her mouth looked small. "I'm going to call Hector and tell him about this, despite he had like less than zero interest in Brightwatch. You'll let me come with you, won't you. It's part of my education." She jumped up and down like a little kid.

"You can be my protégé." He kissed her awkwardly.

"I'll even be your little trick," she laughed.

*   *   *

His mother must have heard them when he accidentally brushed the steel ring hanging near the door, so it swung on its chain to clang against the wall. She acted oblivious to this and went on fussing with her work at the other end of the studio that in the next year would make up part of the American Pavilion in which she and her protégé would have a show together.

"She's just being cool," Nathan whispered to Saffron.

"She is so way cool," Saffron responded. The reverence in her voice irritated Nathan. She didn't hear or maybe didn't accept the sarcasm he'd intended. He approached slowly, and Saffron remained near the entrance. The familiar odors of acrylics, welding torch, cigarettes that was his mother made him shudder slightly. His fear of her wasn't based in memories of violence; she'd hardly ever touched him physically, but he dreaded facing that emotional vacancy, pushing him into a cold, empty corner, where he felt not like a son, but more like a suitor rejected out of sexual preference.

"Did I get here too early?"

"No. It's okay. I'm just fiddling with this model."

She hadn't yet turned to look at him. In front of her two sawhorses supported a plywood base for the architectural model of what looked like a dungeon, built of small squared stones, mortared, holding tiny shackles, ramps, swinging studded carousels, racks, all elegant and threatening when imagined to scale as machines of torture.

"I thought I was just going to make some sketches, and supervise while they built it. Then I got into this model, and really began to enjoy it. It's one eighth scale of this room, a design for a performance in homage to Piranesi. I'm thinking now I might do it in miniature too, and film it. Make tiny marionettes. Or maybe build one to half scale. I've got almost a year to work on it."

"Who's Piranesi?"

"Don't tell me you've never heard of Piranesi."

"I've heard the name, but I guess I'm poorly educated."

"He's the most famous Roman designer and architect, eighteenth century. We had those great books of speculative drawings of prisons and stuff. He's the one who designed that piazza in Rome for the Knight's Templar, where you look through the keyhole of this large gate and see the dome of the St. Peter's. I can't believe you haven't seen that? You've been to Rome?"

"Of course. I don't remember names, though." Nathan preferred to remain ignorant of stuff she knew about; in that way, with her, he was still stuck in adolescence.

She turned then to look at him. He always dreaded her empty gaze that assessed him as a form, just a capacity, a volume, not as a person, or her son. It wasn't even cold, just void, a gaze she'd developed to keep herself from committing an emotion. This was why when he met Miriam, so open emotionally, and available to him, he loved even her tendency to gush. "O, I'm going to miss you, Nathan, so much, sweety. Every sweet little burp, every snore. I'm going to be all wet just thinking about you," she had said after he implored her for a second or third time to come with him. "You know I can't do it, and I would, even though what you are doing is so jerky, but I love you." He held that word, "jerky," against his mind like a kid's sour blanket. Jerky Nathan.

"Isn't this the American Pavilion?" Nathan wanted to irritate her. "Why the Piranesi? Isn't this the American Pavilion?"

She looked away, not back to her model, but to the door where Saffron had got interested in something.

"That's not Miriam. Who is that?" She acted as if she hadn't heard his question.

"She's a friend. I just met her here. She's a great fan of yours."

Isabel grimaced at the word, "fan." She turned back to her model. "I'm thinking of putting some advertising in the real life version—Yahoo dot com, Amazon dot com, dot com dot com, all the dot coms, and Pepsi, and Philip Morris, and Dow Chemical. That should make it American enough for you, sonny boy. I'm doing it also for the baroque media project, and somehow I need to involve the internet. I hate the internet. Lolly calls it male mind mucus. For all this tech you sit on your ass, and delude yourself about power. The whole vocabulary of it is about power, whereas the more time with it, the more you are powerless. You vacate your mind. I've got some ideas for how to use on line in the piece. Maybe I'll sell advertising space, though I hate that idea too, but it's the American way. Pepsi Piranesi. And that I'll build most of it out of styrofoam, acrylic, makes it plenty American. And then my body will be involved on all these machines, and I'll challenge people to experience it in a virtual way, maybe, like virtual incarceration, torture, release. It's American enough, just appropriating the Italian is an American thing."

Imagining his mother, or whoever this was to him, this aging art diva that once gave birth to him, still using her body, probably naked, she was always naked in her art, seemed ludicrous to him, though he supposed that was a prejudice.

"Where is Miriam?"

"You like Miriam, don't you?"

"I like her name. It's very biblical. She seems like an active woman."

"She's so active, she didn't have time to come with me."

"Well, Nathan, if you're here just for what you told me you came for, I don't blame her for not coming. Looking for your father? Give me a break. That closet slammed shut years ago."

They were suddenly into it, and he felt like he wasn't prepared. "For you. It never seemed to trouble you that my father disappeared. I never understood that. Why you didn't look for him when it happened. Not even curiosity. He's my father." Saying that word "father" to Brightwatch filled his eyes with tears. He wiped at them with the back of his wrist. "How could you not care?"

"What makes you think?...Of course I cared. I was

busy, you know, and I was pregnant, but I thought a lot about it; but then I figured if he wanted to come back, he would come back. I got phone calls from Sicily, then from somewhere in Puglia. He didn't sound interested in what was happening to me. He was your typically selfish young guy."

"He was my age."

"So what. That's why I think it's best you leave it alone. When I told him I was pregnant, I can't remember that he even said anything." Nathan had trouble believing her, though he didn't doubt she believed herself. "Those were different times. People didn't just disappear then. It wasn't terrorists, bomb threats, hostages. If it was now, I might have worried more. But it's very easy to abandon a pregnant woman. Tell me it doesn't happen. Then I figured his life was his own, and I had to look out for myself, and for you, of course. I was soon to be a single mother, way before it was popular."

Every time he had to look at the frigid facts of his conception, he felt a cold red sheathe clamp around his heart. "And you wanted me to be a girl."

"Now it's a simple test, they tell you the sex, and you have a choice. Then I had no choice."

The sound of his mother's voice closed in his mind like a fist. It was stupid to ask these questions at all, as if there was hope for anything but pain; but he still felt a need to scrape a small flake of love, of affirmation, off the slag of her callousness. To hear her at all, he knew he should divorce himself from the idea that this was a mother. He couldn't waste regret on something he could never affect.

"Where's your friend?" he asked.

"Lolly, you mean? She's gone to Milano. Some Germans invited her. The Germans love her work. She'll probably sell all of it before her show. It's little objects, like some stuff. I call it some kind of lapidary porn. She's got some of it over there." She pointed to the table Saffron was studying. "My best work is still in performance, but maybe from working so close to her is why I got interested in this model, a cutesy version of my tougher work."

The cranky tone Isabel took towards her protégé surprised Nathan, seemed even a little competitive.

"When my generation was coming up as artists, sure we were strange, but a lot of our strategies had a political edge. Get away from the object, don't produce commodities for the rich. Today the kids will screw the air out of their lungs, drain half the blood from their veins, for a little fame, and money. All we ever thought about was enough money to make our art, and to survive. We believed the art was important, and Artist was a calling." She picked up a circle of copper off her model, and pushed her pinky through it. "Then again, just surviving today takes a lot more money. And art schools have cranked out too many artists. Kids think about showing and selling even before they do any art.

So I do these drawings, and they sell not because they're particularly great drawings, but because I've got a rep. Then maybe someone buys this model, if I finish it. Everything's a compromise, I guess."

As she spoke she moved down the room towards Saffron, who was leafing slowly through a book of sketches.

"You've never mentioned those phone calls before, from my father." The thought of Isabel once talking to his actual father made him feel strangely anxious.

"Why don't you introduce me to your friend?" Isabel approached the table. Saffron turned to look at her, a grin on her face stretched painfully wide.

"Isabel Brightwatch." It felt to Nathan he was presenting a celebrity at a social event. "This is Saffron… Saffron…I forgot your second name."

"Just Saffron," she said, and extended a hand towards Brightwatch.

"So small and white," Isabel said, surrounding the girl's hand in a stained cocoon of work-scarred fingers. "I'm just Brightwatch."

"I know. It's so awesome to meet you. Did your son tell you? I'm a total fan. We studied your work in our performance class."

"He did mention a fan." Isabel looked down at her shoes, as if she were shy.

"I hope you didn't mind my touching all this stuff. I'm like such a snoop. But these drawings are awesome.

And these little sculptures." She pointed at the pieces scattered across the table. "They're way beyond beautiful. I didn't know you did work like this."

Nathan studied the small bronzes, lying around as if spilled from a jewel box, small labial forms, with pieces of ruby glass, or bits of silver chain, or tiny flowers at the point of the clitoris, jeweled and glazed, or cloisonnéd around the lips, ready to be set into plush boxes furnished with tiny scraps of clockwork, varnished wood, sheaves of hair, seashells, fingernails, bullets, Barbie parts, anything small.

"That's Lolly's work. I didn't do them. Don't you find them pretty?"

"O, gross. I'm so gross." Saffron cupped her hands over her mouth. "Sorry. I didn't realize they weren't yours. I'd like to meet her, though."

"I find them pretty," Nathan said.

"Well, I guess." Isabel picked one up, then tossed it back on the table. "She does them from actual photographs. I mean, she really takes closeups of people in the gynecological position. She manipulates the images with photoshop, and then I don't know what else. I think she isolates it and throws it into three dimensions with a really complicated architectural program she has, and then makes these little sculptures. Some Japanese have commissioned them in gold."

"Labial architecture, that's like awesome. It would be great if she could do a building."

215

"I think she's going to show the photograph with each piece. I hope that makes it look a little less precious."

"They're like the entrances to this cathedral we saw in Barcelona. What was its name? Antonio Gaudi. Something Famiglia…Sacred. Working some architecture out of these would be so totally awesome."

"Enter through small cunt to the right," Brightwatch laughed, then spread her arms. "Let there be light. That reminds me. I've got to find someone to help me light my piece, and I've got to find a computer person. You know computers?" She let her arm fall on Saffron's shoulder. "And I'm going to use the internet, or some kind of feedback through computers."

"I know a little bit," Saffron said, as Isabel guided her back across the room to her own model.

"See, at the last biennale, or maybe it was a couple back, this Austrian sculptor, Kresh…something, made a piece; I guess you'd call it his juggernaut piece, a big steel sphere that moved across a room along a track, and people logged onto the website, and it traveled somehow according to the flow of data, and threatened to crash through the wall, and eventually it crashed. Lolly called it some macho melodrama. She says it's just the kind of manipulation the "patriart" world loves today. Like that one she calls the dangerous sculptor, what's his name, who leans these steel plates and balances them with rolls of lead—why do I block his name? You feel so anxious when you're near them, like they are some attack art. I mean, I admire them a lot. But she's another generation. She thinks it's all macho "patriart," she calls it, pumped up, targeted to art world pseudo-intellectual jargon, that condescends to communicate with real people only as a threat." Isabel looked up to see if she'd held her audience.

Nathan watched Saffron who listened to Isabel's words as if they were music, as if she understood everything. He knew he'd get little more out of his mother than he already had, Puglia and Sicily, telephone calls, those were his tickets to travel.

"So what I'm going to do, I think, is have people log on to a website, not my homepage, but specially dedicated, and leave messages—friendly, hostile, critical, favorable, or maybe even different weirder parameters, I haven't totally worked it out, or maybe even random, and then whatever machine I'm attached to will act according to the data being fed it, like the rack would stretch, the press would squeeze, the shackles would tighten…"

"Aren't you afraid?" Saffron asked.

"Fear is a part of what the piece is about, but the threat is to myself, not to anyone else who comes to experience the work; except I think I'll record myself and the participant on split-screen video, so whoever logs in will have to deal with her or his own boundaries of cruelty and compassion, because he can choose to hurt me."

They looked at each other in silence. Saffron took a deep breath, and sighed. "I don't know. That seems over the top. You'll get hurt, the way people are these days. People hurt each other too easily these days."

"I can set the limits." Brightwatch smiled a slight heroic smile. "I won't let anyone hurt me much." She squatted by her model, to adjust something. "Isn't life all about how much pain someone can bear?"

Saffron whispered to Nathan. "Thank you thank you for bringing me here. I love listening to Brightwatch. It's witnessing art history in the flesh."

"History! Brightwatch is still alive. Very cooking, little girl."

Saffron covered her mouth and turned away. "Sorry. I didn't mean to…"

"She's cute. Where'd you get her?"

"Mommy, dearest, please." Nathan feigned a whine. The tension between them twisted sometimes towards the mean, and sometimes towards the comical. He wanted to love her. She always insisted he admire her.

"Get off the mommy," she said. "I deleted that when you left for college."

She couldn't let him even slightly in, not even through an ironic divergence. "Okay. Brightwatch, dearest. Can't you tell me anything else about my father, and then I'll leave you alone?"

She collapsed into a chair, blowing some air out between her lips. "His name was Solomon, okay. I'll tell you this only once, so listen. At the time he was obsessed with a painter named Antonello da Messina, a renaissance obsession. Kind of stupid."

"I know all that. But why do you say 'stupid'? Wasn't this a great painter? A famous…"

"Yeah, of course. Yes. But your father, he thought he could help the world, and change things with this art. Help the world!"

"What do you mean? Help the…With Antonello da…"

"…Messina, da Messina. He was from Messina, in Sicily. He believed there was this lost painting, of St. Francis…"

"I love St. Francis, saint of the birds," said Saffron. "He's at the Frick in New York, Bellini…"

"Yes. Birds. And he thought if he found this painting, or maybe there were more, then maybe that would call attention to Antonello again, and he believed that looking at the Antonello portraits had a special effect on people, the way you look at them. It was interesting, I remember, but I don't remember what he thought, exactly. He thought it could encourage a kind of secular spirituality, he called it. Something about how you look at the portraits forces you to recognize yourself. I don't know, read Cixoux, Bachelard, the theorists. He thought it could help the world. He wanted that. Didn't interest me."

That was more than she'd ever said about his father. Nathan didn't know quite how to digest this peculiarity. This odd idealism. "So mom, what did you think? Do you think he was…?"

"Omigod, you call her Mom. I just realized."

"She's my mother."

"Well, duh. She's Brightwatch."

"No. I don't…" Brightwatch tapped her mouth with two fingers. "You can't help the world. If you try to help the world you only make it worse. You screw it up." She reached into her model and shifted one of the benches, knocking some gears off a tiny machine, as if to illustrate her point. "The best anyone can do is make things little more amusing, life a little more interesting."

"Omigod. Omigod. I know I like totally saw you do that piece. I did." Saffron jumped up and down. "We drove all the way to Bennington. You called it St. Cage, I think, and it was an homage. Where you said all these things you were saying came from John Cage. And there was this part where you had this saint with arrows all in him projected onto your body, and you were saying all these great cynical sayings, and you were laughing. There was something really reassuring, and powerful. And at the end it got dark and your nipples, your lips, your bellybutton, your toenails, all glowed. That was all you saw. Wait…" She grabbed Nathan's arm. "That was a painting by him, by Antonello da Messina. Yes. That was his great painting of St. Sebastian, which we didn't see because we had to cancel Dresden. That was him."

Nathan squinted at his mother, unable to quite digest this information. "So you used Solomon Briggs' painter to create one of your works." He didn't know how to take this. Was it hypocritical? No. Maybe. She'd always claimed that Solomon had no impact on her life, so she'd had no interest in telling him anything.

"Yes, I used an Antonello painting. Yes. He's a world painter. He never belonged to Solomon Briggs, exclusively, I beg your pardon."

"He's so great. Everyone knows him." Saffron said. "Well, not everyone. I do."

"A lot of people spend their spiritual energy searching for god. Your father, Solomon, wasted his energy trying to arrive at a secular spirituality through the way Antonello looked at people in his portraits, or something like that."

"Awesome," said Saffron.

"Why is this the first time we ever talked about this? I mean, haven't I asked you about him? I mean…"

"I don't know, it just never seemed…"

"What else…?"

"Nothing." Brightwatch got quiet. She had lost control of this conversation and didn't like that.

"What did he look like?" Saffron asked, to break the silence.

Brightwatch smiled at her. "He was about Nathan's height, a little plumper, had grey eyes like Nathan's. Nathan resembles him a lot, as I remember."

Nathan recollected the only picture he ever saw of him, a group of friends by the New York Public Library, next to one of the stone lions.

"He couldn't whistle." Brightwatch laughed, back in control.

"I can't whistle," Nathan said.

"I just learned how to do an awesome screech with two fingers, if you ever need a whistler."

"He wore sandals all the time. I don't know? What else?"

"You lived with him. What happened to any pictures of him?"

"That was so long ago, Nathan. What pictures I had got shuffled out of my life."

"Didn't you ever think that I might have wanted them?"

"I think it's nuts, if you think you're going to find him. And it's useless."

Saffron's whistle filled the room. "I'm going to

help," she volunteered.

"Even if I don't find a trace of him, but just come near what his movements were, where he was at any given time, that would be something more than I have, to move inside his shadows, call out his ghosts. Puglia, Sicily, that's helpful." He didn't know yet if the small touch of his philosophy was going to be helpful, or an added confusion.

"He called from Cefalù. I don't know why I remember that."

"That's good. That's better. Where is Cefalù?"

"I always thought it was in Sicily, I think."

"I'll go to Sicily with you," Saffron said, enthusiastically. "I've always wanted to, and the school is going anyway."

"Then the other was from a little town in the spur of the boot, you know that peninsula out into the Adriatic. It's in Puglia, and he was headed to Lecce, down in the heel. I don't know why."

"You remember a lot more than you ever let on before, Brightwatch. Thanks."

"Yeah, well, for me it wasn't so big a deal. We were miles apart. I remember he said "redemption." That's what he wanted from art. I thought, how melodramatic." She pulled a pack of cigarettes from a box near the chair, tapped one out, looked at it, then tapped it back in. "These are Lolly's. I've been quitting." She looked at

Nathan. "I don't mean that like it sounds. It was a big deal. I got pregnant. I thought he was a good match to get pregnant with, and then it became you, and that was a big deal; but he was never a big deal in my life…You know what I mean?"

Nathan couldn't take any push further out onto the edge. Redemption! A heavy snapshot of his father. Nathan was exhausted. "I'm out of here, Brightwatch."

"You're really out on this wild goose chase?"

"My heart knows what the wild goose knows," Nathan dragged that line up from a pool of old songs. He started for the door.

Brightwatch stood up and cradled Saffron's arm as she walked them to the door. "It was lovely to meet you," she said.

"For me it's been a totally awesome privilege. It's, I don't know, it's like I'm here in a dream. I'm so glad we were in that museum, and I picked up your son. It was worth my whole semester in Europe."

"Just because you came with him, you don't have to leave with him. You can stay and work a little as my assistant, show me what you know about computers. Then you'll meet Lolly."

"Mommy, sweetheart," Nathan intoned.

Isabel dropped Saffron's arm.

"Thank you," Saffron said. "Maybe I'll take you up on it some other time. My whole class is headed south to Florence, Rome, then Naples and Sicily, so what I'm thinking is I want to go south with Nathan, then meet up with them down there. It's so way cool, a very open situation, not like school, really. Or vice versa, meet him down there, if Nathan wants."

"Whatever Nathan wants," Brightwatch turned away from them as they went through the door. "Take care of my son."

Nathan stumbled into the gardens around the biennale buildings.

"You okay?" Saffron asked, grabbing his arm. "Don't fall down."

Nathan sank onto a bench, looking out between the trees at the islands of the lagoon. Saffron settled beside him, took his hand into her lap, and leaned into him. The skies were darkening, or clearing up, grey clouds fringed in brightness.

"So do you want me to come with you?"

"What did you think of Brightwatch?"

"Awesome for me, just being in that studio, listening to her; but I can see that for you…Answer me. Do you want me to come with you?"

Nathan said nothing. They walked quietly under the pines. The confusions of a long silence made Saffron insecure. She looked away from Nathan, and talked as if to the lagoon.

"I have to tell you, I was a hooker once; I mean, not

actually a hooker, but I turned a trick. I went with this old Norwegian guy, for money. Afterwards he wanted to marry me, but I thought that was too weird, to marry a hooker. My friend, they called him Muffler, who set me up, would have got me an apartment and everything, but I couldn't see it, getting into that life, and everything…"

"This "Muffler," he was a pimp?"

"No. He was like in college, too. It was lots of money, though." She turned back, to look into his face, but he was staring at his knees.

"Every time I see her I feel like I've been whacked across the side of my head, then whacked again."

"At least you talk to her. I don't know how to begin talking to my 'rents."

Nathan kept himself from saying, "Except when you need money." When she mentioned her parents he felt a sudden pang of loneliness for Miriam. Saffron was younger than he could bear. He would have to get off alone somewhere, and call Mims.

"So do you want me to come with you? Please. I'll take care of you." She laughed.

"I don't know what she meant by that." He slipped his hand out of hers.

"That was between women," Saffron said, coyly. "So you don't want me to come?"

"Why do you want to go somewhere with such an

older guy?"

"You're not such an older guy. I've been with older."

"Do the arithmetic. I'm nearly twice as old. Why do you…?"

"Did you ever run around with a bunch of college women? This is bimbos international. I mean I don't want to diss them. I'm just one of them, and like I do have some friends, but most of the women are so superficial. I mean, they're okay, they're my friends but you're more to my…I want someone mature. I don't think age makes that much difference, do you? I can pay for myself. I don't know, like you feel young to me."

"How do you know I'm not a serial killer, or a rapist?"

"I've had a little rape before. You're the son of Brightwatch."

"Bright calls this a wild goose chase, and she's probably right. And aren't you in school? Don't you have requirements, attendance?"

"It's a pretty open program. I've done Rome and Florence before, anyway. I've never been to Sicily, though."

"Look, this hunt is just something I have to do for myself. I know it's futile, I probably won't find anything."

"No. Not futile. Like I loved what you said about

the shadows of your father, and calling out his ghosts. I was moved by that, Mr. Briggs. You're a very tender person."

Nathan was flattered that she had heard him, had listened to him at all. Miriam, though affectionate and kind, never seemed to hear him, particularly not about this. She had only a little more sympathy for his "cause" than his Brightwatch mother unit.

"That was the first time she ever said anything like that; I mean, anything personal about Solomon Briggs. That he thought that those paintings could help the world. How important is that to know about your father?"

"You can't," Saffron grinned as she mimicked. "Help the world." She almost caught the sound of the Brightwatch's voice, when it recreated the cadences of John Cage's speech. "If you try you will only make it worse—something like that."

"Do you think it's true, that you can't help…?" He paused, realizing he was asking someone fifteen years younger than himself. With a nose ring. SKUNK on her chest. Tattooed lips. Chrome yellow hair highlighted orange. How old was she? Nineteen? Twenty-one the most. Maybe that was good. That was the age of bullshit, when you talked about these things, in college. "She said he wanted redemption."

"I can't tell you about that. I don't know. I'm only

young. Re-demp-tion." She mouthed the word on her pucker. "I like that other word better, when we first met at the painting. It was what? The faces, yeah, obliterated, like…" She moved close and repeated it as if she would kiss him with it. "Obliterated!" He lifted his hand to separate their mouths, and she retreated. "For me this is like such a great reason to run around and look at those paintings, those Antonellos. I'm in love with this art, and Antonello da Messina is one of my secret faves, and none of the other women gets my enthusiasm for it the way…I don't have any of them to talk to. And besides, the Gypsy told me I would meet you, a handsome older man I would travel with."

"A Gypsy?" Nathan stood up, and headed towards the vaporetto landing.

"Yes. It was predicted." She took his hand. "So? Am I in?"

He put an arm around her shoulder, and smiled, but he couldn't answer. She was so young, almost a child, but so precocious, sophisticated about the art. It would be precious to have her input, and he felt a real hunger for the sympathetic companionship she promised; on the other hand, that she wanted to travel with him rather than with her peers might be a premonition of trouble ahead, some instability, some great neediness. Among qualities he acknowledged in himself, fatherliness was not one of them.

"Venice is so a dream. You know we were told they used to call it La Serenissima, the most serene," Saffron said, looking down the quai at fragments of the city visible through the mists.

"I wonder how serene it will be as it sinks."

A slant of golden light kissed the facade of San Giorgio Maggiore.

Saffron threw her arms around his neck as if she wanted to kiss him, but she didn't. "It's not like anyplace else on this planet, anyway. If I ever dreamt of going to Venus…"

The boat arrived, soundlessly. "Come on, Saffron," Nathan helped her onto the deck of the boat that would take them away from the island of his mother.

"But this is…" She looked up and down the oblong deck. "What kind of a boat is this?"

"We have to go below."

"Does this mean yes? You're taking me with you?"

They descended a spiral stair to the cabin below. Benches were arranged along the sides, and in parallel rows down the middle of the cabin. A dim red light illuminated the passengers. Some people gathered around and took turns peering through what looked like a periscope.

"I think they're speaking Russian, some language I don't know," Saffron whispered. She looked around at the other people, and the thick portholes. "Is this what I think it is?"

"Probably. What do you think it is?"

"A submarine? Under water boat?"

"Well, the tide is high, and the waters are deep."

As the light went from red to green the craft pulled away from the dock, and they sensed its tilt and descent. The big diesel vibrated through their bones.

"This is not to be believed," Saffron said, and squinted into the murk through the porthole, then she patted Nathan on the leg and got up to take her turn at the periscope.

"Sewage, big buds of sludge, actual garbage, swill from restaurants." The voice of a tour guide crackled in English over the intercom. "There on the left goes someone's boot, and a raincoat, yellow. Did anyone catch the label? Whoops. A whole lifeboat."

"Tonino Teodoro, I think, is the label," a passenger offered. "There goes the other boot."

Nathan heard a thump against the hull near himself, and saw something vaguely dog swirl by. "Some days they drown the dogs," the guide's voice offered.

"Who are they?" Nathan asked.

Saffron returned, "You should look through the periscope, still some of the domes left to see. Whoa!" She pressed her face against the porthole. "Wasn't that that famous Titian?"

"Those seated on the right side of the cabin might notice the dome of a small synagogue from the ghetto, passing, once built on top of the modest apartment house. The Jews were welcomed to live in Venice, with certain restrictions, a curfew, but they could not build any new buildings, were given no land for their synagogues, so they had to put them on top of the modest buildings that were already there."

"Look, wow!" Saffron pointed into the murk, as they went through what looked like the arch from the Rialto bridge.

"This sure is the great way to see Venice, but I didn't expect it so soon," Nathan said.

"Everything jumbled, like Venice soup. Omigod," Saffron exclaimed. "I just visited all those. Those are from the Peggy Guggenheim. Those are out of the Gianni Mattioli collection. A Morandi. I loved that. And here come all those futurist works. Balla, the Carlo Carrà Interventista Manifesto, Boccioni."

"So the futurists are in the past. How do you see through all this murk?"

"My God, that awesome Mondrian. And Giacometti. And here comes the Henry Moore. Look out."

The sculpture glanced off the hull, followed by some sizzling neon almost extinguished.

"A Jackson Pollock! A Mark Rothko!" Saffron's enthusiasm for the works almost negated the catastrophe that had sent them into the flood. A submerged tide of the twenty-first century was coming, an enormous wash of technology and waste, a mass of difference.

"We apologize," said the guiding voice. "For the unpleasantness. The nets at the mouth of the lagoon are designed to catch these unfortunates, but so many are caught in the currents that a lot of them still get through."

Saffron covered her eyes as mutilated bodies drifted through the slowly tumbling trio of Robert Motherwell canvases, the Fernand Léger, the disturbing Max Ernst fantasies. One seemed to embrace and dance with an elegant small cubist *quelque chose* by Georges Braque.

"These must be terminated population from Srebeniça, or Bosnia, or Kosovo. Could they be Algerian? No. It's hard to remember how many the people have been." Nathan said.

"Please. Let's get out of here."

"Soon."

"Can't I go with you?"

"You are with me."

"Watch how they prance," the voice instructed. As if in slow motion, the mighty horses of St. Marks galloped by the portholes, parting clouds of murk, spinning art and corpses in their wake. La Fenice. La Fenice spun by like a Tibetan prayer wheel. The exhale from the flared nostrils of the great steeds rose like tremendous tears through the brownness, like dream eggs that floated upwards and away.

MILKS

MILKS

The dingy train station at Foggia, with its collapsed benches and grey walls of peeling grime, its desolate high ceilings, and unlit corners, felt anyway like a release from suffocation. Sicily had been like a collar tightening on his throat. It was probably all in his mind, but now he felt free of Palermo, free of dreary Messina. Now he knew he was really on his way to find what he had set out to find, one way or another. The joyous reunions that filled the station lightened his mood—all the migrant workers returned from Milano, Torino, Germany, Sweden, Switzerland, glad to see their families again. This tide of joy was an inundation of confidence, premonitions of success. Free of Violeta, free of Annelino. Rid of the dismal Sicilian silences. His Sicilian acquaintances dimmed like figures through a haze.

Here people slapped their chests with emotion. Dark, sturdy men descended from the trains in their durable brown wool suits, in their black *basquis* or their snap brim caps, their shoes without laces. They embraced their families, they tossed the scuffed cardboard suitcases and boxes bursting with gifts onto the roofs of tiny Seicentos and sweet old Topolinos. Children squealed and grabbed their pappas. A plump girl child rushed Solomon and embraced his leg. She smelled like a carp. Then she looked up and yelped when she saw he wasn't her uncle. She was rescued by a brightly painted *traino,* pulled by a mule. It turned into the circle, its two wheels as tall as Solomon, and a young man jumped off, grabbed the girl, and threw her onto the burlap sacks full of greens, next to the luggage.

This was where he would pull his inside straight, his best hunch yet, where he would find the great St. Francis paintings, paintings to begin to heal the world, why not.

He searched for the station-master once the crowd cleared out. First he would go either to San Giovanni Rotondo, and look for this Padre Pio, or to Peschichi, where Mario's family was expecting him to show up. He spotted the uniformed man behind the wicket. His outfit had been made for someone much larger, so he looked like a child dressed up. With his back to Solomon he sorted, stamped, and spindled a huge pile of official papers.

Solomon tapped on the counter, waiting for the stationmaster to turn around. He thought about the ride from Napoli to Pescara, and then standing all the way south to Foggia in the heat of the second class car, the train full of migrant workers. They pressed against him, staring, and made him explain where he came from. "America, ahhhh. America." And why was he coming South? American tourists don't come to the Mezzogiorno. Why did he ever want to leave America? Ahhh, to look for a painting. He should go to Alberobello, see the trulli. To Martina Franca, eat lamb testicles. Go to Lecce, very beautiful, many paintings, the Florence of the South. To Capo Santa Maria di Leuca, the tip of Italy, all the villas owned by *gran signore.* There from the very tip of the *Salento,* the heel of the boot, you can smell Africa, cinnamon, cardamom, myrrh and ambergris on the winds. And you will go to see Padre Pio? You believe that? The church, the priests, hypocrites. They want the poor to stay poor, and ignorant, the people groveling under their control, thieves worse than the mafia. They suck our blood. But Peschici is beautiful, yes, high on a cliff. Like an island of Greece, they tell me. Yes, said another, gesturing with his hands in his jacket pockets. I've been to Greece—the white houses, blue shutters, and calamari, eat the calamari. No, eat the *triglie,* said another. He is American. He can pay for the *triglie.* The best fish in the whole world.

The man behind the wicket finally turned his head, and cast tired eyes on Solomon. His face was thin and drawn, with the heavy shadow of a beard, his eyes so close together they almost crossed, and most surprising was his nose, crooked, notched, as the immortal nose of Federigo di Montefeltro, Count of Urbino. He had been a great warrior, who when he lost an eye in battle had part of his nose removed so he could see across his face. He was also a man of great learning and culture, who had one of the biggest libraries in all of Italy, who had commissioned many works by Piero Della Francesca, and Solomon imagined he might have commissioned a St. Francis by Antonello, had he ever met the great Sicilian master. There was nothing to say he hadn't. How could he resist? Paint it, Antonello, for the Duomo to be built in Urbino, or even for the cathedral in Assisi. He was proud to get his own crooked nose into the renderings of religious subjects, as it was displayed even now in Milano, at the Brera, in Piero's great *Madonna and Child On Her Throne*. Such was the nose of this stationmaster, so that Solomon took it as yet another sign that he had come to the right place.

"I need to go to San Giovanni Rotondo," Solomon said.

The man straightened his uniform jacket, adjusted his cap, checked his watch, and approached his side of the wicket. "Ah, *caro signore,*" almost singing with condescension and compassion. "Between where you want to go, and where you can go, always a question of schedules." The corners of his mouth drooped serious and weary. He leaned over the wicket. "Where is your group? You are alone?"

From the back room a woman entered and stared at Solomon from behind the Station Master, her mouth hung slightly open, eyes wide, as if something she saw in Solomon had startled her.

"Yes, I'm alone," Solomon responded.

"Where is your wife?" The woman was loud.

Isabel was probably going to have his child, but Isabel as a wife didn't make much sense to him. He figured now that she had been only an excuse for him to get to Italy, and do what he had to do. He'd come this far in life without marriage, anyway; and he didn't want to bring up Venice, a little pretentious, nor did he want to mention Isabel as an artist. "I have no wife." The melancholy in his voice was unintended.

"How can you have no wife?" The woman's voice echoed through the empty station as if through a loudspeaker. She stepped up to stand next to the Station Master.

Solomon didn't want this conversation. "I'm not married," he said, curtly. "I want to take the next train this afternoon for San Giovanni Rotundo."

"Who takes care of you?" She roared. "How does a man live without a wife?"

"Angelina, quiet. He can hear you." He shrugged at Solomon. "Her father was deaf, and she's a little. Anyway, you can't go to San Giovanni Rotondo," said the stationmaster. "No trains go there."

"This is my husband. I take care of him. Look at him. If not for me, what would he do?" Herself was a small round woman, also in a state railroad uniform, grey trimmed with red, though hers was a few sizes too

241

small, so her wrists stuck out of the sleeves, her flesh folded over the skirt. She couldn't close her jacket over her stained blouse.

"Maybe there is a bus?"

"You have come to see the saintly Padre? Padre Pio?" the man asked.

"I've come to look for a painting." He didn't know why he mentioned this.

"You are not a Catholic." the woman blared. "During the war many Americans came, and they were not Catholic. And they married the Italian girls."

"No. I'm not Catholic."

"Then where are you from?" She shrieked, pushed her husband aside, and leaned towards him.

"America. The United States."

"Ahhh. Then you know Fiorello LaGuardia. He was Catholic. He was Italian, LaGuardia. There are Catholics in America." She smiled, her voice simmering down.

"Protestants," said her husband, shrugging meekly.

"Fiorello LaGuardia was a good man. He was Catholic. He came here to see Padre Pio, and he saw all the poor people, and the suffering pilgrims, and he met the saintly father. He was president of New York City, and here he built a hospital for poor sick pilgrims. In America…" She screeched again, and rubbed her thumb over her fingers in the gesture that meant money.

"I don't need to see Padre Pio. I've come here to find

a painting, a particular one of St. Francis, by Antonello…"

"He will be a saint, just like St. Francis," said the husband. "He has the stigmata. I saw it, once. I saw him through a mirror. You should try to meet the saintly father. There are always many many paintings everywhere, here in Foggia to see, or you can go to Monopoli, or Bari, but there's only one Padre Pio. So why would you go to Monte Sant Angelo for a painting? But to see the stigmata! The saintly father! Tell him you are from America. Tell him you knew Fiorello LaGuardia. One bus a day goes, only in the morning."

The Station Master wasn't wrong. He just as easily could look in Martina Franca or Monopoli. Thousands of places to search, but only one where it gathered dust in its beautiful obscurity. Thousands of small archives, niches, closets to hide a painting. He'd already looked in Cortona, in Spoleto, where there was a Madonna and child by Antonello's son. And once he'd gone to look in closets in the museum in Bergamo, but the curator would not cooperate. And he'd looked in Gubbio, shoved up against its hillside, and he'd searched as much as he could in Orvieto, where Beato Angelico and Luca Signorelli had left their marks. There he'd eaten tagliatelle with truffles, and some succulent pheasant. Bonus meals along the way. He'd sniffed around in Spello, where J.P. Morgan's favorite, Il Pinturicchio, had left some chapels. But now he was sure he would find it somewhere here in the South, a great place to lose the art, il mezzogiorno.

It had been sitting for five centuries, waiting for him to uncover it, when the moment was right. And this was the right moment to bless the spirit of the new world with the as yet unassimilated genius of the old. It was hanging somewhere, maybe overpainted and overpainted. This place felt good. He would see right through to the real thing. It well could be here, in the lair of the future saint. Antonellus pinxit. Mine is a strange faith, he thought. It moves on hunches. He spent his small inheritance on these speculations to keep him moving place to place, to bring him here to steamy mosquito bogs of Foggia, once famous for malaria, and what else? Bauxite, maybe? This was 1964, after all. Even bauxite had done some damage. A poor world with Kennedy assassinated. A rich world with Martin Luther King on the march. A new spirit percolating through everything. So he looks for a painting that might or might not exist. But yes, it exists. Yes, it has to be retrieved.

They mentioned that there was a bus in the morning to take him out onto the spur of the boot, the Gargano, a place he'd never payed attention to before, not until Mario Chiodino, his neighbor in Mestre, told him about it. He knew Mario, who planted and harvested artichokes to sell in Venice, only as the contadino who worked the land around the place they rented. He seemed a good man. For Solomon this was the perfect guy off whom to grab a hunch; someone who hadn't even heard of Antonello. His buddy Isabel did her art, he went out to find this painting. Civilization still haunts the earth. Antonello knew how to see the human being with absolute clarity, and his paintings still protect that information, those vital ambiguities—how the person occupies space, how spirit reaches out to the viewer through the eyes. He wished he could express it accurately. The harmony of interior and exterior space. Disharmony. Words don't find it. Just look at the paintings. Sit down at the poker table with all of Antonello's subjects, play a few hands. They know you, looking at you crooked but direct from the paintings, and they are waiting for you to make your hopeless move. They can skin you like a squirrel, just with their eyes. They know more than you about yourself. And by way of love Antonello gave us this Mary, how the Sicilian Hebrew Virgin Mary really looks as she begins to understand she has conceived the son of God, how she looks within herself, yet reaches that hand out of the picture, maybe to greet us, maybe to ward off the angel Gabriel. And if Antonello did do a picture of St. Francis receiving the stigmata, for instance, it would be worth everything to know how his genius saw and understood the face, and the spirit of the man, what this miracle means to himself as he renounces the luxury of his inheritance. The ability to see people clearly, and so deep, and make them move so forwardly to the viewer, has been lost in the world, or eliminated, passed into an oblivion of storytelling, limiting speculations, if this gift has ever existed anywhere else but in Antonello.

The stationmaster and his wife watched him, as if waiting for him to stop thinking.

"Don't worry about painting. Better a nice woman." The Station Master's wife blared out as she came from behind the window, and squeezed Solomon's arm. "A good wife to cook, and mend your clothes." She turned to her husband. "Maybe Gianinna?"

"No. She has a beard."

"Then Arabella's daughter, the fair one, Sofia."

"She's young enough, but a little bit crazy. Very pretty. Maybe…maybe not a virgin."

Solomon started for the door.

"You come back tomorrow," said the wife, almost whispering as she grabbed the brim of her cap and flipped it towards him. "We'll have a nice wife for you." She finished with an echoing whoop.

*   *   *

The Gargano promontory, a little known jewel on a boot studded with gems, actually the spur on the heel of that boot, is a limestone escarpment that rises from the tableland of the province of Puglia and thrusts its white cliffs out above the

Adriatic, cliffs fringed with white sand beaches.

Solomon read this in his French guidebook, as he stood on the bus crushed against several dozen women dressed in black. He had battled them, and their children, their goats and chickens for his place to stand on the bus.

Unlike most of the Puglia region, the Gargano is mountainous, with virgin forests and ancient olive groves. The blue olives are surrounded by red poppies in the spring, and golden dandelions the people harvest for food and wine. The forests are home to wild boar and lynx and deer. The pheasant, grouse, and partridge make it a great destination for sporting hunters. The coast is dotted with quaint fishing villages, where informal restaurants serve generous plates of merluzzo, triglie, squid, and a fritto misto of tiny fish fried in batter, a delicious specialty of this shore. The peninsula is home also to Monte Sant'Angelo, a monastery where the holy Padre Pio, a saintly priest soon to be canonized, lives in seclusion. The Romanesque churches found…

He went to Peschici first, to look up Mario's family. The village sat several hundred feet above a pristine white beach and clear sea of liquid emerald. Solomon could feel, looking out over this, the sadness Mario must have experienced, leaving such an exaltation of a place for the dull wastes of Mestre. Below, on the long curve of beach, was a lean-to over a small stove and a few folding tables, where a couple of women fried battered fish to a crisp, golden sweetness in olive oil, and chased their children playing in the sand. The smell of the hot oil wafted in waves all the way up to the small belvedere where the bus had let him off.

He walked down the narrow, cobblestone street that splintered off the main road to the shore till he found the address, number 129, a house with a blue door. He hesitated, staring at the door. Smells of the fish fry and sea spray breezed up the cobblestone alley from the shore. Mario had told him there was an older brother, a little sister, the mother, and the dim memory of a father who had made three kids, then left to be killed in the war. Just talking of them had brought Mario to tears. Solomon didn't know Mario well enough to feel easy about introducing himself. His arm felt like a 500 pound weight to lift and knock on the door. He waited, then heard shutters thrown open above his head.

"Ma, signore, chi cerca, per carità?" A young woman leaned out into the sun. When Solomon explained that he had come from Venice with a message from Mario, she rushed down and threw open the door.

"S'accomodi, entra, per piacere. Entra, entra, signore."

"You must be Iera?"

"Si. Si. Eccomi, Iera." She grinned widely, a family grin, that turned her face into Mario's, though several years younger. She took Solomon by the sleeve and led him upstairs into the parlor, where an older woman sat on a stool kneading a wooden paddle through the cheese in a small tub. "Mamma," Iera said. The room smelled of goat and brine. The parlor furniture was covered with newspaper while the room was given over to processing the mozzarella, Iera explained. "We have no shed to do this, so we have to do it in the house. Not so elegant. I'm sorry."

The mother put down the paddle and started to pull fistfuls of cheese from the mass, rolling them into balls that she dropped into a bucket of brine, cursing all the time. "Quante capre. Quante capre. Maladette capre. Damned goats. Too many goats." She looked up at Solomon. "Who is this?"

"It's a friend of Mario, Mamma. He came from Venice." Iera took the paddle from her mother's hand and helped her to stand up. She sat down herself to work the cheese.

The older woman stared at him, a thin smile on her dry lips. "S'accomodi, signore. Make yourself comfortable." She smoothed the newspaper over the cushions of the couch. "I'm so sorry, signore," said the old woman. "We are poor people, have no place else to make the cheese, and you cannot stop or else all the milk…wasted." She squeezed Solomon's arm, patted his chest as if he was a pig she was going to roast.

"Tell us your name. What is your name?" Solomon said his name. It was difficult to look at the old woman, she was staring at him so intently. "Yes, Solomon. Tell us about Mario. Iera, listen. He will tell us about Mario."

Solomon didn't know what to say. He didn't want to tell them how their son and brother was scratching through hard times. He fabricated a line of half truths, of how well Mario was doing, his good job, the good land, saving money, his nice house with Angelica, how happy they were. Iera grinned broadly at the good news and, as she worked the cheese, she stole looks at Solomon. Her beauty and youthful charm encouraged Solomon to embellish the picture. Yes, they had a refrigerator, yes a short wave radio, yes a house with three rooms, yes a car, a seicento, yes a big horse to pull the plow.

As he talked, the older woman seemed to embrace him with her eyes.

"Don't look at him so much, Mamma. It's not polite."

The old lady leaned forward, hooked the back of his neck with her hand, and pulled him towards herself. "You are so very fat, and so handsome."

Solomon always thought of himself as a skinny guy. He tried to pull away from her grip, but she was strong, a wiry old lady, and he was forced to look down at the black of her dress. She smelled of goat and rosewater.

"We are happy that you have come from Mario. Welcome. Welcome. Iera, look how fat is your future husband. You are so welcome here. So handsome." She released Solomon's neck so his head sprang back as if whiplashed. "And so, mister Solomon, you like Iera?"

"Mamma, no." Iera blushed.

"She is very strong, a good young woman. A wife for your whole life."

"Mamma! Basta!" Iera turned the stool so her back was to them, and continued working the cheese.

"Mario told me about Iera," Solomon said. Something pleased him about the thought of marrying this pretty girl he hardly knew. It was about time he married, he could hear his dead mother saying from her perch.

"So you will marry Iera," the older woman said, fiercely.

"Yes," said Solomon, thinning the conversation into a silence filled with the slaps of cheese against the side of the tub. No, he thought. "Yes," he said again.

He thought of Isabel, working in Venice on her own, carrying his daughter, or maybe his son. This was the second time since he'd arrived here that the idea of marriage swelled up to fill the space. He saw how beautiful Iera was, and so full of yearning it spilled over and made him yearn for her. She would be such a tender wife. He was certainly of the age when he should get married. Isabel wasn't a woman to marry. She didn't even want to be a wife. And he didn't know if he wanted to be a husband. Not hers, anyway. The child, if it was for real, would help him get closer to Isabel, close as he thought he wanted to be. Fatherhood would shine some warmth into his life, end the murkiness of self-involvement. He would dedicate with her to raise a child. That wasn't too idealistic. But he could do the same with this girl. Children were not hard to make. And this was more like he always had thought it would be—meet someone, boom! Marriage surprise. That the one he met would be making mozzarella cheese, he grinned, that he could never have predicted. He had once thought he wanted Isabel to let him get closer to her, even to serve the talent he admired, and to feel her reciprocate with the kind of passion he knew she was capable of, that she sometimes loosed on him, a dedication to him in the moment when they made love; and he would hope for her to release herself from her own self absorption into that same passion, so they both could expand through their lives as lovers, and as parents together. He expected too much. She had her art, after all, behind which she kept him at a distance, helped her evade whatever commitment he'd ask to their being a "couple." He didn't even like the word, himself. In fact, all the reasons that made her difficult, made him respect her all the more. But surely she wasn't right for marriage. And his current passion for Antonello, which though she somewhat ridiculed it, he suspected that was what allowed them to stay together, that he was this preoccupied. To some of his friends it looked like he demeaned himself to be with her. "Why don't you get your own life, Sol?" Maggie, his movie buddy from Detroit often said when he confided in her over dinner, before the show. But Solomon felt this was enough, a life that Antonello made richer. A child might take everything further with Isabel, but marriage made more sense with this sweet dark stranger. Isabel had been the most interesting ride he had found so far, but he didn't know how much further he could take it.

Tonino arrived, straddling his tiny, three wheeled Vespa truck, jugs of goat milk strapped into the bed. This was a small dark man, wiry as his mother, quick and energetic. He had none of the softness, the kind smiles of Iera and Mario in his looks. "Oh, you are such a good man to come here to see us," he said, shaking Solomon's hand. "And how is Mario? When does he come home? It is so good to meet you. You come from Venice. You are from America? Mamma mia, all the way down here to see us. Why do you come? You have relatives here?"

"He comes for Iera," the mother said. "He will marry our Iera and take her to America."

"Mamma, basta. Stop. Don't talk. He doesn't know." Iera tucked her bare feet under the hem of her skirt.

"Zita, scema. Keep shut your mouth, you silly girl."

"Don't listen to them," Tonino said. "Unless you want to marry. Do you want to marry Iera?"

"Yes," said Solomon, ready to keep the option open. He felt just a twinge of guilt, because for him it was a fantasy from which he could easily disappear.

"Then Iera is a good woman, if you want to marry her, but don't listen to mamma. She wants to arrange everything."

Solomon stayed for dinner, and explained finally that he was interested in looking for the painting in San Giovanni Rotondo. Antonello's painting. The mamma shrugged and left the room when he talked about it. Iera said she had never been to San Giovanni Rotondo, as if it were somewhere far away. She said she was afraid of Padre Pio, didn't want to see him. He would make her sick, she thought. Her brother explained that she had it backwards, and Iera smiled at Solomon, as if she had made a great joke, a smile that could squeeze honey from a stone. Tonino gripped Solomon's arm, enthusiastic about the idea.

"Good, very good. You will find the painting there, I have no doubt of it. We can go there tomorrow on my Vespa and you can stop to see the goats, because they are near the monastery. And when you see them you will be lucky, because then you can meet Aldo and we will let you invest in the goats, and we will show you how we become rich; and I can take you into the monastery, because I deliver goat milk to the saintly father's cook, and I take them the cheese. The saintly father loves the fresh goat mozzarella, even the salty mozzarella, because we make it so delicious. You can take some back with you to America and we will make a business, sell our cheese in America. We can have big business in America. Mamma, are you listening?" He shouted into the kitchen. "We make big business in America. Our goats will fly in America. I can come to America, and I can become the richest American goat industrialist."

The next morning Iera saw them off. The yearning in her smile, in her eyes, made Solomon ache. She was so frighteningly beautiful.

"I will come back, for you," Solomon said, and he meant it.

"For me?" She cradled his hand in both of hers.

"Yes." He felt the warmth of the womb her palms made around his hand push deep into his loins. "I will come back here for you and we will…" He couldn't say it.

"Marry." she said. "Marry me."

"Yes." He hardly recognized himself, talking like this. Thinking like this. He meant it, and indulged himself in the pleasure of her obvious joy. Her parting kiss on his cheek was huge and warm, and he felt it there for hours as they rode, and many days later he could still recall how it felt. The day was calm, the Adriatic an emerald drum. They rode out towards Monte Sant'Angelo under an amethyst dome of cloudless sky. Seated in the bed of the little scooter/truck Solomon thought this is the colors of heaven. The little Vespa wheezed over the hills, and bumped on dirt roads through the virgin pine forests, through ancient olive groves, ancient olive trees twisted and hollow. The Vespa almost bucked him out of its bed, into the trees. He could have been living here forever, riding the bed of tiny Vespa through the olives. Their contorted old trunks folded on themselves, as if they hid centuries of secrets of joy and misery. They turned off the gravel road, onto a track that wound through more twisted olives to a tiny cottage, the walls like heaps of stones that seemed to have rolled into place on their own. Chickens and guinea hens pecked around the yard. A rooster flew to the peak of the roof and crowed. On the slopes a wandering of goats bleated down at the stranger. Two young billies came over to tug Solomon's shoelaces untied, then stepped back to laugh at him.

"Eccolo, Aldo," Tonino exclaimed, as a tiny man sprang out from in back of the hut, bounding towards them, much like a goat himself. A black goose, with a string of mottled goslings complained behind him.

"Aldo, this is my friend. He is Mario's friend, come from Venice. All the way from the United States. From New York, Aldo. Fiorello LaGuardia. We make business with him, sell our cheese in America. American industrialists, Aldo." Tonino leaned towards Solomon, to whisper, "He won't speak. He is mute, he'll never say a word, but take his hand."

Solomon took Aldo's extended hand, large, powerful hands on so small a man. He touched Solomon's hand softly, without squeezing it, then suddenly pulled it away, and clapped. Solomon recognized Aldo's face from somewhere. He understood where only after Tonino explained that Aldo had come from Sicily. It was an Antonello face, one he had recently seen in a dark gallery in a monastery in Piacenza, a portrait of Christ called *Ecce Homo,* one of several portraits Antonello did, using the same model he did for the one in the Met in New York, a kind of Rocky Marciano puss, thick nose, full lips, that looked like it had taken a few shots in its day. It was the look of a Sicilian fisherman who had perhaps been chosen to play Christ in a passion play, then suddenly flipped over to believe this was not a role, but he was actually The Christ, and this was the real crown of thorns on his head, and his scalp bled, and the cross was a real weight, and he looked out at you, with those eyes of terminal despair, the folly, the tragic injustice and disappointment of the actual crucifixion. That portrait gave us this transformation, showing the perfect tears on his cheek, and even one that had fallen to his chest, still a perfect droplet in form, as if once Christ expresses a tear, it maintains its form forever. This Aldo bounced around like a comic version of that character, a Harpo Marx goatherd Christ whose every move seemed like play, as if he was one of the goats on the hillside.

"Come," Tonino said. "We will show you the special goats. Aldo breeds them. They are our miracle, and they will make us rich." Solomon followed them back of the house, down a little dip to a small corral that held about a dozen goats. There was something strange about these, a little deformed.

"These are Aldo's genius. He is a genius. You know, he'll never say something, not a word, but he will do miracles. He will make us rich."

With explosive spryness Aldo leaped across the corral to snatch one of these goats by the tail. These were more skittish than the others, not so friendly.

"Look," Tonino said. "How strong and quick Aldo is. He knows the goats so well. He knows."

Aldo set the bleating brown and white goat down in front of Solomon. A jackdaw settled on a fencepost, watching and chuckling. Several others chak-chakked into the olive trees. The deformity Solomon had noticed was that their front legs were much shorter than their rear, giving the torsoes of the goats a slope that added to the impression of deformity. Part of those front legs seemed to be growing upwards. Tonino bent to kiss the deformed shoulder blades. "These will be wings. He is making the goats with wings." Tonino spread his arms. "These goats will fly like birds. No, they will fly like bats."

"Why? What good is flying goats?"

"What good is anything, *figlio mio?* Flying goats is good, and that is Aldo's genius. He sees that. He uses the bats, I don't know how. There is something he does with the bits of the bats and pieces of goats. I don't understand what he does, but in that little hut, he won't let you in, I've never been inside, but he does this. He is a miracle, Aldo. Speaks not a word, but he is a genius."

"If God intended goats to fly," Solomon was aware of his own banality. "He would have given them wings, I guess."

"Yes, my boy, we are all manifestations of God, so if Aldo succeeds to make these goats that fly, it will be God's work."

"So any evil a man thinks up can be God's work. Anything nasty that he does? Mussolini and Hitler? Ethiopia?"

"Ah, *figlio mio*. Evil is a different story. It is not evil to fly a goat, you will see. Go, Aldo, get your apron, the milking apron." Aldo bounded back towards his house. "I don't understand Mario, my brother, why he leaves this place. This is his home. His family is here. This is the olives, the forests, the goats, the beautiful sea." Tonino waved his arm at the jackdaws, "Shut up you delinquents." They chak-chakked louder and flapped from branch to branch. "I know you, you thieves," he shouted.

He put an arm around Solomon's shoulders and rhapsodized again. "And there is the sea, like emeralds, the sea, and the beaches here white as goat milk. Certainly there are beautiful beaches by Venice, but not like here, dear Solomon, as you can see. There it is crowded with strangers, but here it is pure and tender. This is family. This is his goats. Tell Mario all of this. He will listen to you." Tonino grabbed Solomon's arm, and looked into his eyes. "Dear, dear Solomon. Ahhh! Here comes Aldo again."

Aldo had donned a large, awkward apron with a broad-mouthed tin funnel sewn to the front. "This is the milking apron Aldo invented," Tonino said. "For the flying goats. This is how profound, how free is Aldo's genius. Sometimes the simplest idea is the most important. Here it is, the milking apron for the flying goats; you see, with this apron you never have to bend. You can milk standing up. It is not easy for some people to bend so low to milk the goats. Aldo, yes, or myself, yes, we are small; but Americans, for example, like yourself, even bigger than yourself, very large Americans I have seen, who would suffer to milk thirty goats, be so bent over they never straighten up again."

"There are platforms. You can raise the goats up for milking." Solomon had seen this somewhere.

"No. No. Not platforms. Wings. Wings." Tonino said vehemently, as Aldo waved his arms around and shook his head. He had understood. He made a gesture, snapping his hands away from the goats. "A platform is outside nature. The goats must be free. Once our goats can fly, using Aldo's apron you can milk them standing up, no problem. It will be natural as a baby at its mother's breast. The goats free. And you wear this apron so the milk squirts against the chest plate and flows down through the tubes into your bucket, which you can pull on a small cart harnessed to follow behind you. So everyone can milk the goats. It is magnificent. And goat milk is the best, white as clouds, very healthy milk for you, and for the babies. So easy to digest. Generations of health, and happy families. And the cheese." He kissed his fingertips. "Ambrosia. It is the best in the world. Goat cheese brings justice to the world. Everyone will take the cheese, and the milk of the goat will flow through all of Europe, making people free from hunger and fear; and my dear Solomon, an ocean of white, the wine of the goat, will flow even to America. Ahhh, America. We will sell it to America, sell our goats, our aprons to America, and we will be rich. Imagine a skyscraper of goat cheese in New York City. Fiorello LaGuardia. Tell this to Mario, when you see him again. He should come home. His goats, his fortune waits here for him."

Aldo released the little goat, and they both squealed as it stumbled back to the corner of the corral where its sisters and brothers huddled, baring their teeth and hissing in a way very ungoatlike.

They ate some hard bread, salami, cheese, and tomatoes, then they mounted the Vespa again, and set off on a narrow track through the woods, Solomon in back, clutching a bucket of milk. Flies landed in the bucket, buzzing across the white surface. Golden butterflies flecked the air as the Vespa descended to the monastery.

"Look, dear Solomon. San Giovanni Rotondo. The baptistery is round, rotondo. Look, how beautiful it is. Built on the temple of Jupiter. You know that. An ancient temple for the saintly father."

Solomon was happy to learn that this place had been built on a Roman site, the baptistry then fifteenth century, and then the monastery, layer on layer of the sacred. For some reason it made his prospects seem better. Surely here was the place to find the St. Francis by Antonello that had been hidden so long. This was a simple building of limestone blocks, surrounded by a wall, a fringe of broken glass fixed in mortar along the top. It was settled into a clearing of the dark pine forest, and lay in the sunlight like an ember in its ashes. Tonino entered through the gate he used to deliver his milk and cheese. The silence here made him feel happy, and secure. In Padova he had descended into tunnels dug during World War II for protection from the bombing, the treasures still there, and he was sure he would find it; in Bergamo, at the Cararra Academy Museum, he inspected room after room, accompanied by a hostile curator, who wouldn't open some of those rooms where Solomon had the feeling there might be a clue. The more he insisted, the more the curator thought he was crazy. That curator was keeping the discovery for himself, and that was okay. As long as the painting was eventually revealed, all the curators of the world could get the credit. At the Certosa di Pavia he had climbed the campanile to the small storage rooms, sure it would be there. In every place there was the excitement and anticipation on the way, then that vacant feeling of nothing left to breathe, as the doors opened, and revealed the emptiness. The negatives accumulated. That nothing at least was something! A process, anyone might say, of elimination. Perhaps there was no such painting in the world. He was narrowing it down. Perhaps his search was just futile, wasting the chambers of his heart. Waste on, he thought. Waste on.

At any of these sites he could have taken months to thoroughly search, but he believed that just as he was looking for the art, the art was waiting somewhere for him, and that there would be some sign, an aura, an indication that would speak to him—dig deeper there, look further here. This one is overpainted, can't you see? There's something behind that canvas. There's a secret panel in that room. He would one day dust something off to find an arrow pointing ANTONELLO THIS WAY / ST. FRANCIS THIS WAY. He believed a moment would come, a moment he could recognize, like a pull. He'd be sitting on a jack and a nine, and pull anyway— the ace of diamonds, and pull again, because it was the moment—the ace of hearts,

Tonino left him in the hands of Frate Pumkin, a tall, blonde monk who had left the Orthodox church in Russia to be with Padre Pio. The monk said he would be happy for the opportunity to practice his English.

"Brother Pumkin, I have a special request because I am looking wherever I can, for a painting I think has been lost, but still, somewhere…"

"Poomkin," the brother corrected. "No Pumkin."

He led Solomon to a small windowless office, many pictures of Padre Pio on the walls, the future saint visited by notables—Pope Pius II, Fiorello LaGuardia, Danilo Dolci, Al Capone, a cycling champion, and some simpler people like a woman on crutches, an aged sheepherder, a mother and child, the little girl holding up to the saintly father a basket of huge lemons. Frate Pumkin settled behind his desk, took a drink from a cup sitting there, and signaled Solomon into a seat across from him.

"For why are you here?" asked the handsome brother. He wiped some goat milk off his moustache with the sleeve of his cassock.

"Like I said, it's a little strange. I am here…I am looking for a lost painting. Painted by Antonello da Messina. Or it could even be a whole altarpiece of the story of Saint Francis."

"You want this painting of St. Francis?"

"I don't want it for myself. I want to see it. I want to find it and bring it to the light. It will be important…"

"Important?…"

"…for the whole world to see this wonderful painting, by this great…"

"The world won't look at nothing…" The brother stroked his chin. "Why don't you go to Messina? He is da Messina."

"I was in Messina. Nothing is there. My intuition tells me."

"Intuition…?"

"I go by nerve, a hunch, my instinct. I trust it."

"So you think it's here? Your nerve tells you Monte St. Angelo?"

"Yes, now I know it's here. It most certainly is." Asserting this certainty made Solomon a little dizzy.

"Everything from God," said Frate Pumkin, readjusting some papers stuck into a corner of the desk blotter. "We have no paintings here, not even a few paintings. Here we have the living saint. Not canonized yet, but soon saint, nonetheless." He said "nonetheles" as if he was trying the word for the first time, then he grinned as if proud of his success at pronouncing it.

"Good," said Solomon, shoring up his courage. "I am sure the painting is here. Signora Bompani sent me to San Giovanni Rotondo from the archives in The Vatican, as a most likely location here," Solomon lied. "I have here a letter from the gracious Signora." He fumbled in his pockets, as if looking for the letter.

"No. No," said Pumkin. "Don't troubles." The brother got up, blowing his nose in a large blue handkerchief, then wiping at his forehead. He slugged down the rest of his milk. "I am often too hot here in Southern Italy. In Vladivostok, from where I come, never so hot. I walk here all the way across the wide Russia. You know where is Vladivostok? At seminary I was there, to take care of my grandmother who live alone there, was why I chose to seminary there, and because it was far plenty enough from Moscow; then I hear the Soviets come to close my monastery. I know I must leave. It was smart for me that I did. Other brothers, monks, priests, sisters, they be sent to work camp in Siberia…You know about work camp. To die."

Solomon waited as if to hear what relevance there was in this for his own search, but the brother dropped the story for the moment. "So I show you what is here. Nothing. No painting. No Saint Francis. Living saint here." Brother Pumkin led Solomon to another room, an empty monk's cell furnished only with a crude wooden bed, a stool, and a sink. He opened the closet and pulled out a banner—of the kind they sell to tourists in Assisi, with a representation of Saint Francis, arms spread, looking to the sky. "Only this. Here Saint Francis." He pushed the banner at Solomon, who didn't want to touch it, though he took some encouragement even from this cheap souvenir. Pumkin replaced the banner in the closet.

"I come here out of dear Orthodox Church, out of seminary. All the way walk from Vladivostok." He leaned in at Solomon so their faces almost touched. "I walk across all of Russia, all the way I walk. Carry sick grandma on my back."

"I'm sorry, brother Pumkin. It was so difficult for you." He turned his head, not realizing their faces were so close, lightly brushing Pumkin's nose.

"Poomkin," the brother corrected again. Solomon lifted his hand to ward off Pumkin's sour breath.

"Are there other rooms, or storage caves?" Pumkin's face was so near that Solomon feared he was going to kiss. He stepped back, but the brother closed in again.

"We have no food, drink water from puddles in the road. Sometimes I steal chicken from farm, and once a fat goose I cook by the road, to feed the Marushka, my grandmama. We walk every day, yes walk, and I feel her going away. She gets lighter and lighter on my back. She wants go back to Drovnyh, her village, outside Moscow, then she stops to breathing. I put her down and look, and don't feed her no more chicken. I carry her few light bones like a bird to Drovnyh, and I bury her at night, a muzhik in the earth of beloved mother Russia." Frate Pumkin pulled away from Solomon as if he was suddenly revolted by their proximity. As he left the room, he wiped tears from his eyes. Solomon followed him down another corridor. Grey light sifted through a narrow window high on a far wall. They stopped by a large double door, closed with a lock and hasp. Solomon touched the lock.

"Can you let me in here?"

"You don't go in everywhere. This is a monastery." Pumkin wiped the lock off with his handkerchief, as if removing Solomon's fingerprints.

Solomon leaned close to Frate Pumkin's face. "Brother Pumkin," he said. "Open this door. I am looking only for the painting, for some clue to the painting." He surprised himself by kissing the brother on his cheek.

Pumkin jumped back, as if startled, shook his head, and wiped his cheek. Without a word he found the key on his ring, and opened the door. It was a storeroom for some old pews, some insipid nineteenth century paintings of the holy family, an adoration, a crucifixion painted on black velvet. Solomon looked at another double door at the far end of the room.

"I cannot this one," Frate Pumkin said, placing his hands on Solomon's shoulders, as if he would embrace him. "I am sorry man."

"Frate Pumkin, I have come all the way from the United States, from the city of New York City, to look for this painting. In the British Museum in London, where they hold the *St. Jerome In His Study,* and a portrait, self-portrait, I found a scrap, only a piece of parchment, and printed there, *San Francesco…Antonello Pinxit*. Antonello Pinxit, Frate Pumkin." As if on cue some dim organ music seeped through the walls. Solomon and Frate Pumkin embraced, like two men. Solomon felt a sob shake Pumkin's body.

"I cannot this door," Pumkin said.

"You will do it, please."

"I cannot."

Solomon undid the rope belt of Pumkin's cassock, and without protest from the brother, pulled off his keyring. Pumkin slouched back against a stack of pews, as Solomon tried each of the keys in the door. It was an old lock, a large keyhole, so there were only nine of the larger keys that would fit. He tried each of them twice, and then a third time. None of them worked.

"Pumkin, which is it?"

"Poomkin. Poom…Poom," A mischievous grin crossed his face. "No key, Mr. Solomon."

"Pumkin, I just…?" He turned the handle and pushed on the door. It was open.

"Some doors, they open for yourself," Pumkin said with a pompous lift of his chin, and turn of the head.

He pushed harder on the door, and it moved a clutter of folding chairs enough so he stepped into a deep closet. Even in the darkness, he knew it was full of something. The switch by the door lit a dim incandescent bulb near the ceiling. A large table filled most of the space. The tabletop held a replica to scale of the island of Manhattan. There were even, down Fifth Avenue, replicas of the traffic lights with a tiny figure of Mercury holding his caduceus on the top of each. Against the wall was a portrait of Fiorello LaGuardia, the "little flower," the New York mayor he remembered as a kid, famous for chasing fire trucks, for reading to kids on the radio. Scrapbooks and journals were scattered around on smaller tables, with tributes to the mayor, pictures of himself standing in front of the pilgrim's hospital that bore his name. Framed photographs stacked against the wall showed the mayor with the saintly father, with the pope, with other religious notables. Other paintings of "the little flower" were leaned neatly in rows, by boxes full of souvenirs and stuff from New York City.

"Nothing here," Solomon said.

"There are many rooms, and the day is still long," Pumkin reassured him. He led Solomon through the rest of the rooms of the monastery, and in to the baptistry, some of the rooms below ground, built into the walls of the ancient temple of Jove. Solomon had to let his intuition go again. Another failed hunch, but Frate Pumkin's mention of the Duomo in Lecce gave him some hope, and a large cathedral in Galatina, a pure Romanesque in Otranto—other places to continue his mission.

"Don't be discouraged, Mr. Solomon. Could be worst thing that happens is you find this painting."

"I'm just a little tired."

"You find the painting, and you become a slave to notoriety. you become too famous. Everything in the hands of God, you know."

"Yes. The hands…"

"You can sleep here at the monastery, but first I will show you one more thing."

"What about Tonino?" He suddenly felt Iera's kiss, as if it was freshly branded on his cheek.

"Tonino left long ago. He will be back tomorrow morning to deliver the milk and cheese. You can stay here no charge. And we will give you the food. So now you come with me and I will show you."

"What will you show me?"

"Some saint, I will show."

He pulled on Solomon's shirt to lead him through the hallways to the front of the building, and at the end of the hallway he parted some curtains to a narrow corridor that ended at a closet. Pumkin opened the closet doors, and they stepped in. They were in complete darkness until after admonishing him to be quiet Frate Pumkin unlatched some shutters that covered a carved wooden latticework, where the light sifted through, illuminating the face of the Russian brother, who with his chin gestured to call Solomon's attention to what was in the room behind the latticework. A priest was settled onto a wide chair upholstered in purple velvet, as he blessed a trembling woman, dressed in black. Solomon watched in amazement. The room into which he looked seemed filled with a different energy. Pumkin placed a hand on Solomon's shoulder. "Yes," he whispered, as if he knew the question Solomon might ask.

The priest, in the simplest cassock, tied with a rope, his feet in sandals, blessed the woman, who backed away from him on her knees, and went out the door. Surely this was Padre Pio. He turned slowly towards Solomon at the latticework, as if he knew they were there. He faced them, a grin on his radiant, bearded face, that matched Pumkin's grin, and Solomon's as well, for he felt himself grinning. You might even call that grin mischievous, holy mischief, he thought later. The priest lifted his hands to look at his palms, and then turned the palms towards Solomon. The sainted padre had a look of total astonishment. Solomon felt pain in the palms of his own hands, that traveled down his side, weakening his legs so he feared he would fall through the lattice if Frate Pumkin wasn't holding his belt. Thus Solomon saw them, the stigmata, if that's what they were, like fresh wounds, a slow stream of blood from each, down the wrist, and Solomon held his breath to keep from gasping aloud. When he tried to tell Iera about it the next day, she didn't want to listen. She ran away, down to the beach, where she joined the women who fried the fish.

Later he doubted that he'd seen this at all in real life, but as if it was a painting; then he thought, that was it, Padre Pio had shown him something he needed to see. This was how St. Francis would look in the painting, a look of astonishment, innocence at his own witness to a miracle he hadn't expected, couldn't have asked for, couldn't explain, as if it wasn't happening to himself even though it belonged to himself, and then what he knew was that it had to be offered to the world. The painting, St. Francis, by Antonello, would look like that.

AY YAY YAYAY

AY YAY YAYAY

Manfredonia was not on the list of towns he'd gleaned from Brightwatch. Peschici was, and that was where they were headed; but now they were in Manfredonia, embalmed in traffic. "We're not in Venice anymore, Toto," a desultory Saffron said several times. "Nope." This was a narrow squeeze of streets at seven-thirty rush hour. Too many small cars. Greasy air, hot as a bakery. In the cockpits of their Fiats the Manfredoniani yakked into cell phones. "Like we're in a maniac world," Saffron had said in Naples as they walked through the great Galleria that felt like an immense aviary, where people, both hands set free by the new cell phones, gestured wildly into the communication abstract. Or it felt to Nathan and Saffron like they were diving through a forest of human anemones, flailing arms, shouts into the air, people who seemed engaged in arguments with themselves. Any crowded piazza now could look like a madhouse of remote intercourse, like this was the end of the world. To live in the Here and Now wasn't possible since everyone was married to a cell phone; *there* and *later*, so close in your pocket, in your hand, so much sexier.

Naples hadn't been on his list, but Saffron convinced him to go there. She needed to chalk up notes on

Napoli for her required journal, traveling with or without her classmates. It was okay for Nathan. He'd heard stories both of enchantment, and of fear about the city that has the slogan, *See Naples Then Die*. In fact, they had their first nasty experience when they left their rented Daewoo subcompact parked for less than two minutes, herself to find a place to pee, himself to ask directions to their hotel. Someone was instantly on the job, to jim the door open, snap the trunk latch, and grab her backpack, and his small bag too. No pain. No damage. Nothing but false solicitousness and insouciance from the citizens on the street.

"We are so sorry, signora. The thieves are very bold these days. You stop one of them, and there are so many others, just like in our government. It's a disgrace. It's the drugs, everywhere the drug addicts. It makes thieves without conscience or honor. We are so sorry."

Nathan ran up the street, looking into doorways, then came back. "Where could they have gone so quickly? Not even two minutes."

"Signore, in Napoli two minutes is a lifetime. Forget about it. It is a pleasure to forget. Go to Capri, signore, and beautiful Capri will help you forget."

Saffron lost her journal, and some books, and pictures of her mother and sisters, and an especially rare one of her father playing violin. Over that she was inconsolable. He was concertmaster with the Pittsburgh symphony, she herself an accomplished though reluctant violinist. It bothered Nathan, too, to lose his favorite Les Copains cotton sweater, though he still felt lucky to have his passport and credit cards. And wisely Saffron kept vital documents and her travelers checks in a pouch hanging between her breasts.

They looked into each other's frowns until a smile broke out, as if one smile on both their faces; then, as if by the flip of a switch, they both turned giddy. The little god of non-attachment that presides for better or worse over tourists in Naples, lifted the weight of loss from their hearts. After all, this was just some things, and they had suffered the loss together. That was like a nice bonding, and they became inebriated with it, and unembarrassedly affectionate. It was as if the thief had stolen as well whatever barriers their age difference still posed. Like newlyweds they clowned together in the *forciella*, bargaining like crazy in that dark winding labyrinth of contraband and stolen goods, to get whatever they could pick up on the cheap; in fact, Saffron bought back at a decent price her own copy of *Bogeywoman* a tasty stew of lesbian veal by Jaimy Gordon, pages not even soiled in the hands of the thieves, her Amazon. com placemark still installed. "This is a book you don't find every day in English here in Naples," the bookseller said. "Not even in New York," Saffron agreed.

When Nathan caught the urchin with a hand snaked into his pocket, and the kid said, "I'm sorry, I thought you were my father." He embraced the kid and pulled Saffron into the embrace. "And this is your mamma."

"*Che mamma, managgia gli Americani,*" the kid exclaimed.

Nathan slipped him a ten thousand lire note.

"Ten thousand? *Carissimo signore, Americanissimo signore,* my brothers my sisters, what can I feed them, not even one etto of baccalá, a half kilo of tripes maybe, with this ten thousand. Mamma in the hospital. Pappa and the *merda.*" He gestured to imitate shooting up. Nathan gave him another ten thousand, and the boy skipped away, disappearing up some steps, into a narrow slot of a street, through the drying laundry, the toddlers tethered to the really big mammas of the poorest alleys.

That people called her signora at first bothered Saffron, though she knew it was out of politeness or confusion. At first she had responded, "I'm still a signorina, thank you very much," (*Vi ringrazio tanto, ma sono ancora signorina*). Then she got tired of that, and sullenly accepted the idea; but finally in Naples she started to enjoy it, being Nathan's wife, the spouse tattooed and pierced. She thought it was way cool that she had picked up in Venice not just a great looking traveling buddy and excellent lay, but a chance to play wife to someone who wouldn't get too serious about the charade. After all, there was this Miriam about whom he was so tediously honest, his alleged fiancée, for whom she couldn't help but harbor some competitive jealousy, and would for as long as she was with Nathan. But this was altogether great for her because she could play wife, and when the time came they could split, she could leave him, no lawyers, no trauma involved, a seamless divorce. They had a kind of pre-prenuptial agreement. What kind of wife would she be this week? The sexy wife. The passionate devotée wife. On Capri she showed off her wildest sexual appetites and ingenuity, as they spent most of their time rocking the bed. Maids and bellhops lined up outside their door, and applauded as they left their room in the afternoon to explore the famous island grottoes.

But that was Capri, and this was gridlock in Manfredonia.

"How do they call this place? Manfred…?"

"Manfredonia."

"When will we be out of here? I can't breathe. I have to go to the bathroom. When will we get moving?"

"As soon as the traffic moves, dear."

"It doesn't even sound like the name of a real city, Manfredonia. I need to shit." When she exhibited frustration and irritability, like a little girl, Nathan wished he was alone, or back with Miriam. He had got into this with her because it promised to be a sweet fling, but he had no patience for this kind of mutual torture. The cars in front and the cars behind wailed their horns. They were stuck forever in this canyon of noise and smoke.

Scooters and motorcycles squeezed by between the shopfronts and the cars, coughing exhaust through the window.

"Close the window. I don't want to die of lung cancer in…What's the name of this damned town."

"Stop your whining. We cook in here when I close the window."

"Stop your whining, dude." She did a nasal imitation of his voice. "Why are we in this, what is it…something…donia?"

"You know."

"It sounds like…Isn't it like the name of the country in some Marx Brothers movie?"

"No, I think that was Lusitania…no, Caledonia…Pennsylvania…Transylvania."

"Funny, not, Briggs. This place would be like an insult to good Count Dracula. Anyway, it sounds more like that, not like any city." She slumped down in her seat. "We'll never get out of this alley alive, Briggs."

"Come on. Shut up." They jerked ahead a few meters.

"Like, don't tell me to shut up. You shut up." She covered her face with her hands. "I shouldn't have come with you. This is supposed to be my so-called education. I'm not learning anything here, stuck in traffic with a geriatric. Sorry!" She tried to hold back, but her knives were already in the air. "You don't even care that much about your damned father. What good will it do, even if you find him?"

"Don't go there Saffron. I don't need this from you."

She blew out, flapping her lips. "I came along to look at paintings. Whatever happened to Antonello da…wherever? Who ever cared about going to Caledonia?"

"Manfredonia, damn it. Remember where we are. You can get out of the car right now, my child. Go. Get out. Leave."

"You want me to leave?"

"Go."

She opened the door, and stepped out. The backed-up drivers honked like hell, and leaned out their windows. Catcalls and whistling filled the street. She turned back to look at him. "I hate this," she mouthed, looking as if she'd meant to say, "I hate you."

She flipped a bird at her taunters, looking up and down the narrow street, then she did something that totally startled Nathan, and made him feel older. She dropped her pants to her ankles and squatted at the curb, and what began as a trickle turned into a golden inundation. A face appeared through the curtain of the hairdresser in front of her, and two short heavy men stepped out of the electronics shop adjacent, and waved their arms. Then he saw her about to rise, the noise of derision rising as she did. A tattoo across her lower back was a line of elephants joined trunk to tail. She squatted again. The tattoo started to move. Another face, hair in curlers, appeared in the window, shouting. Nathan turned away, as he saw her squeeze off a neat loaf of chocolate brown right near the car, followed by a pair of curly cigars. "Let's see," he thought to himself. "This is Thursday, the 26th of May. In New York we'd be thinking, Robert Moses Park." A little girl came out of the electronics shop and shouted something. Nathan looked for an opening. If there only had been one, he'd have driven away, left Saffron in her mess. A woman covered the little girl's eyes with her hand, and pulled her back into the shop. All down the gridlocked street people got out of their cars to see what Saffron was doing. They stood on their hoods. They balanced tippytoes on the roofs of their Fiats and waved their arms. From the apartments around people sloshed their mop buckets over her, slopped their garbage down on top of her. Flying low, the local helicopter opened its slurry bucket and released into the traffic a shower of promotional fliers—DENTRO C'E INTEL. A mattress, reeking of something, landed on her back and burst into flames. She shrugged it away, stood up straight, yanked her pants back up, and turned to her tormentors, lifted both arms with her fingers in the victory 'V's, "Viva America, Vive l'Amerique, long live the United States of America."

Nathan didn't know what to think.

Just across the Adriatic, from a tiny half-moon beach

west of Tiranë, between Durrës and Lezhe, Vjolka, who came down from wild mountains near Gramsh, and Pandeli from Korçe, and Agrom who moved to Tiranë to be with his lovely Zenepe, slid a long boat into the Adriatic, and began to row towards Saffron. It wasn't that they didn't love their country; of course, they did. They had that in common, proud to be Albanian; but they deserved a better life. They also had in common that they were sick of war, and of poverty. They had fought the war in Kosovo, and had returned, and knew a wider war was inevitable in these accursed mountains. They had seen what a better life could be like on Italian TV, and they wanted it—the touch of prosperity, a life without stupid murder. They pushed off and started to row powerfully towards that better life in the industrialized world. Zenepe waved to them from the shore. At the last moment she had decided not to chance it. She was poor, and certainly they had few prospects in Albania, but she didn't like the sound of the word, *"shperngulje."* She waved at the men, and blinked the tears down that tickled her cheeks. At least they hadn't forced her to go with them. They could have hit her on the head.

Was Saffron just ill-bred and gross? Was she some kind of femme rebel? Was this today's youth? Nathan didn't want to judge her. Sometimes she seemed just the bright young woman who flattered him with her company; but other times, now, for instance, she acted like a total alien, from a generation of mutants.

She opened the Daewoo door, and was about to climb back in. "They hate me so much. I love it." She leaned to kiss him on the cheek.

"Holy crapola, Saffronski, you can't…Wait! Watch the seat. Don't…" he said.

From the canvas shopping bag she had bought in Naples, she pulled out a roll of toilet paper and shook it at him. "Like, duhhhh!" She sat down. "The first thing you have to learn about me, Briggs, is that I'm totally ecological, I'm clean, I'm organic. Besides, it's only a rented car. You don't have to be so fussy."

"That was a disgusting…I mean, what you did. How could…?"

"…Ts wonnaful, ts wonnaful, ts wonnaful, goodbye my baby…dit dit ditta ditta dit," she sang in a growl, and swayed side to side. "Don't you love him?"

"Who?"

"Paolo Conte. I thought he was a your generation kind of a thing."

Nathan hated her bringing up the generations. "So your generation craps on the street, anywhere it wants to, Saffronski?" He had to acknowledge with this new nickname that through this he'd actually grown fonder of her. Seeing her smile, he could read her as innocent or knowing or vindictive or shy. He felt a muddle of loathing and pride. Maybe love had something to do with it.

"It was awesome, and totally empowering. I always wanted to do that. Have you ever let a woman piss on you, Briggs?"

"You wanted to do what?"

"I wanted to be...forget it. I can't even say it. He's from Genova, you know."

"Who?"

"Paolo Conte. He's awesome. We're not even anywhere near Genova. This is the South. Like I don't even know where this is. But haven't you even been to Genova? Briggs, get a clue. Like, there's a painting by your father's Antonello there, in the Spinoza gallery, or whatever it's called. It's an Ecce Homo, a portrait of Christ just before the crucifixion. Like there's one of those at the Met in New York too. A really powerful one."

"How do you remember all this?"

"I just do. I've always had painting as my first love. And didn't you ever go to see that great portrait in Torino? I did. It's like the world's most absolutely grown-up guy, and he looks at you and you know you want to hide, but he won't let you get away with it."

"So what was it that you always wanted to be?" Change the subject. He sometimes felt bullied by her cultural knowledge, because often she seemed to know everything, at least a lot more than he did.

"What? O, that. Well, okay, but like don't take this the wrong way. I've always wanted to know what it was like to be an ugly American. My mom is such an ugly American when she travels, and so I'm like, get real mom, this is the world. It's not Scottsville. And she's like bossy and stupid and so like rich lady. But now I've done something makes me feel ugly, just like mom. Not really, though. But this connects me with my roots. The ugly roots. That's important, Briggs. I feel better."

She kept him off balance. Half the time Nathan didn't know when she was kidding. "When the carabinieri show up any second, what will you say to them? That you feel better?"

"That I'm your daughter, and you told me to do it." She checked her face in the visor mirror. "You didn't answer my question, my woman piss on Briggs question. Or to defecate upon you? Have you ever had a woman do that?"

"Oh, Saffron."

"Right, see. Didn't we promise for better or for worse? My boyfriend, Aaron Voronsky, used to like to bleed on me. It was awesome. He'd cut himself and bleed, and make designs. He should have been an artist. Maybe he will. Do blood art. Blood is so beautiful. Would you like that?"

"Saffron, please stop."

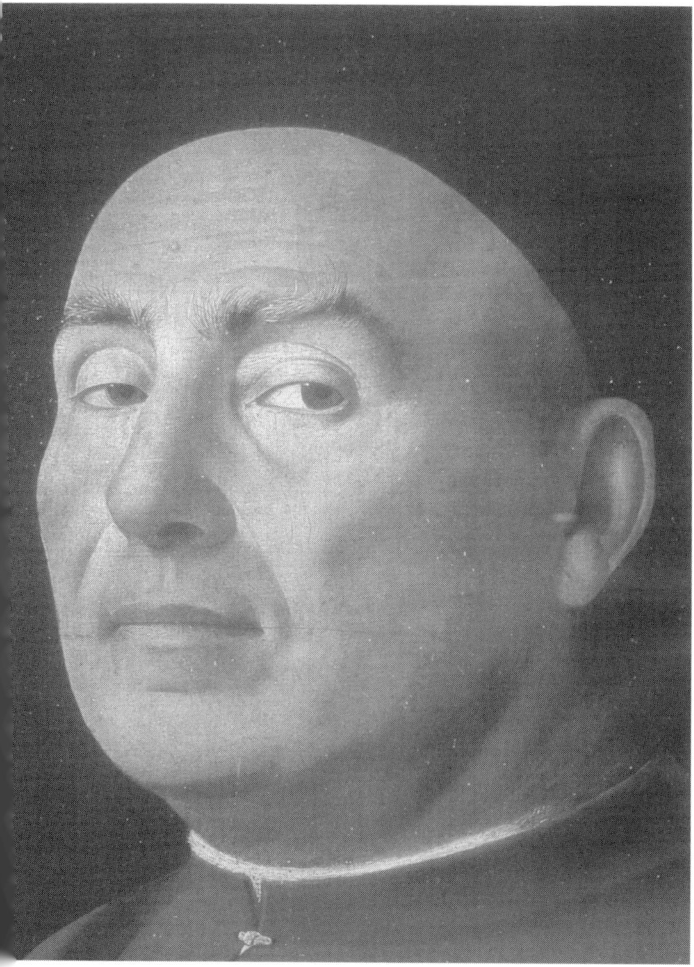

"You're sooo, like I don't even want to hear about kinky. What do you think Dracula is all about?"

People out of the shops bent over the car, and gaped like tourists into an aquarium. Twelve citizens copied down the license plate. They took snapshots. Digital cameras pixeled the pair. Someone whipped out a camcorder and a tripod. The light was bad, the wind was wrong, it was going to rain. They slapped the fenders and windows, made threatening gestures. In the Adriatic the swells were great, and the refugees rowed into the wind. A tall kid with long arms squeegeed their windows with grease, and demanded money. Where were their brains? What do they expect?

"How did you talk me into letting you come along?" He was finding it hard to breathe.

"Don't worry, I'm getting out as soon as there's an opening. Anyway, I so expected to be looking at art with you. We don't look at anything. That's like one of the most important things to me. I mean, thank you for helping me meet Brightwatch, but now I want my education again." She looked in the back. Seven young boys stared at her through the rear window. "Where were we supposed to go from here, anyway?"

The traffic started to ease in front, and many cars crawled away. The crowd around their Daewoo dispersed as everything began to move.

"Look, they're cleaning it up. It's so cool how that happens." She leaned back against the seat and took a puff from an imaginary cigarette. "I used to smoke. I'll probably do it again. I liked everything better when I smoked. So where, did you say? Whither goest we?"

"Peschici, on the tip of the Gargano."

"That sounds like a place. More like a real Italian place." She settled back into some thoughts for a few moments, as they started to accelerate. "Why are we going there?"

"You know. It's on the list."

"Ahhh. The famous list."

"Saffron, no sarcasm, okay. You know what I'm doing here. I don't want to have to defend it. You begged to come with me."

"And you wanted to fuck me. Boring!"

"I suppose you didn't want that. They were your condoms you brought along. I really had to force you, right?"

"You'll never find your father. Not by yourself, like this. You need to hire a professional, a detective. Anyway, I thought condoms would be hard to find in Italy, so close to the Vatican. This is just stupid."

"When I want your advice, I'll ask for it, Saffron." They broke out onto a wider road that circled the town, and traffic began to move. "This is the way I'm doing it. I have to look for him myself."

"Well, if you ask me, it's dumb."

"I never asked you."

"Next time, ask me." She kissed him on the cheek.

With the release from gridlock they slowly mellowed—
a Bernoulli moment—swifter the traffic, lower the pressure. Because it was late they stopped at a hotel on the industrial fringe of Manfredonia, the Jolly-Texas Hotel, with modern, motel-like rooms—single beds they had to push together, telephone, television, modem, minibar. Nathan automatically hit the remote, and Saffron pulled the plug from the wall. The screen sizzled. Their window looked out on an odd windowless factory that manufactured some part for something somewhere else. It was illuminated with mercury vapor lamps. They closed the windows and pulled the drapes against the noise.

"Who you calling?" Saffron asked when he sat down with the phone.

"Miriam."

"The fiancée. Are you going to tell her about me?" She smiled mischievously.

"Not tonight. When I get back, maybe."

The part she played here pleased her, despite this twinge of jealousy. That she could be some kind of faux wife for these moments, and also the illicit lover, was a thrill. She had little at stake. As he dialed, then waited with the earpiece to his head, she slowly stripped, and danced in front of him. He turned away, tried to wave her out of sight as the call was ringing through in America. She found her sunglasses, also bought in Naples, and looked in the mirror at her naked image darkened.

Then she hooked an earpiece through the ring in her navel, and danced back in front of him as he was talking, a comic routine, the glasses hanging down from her bellybutton. He made a gesture, and turned his back. "I'm in Manfredonia." "No. Not Macedonia." "I never heard of it, either." "Great. That should mean a big bonus."

"Baby, you and me we ain't nothing but mammals / So let's do what they do on the Discovery channel." She pronounced for him after he hung up. It was hard for Nathan to smile, with Miriam's voice still in his ear. Saffron felt much better. The special thing they had together for however long they'd had and will have it, seemed special again. It was cool to be traveling with someone so focused, so serious, and so fun. It was cool to go to these weird places, where no one else had ever been,

Later they snuggled close in bed and she whispered apologies in his ear.

"Sorry for what?" he asked, his back to her.

"For fooling around during your phone call. That was like a little catty. It was nasty of me. It's my big fault to get nasty sometimes."

"No," he said, reaching back to pat her. "That was fun. I deserved it. I shouldn't be calling Miriam while you are standing there."

She loved that concession, something someone older could do, but maybe not one of her younger dudes, though those wouldn't be in a position to make such a call. "And I'm sorry for dissing your search for your dad. And for being like so cranky in the car." She reached across his hip, because she suddenly had the urge to touch his prick. It lay cooling against his thigh under the pale blue paisley boxers. At the touch of her hand it started to swell. "Ooooh!" she said. "Nothing but mammals."

"What are you talking about?" he asked as he lifted his pelvis.

"What they do on the Discovery channel. It's a stupid song. I can't get it out of my head." She leaned over to watch how his Sinatra had popped from his shorts, as if to say "buona sera" on its own. She'd taken an interest in penises from the time she was twelve, and had discovered in the room her mother called her private sewing room, a secret collection of dildoes in a locked cedar box, hidden under her mom's antique fainting couch. She called it Lucy's Crayola Box. Lucinda was her mother's name. That was in Connecticut. Her mother never sewed. It wasn't as if this was just an interest. The Mick Jagger thing did frequently excite her; in fact, she had seen plenty up close now, and she'd already had some exceptional moments with them, called them each by some old singer's name. She called her old boyfriend Voronski's penis Sting, and that seemed to flatter him a lot. By the time she was thirty, she expected to see many more, because the beat goes on. Unfortunately except for her mother's crayolas each of them usually comes with a man attached, who often couldn't tell himself from his Stevie Wonder. Some day she would write about this, in a book she would call The Book Of Men—cute little purple-rimmed cap, the faux muscularity of the shaft, and the anxious comedy of its random stiffs and wilts, the various lengths and thicknesses, and the complexes attached to all that. It made her glad to be a woman.

"Hello," Nathan said, waving a hand in front of her eyes. "Where are you? What's going on in there?" He tapped her forehead. She looked great to him, when she was thoughtful. It added some complexity to the unrelenting freshness of her youth.

"Nothing, really…not anything important, just…" She wouldn't mind talking to him about things like this at some point, if they got to know each other longer. It would be a point for discussion with someone like him, a dude with life experience. But since this was their last night…

"Come on, Saffron. I can see it." He tapped her forehead. "Something is computing in there."

"It's just…Sweat baby, sweat baby," she mumbled, then leaned forward to rub noses with him. "We had our first real squabble," she said. "I like that. I thought our marriage was about to break up."

"You almost walked away."

"Yeah. Where would I have gone?"

"Instead you took a…"

"I know. That was so gross. But wow. Excellent, I felt after that."

"So what are you thinking now?"

She leaned over. "This…" She licked the purple rim of his Mel Torme, maybe that was the better name for this one, then kissed the tiny mouth, and got the first taste of salt on her lips. Then she sheathed him between teeth and gums, took him in her mouth. That usually stopped the questioning. It always felt weird at first, taking one in her mouth, kind of impersonal, to feel some Michael Bolton swell against her lips and teeth, gag on it, like she was sucking on some inflatable plumbing; but then the sound of pleasure from him, an ohhh an ahhh or the whisper of her name, and a tug on her nipple ring, and she would start to get wet. She appreciated the way he relaxed into the sex, into slow moves, unlike most she'd been with, who were so quick and impatient, so frantic. He was the oldest man she had ever been with. She wondered if she could go with someone even older. Probably not. This was weird enough.

"Let me do this," he said, and he pulled out of her mouth, and rolled her over so he could sniff down into her vagina. The rings on her pierced labia pressed against his cheeks.

"Ouch, wait, stop," she cried, as the catch of one large gold ring snagged his moustache. "Oweee. That never happened before," she pouted.

"Sorry."

"It's not your fault. I have to get rid of those," she said.

"I should shave my moustache," he said.

"I can't imagine you without a moustache. But do they feel any good when you go in?"

"No," he said, smiling to see her face so concerned. "I don't think they make much difference."

"I should have put a stud in my tongue, like Deborah. That would feel good, wouldn't it. But I couldn't deal with that."

"What if I got a stud?"

"I can't imagine that, Nathan Briggs. But, I have a friend, Eloisa Queenly, who goes to Bryn Mawr, she likes to stick needles in her clit when she comes."

"She does not."

"She calls it Arnold, because it's so big. I mean, really. She has a website. She shows how she does it, if you subscribe. I can give you the address. It's eloisa's prick.com. All lower case. She'll send you a tape. She's practically payed off all her college loans. She bought these acupuncture needles. Arnold is like enormous. She let me lick it once." She paused to see if he would have a reaction. "It was almost a Pavarotti, it was so like, out. For a while she wouldn't date anyone but acupuncturists, or at least guys who were going to acupuncture school. That's an unfair limitation, don't you think?"

"You're making this up, Saffron. Why are you telling me this?"

"It's because we're not looking at art, Briggs. It's like so important to me, I told you. I wouldn't be thinking about stupid stuff. As soon as I stop looking at art my mind dives, like into the gutter. I'm so…I thought we were going around to find all the Antonello da Messina paintings." She lifted his head by the hair, and looked in his face. Maybe she was telling the truth, and maybe she wasn't. He was right about some things, she did like to make stuff up. He needed to be shocked, anyway. There was something dead in him. Maybe that's what was hard about hanging with an older dude, you have to deal with what has already died in him. Maybe that was true, maybe not. "Do you think there's someone somewhere who is making everything up, like someone writing all the time, like in the Akashic records? More famous than Erica Jong? Smarter than Kathy Acker? Grittier than Eileen Myles? 'Oh shut up, Saffron, and Briggs, grab my grapes,' as Grandma Denes might have said." She pushed his face back between her legs.

Nathan curled his tongue and sparred lightly with her clitoris, so she giggled. "Don't stop now." She held his head down. "I love this so much," she sang out, as he pushed himself into her.

Nathan had difficulty making love this time, and could only fake some passion whenever she opened her eyes to moan or smile at him, herself looking so innocent and young to him; but he couldn't escape the sound of Miriam's voice, not anything in particular that she'd said, but the sound of it. The word "unfaithful" entered his mind. That was ridiculous. They weren't even married yet. He had been stupid to call her at all, and kept recollecting those sounds of indifference in her voice. There had not been one hint that she was pleased to hear from him, though she eagerly told him about an account she had cinched. If he was really being unfaithful to anything, it was to this experience here and now.

When they were done Saffron rolled onto her side, her back to him, singing some vague tunes as she fell asleep. He lay awake, appreciating the separation, touching her lightly and staring at the tattoo on her shoulder of Popeye and Olive Oyl. Why had she chosen that? He would have to ask her. Wasn't it Max who had said that a woman with a tattoo can never be naked? He was drawn to the window by a sound outside. Lights from the factory were out except for the mercury vapor lamps in the parking lot. He cracked the window and heard a high-pitched hiss, and then a bleating, like sheep, or a strangled goat, almost out of audible range. At least it was a sound of nature, not an internal combustion engine, or diesel clatter. Some huge bats were flying at the edge of the light. He saw one pass through the light of the mercury vapor lamps, its translucent wings filtering the light to pale blue. "Big bats," he thought, closing the window again. Saffron looked more like a child when she slept. He hadn't thought of her that way before, and it made him uneasy. She was a child, her thumb almost in her mouth, the thumbnail touching the ring that pierced her lower lip. She looked like she felt safe, her body half out of the covers. That made Nathan feel strong. There was something fine and empowering in the old idea of protecting your woman. What Max had said was that no woman was ever really naked. That was it. But Saffron looked so pink, so vulnerable. Must be something Max had learned after marriage.

The next day was clear, sky blue, cheerful day. They wound the Daewoo through the olive groves, and along the limestone cliffs of the Gargano, heading for Peschici. Saffron trailed her hand out the window, feeling the wind. "I wish I had my laptop," she said.

"Was that in your backpack too?"

"Nope, thank the goddess. I left it with Deborah. Probably in Sicily by now. I have to like go to Sicily, whether you do or not. I thought when we started we would have looked at more paintings by now. That's what I'm interested in. I'm paying tuition for that. There are like a lot of paintings by Antonello da Messina in Sicily. That's where he's from. Aren't you going to go there?"

"Maybe."

"Won't you miss me?"

"Of course. I think I will. Let's not talk about it."

She touched his face in a fond, almost maternal gesture. "Your dad must have gone there. Anyway, I'll meet up with them in Taormina, I think. I'll check my email then," She moved her fingers as if striking a keyboard.

"So you get a lot of email?"

"Doesn't everybody? Look at that awesome olive tree. How do they get so twisted? Sometimes I can't believe this place is so old. Don't you get a lot of email?"

"My secretary does all the estuff. I have trouble even looking at the screen. I like talking face to face, like this, people to people."

"People," she said, fluttering her hands in the air, as if to indicate that for her people were dispersed throughout the ether. "So the web would be helpful, more than email, we could go to Peschici first, and know all about it before we get there."

"You don't go there on the web. When you're on the web, you're only on the web, sweetie. You're not anywhere else. You don't go anywhere. You're on your butt, in your seat. You're staring at a screen."

"Oh, Briggs, you're so…just eat my cold paprikasch, as my grandma Denes used to say. You are a hopeless ancient person. Go back and live in your own century; I mean, maybe you're too old for me, but you're young enough to have been on the rise for the swelling of Bill Gates. You could have been one of the original nerds." She caught him grimacing. "Maybe not. A nerd is like a good thing, you know."

"Can I ask you something?" He needed to change the subject.

"Ask away." She kissed him on the cheek, in a great mood because she felt they had come to an honest equilibrium, and she had been able to establish that she was leaving some time soon, to head for Sicily and her classmates. For some reason it had been hard for her to express that.

"What is that Popeye and Olive Oyl tattoo on your shoulder blade?"

"Oh, that one's not finished yet. It's like a Magritte thing we're doing. When I go back we're going to put a pipe in Popeye's mouth, and that's why Olive Oyl is like pointing. She'll be pointing at the pipe, and then we'll put some words in, like, *"Ceci n'est pas une pipe."* That's like French. I bet you know where that comes from. It's fairly famous. At least, we look at it in modern art history."

Nathan shrugged.

"O Popeye, my hero," she squeaked, and stretched her neck to kiss him on the cheek. Talking about her body decor always lifted her spirits, and made her affectionate. "Well, like, you know who Magritte is?"

"Yeah. I think I've seen…."

"He's this Belgian surrealist painter, from Belgium. Modern. Like, dead, though. Well he did a famous painting, or it's a drawing, I don't know, of a pipe, like a tobacco smoking pipe, with those words under it, or maybe they're on top of it. *This is not a pipe..* So what is it? A drawing of a pipe? What is that? But Pipe (peep), that's slang for penis in French, so like Olive Oyl pointing at Popeye's pipe and laughing, that's a statement. It's like my own feminist tattoo that I made up."

"Okay. Like, thanks. That's awesome," he said, awkwardly. "I didn't expect all that much explanation."

"Why? Did you think I was being just decorative? Are you afraid of feminists too, Nathan Briggs?" She poked him in the ribs.

He flailed out, and pinched her nipple.

"Ouch! Pig," she chirped. "Oooh! Look at that." They rounded a bend and Peschici came into view, all white in the sunlight on its limestone cliff, submerged in a liquid blue sky. "This is like Greece. I feel like I'm in Greece. We weren't going to Greece on this trip. That's for the Ancient Civ. course when they give it. That's supposed to be awesome."

She paused for a thoughtful moment, then laid an arm lightly across his back. "I'm going to ask just one favor before we split up."

"Split up?…"

"Yes. I go to Sicily, and you…I want you to help me color my hair."

He looked at her hair, and noticed the yellow was almost gone, just a frosting on the end of some lustreless brown. "I'm not a hair person. I've never done that."

"It's easy. You can do it. I do most of it myself. I just like to have a friend, you know, when I do it." She tousled his hair. He knew that asking him to do this was a further show of her trust, but it didn't feel comfortable to him. "I know you've got it in you, Briggs. Color hair, get kissed by young bimbo." She planted a big wet one on his cheek.

They climbed the switchbacks into the village, then squeezed into a space between two reisebüro buses, and got out of the car. On the belvedere that overlooked the beaches the Germans were all speaking German. Nathan and Saffron leaned on the wall to look down on the half-moon bay. Tour buses were parked on the road down below from one end of the beach to the other. As far as they could see bodies lay side by side, grilling on the beach.

"Do you think those are all German bodies?"

"I am the great god Melanoma," he shouted across the bay.

"Don't. You are not."

A group of hefty tourists armed with camcorders and cameras emptied from one of the buses in back of them.

"Ich bin Melanoma," he shouted louder.

"Stop it, Briggs. Shut up. You're embarrassing me."

"Hey, embarrassing? A crap on the street in Manfredonia wasn't embarrassing?"

"That was a necessity. I guess that bothered you, didn't it?" She shrugged. "Besides, that was Manfredonia, and this is the fatherland."

"You're not German, Denes. This isn't Germany, need I remind you?."

"We're Hungarian, most of us Deneses. Even Prince Klemens Von Metternich ate the occasional goulasch, Grandma Denes like to say."

Nathan had only a vague idea of who this Metternnich was. "But you're right about one thing, Saffronski, you look at any beach now in the Mediterranean and it looks as if the Germans won World War Two."

"I think the winner was the sunscreen glopmakers. Like I wasn't even born yet for any war."

"Not me, either. I toddled through Vietnam."

"That's something we have in common, Mr. Briggs. We are both without wars. My dad almost had to go to Vietnam." She pressed against his arm. "That would have been awful, he's like a totally peaceful man. He's an artist." He pulled her closer. Maybe it was the sea. The sky. He was having feelings.

"That doesn't look very appealing down there, Briggs. Usually I see a beach and like I want to rip off my clothes and just dive in. It must have been really spectacular here once, before it got like discovered."

"It still is."

"Not with all this tourism garbage. Manfredonia, at least, was real."

"Now suddenly you like Manfredonia."

"Let's find a restaurant and settle this over a nice lunch." She put her arms around his neck.

"Settle what?"

"Our differences, dude," she kissed him.

"What differences now? We don't have any."

"Well, good. I think I agree. Then we can just eat."

With her friendly manipulations she was sometimes so nimble he felt just old and slow. He wasn't old. He was in the middle of his life.

They found a small restaurant down the hill, on a side street, called Pesce Peschici. The dining room was layed out on a terrace on the roof, under a canopy of bougainvillea. Only six other people sat at another table on the opposite end of the terrace. They looked out over the roofs of buildings that blocked the beach view, and the tawdry developments of cottages and hotels, but they could see the Adriatic's sweet limpid green.

A small, thin woman, who was probably younger than she looked, was the only waitress, sliding around in black Chinese slippers, black dress, greying black hair pulled back in a tight bun, that emphasized the creases in her joyless face. She moved with cranky deliberateness, serving the large table without a word. At first she ignored them, using the old waiter's trick of slipping the eyes past a beckoning hand as if she didn't see it. When she finally acknowledged them, she looked like she had received some kind of shock. She sat down at another table, and stared for a long time.

"What's she doing? I'm starved," Saffron said.

When finally she came over she said, simply, "Pesce? Fish?" They agreed to fish.

"I love this restaurant, that we have it to ourselves" Saffron said. "All the other people must be eating down by the beach." Light through the flowered canopy cast violet shadows on their faces. "Though did you notice how that waitress looks at you. That's weird."

"I didn't notice anything."

The waitress brought a basket of bread, and a plate of sliced tomatoes and snowy white cheese, sprinkled with oil and basil. "Mozzarella," she said. "I make."

The woman lingered at the table, staring at Nathan as if she had something to say to him.

"I see what you mean," Nathan mumbled through his teeth.

"No buffalo mozzarella. Not vacca, cow, no. Capre. Goats cheeses. Mozzarella goat. I make this. Very good." A smile brought up all the wrinkles on her lean face, her dark eyes moist, as if the cheese held some secret yearnings and disappointment.

They realized at the same time that she wouldn't leave them alone until she saw them taste her cheese, so they both did so, and complimented her. She widened her smile, and patted both of them on the shoulder. Her hand lingered on Nathan's, sliding off slowly.

"What was that about?" Saffron asked. "Maybe I

should leave you two alone."

The waitress brought them bowls of spaghetti with mussels, then occupied herself serving the large table. The chef, who seemed slightly older, wiry and stooped, same sharp features, probably a brother, came to the door of the kitchen and wiped his brow with a kerchief. He stared at Saffron and Nathan, his lips and nose in a rodentine twitch. When a group of four arrived on the terrace, he shrugged and returned to his stove. The mussels had a bouquet vaguely sewerish.

"What is there so weird about this place? I really like it, I mean, mostly. It's pretty, and delicious so far." Saffron leaned forward to touch Nathan's hand.

"Ecco il pesce, frutta di mare…," interrupted the woman, as she set down a great heap of gold, whiffs of olive oil and garlic. She pointed at each item on the plate. *"Polpe, triglie, merluzzo, sarde, acciughini, calamari. Va bene, signori?"*

"Grazie, signora," Nathan said. *"Ci porta, per piacere, signora, un mezzo rosso."*

"Signorina," she said. *"Sono signorina, ancora,"* she replied, and turned on her heel and left as if insulted.

"That was what you used to say," Nathan kidded. "I hope she remembers the wine."

"The way she looked at me now, like, I don't get it. Is she like all, oooh, mamma mia, tattoos, bad girl."

"I doubt that."

"Like there's some woman thing going on, but I

don't know what it is."

"Nothing's going on. I ordered some wine."

"It just makes me feel weird." She looked over at the waitress standing at the door to the kitchen, with her hand to her mouth, still staring at them. "I guess we can't ask her to stop staring."

"Saffron, hey." He touched her face. "Just look at this golden mountain of fried fish and stuff. Look at this platter. It's our golden opportunity to gorge. If we eat all this fishy matter, we'll have to swim away to another planet."

"Outstanding, Briggs. Science fiction feast." She swept some onto her plate, and the wine arrived, and they sucked it down, and ordered more. They were happy to be together then. Life felt good.

After a conversation at the tourist kiosk in Pechici that assured them everything was booked, they returned to Manfredonia. The manager of the Jolly-Texas Hotel welcomed them back as if they were old friends, and escorted them himself to what he said was the best room in the hotel.

"You look very tired," Nathan said to the man, a small person, with a weary unshaven face, who looked unhappy even as he grinned. "Everyone is tired, signore and signora." He nodded politely to Saffron. *"Cari amanti miei,* no one can sleep any more, sadly, sadly." He opened the door for them into a large rose-coloured room. The centerpiece was a massive, canopied, heart-shaped bed, the bedclothes and veils draped from the posts all rose colored, patterned with orange and purple flowers, and a flock of stuffed finches, warblers, lovebirds, canaries, wrens, orioles, sat on perches around the room, as if on a set for some miniature Hitchcock. The manager pulled out an aerosol, and sprayed the room with a scent of roses. Above the bed a heart-shaped mirror was illuminated by a fringe of tiny bullet shaped lights glowing rose. "This is our Las Vegas honeymoon Texas room. Very nice. Best room in Jolly-Texas Hotel." He pulled open the drapes of the double double window. Their view was onto the swimming pool, over a wide band of grass that looked suspiciously like astroturf, and a wall of tufa and fig cactus, rescued and preserved from the construction of a sprawling factory beyond. The factory looked abandoned now, most of the windows broken out, half a gate swinging open, one pole that held a vapor lamp bent almost to the ground.

"Very nice. Thank you, signore…signore…"

"*Ah…Liscio…sono Liscio, mi chiamo.*" He smiled his sad smile, and shook Nathan's hand. "But of one thing, signora, I must alert you. Just one, which is why we get no sleep." He addressed himself to Saffron, as if he expected more understanding from a woman. "It is the *caprestrelli*. The accursed *caprestrelli*. Which is why we are so tired, why we don't sleep in the night. They come out at night. *Maledetti caprestrelli.*" Through all of this he maintained his smile, because being cheerful was part of his job. With one last wide grin, and a bow, he left them alone in the room.

They slowly peeled off their clothes and lay down in bed, looking at themselves in the heart-shaped mirror above. They were in a nice place now, emotionally, Nathan thought. A satisfied and friendly place. The mirror made them giggle together, softly. She took his hand. She knew this would be their last night together, and that was all right. They played with each other's fingers, and occasionally turned to each other and lightly kissed. They lay together waiting for darkness, breathing lightly.

"You know, I suddenly had a great thought," she said. "About that waitress in Peschici."

"That still bothers you?" He leaned over and kissed her.

"No, not bothers…but, listen, do you have any pictures of your father?"

Her bringing up the father surprised him. "Not…I looked at one that Brightwatch kept, but it was a group picture, with herself in front, and she pointed out some of the other artists, like Nancy Graves, and Charles Ross, and Robert Smithson; I remember the names because my mother talked about them a lot. Michael Heizer, and my father was in back, and he wasn't completely in focus."

"Could you tell that he…? Did he look like you?"
"Why?"

"Well, like, did he or didn't he?"

"From what I could tell. I mean, I don't really know how I really look, but…Yes, I guess he did."

"Then that's it. Your father met that woman, that waitress, once, and he made a big impression on her once. She probably fell in love with him once. I can imagine it, when she was a young girl. I'll bet she was attractive then, and he came through the town. There weren't like so many tourists at that time. She wanted a way to escape what looked like a dead end life. He was so handsome, the way you are." She squeezed his hand. "That's why she said she was still a signorina, with all that bitterness in her voice. She was in love with your father, and you look just like him, and she remembers. Do you see what it is?"

Nathan felt a shudder up his back. That she'd been thinking about this at all brought him nearly to tears. And she was probably right, this young woman he had so recently met. Miriam had never put any thought into this. As far as she was concerned finding the father was his own foolish and private quest.

"What do you think I should do?" he asked, feeling helpless.

"You should…It's obvious. You need to talk to her, to find out everything you can. She could know, at least, where he went from Peschici. She's got to know something. If I'm right. Who knows?"

He kissed her hand, watched himself in the rosy

mirror above the bed, kissing her hand. "Thank you." She smiled at him, and he wanted to keep that smile forever in a locket. If only there were still lockets. They started giggling, to see both of themselves encircled by the mirrored heart above them. He felt younger, as if he'd just been born.

"So what have you been expecting? That some day you would knock on a door somewhere, and your father would open it?"

"No." He shook his head. "Yes. That's what. No. I don't know. I just decided to look for him."

"So it's like a new hobby? It's a recently acquired preoccupation?"

"No. I always thought about him some, but I felt impotent to do anything."

"And now? Look where it's got you now."

"It's got me here with you, with Saffron Denes," he said, making an evasive move. "That's good. That's not bad."

"No, not bad at all. You know, now I'm like, what does he do in real life. What does Mr. Nathan Briggs do? We never talk about things like that."

"It's not important. This is real life." He saw both of them inside the rosy mirror, lying on their backs and talking. This mirror could make anything in the world seem ridiculous. "I make money for people. That's what I do."

"Are you good at it?"

"Yes."

"That's good." She blew him a kiss into the mirror. "Are you rich?"

"No."

"That's good too. I hate money."

"I don't think so, Saffron. Money isn't something to love or hate. It's best to understand it." He didn't want to sound the way that sounded.

"I don't want money. My family has money."

"That's obvious."

"Shut up. It's meaningless, and I can't see it's done any of them much good. Some of them are very mean people."

"It seems meaningless only when you have it, sweetie. If you don't it takes on plenty of meaning. Lack of it can rule your life."

"It rules your life if you have it, too. I'm not talking about my dad. He's the poor one. He plays the violin. He's an artist. That's why he left mother, because she has all the money, and she thought that meant something. She used it. She started to hold it over his head; but like it doesn't mean anything. I mean, I love mother, but…" Saffron twisted the ring in her bellybutton. Nathan took her hand.

"Sweetie, without your mama's money, you wouldn't be here. That's what makes this possible, you here with me. Money keeps you here, instead of sitting somewhere in a cubicle under fluorescent lights at a work station, playing video games in your slack time, battling carpal tunnel syn…"

"Briggs, I am so not enjoying this conversation. Shut up! You're not any better than me just because you grew up poor."

"You'll always go back to your money; in fact, you never left it."

"Shut up. Just stop, shut up."

"Don't you worry, Saffron, I can stop on a dime; but you know I'm right."

"Please! SHUT UP!!!" She banged her fist on the bed.

He did stop, felt relieved to be able to get off it himself. He watched her in the mirror, lying with with her eyes clamped shut over her anger, her breathing shallow. He moved his hand to her belly and breathed with her, taking her rhythm, slowing it down, deepening both their breaths. She opened her eyes and covered his hand with hers, and he turned then to look directly at her.

"You're beautiful, Saffron. You know, I really love you." He hardly ever used the "L" word, not even with Miriam. The sound of it made him feel like he was a character in some sappy romance novel.

She turned to him, and they moved together into an embrace, kissing and kissing. She pressed herself into him as if she wanted to melt their bones together. "I love your body," she whispered. "Your cock, oooh…," she whispered, and twined her legs around his, flexed her ankles against his calves.

"You make me feel so young," he sang, and laughed.

"We're starting to talk like characters in a Judith Krantz novel," she grinned at him.

"I've never read one. What are they like?"

"Me neither, but you know what I mean, gushy love. I suddenly love gushy."

"I do really really love you," Nathan said.

"Please don't say anything too romantic."

"Why not?"

"Because."

He leaned back to look at her, till she answered the question in his look.

"Because it only hurts in the long run."

"But what I feel…I do…Ahhhhrrrggghh."

She squeezed his balls to stop his voice.

After they made love, they separated and he looked at her face, streaked with tears.

"You're crying, sweetie." He wiped her cheek.

"No. I'm happy. It's just that I always wanted to make love like this."

"How is this?"

"I always dreamed of one endless slow long excellent stroke, an endless long single perfect stroke, half the hour going in, half hour out, all electric sweet and ecstasy. And we're like pilgrims lost in one sweet struggle to be released." As soon as she said that she realized how hokie it all sounded, as if she'd read it somewhere stupid.

"Oh. Now you're getting too romantic."

She was in that kind of mood. Why stop? Another day and she wouldn't be able to say anything at all to him. She'd be somewhere else. "Because I really love you so much. Like, really love. I mean, I admire you as a person too. I never felt like this before," she said, and took it further. "Like we're the first people ever here in a new world called Manfredonia, and we're like so ready to start the planet again. What should we call it? Maybe the Planet Mazel-Tov. Deborah always says that. I like the Jewish words."

"Saffron." He felt a flash of panic, at the commitment he imagined attached to her enthusiasm. "We can't...I don't have the...I feel this, I love you, but..."

She slid a hand across his mouth to hush him. "I just want to say these things. And it's because I'm like leaving you, and will be leaving us behind. I've known you like less than anyone in the world, and I feel like we know each other better than everybody. It makes me want to cry. So I'm going to have to color my hair before I leave. These are just things to say before you leave your lover. My gypsy didn't tell me I would fall in love, she just said I'd meet you."

"Was there really a gypsy?"

"She never told me I would have to leave you, and

that it would hurt."

They lay together quietly for some moments, looking into the mirror, as their tears turned to laughter.

"This is such a ridiculous room," she laughed. "Were the fifties like this?"

"I couldn't tell you. I wasn't here for the fifties." He raised up on an arm, and looked at her. "I never expected the pierced and tattooed generation of girls could be so romantic. I would have expected cynicism. Sarcasm. Jaded reactions."

"We're women, Nathan Briggs. And you know me. And it's not like we're cynics. We believe in ourselves. And when you, like, think about it, didn't you take advantage of my innocence?" She looked at him from between her spread fingers, then lowered her hand to reveal a broad smile. "It's because I own myself, Briggs, that I can leave you at all. It's not easy. Otherwise I'd be like a woman who snaps myself to your belt, and lets you pull me around forever. And before forever you'd be bored with me, and like I wouldn't even acknowledge that I was bored with you too. You'd be old, and I'd hate…"

Nathan touched her lips. "Shhhh…" She locked his finger in her teeth.

"I'm sure we'll always know each other. Ouch." he said.

She released his finger. "No, Nathan Briggs. We'll always know we knew each other."

Her mind again passed the more subtle thread through their weave. They both dozed off smiling, until a noise woke them up.

"I was dreaming about my father," he said.

"Solomon Briggs, I like that name."

"No, I was dreaming that I find him trapped somewhere, or lost somewhere with amnesia." She wiped a tear from Nathan's eye, and kissed his cheek. "And I rescue him and take him back to New York with me."

"Why does he want to go back to New York?" She wipes another tear.

"I don't know, but that's what I do. To take him back. To help the world."

"You can't help the world in New York, Nathan Briggs. You can't help the world. That's the rules."

He lifted a fist as if to pummel her, and then he embraced her, and they rolled back and forth, laughing, until a sharp noise, and then another, stopped them.

"What is that?" She turned away from him and sat up.

A sound repeated, just outside their window, like a railcar braking, like a population of terrified children. Something glanced off the window, and let out a frightened call. This had been going on for some time, they realized, but they had been so absorbed in each other, they'd been oblivious. He jumped from bed, and pulled back the drapes. Night had settled in, but the window was illuminated blue and silver like an LCD screen, and across it flew some strange and mournful creatures, such as neither had ever seen before. They were larger than any bird, with bat-like wings, but too large for bats. Their bodies like goats, but too small to be goats. Their eyes that glanced deep into the room as they flew close were like red and gold agates, crazed goats' eyes. When they saw the two naked humans, these creatures cackled and screeched, assaulted the couple with laughter and derision. Nathan and Saffron saw each other naked, and were suddenly ashamed. Each popped a banana leaf off the plastic banana plant near the window, and covered themselves. They called the desk, and the manager was at their door in a few seconds.

"Ah, signori, it's what I told you. It's what I told you. *Cari amanti Americani.* The caprestrelli. No one sleeps. A blessing to be deaf, and not to hear their horrible noises. And not to see them too would be a gift. I don't even mention the stink."

"Why don't you just get rid of them?"

"Ahhh, if only we could, signori, but we cannot."

"There are nets," Nathan said. "Mist nets, I've seen them used to catch birds and bats. They stop everything that flies."

"Not the caprestrelli, signori. We try everything to trap them, we can't trap them. We try to shoot them, they won't be shot. We follow them at dawn to find out where they sleep, but no one has ever found one. No one has ever touched one, but who would want to, signori? Since they have come, no one has slept." When Saffron saw he was weeping, she put an arm around his shoulder. "I would kill all of them if it was in my power, and then I would go to sleep, sleep on this beautiful bed here. I would sleep through the night, and the next, and the next. But they fly, they fly and make their sickening noises that you don't want to hear, but you can't ignore, and they drop their caca (please forgive me) anywhere they please. And that foul milk, they leak out what is a milk that smells like fish rotting in the harbor, like a heap of mutande from filthy old men. I am so sorry, signori." He stepped to the door, then turned back before leaving. "I wish you good sleep signori, but I pity you. The more you know them, the less you sleep. I am happy you came back to stay with us, but I am so sorry for this. *Cari, cari amanti.*" He wiped sweat and tears with the back of his sleeve.

"It's not your fault." Nathan laid an arm on his shoulder, and Saffron stroked his hand. "We can handle it," Nathan assured him.

"I don't know. I don't know. *Cari amanti miei.* They are increasing. Soon they will be everywhere in Italy, stealing our livelihood. They will cross the Adriatic and inflame the Balkans. Insomniac Serbs and Croats and will chop each other into sausage. Finland will wake up once and for all. Every cell phone will ring in the middle of the night, and blabbermouths and blabbermouths. In France, in Spain the fools will run out into the streets and bite the bulls. In Portugal the turtles already have risen from the sea, and have begun to scream. They want to fly away. The Ukraine will be a fury of hell without sleep. And Russia, the great Russian bear will rise from hibernation and never sleep again. The Germans will march again in their great hobnail boots. Soon Africa, soon China, soon the whole world will explode with insomnia for these caprestrelli. These accursed. These *maladetti cadàveri di putane.*" He closed the door.

"Ay yayay yayay," said Saffron, after the manager was gone. Bluish shadows crossed their faces. "The world is over, Nathan Briggs." She dropped her towel and without thinking, pressed herself flat against the window. The caprestrelli, excited by this flat nude American girl, flew and flew at her, then screeched back into the shadows. "What did you do with the remote? Switch them off. You lost the remote."

"Shhh. Be quiet. I'm thinking."

What of Agrom, Pandeli, Vjolka? What of Bardhyl and Fatos who almost went with them? What of the beautiful Zenepe? It was Pandeli's turn to give up the oars and sleep. He dreamt of the mountains, of leaving their letterpress where they printed poems, and climbing a hill to a stand of blackberries, and of picking the sweet dark bunches from the thorns, and then they stopped, and he pushed one through her lips, and then with his lips sucked the sweat off the fine hairs of Zenepe's moustache. He dreamt of the moustaches of Italian virgins. The night was dark. The waves tossed and spun their little boat like a toy. The light, if it came, would start at their backs. The hope, if it appeared, would be in the direction of Saffron and Nathan.

"I know what this is," Saffron said, her lips pressed almost against the glass. She liked the cool taste of it. "This may be The Wozzard of Izz. And what are you talking about thinking, anyway, you don't know how. Just give me the remote."

"Saffron, this is not a movie. It's not TV. This is happening."

"Okay, you prove that."

"Okay. Here." He slid open the door by the window, and the decibels barged in, and the air thick with stench made him jump back. "See?" One of the creatures flew into the room, and hovered a moment, chortling, squeaking, dripping its foul smelling milk. It stared into Nathan's face.

"Don't look at me, you misery." In defiance he faced this perversity. It seemed to want to speak to him. Up close its face looked almost cute. Where was it ever written that evil could be cute? "All right. Speak, cute beast. We listen. Speak," Nathan implored. It opened its mouth and sent a gust of goatish guano-breath into Nathan's face.

Saffron tried to get away from the window, but the creature flew hard against her, crushing her flatter into the window. As it raised and lowered its wings she felt it press and release her body. "Get off me. Get off me, you bitch. Don't let it fuck me. Please, Briggs. Get this thing off me."

Nathan wanted to rescue her, but was lost at what to do. He grabbed a wing that slipped away. He beat it with a floor lamp, but that didn't phase it. He was afraid to hurt Saffron. Another was flapping at the door, and he had to fend it off with the lamp.

The creature nipped at Saffron's ear, making a high-pitched eeee eeeee sound, that shuddered her body like new chalk across a blackboard. "Shut it up. You smell like puke, like a bathroom in a frat house. Get off my back, you piece of slime pig flying bat goat godzilla meets mothra shit." The creature suddenly backed off, and flew away, as if it had been insulted. It left a coating of chalky milk to putrefy on Saffron's skin. "Why did you open that door?" She cried and scratched at the crud on her body, but it was imbedded like when she used to paint, the colors stained into the skin after days at her studio. "I didn't need to know about this. I don't know anything. I knew we shouldn't have come to Manfredonia. What can we do now? Do I have to soak myself kerosene and Tide? I'll need sandpaper to get this off."

He pulled her back to himself, and stared into her eyes. She stank, worse than a hospital sewer. The creature's milk had obliterated her tattoos, but Nathan didn't want to tell her. She was trembling. He thought it would embarrass her, and be rude if he held his nose. As the older man he should be able to reassure her, but he could see in her eyes the strange brouhaha that was her soul. It made him feel useless to help. That stench seemed even to come from both of themselves now. He was willing to share it. He was glad now to have it with her, because it was his fault, after all. He had brought her to this place, now a room of corruption and stench. Outside the room, the world stank too. "I don't think this should stop us, Saffron." He sighed, pulled her to his body. "This can't be the way the world ends."

"Ayyay yayay yayay." She whimpered, and backed away from him.

Nathan spoke, hoping his voice, the steady voice of a man in control, could comfort her, make it all easier. "These caprestrelli are accidents of mind, or enigmas of the heart. Maybe they're analog or maybe digital. They are the loons of desire, the kestrels of snappiness. They are happy doom gliders, I believe. They burrow into the flesh of the night. How many chips do they devour? How many bytes make them execute? How many of any are these missiles of ought, teased from some new lamps of cosmic boredom? Are they the flukes of mind?

Are they riddlers of the heart?" That sounded pretty good to him, in this time of adversity.

Despite his words she began to feel calm, and listened compassionately as he struggled to articulate his whatever. Men talked this way, particularly older ones, she found. They couldn't help it. She liked it, because she would remember and use it when she wrote her Book Of Men, which she intended to do as soon as she graduated. Now that she had made real contact with one of these creatures, and had got rid of it, and was still herself, she had some confidence.

"Whatever," she shrugged, in reply to him. She knew she was young. Her fears had passed like a sock pulled off a foot. Finally, she couldn't take it seriously. She wasn't afraid any more. Everything was just as weird as everything else. And Nathan Briggs? She was leaving him anyway, to go back to her classmates. She'd been to many many horror movies much worse than this. Wes Craven was worse than this. *Blue Velvet* had been scarier. What about Jason? Even *Rosemary's Baby* she'd seen once, was scarier. In fact, it was almost as ridiculous as *Night Of The Living Dead*, original or remake. She just had to get rid of the crap it left on her body. That was gross. Now, first things first.

She reached into her Napoli Nature Conservancy bag, and pulled out a tube and a comb. "This is my new color." She waved the tube at Nathan. "Come help." She sat down on a straight-backed chair that felt as if no one had ever sat there before.

"I've never done this, like I…"

"It's okay. I do most of it. I just comb it in, and you make sure it gets everywhere, and it's even, especially in the back." She squeezed a worm of the gel onto the comb, and started it into her hair.

"I can't do this," said Nathan, looking out at the spinning world.

"Briggs, you can do it. Just do it."

How can it be this easy, he wondered, as she handed him the comb. The color was a silver blue, almost precisely the color of the light outside the window, where the creatures still flew. Azzura Volpe, it was labeled. He worked it through her hair, and liked the way it felt. This was one small pleasure that made a crisis bearable. Thank G-d for hair.

She squeezed his hand when she thought it was enough.

"Is this a color you got in Naples?" he asked.

A tiresome queston. He was weird, and getting older. Could be all this just had been her comeuppance for hanging with an older dude. She thought it was cool that she would head back to chill with her classmates tomorrow. If she could get herself smelling sweet again, that would be great. It would be really bum to have the first thing they noticed about her be her smell.

For now she had an idea for Nathan and herself, a sweeter way to closure. This was it: "I know what we can do. It would be radical now that it's all over; I mean, you and me. We can get dressed up in our best clothes and meet somewhere, like at some elegant restaurant in Manfredonia."

"We don't have any best clothes. And I don't know if there's even an elegant restaurant in Manfredonia."

"Be happy, don't worry. We can go dancing. Whatever we wear is our best clothes. We'll dress in the memory of our love." She couldn't believe she said that, but she was psyched that she did. "We can make everything up."

"I don't know where they dance in Manfredonia. What do you do, ballroom dancing? Isn't it back in fashion?"

"For sure, Briggs. Just a half hour ago. I took lessons from Anorexic Aldo, but I didn't like it. I don't like to be moving backwards." She kissed him. "I'll ballroom if I can lead." She kissed him again, and then withdrew, slapping at her nose to chase the smell away. "And then everything will get so corny. We can stink the place up, and watch them all be polite. We can be very polite, and stinky. I want to be polite with you. I want to be corny with you. And we can go together and have our last supper and our last dance. We can pretend we haven't seen each other for years, and here we've run into each other in Manfredonia. Who would ever imagine Manfredonia?"

They looked out the window, at the winged chimeras that sailed across the screeny expanse of glass; their goat-bleats, their hissing, their screeches drilled into the nerves. Whatever, whatever. Saffron ran her palms lightly over the shimmer of her new color. It would feel better when it dried a little more. You had to get used to it. Anyone gets used to everything.

Translucent wings spread like veils to brush across the swimming pool, the astroturf, the abandoned factory; translucent wings for us to obliterate the moon.

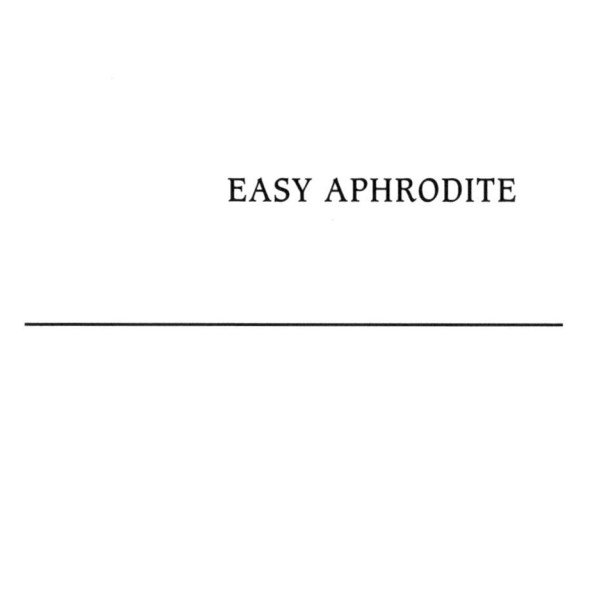

EASY APHRODITE

EASY APHRODITE

It was like an inertia that made him loath to enter a city named Lecce, pronounced like the Spanish word for milk, city of milk in the middle of the heel of the boot. He felt a peculiar apprehension. Fear of milk. It was the actual end of the line, and Solomon dreaded getting off the train. This city was without a harbor, without a river. How did they decide to put a city here? It was not at the foot of some mountains. It was in the center of a peninsula, the limestone shelf that was the heel of the boot. Little soil, so little agriculture. A bit of tobacco, some olive plantations. Puzzling, to build a city here. Solomon could tell his friends he'd been all the way down into the heel of the boot to look for the painting. Italy was convenient, in that you could always locate yourself somewhere on a boot. Shaped like a boot, famous for shoes, Isabel loved to say. He would go back to Iera with a pair of wonderful shoes for her small feet. He knew no one else who had been this far south on the Adriatic. What for, all the way down in the heel, they might ask? To find a lost painting by Antonello da Messina. Why? To see St. Francis as Antonello understood him. Why so far down into the heel of the boot? Because if this painting exists, as he was betting it did, it would be in an unlikely place. Lecce was that, an unlikely place.

He dropped his bags in the shade of the train station, and stepped into the sundrenched turnaround. The sun like a hammer drove him back into the shadows. He watched a tiny Topolino pull up, Italy's postwar answer to Germany's VW bug, a two seater coupe that looked like something Mickey Mouse might use to impress Minnie; in fact, Topolino was what the Italians called Mickey. Two dark skinned men got out, probably a father and son, dressed too warmly in brown checked wool suits, because they were headed north, frayed collars on their white shirts, black shoes without laces, no socks. They helped a woman all in black and two little girls in their prettiest dresses squeeze out from behind the seats. The girls hugged and kissed their father and brother, then followed the men, helping with their suitcases, into the station as a local cop chased them, waved his arms, shouting that they should move the Topolino. He threw up his arms in frustration and came towards Solomon, stopping about ten feet from him to size him up.

"Salve. Your identity card, please," he said as he approached. He was a slim, unshaven man, his face gaunt as a skull. His stained grey uniform, with faded red epaulettes, looked like he never took it off. He stroked the gold badge embroidered onto his pocket, to make sure Solomon was aware that he actually was empowered to assert the authority he seemed eager to exert.

"I have no identity card."

"What?" His face turned red. His neck stiffened with outrage.

"I don't have identity card. I have a passport."

"But, signore, how do you know who you are with no identity card? I must confirm your identity. How will I know who you are?"

He was like a comic vestige of fascism, living in confusion after the failure of Mussolini. "I'll show you my passport." Solomon opened a pocket of one of his bags.

"Not acceptable. No good. You must have…" He snapped his head away when a ruckus erupted behind him, and he rushed off, waving his arms, shouting at some people shouting back at him. They had pulled up in a high-wheeled traino, and the mule was kicking as they unloaded the suitcases. Now the station was filling with families, sending guest workers north to Torino, Milano, Germany, Sweden, Switzerland, on the overnight train that left at three forty-five. The men were all overdressed anticipating the northern climate, with wool caps on their heads, and the women, dressed all in black, ran around like ants tending their eggs. Children played amongst the melancholy adults in their most colorful clothes. The sun was punishing, but the people didn't seem to feel it, as they said goodbye to the fathers, the husbands they were exporting to work in the coldest places.

He noticed then a line of horse-drawn carriages, the kind called Broughams, that he'd seen before only in period movies. Perhaps they were waiting for someone important, or maybe they were shooting a period movie here. He often thought, when he turned certain corners anywhere in Italy, that he had stumbled into, sleepwalked onto a movie set. Then he saw people negotiating with the drivers, and climbing into the carriages, and going away. These were taxis in Lecce. Perhaps this was the last city in the modern world with taxis like this. He heard himself chuckle with pleasure at this, felt a little strange, knowing there was no one to reassure him that he wasn't hallucinating into a time warp. It was nineteen hundred and sixty-four, after all. The horseless carriage had been predominant everywhere else for more than half a century. This was a genuine tourist's dream, but it also raised his apprehension, as if something weird and dreadful was about to happen. He'd had this unreasonable fear in Sicily. Could this time warp settle onto his being, spread its feathery suffocation over himself like a great brooding hen.

After the three-forty-five pulled out, and the square was empty, one of the coaches approached him. "Can I be of any assistance, signore?" the driver asked from his seat above the compartment. Solomon realized he'd been standing there for a long time, in the cool of the shadows, practically asleep on his feet. The station square was virtually empty now. The driver climbed down, a small, stooped man with large hands that seemed permanently hooked from holding the reins. "Maybe a nice hotel, signore. A cool hotel. A nice girl in the bed." He grinned, unctuous as an undertaker in his black suit that matched the exterior of his brougham, and a greasy green tie over a soiled white shirt. Solomon noticed when he swung the door open that the tie matched the worn plush interior. He stood there, grinning, waiting for Solomon's response.

"Yes. Thank you. Yes. Where is a hotel?" Solomon's voice burst out, as if he'd been startled out of a coma.

"Don't worry, signore," said the driver, as he carefully placed Solomon's bags on a rack in back of the coach. "Everything is fine. Everything is going well. The world turns slowly. The tide comes in, the tide goes out at San Cataldo. Sometimes a little wind, some rain, maybe a scirocco brings sand from the sahara. Don't worry. This is an old place. Aphrodite will take us there." He patted the nose of his horse and she blew a quiet whinny. The driver helped Solomon into the carriage. He felt clumsy. He had never climbed into a carriage before, and fell forward onto his belly on the seat. "Ah, signore. Do not fret. The wives are at their stoves, and the sauces are simmering. And the pasta water is about to boil. Have you tried the orrechiette? Orrechiette col cima di rape. A specialty here in the Salento. Do not worry. Everything is ready for you. In the casks the wine ages slowly. This country is a very old country."

The more the driver insisted he not worry, the more it seemed there might be something to worry about. It smelled very old inside the carriage, as if the worn plush fabrics held on to a whiff of every passenger who had ever settled into these seats. For how long? For centuries? The cab rocked a little as the driver climbed back up to his seat, and then with a soft command and crack of the whip they jerked ahead. The carriage rolled noisily, hooves thudding on the asphalt, spread thinly over the old cobbles. Solomon pulled the curtain back from the window, a gesture he'd seen in so many historical movies, in westerns, in Madame Bovary for example. Peering out he easily imagined again he'd left his own life and was moved into someone's film. A film about what? About Solomon? About Antonello? He had no time to pursue this speculation because only two blocks from the station the carriage stopped, and here was the hotel. He could have walked, and saved the fifteen hundred lire the driver asked for this two minute ride. Solomon protested. The driver replied graciously.

"Consider, signore, how we protected you from the heat, Aphrodite and I. And from having to carry your bags all the way from the station. And this is an economical hotel, and good hotel too. I take you into town, and you pay much more money. We will come back in the evening, Aphrodite and myself, after you take a nap, and after I go to see about Siegfried, and then with your permission we will take you around, and show you the glorious baroque of Lecce, the pearl of the Salento, the Florence of the South, like ancient Athens. We will take you to the Roman Arena, to the Duomo, to Piazza San Oronzo, to the famous column that marks the end of the Appian way, one here, one in Brindisi, to the baroque church of Santa Chiara. Leccese baroque is a special beautiful baroque, because the stone, the tufa, is so soft, signore. You carve it like butter. And the arch of triumph, our own, that we call Porta Napoli. Aphrodite will take us everywhere. Everywhere, signore."

"Well, I was thinking, I like to walk around and…"

"So, why have you come here to Lecce?"

"I don't really need a whole tour. How much would you charge?"

"For you, signore, because you are American, and I love the Americans, ten thousand lire only, and three thousand for oats for Aphrodite. And sometimes she will eat a zucchini. So why did you come here to Lecce, so far in the south? Tourists, Americans don't often come. During the war years we saw many American soldiers, good people, generous with their mild cigarettes, but not so many in these years. Now there are some American servicemen in Taranto, but that is a secret. A few of them come here sometimes to find a girl, to eat a nice meal. In Lecce si mangia bene, si spende poco. Eat well, spend little."

"I came to look for a painting."

"Ah, signore. Many paintings. Many paintings here."

"By Antonello Da Messina. I am a student of his paintings."

"Oh, from Messina. I understand. I understand. But Messina is in Sicily. You are in the wrong city, signore. But this is a lucky mistake. The Salento is beautiful, a very old country. And all of Puglia is beautiful too. You should go to Alberobello, see the trullis. But this is not Sicily. Sicily is an island, signore."

"I think maybe this certain painting could be here," Solomon said, as if every day he had to convince himself again.

"Good. A painting. Yes. You should go to Galatina, especially in these days for the festival of Pietro e Paolo. You will definitely see something there, paintings as well. and it's closer than Sicily. But first you will let me show you this city, of Lecce. You have mistaken your direction, but you must profit from your mistake. This is your opportunity to see a place so beautiful. To learn about *il barocco Leccese.*"

"I don't…"

"No. No. I come back. Don't decide now. I must go see about Siegfried. Don't decide now. Six o'clock I come. Have a nap. Have a nice girl here. Then seven o'clock I come back. Yes? Yes, of course."

The driver carried his bags in to the desk, had a brief conversation with the woman behind it, told Solomon she wanted his passport, then left. Siegfried? A strange name, Solomon thought, to be evoked in Southern Italy.

Solomon laid the passport on the counter, then peered into the darkness of the hotel lobby. It looked as if the old tattered elegance of the carriage had been expanded in every direction to create this. Dark drapes covered all the windows, and the coatings of the large mirrors were peeling from behind. Except for one settee, on which two old men sat side by side, staring at an empty checkerboard, as if they were trying to remember what game they were playing on it, all the furnishings—sprawling couches, love seats, coffee tables, upholstered benches, easy chairs against each of the four columns by the imperial stairway—were covered with black dust protectors. A huge chandelier centered over the stairway, candles still leaning in the blown glass candleholders, was lit only by three dim lightbulbs, their wires wrapped around the glass branches.

"Please follow me, signore," said the woman who, after writing in the register, came around from behind the desk, and grabbed his bags to lead him up the stairs. *"Ascensore é guasto,"* she said. The elevator was busted. She was a tiny woman, but she carried his bags without effort. Another woman, just as small, jumped like a troll from under the stairs, and grabbed the key from the first, and ran on ahead.

They led him to his room on the first floor, halfway

down a long corridor, dimly lit by one bare bulb. The corridor was very quiet. He couldn't tell if any of the other rooms were occupied. His was a large room. The vaulted yellow ceiling seemed higher than the room was wide. It was sparsely furnished with two narrow beds, their springs of steel mesh, a table, a mirror, an enameled portable bidet on a wobbly stand, a picture of the Eiffel tower on the wall across from the beds. A toilet was his to share down the hall and a shower, also in the hall, available only in the morning at extra cost. The walls were painted an institutional green, bordered with a blue pattern of leaves where they met the ceiling vault. At one point the painter had extended the leaves as a vine up into the vault, the vine intended to surround a child's body that had been palely sketched in, and abandoned. The maid parted a yellowed curtain, and threw open the double french doors onto a narrow balcony, and pointed out that in one direction you saw the train station, and in the other the wall of the old city. She dropped the heavy, double-bitted key into his hand. *"Va bene, signore?"* She grinned at him. *"La camera va bene, si? Aria. Si respira bene. Tutto."*

"Si, va bene. It's good." He tipped them each five hundred lire.

"La Bella Piumina viene subito, signore," said the desk girl. "She come soon."

The two women stood in the doorway and watched him open his bag, and pull out a book. They watched as if they had never seen anything like it before. He sat on the edge of the bed and waited for them to leave. They lingered.

"Thank you. *Grazie.* That's all I need." He gestured to send them away, but they still lingered as if they didn't want to give up the entertainment he provided.

"*Via, per cortesia,*" he said, with a more emphatic wave of his arm.

"*Scusi, signore.*" The desk clerk took the maid's arm.

"*La bella Piumina é Napoletana, bella, grassa, gradevole,*" said the maid. "*Viene subito. E impiegata adesso, fuori albergo.* From Naples. Very good."

They finally left and closed the door, and Solomon opened the novel he had brought, *In Sicily,* by Elio Vittorini, with an intro by Ernest Hemingway. Sure Hemingway liked it. The dialogue could have come right out of one of his own novels. The rural Sicily that Vittorini wrote about was nothing like Solomon's brief experience of the place, though he had seen there some rural superstition at work. The book had its populist, leftist political side, but underneath that was a current more ancient, mysterious, mythical. Solomon never could have got at that in his ten days there. He thought of Antonello, coming from that place, but outside superstition, and myth, and dusky legend. His painter asserted a clarity of observation and understanding of human psychology, totally rational, even if enormously complicated. The mystery he painted was the mystery of human discernment and ambivalence. Each of his portraits catches the subject at a nexus of insight and discrimination. They look at you. Often you are intimidated because you fear they're smarter than you are. They know something about you that they will never reveal. Entertain us with your next move, they seem to be saying. Everything drove him to think of Antonello, and then he thought of Iera.

He fell asleep with Vittorini open on his face.

The knocking on his door became quite loud before he opened his eyes again, and he swatted the book away, as if it was some animal that had settled there to suffocate him. He stood up and glimpsed himself in the mirror, this wreck of a traveler, so skinny in his shorts.

"Eccomi, La Piumina," said the apparition framed in the doorway. He staggered a step back as if blown by a sudden gust. Here was an ample young woman, barefoot, draped in a black lace mantilla, and some lacy nothings, like a sheer red bra, and ruby lace panties, her lips also deep ruby in a precious pucker. Her great bosom swelled as she looked at him, and threatened to flow over the fringes of lace. She hardly seemed to move her mighty thighs as she stepped into the room, and shut the door behind herself.

"You are Americano," she sighed, and arched her back. "Don't be so worried," she touched his face. "I am a woman for you, very nice." She tested the bed with her hand. "Signore, I am very nice for you, la Piumina." She lay back on the bed, her flesh like a liquid across the sheets. She unhooked, and the red cups of her bra flopped to each side like vestigial wings.

"Non esiste amor." A voice rose through the window from a bar below. *"E soltanto 'na favola."*

"Two Americans came here a week ago from Taranto. They were military, from the air base, the secret missile base in Gioa del Colle. Are you from the military?"

"No. I'm not, not at all." Her smell, perfumed and acrid, filled his room with confusion. She was almost nude on his bed, just a girl, though her fleshiness made her seem ageless. A spark woke up his groin, and surged up his spine. This was not usually his type, a surprise, this dark Rubenesque.

"They were black men, dark as your shoes, signore. What is your name?"

"I am Solomon. Solomon Briggs."

"Breeges, So-lo-mon. Ahhh! *Salomóne, dalla Bibbia. Bello.* Very beautiful. You are very wise man." Her smile was sweet, and made her look truly innocent, though the dark eyes surrendered none of her mystery. "But very nice gentlemen these Americani, Reginald and Harry. I had never been with so black men before. Very gentlemen. Very cultivated. More than the white ones who come, who are so disrespectful, so nasty. I don't go with the white ones any more, only with you, signore

Salómone."

She was totally relaxed in the bed, like an actor in the lights of a familiar stage, easy with her monologue.

"One of them, Reginald, had studied all the history of the Salento, and wanted to know from me if the Saracen people were black. I didn't know, signore Salomóne, but you are wise, and you know. Were the Saracen people black people? Were they black like the Moors?"

"I don't know anything about the Saracens."

"A pity, and here you are Salomóne, and you don't know. When Reginald comes back I want to tell him something. Yes, the Saracens were black people. No, the Saracens were not black people. He is a very good man, and a very cultured Americano." She smiled at Solomon, and raised her hips to roll her panties off. She had recently shaved. There were abrasions where the razor had scraped too close. A small triangle of black hair covered her mound.

"I don't know why…What brought you to my room?"

La Piumina laughed, and the laugh made her seem more ancient. "This is my profession. I am putana, professore." She giggled coyly. "La Piumina is always here for this thing." She lightly stroked her vagina, and let her fingers sink in. "I sell you the flavor of the fig." She held out two glistening fingers. "Here. Taste. We make love. Nice nice love."

"What do you mean when you call this love?"

Solomon felt uncomfortable. He had never really been with a whore before.

"*Ehhh, giusto, signore.* You are right. *Che cazzo è amore.*"

"I never asked for anything...for you to come."

She smiled the wise, coquettish smile of a woman who knows her way around men's resistance and insecurity. "It was Aldo, your driver, professor, who said you waited for me here, and so did Agnina and Marinella, and here you are. Weren't you waiting for me? Here all by yourself? In the middle of the day. Alone in your room. You know you want La Piumina."

"I don't...I don't say I don't want..." He was embarrassed. Was there an etiquette to this situation? She was a whore. He could throw her out. He really hadn't "ordered" one, and didn't really want one, except there was something intriguing about La Piumina herself. In his mind was Iera, whom he hadn't even touched. And further back, Isabel, whom he had perhaps once too often. He didn't need a whore, but he didn't want La Piumina to leave. It struck him comical how she immediately relaxed onto the bed, and she seemed a really tender person. He felt the familiar stiffening between his legs, and respected that. It wasn't just automatic any more.

"Have you ever had a Napoletana, professor? A Neapolitan woman?"

"No. I can't say I...No, never." He wasn't comfortable that she had started calling him *professore,* sensed a slight nod of condescension to his inexperience.

"Then you should try this." She spread her legs and parted the small lips, to let a snack of pinkness out from the tawny flaps between her thighs. "You will spend very little, twenty thousand lire only." She thickened her tongue, and let it moisten her lips. "Come. On top of me here. Don't be afraid. I am very nice. I am clean. My skin is pure, like silk. I help you, Mr. American Salomóne."

He hesitated. She stroked his arm with her fingertips. "If you don't take off your pants there is nothing I can do for you."

When she had first come into the room he couldn't imagine touching her, she seemed so gross and unappealing; but now, in the bed, her flesh looked comfortable and inviting. He stood naked above her. Her smell was pungent and sweet, drilling deep into his senses. Dark eyes tugged him down, as if to float him on her pool of smooth skin, smooth and dark as a first pressing of oil, her nipples stiff, deep brown, like a nibble of leather, and as he traced his fingertips across her belly she moaned. "O, signore. O, amore."

A thought of Isabel entered then abandoned his mind as she held his hard cock that swelled further against the pressure of her fingers, and "Piumina" he said, as she eased him through her moist warmth. Startling him was such agility in a body this heavy, more passionate than he ever anticipated a professional could be, her sighs like broad organ chords, and she whispered soft affections in his ear, in a dialect full of shushing sounds like the sea. Surging up under him her belly and breasts were soft and powerful; he lost himself into the insect brain in his spine, hips pumping, pumping. She was so open and wet he felt that with one powerful suck she could have all of him down, pull him inside herself to smother there forever. This was the mythical charybdis he thought he had avoided when he crossed back to the continent over the Straits of Messina.

For a while they lay exhausted, touching like real lovers. He tried to locate on his cheek the imprint of Iera's kiss that had lingered so long, but he couldn't find it now. Piumina's smell, a pungent diesel of flesh, mingled with his own sweat and filled the room.

"Are you always like this?" he asked, after his breathing calmed.

"What is this?"

"So excited, so passionate. Don't you get tired?"

"This is my profession, *professore*. Dear *Professore*. Sometimes I make love."

"But every day? You must do this so many times."

"No. I don't make love every time. Most men don't want love. They want to fuck. I can just lie here for them, I don't have to be anything but their nice portion of *pasta alla ficàia*."

"And for me?"

"You are like a schoolboy, *Professore* schoolboy, his dick dry as a sick dog's nose, very sad, very lonesome. Sometimes when he is sad, and I see it, that makes me feel something inside, not pity but saucy, tasty. It makes passion in me. That was for you."

"So Piumina, you are like a doctor, then?."

"You can take the doctors, and shove them up your ass. I am a whore! What I do for you, is done by a whore. Remember that."

"Thank you, Piumina." Solomon felt good, as if he had been washed ashore on a beach, and some gentle waves lapped and lapped his body.

"You pay me, mister Salomóne. I don't need your *grazie*. Pay me for the fig you consume. You were the lonely man, very sad, and now you are happy like a little pig, and not so lonely for a moment. So what do you think this work is I do? You think I am like a daughter of pricks? Sometimes it is like nothing. Easy, and I love it, and I do good for someone, a little bit. And I get pleasure from it too, sometimes. It is a gift from heaven, when you take pleasure from your work. Every day most people are slaves to earn a little bread. And look even at these fine women, in their fine clothes, with their fine children, and fine furnishings in their salottos, that only princes once could afford. These fine ladies become slaves to marriage, to their husbands. I am a naked whore, and a free woman, Mr. Salomóne. Few women are free in this beautiful miserable Italy. This is a dog's paradise, and the dogs suffer here. Freedom is what I have."

"Freedom is like a muscle, Piumina. It needs to be exercised."

Laughing at him, she grabbed his dick, "This is the muscle, *professore*. A man is a slave to his little organ, his tender piece of veal." She swung off the bed, and went to the sink to splash water on her body. "You are the philosopher, professore Salomóne. I am La Piumina, a whore; but no one makes me out ignorant for that. About my life, I am shrewd." She tapped her forehead. "I chose this small city, so stuck in who knows what century, ancient minds, a feudal mentality. Here I can be independent. In Naples where I learned this profession, too much competition. They are masters of survival, my Napoletani, and before you wake up they see a hundred ways to take your money. They sell you the hair off their grandmother's cunt if she is dead, and if she still lives, they sell you an option. Everything with good humor; but there is danger, too. A whore on the streets can soon be meat for the crows. You understand me, professore?" He mumbled his affirmative. The strength of her assertions had erased his rosier mood. "Those sailors— Americans, Portugese, Africans, strange things they ask you to do. I had to work for a manager, what do you call that? A pimp. May the spiders gnaw through his ears, the maggots eat his brain. Or I could have gone to a house, where you work, they feed you, a little bit they protect you, but little money in your purse. This is better here. Sleepy old Lecce. I work alone. I am free. My business is my own business. The other whores are friendly enough, almost a family. Several of them, old girls, were part of the old *quindicina*. That was when our profession was on the up and up, and the government organized the whores, and rotated them town to town every fifteen days. So they are relaxed. We don't disturb each other. With a little cunning I manage the police." She made a gesture with her fingers to show that by cunning she meant money. She washed her feet in the bidet, then filled it again to squat and wash her working parts.

Solomon turned away because now she looked unappealing. He couldn't even imagine the intimacy of a few moments before. People were most attractive in the middle distance, he often noted, where desire blends with illusion; and even the most gorgeous woman, the most handsome man, moving towards you from across the street, could become ordinary, or even frightening up close, when you glimpse the strain the commitment to appearance puts on the facial expression. Something nasty in the eyes. Mouth held like a beak, like a challenge. A disdainful flare of the nostrils. But with La Piumina, closer had been more attractive. Maybe that was why she was La Piumina.

"So why have you come here to this little town, Mr. American? If you are not from the military?"

Solomon laughed. "I have come to look for the painting of St. Francis, by Antonello da Messina." He loved dropping those words into the backwash of what had just happened.

"Ah, St. Francis," she repeated. "You can go straight up your ass with all these saints. That saintliness is their living, okay, their own business. This mongrel world the rest of us are born to won't support too many of them, thank God. St. Francis was born rich. Most of the saints are born rich. He also was born without an asshole. He would never have known La Piumina, and I would have avoided him. I have no compassion for this willful innocence, self-righteous abstinence. Go shove it up your ass. St. Augustine, maybe we could carry on a conversation. He knew some flesh, and lived a while in my world. He might understand me, that I want a city full of human beings, not saints without pricks. And as for the Magdalene, she was savvy, almost a good Napolitana. She knew how to profit as the whore of Jesus." Talking had put La Piumina in a buoyant mood, almost singing. "If you want to find St. Francis, talk to the driver, Aldo. He lives just outside the city, and people say he has conversations with birds, just like St. Francis. And that he and his friend, they have hatched many eggs."

She looked into the corridor, and laughed at the world out there, a fat young woman now, in stained wrinkles of lace, someone who might bring you a plate of pasta in a restaurant, nothing seductive about her. But she left Solomon relaxed, with a broad grin on his own face. It wasn't till he was putting on his shoes that he remembered that she never asked him again for money. He put three ten thousand lire notes in an envelope, and left them for her at the desk as he went out to take a walk into town.

"Ah, mister," said the driver, who was waiting for him outside the hotel. "You are ready now for a ride with me into Lecce."

"I'm going to walk," Solomon said. "It's cooler now."

"No. Not to walk. Come. Ride up here beside me. Sit here." He patted the seat next to himself. "From here you will see everything. Aphrodite will take you and show everything. And I will explain for you the beauty of our city. From up here you will look on all the elegant Leccese girls. You call them birds, is it not. Famous in the whole world. This is an opportunity for you."

Solomon gave in. He pulled himself up to sit next to Aldo, and they started off into the traffic, just a few cars, some light vans, some three wheeled Vespas with truck beds. "You should enjoy this ride, signore. Soon I am extinct, like a bird, like the auk. No more ever such carriages again, only the filthy machines. Look at them, signore. How shall I call you?"

"Solomon is my name. Salomóne."

"Ahhh, Salo. I am Aldo. So look, there is the wall of the city. And what good will they do, those machines? To stink. Fart their filth into the air. For this carriage you can't even find a wheel any more. An axle? Never." He flicked his fingertips under his chin. *"Niente."* They crossed the main boulevard that circled the town, and paused outside the wall.

"This wall goes almost all the way around the city, with several gates. This one is Porta Napoli." Aldo yawned, and stretched, then they continued through the arch into the old city. "They call this our arch of triumph." They stopped again on the other side. "Look how different," Aldo said, pointing down the ancient street. "Carriage feels accommodated in here. Aphrodite holds her head higher."

It was twilight, the evening alchemy, as if the walls had been gathering light all day and turning it to gold. Aldo leaned forward to whisper in dialect to Aphrodite. The mare shook her head, and snorted in response. Aldo yawned again, and laid the reins on Solomon's lap. "Signore Salo, you should drive. I've already told Aphrodite where to go."

Solomon touched the old leather of the reins. "I've never done this."

"Aphrodite takes care of everything. She is not a machine. Don't worry, Mr. Salo. The evening is beautiful. The air is rich. Look. Look at the swallows. It is a fine time, when all the grand signore of the city are dressed, and they are walking slowly, taking their passegiata. And the swallows sweep the insects out of the sky." He moved the reins to Solomon's hands.

"I don't know even what…"

"Aphrodite knows everything, signore. She knows where to to go. She knows about you. She knows what to do." Aldo touched the mare's flank with his whip, and they started forward. "See, Mister Salo, it is all…" Aldo yawned again, looked at Solomon, blinked a few times, and gave in to sleep.

Solomon let the reins lie loosely in his hands. Perhaps it was from a movie that he remembered this was how you did it. Palms up, reins loose. At the unfamiliar touch, Aphrodite looked back at Solomon, and shook her head again. With her high pitched snort he was sure she meant to tell him she was in charge. They kept going anyway, funneled into the narrow street that lead to Piazza San Oronzo, in the center of town. On the cobbles Aphrodite's hooves made a pleasing music. It was the magic hour from sunset into twilight, when the heat has finally loosened its grip, and the finest people put on their finest clothes, and step from their kitchens and drawing rooms, and onto the streets, to announce their wealth, display their elegance, flaunt their position, and to pay their respects with courtesies, bows, and handshakes, and carefully worded chattering.

Aphrodite trotted briskly, her hooves continuing the

ancient rhythmic tune on the paving stones. They passed fussy old facades, heavily ornamented doorways, balconies supported by grinning caryatids, maidens that looked confused, as if they had never expected to be carved of stone. The ease with which you could model this tufa allowed for a decorative gibberish, they called baroque. Aphrodite slowed on her own and pulled to the side whenever an automobile needed to pass. Families strolled and conversed. It seemed everyone was on the street. Beautiful young daughters were excited by the evening, and the prospect of meeting some handsome young man, his sudden elegance when they turned a corner. It seemed all tightly controlled, impenetrable, a mesh of ancient signals. For Solomon this was a strange intoxication to be alone, like floating above this crowd. It would have been nice to have Isabel with him here, to lean against her and affirm the reality of all this, the murmur of people, the posturing and gestures, the lights slowly coming on, the narrow streets, the shops lit like boudoirs, and above everything, across the deepening blue of sky, weaving a constant racket, swoops of what looked like all the swallows in the world crosshatched the blue with their darkness. Iera he tried to imagine with him, but Isabel at his side made more sense, someone to reassure him that this warp of paradise, this cul-de sac in time, an evocation of minds past, was real and not so dreadful. What did he dread?

Aphrodite pulled the carriage onto an open square in the center of town, irregular in shape, crowded with people, an Upim store on one side, people seated at cafés around the piazza, sipping their aperitivos, strolling over the mosaic of the wolf (Lecce meant wolf, Aldo told him, in Leccese dialect) past the famous column, silhouetted as they crossed in front of a small, closed pavilion, lit like a furnace from within, and then, where Aphrodite came to a halt, the excavation, part of a Roman amphitheater, a stone balustrade curved around it.

"Ah," Aldo lifted his head. "Piazza San Oronzo. Yes. Look, over there. Santa Croce." Aldo pointed at a cathedral, the wide facade an intricately decorated confection. "That is why this is the Florence of the baroque. Mr. Salo, you find yourself now in the Athens of Puglia. The column there. The Roman Amphitheater here." Otherwise, Solomon noted, most of the square was surrounded by buildings in the bland fascist mode of the thirties.

"Aldo," Solomon placed a hand on his shoulder, to take advantage of this conscious moment. "Where would I go to look for a painting? Some archive, or storage where they would keep old paintings?"

"Paintings, of course." He took the reins. Solomon could tell by the way Aldo let the question lie, that he wouldn't get an answer. He pressed anyway.

"A painting of St. Francis, yes. Maybe hidden somewhere."

"Ahhh, St. Francis." Aldo's face was suddenly illuminated by headlights. "Aphrodite, ch ch," He clicked at the mare and she started to move again.

"It would be by Antonello. Antonello da Messina. But painted over, probably. It would be hard to see. But I thought you might know, since you drive everybody, even the priests. Maybe an archive, a collection, a church repository where, I don't know…I thought you might have some idea, as well as anyone."

Aphrodite took them quickly away from the piazza, Aldo still half asleep, holding the reins. They passed some ordinary shopfronts, then more modern residences, then moved along another part of the city wall, and into a construction zone. "This will be the Piazza del Millecento, when they finish. If they ever finish." He smiled with eyes shut. "Very big, very big city. Lecce will be like the Torino of the south. Like New York City, yes. So you tell me, Mr. Salo, what do you think? Does Lecce grow, or does the world shrink?"

They rode west into shadows beyond the town, towards a lavender horizon. The narrow road stretched between stone walls and dense boundaries of prickly pear. Tangled paddles of the cactus mimed an awkward shadow-play as they passed. Solomon felt strange, a disorientation of place, and a greater disruption of time.

When was this reality? When would he have had to be born to live this? Where were they headed? His courage paled, though he didn't know for what he'd need courage.

"Maybe you could take me back to my hotel?"

"I take you to my house, just a little way from here."

Aldo against the cobalt sky looked like a silhouette from a different age. "My hotel," he said, but feebly. He'd need something. He didn't know what, maybe courage. But why? There was no threat. He would come out of this all right. There actually was no "this" to come out of. He wanted to come to know Iera better.

Aldo whistled in a minor key, some doleful melody, drawing stars out through the weave of twilight. So sad, these stars. The evening air was liquid and clear. This was an adventure. He could drown in this atmosphere. Birds nearby responded to the whistling with their own melancholy songs. The upper limb of a full moon swelled behind them. They turned onto a lane between two long rows of tall umbrella pines that formed an arched procession leading to a small squared house built of tufa block, two windows dimly lit. From a beehive clay oven outside the front door a thread of smoke curled up to lassoo some stars. An old fig tree flexed its thick arms over one end of the house. Some guinea hens, disturbed by the arrival, complained in their roosts. Aldo answered with an almost identical sound, and they calmed down. He talks to birds, Solomon remembered. The moon that had swelled at the horizon now was down to size.

A scent of fresh baked bread pulled him into the front room. Several loaves sat on a long wooden table, in the center, next to a bowl of fresh figs. Aldo sat down on a three-legged stool next to a bottle of wine and some glasses, pulled a hunk off one of the loaves, and handed it to Solomon, sliding a stool his way with his foot.

"Salo, come sit down. Siegfried baked today. Good bread. And these are the last of the fiorone, the first figs, the best." He reached over to the old sideboard to grab a wheel of pecorino. "Cheese." He sliced off a wedge and handed it to Solomon. Solomon noticed a chart on the wall of Audobon quality prints of birds, most of them extinct. Birds and their eggs. There was a slender-billed grackle, and the Labrador duck, and there was the melancholy dodo, one foot on its speckled grey egg. Siegfried? Someone named Siegfried lived with Aldo? "You must thank Siegfried," the coach driver said when Solomon thanked him for the bread. "I think he's baked some focacce, too. And you must thank Aphrodite. She eats a few oats, and some hay, and what she makes nourishes the garden and the fig tree. No machine will do that."

Moaning filtered into the room from elsewhere in the house. Solomon looked at the coach driver. "What?..." It was a woeful singing, like a man in pain, no, like someone resigned to pain, who had been suffering plenty over time; almost a song, like some blues. There was a song he'd heard before.

"Vor der Kaserne / Vor dem großen Tor…" Each line of the song was followed by a moan, increasing in volume, till it faded to a whimper. "Stand eine Laterne / Und steht sie noch davor…"

What was that tune? Solomon was sure he knew it. "Sieg…Sieg…fried. Is that Siegfried?" It was difficult to say the name, that northern name, so far south, so deep in Italy, so close to Africa. How many Siegfrieds died, were wounded under Rommel in North Africa?

"What?"

"Ja ootab, et me tema all / taas kohtuksime tänaval…" and again the tune. He'd never heard that language.

"That. Is that Siegfried?"

"Ahhh. Siegfried. Yes. I don't even hear him any more, you know. He makes this noise, this song, these moans. I am so used to this."

"Con te Lili Marlene / Con me Lili Marlene…"

Of course, that World War II song. So Marlene Dietrich. He stood up to look for the singer, but Aldo held him back. After a few moments they heard a stunted "Haha!" like the kachunk of a cash register, followed by a strumming of laughter, "hahahahaha." "Now you come to meet Siegfried."

The next room held a bed and a dresser, and many

more pictures of birds on the wall, and through a beaded curtain covering a doorway to a smaller room, Solomon saw him squatted on his haunches over a nest of rolled blankets, sheets, leaves, wool.

"Outside the barracks, by the corner light / I'll always stand and wait for you at night." He sang, opening his arms to Solomon. In one hand he held a dark brown egg, smaller than a chicken's, larger than a quail's. "Nestor Productus," he said, with gargled r's and hard esses. "Norfolk Island Kaka," he said. "For you, Lili Marlene / For you, Lili Marlene," he sang to Solomon. He clambered from the nest protecting the egg which he held up for Aldo to see, before he set it next to other eggs in a cushioned box on a tripod stand. He picked two and held them up, one in each hand. This was a tall blonde Siegfried, slim neck with pointed adam's apple, haunted in the face. His skin was white, and his eyebrows blonde. His lips were pink and moist. Was this the advent that Solomon had dreaded? His eyes steel blue. His teeth were pearly white. In each hand, his arms spread wide, he now held an egg. Aldo hugged the taller man, laid his cheek against the hairless chest. "Nestor Productus. I have brought Nestor Productus, Aldo."

"He is eventually going to bring the Great Auk," Aldo explained to Solomon. "That is his goal."

"Pinguinnis Impennis," Siegfried said, as he offered Solomon his hand to shake. "I vill some day." He narrowed his steely eyes. Had Solomon dreaded that stare? "Ze great Auk, I vill."

"I don't get it," Solomon said. He wanted to get away from this place, to be alone, lying in the bed, listening for La Piumina in the hall. He had never thought he would ever be homesick for an hotel room.

"He is making eggs. Siegfried has learned to make eggs."

"I am. I lay zee eggs. I lay zem. I will one day lay zee egg of zee Auk. It is big. It is a difficult egg."

"How does he? Does he actually, you know, lay eggs?" Solomon asked Aldo.

"I am Cherman. I have zis talent. I lay zem. I am Cherman, from Dusseldorf," Siegfried stretched with pride.

"Do you…Are these eggs fertile?" He was slightly embarrassed to ask this.

"He came here from Germany during the war, ran away from the army, from the Wehrmacht," Aldo said. "He knew what they were doing, and he couldn't tolerate it."

"It vas evil. It vas cruel. I could not participate. I could not tolerate zat."

"And he came all the way to Lecce, rode a supply train part of the way, and I met him just as I met you, at the station, with my carriage. Aphrodite was younger then. She was very sleek. So Siegfried told me his story, and I brought him here, and he has lived with me ever since."

"I am very grateful," Siegfried said.

"Then he discovered he had this talent. It was a surprise to himself. What would you think if you were suddenly laying eggs? At first I didn't believe it, that he was as good as a bird, to make eggs."

"How does he do it?"

"I am Cherman."

"He is German. I don't know."

"Beware the Germans laying eggs," Solomon said, without thinking.

"I did not vant a final solution, a holocaust, nix. Zere is nothing so bad in zee Chews."

"All the guinea hens outside in the trees, they are from eggs that Siegfried gave, so he can, he makes fertile."

"I am a male. Zis is not so strange. I will make zee Great Auk again on zee earth, zough it cannot forgiving everysing my people did. Ze holocaust was big enormous mistake by ze fazzerland. But I will make zee Auk again to walk zee earth, and zat vill be mine gift. It vill be Chermany's great gift back to ze vorld."

"You see," Aldo said. "The Germans can do it. They can do everything. Whatever you might say about the Jews, and the Gypsies, and the, you know, nice boys." He made the sign with his fingers against his cheek that

365

in Italian gesture language means that someone is queer. "You have to admit they were a problem for a long time, and the Germans figured it out, how to settle this problem, and maybe it was evil, yes, but they found a solution, and it was efficient. No one else had the solution."

"Aldo. What are you saying? My family is Chewish. If I…" It bothered him that he had unintentionally imitated Siegfried's pronunciation.

Solomon thought he saw something, a morbid grimace flicker across Siegfried's expression. "We know that the Germans are very smart. A German can do this what Siegfried does, and maybe there will never be an explanation. We may never understand how Siegfried lays his eggs."

Somewhere evil moves in its invisible boots, right now, all the time. Somewhere else a German defector lays eggs, a horse fertilizes a fig tree. A child maybe swells in Isabel. Iera perhaps dreams of Solomon, and Solomon thinks of Antonello's portraits, not products of the artist's perception, but as tools of perceptivity, how each one looks out at you, at Solomon, and makes him need to know himself.

"Tadorna Cristata," Siegfried pronounced. "Zee Crested Shelduck. Campephilus Imperialis, zee Imperial Woodpecker. Chlorostilbon Bracei, Brace's Emerald. Siphoris Americanus, zee Jamaican Poorwill. Sceloglaux

Albifacies, zee Laughing Owl. Moho Nobilis, zee Hawaiin Oo. Chaunoproctus Ferreorostris, the Bonin Grosbeak. Turnagra Capensis, zee Piopio. All of zese and more, until ze Great Auk itself, I shall bring back as a gift for humankind, to begin us ze redemption of my Chermany, my poor, misunderstood Chermany. And zhen, as soon as I have ze capacity, I shall lay zee Great Auk egg, and even if I do not find zhat capacity, zis shall be my final act, my last sacrifice for ze Fazzerland."

"The Great Auk," Solomon repeated to Siegfried's moist pink smile, over pearly pearly teeth. "Did St. Francis ever talk to The Great Auk, do you think?" Solomon looked to a blank wall and visualized a painting of St. Francis talking to the Auks, a painting by Antonello. A great fresco by Antonello, the mild mannered saint, talking to the Greatest Auk, saying it in Cherman.

A silence thickened in the room as Siegfried turned to straighten out his nest. Solomon backed out through the door, out of the house, and into the moonlight. Aldo followed him. A chill swept the peninsula. Stepping onto the silvery ground was like trampling the hair of the northern graces, who now leaned south, back over the continent from their fjords and glaciers.

Aldo took the feedbag from Aphrodite's muzzle, brought the carriage around, then climbed back onto his seat.

"Come," he said. "Now we take you to the hotel. In

town they are showing *Eight and a Half*, and it always takes a year or more for the films to get down here to this little Lecce, especially these films by that accursed sot, that pig, Fellini. But many people will be there, because they are so hungry to see this garbage, the miserable life of Rome, of Via Veneto. If our beloved Benito were still alive, this abomination would not be allowed. But what can I do? I must be at the theatre in time to take home some of the swine who watch such film.."

Solomon climbed up next to him again, more nimbly this time. At the end of the lane of umbrella pines, Aphrodite lifted her tail and released into the moonlight several cylinders of pure gold. The air was redolent of wild marjoram, a scent sweet as the night. She turned back as if to smile at Solomon, and then she whinnied, though it was more like a cough or a roar; and then they rode towards the glow of Lecce, dulled by moonlight, behind the good cheer of the old mare, tossing her head from side to side like the young chestnut filly she once had been. Solomon was sure the music in the air was Aphrodite's song.

"Aldo, is it unusual to have such a horse, that sings?"

"Not so strange," Aldo replied, sitting alert and erect at the reins. "But a horse that will turn straw into gold, now we think that is unprecedented, and you will never see it again, Salo, in these confusing years to come."

PIGS

PIGS

He felt her absence in bed, and then the tease of her vacancy riding shotgun in the rented Daewoo. This vacuum sucked him after her, a spider down a drain. He drove mumbling alone, from the heel into the toe of the boot, then onto the ferry at Villa St. Giovanni, and arrived in Messina before he realized he was going anywhere. Nathan followed his memory of her breathing the name, "Taormina," up the cliff road into that ancient tourist town. He found her in none of the hotels, nor caffes, nor did he see her in the evening there in the discos of Giardini-Naxos, nor when he trudged fully dressed, staring at women like a maniac voyeur, down the bikini beaches, looking for a flash of her kryptonite hair. Had he forgotten what she looked like? Had she been just part of a dream?

"A beautiful town, this Taormina," he ventured conversation with a young man who had winked at him at a refreshment stand near the beach. Nathan described the girls, and asked if he had seen them. A shadow of disappointment crossed the young man's face.

"Yes, a pretty town for you, but for the Taorminiani." He gestured, a scrape below his chin with his fingertips, which meant *"niente,"* nothing. "I was born here. I love Taormina. But I can't afford to live here.

There's no work here. Who can buy a house here? The Americans. The Germans. How do you raise a family? Who's in control? The mafia, maybe. The government. Same thing. Who can say?" Yes, he went on when Nathan insisted, he'd seen the group of girls, one with hair silver and blue as that. So many groups of girls come to Taormina, beautiful American girls with long legs and money. "I want to go to America. I want to find an American girl with money and go to America." He winked at Nathan again, just to make sure. Nathan gave him his card, which the young man puzzled over, then slipped under the elastic of his bikini.

Under Etna, great mother volcano, and on the beaches around Catania, he searched in futility; then he left the car and grabbed a bus to Enna, thinking that on foot there he might have better luck. He acted like a desperate fool. So what? He took a taxi out to the sacred lake Pergusa, where the myth has it that while picking flowers near the pomegranate trees, Persephone was raped, then abducted by Hades. Every year her mother, Demeter, returns to reseed the land around the lake, though it's now paved, a motor speedway, and the ritual is international formula car competition; and now Nathan thinks "these girls, these girls, these girls might love speed." But he didn't see them there. In Siracusa he found the Gran Hotel Politti, where they had stayed, and he followed the lead from a desk clerk and went to Noto because she had heard them speak of stopping at that old baroque town, then he went back to Messina, and to Palermo, as he slowly abandoned his faint hopes.

He felt a curious relief at never catching up with her, that he had saved himself the humiliation of Saffron's rejection and her friends' ridicule. He could hear her voice, angry that he had followed her at all. She was young. She wouldn't be flattered. She wouldn't be understanding. Why should she be? What right have you, she might say? Following me? Her self-righteous indignation so hypocritical, and not really Saffron. Or maybe she'd feel some slight thrill of power, because to her classmates he'd look like a pitiful older guy, panting after her out of his mid-life crisis. They'd make her bust him for stalking. First she had begged him to let her travel with him, and now he was the one gasping. So now he found himself almost inadvertently on the sad, beautiful island of Sicily, a place of bitter history, and the most delicious sweets. And now he had nothing to do, really, since he was wary of subjecting himself to whatever mortification he'd suffer if he found her. Pressure from her peers, and not her own vindictiveness, would probably twist her into her cruelest stance as a young woman preyed on by an older man. It made him wince, and laugh at the same time, to imagine Saffron as prey to anything. More pity to the hunter.

To run into her somewhere under Mount Etna, that would have been too stupid, too grossly symbolic. The embrace, the eruption, the giggles as they ran to escape some sizzling lava. He thought of her as a kind person, actually, in the core of her being, though pressure from her peers and the discrepancy in their ages would make it impossible now for her to be really kind to him. But what did he know? Maybe if she saw him, she would fly into his arms. Maybe. Corny circumstances like in some easy sentimental movies that made him weep. Every sentimental movie. Maybe she felt his absence as painfully as he did hers. And just for relief, in front of her friends, in front of the chaperones, the professors, the paintings, the ancient ruins, the delicious cannoli and sfogliatelle, the varnishes of coffee, she would rise up, and fly into his arms. He hadn't found her afraid to embarrass herself otherwise; just the opposite, in fact. She could fly. They had been through plenty together in their brief acquaintance. What more could love be than what they'd had? Like those caprestrelli they had experienced together in their mutual daydream, she too could fly. Why wouldn't she? He was an incorrigibly romantic, old fashioned guy to think this. But it wasn't impossible.

So he was suddenly in Sicily, and decided to take advantage of it? He'd never been to a Club Med before, and here was one nearby, in a town called Cefalù. Club Med was something other people did, not himself, but this turned out to be surprisingly pleasant, a thatched south pacific style paradise on a spit of land removed from the ancient melancholy that was Sicily, at one end of the shallow cove of Cefalù. He had a view from his half of the thatched duplex cottage he was able to rent for a week of the Norman cathedral squatting in the distance on its hill in the midst of squalid stone houses piled up the cliff. He felt no need to visit the town.

He bought a week in this paradise, the only single man alone in a world of couples and families. That was not what he'd expected at Club Med; but this was an opportunity to hang out on the beach, take a few stabs at the sport of windsurfing, relax. Moss was the windsurfing instructor, from South Africa, tanned and buff, with a gold Star of David swinging on a leather thong from his neck. He seemed to love working with Nathan. "Let the wind do it. Feel the wind push you up. Hug the wind. Become part of your sail. Don't push against the mast. Keep your knees bent. Gevolt, Nathan. Feel into the wind like a new lover." His South African accent sounded peculiar, especially when he lapsed into his few Yiddish words. He liked to press his body against Nathan, to illustrate what the wind should feel like.

"Don't you know it? Can't you tell that he's gay?" said Elsa, the Danish Yoga instructor, tall and tanned, her hair bleached almost white from the sun. Nathan was the only one in her afternoon class. "He thinks maybe you are gay too. Are you gay?"

"Give me a break. Not gay."

"Well, he likes the straight men. That's why no one likes him in town. I don't blame him. I like to seduce the straight men too."

She led him through an awkward performance of the morning salute to the sun. She obviously knew very little about yoga.

"How did you get here, to this Club Med?"

"I'm taking a break from my education."

"Studying what?"

"How do you say animal doctor? Veterinary. Yes. It's a long struggle of schoolwork, and too much stress."

"And how did you get here?"

"First I went to Greece, for my job. I chaperoned two carloads of brood sows, and three huge breeding boars." She spread her arms to show how big. "We were on the train together from Copenhagen to Athens. That was free transportation, plus a little stipend."

"That was a very long trip with pigs."

"I love pigs. These are very good ones. They are so smart. They go hwnnn hwnnn." She snorted and laughed. "And the boars have balls like melons." She raised her hands as if hefting them. "I fed them. I slept in the same car with them."

"You must have been happy to get off the train."

"They were happy too. It was over two weeks. We were quarantined for a week on the border. My pigs were so confused."

"Then how did you get here?"

"It's not a problem. The Mediterranean is a small ocean, on which the Phoenicians even figured it out.

They made boats, many small boats, and they float usually, and they go," she laughed. "Today you just have to look at the internet. You go to Club Med, and they they hire people, and I found this one here that needed yoga instructor, so I would come here to teach yoga. I found a Turkish boat that went to Bari, Brindisi, Cefalù."

"I hate to say this, but you don't seem to know much about yoga."

"In Copenhagen I took a class, and I have a book. Nobody cares. I am a blonde." She flipped her hair dramatically, and laughed.

"So now do you miss the pigs?"

"Of course not, except I miss their balls. I like the pigs."

A swarthy youth slipped into the doorway, scowling. He looked small and dangerous. "Baldassare," she said. "Avanti. Come in."

The young Sicilian didn't seem very happy to be introduced to Nathan. He brushed by him, and hooked an arm around Elsa's waist. She patted the top of his head, which hardly cleared her chin. "The class is over, Nathan. I have to go with Baldy. I'll see you maybe tomorrow, or the next day for another lesson." She winked at him, and her young man friend set his jaw, and growled, "Arrivederci. Piacere." He didn't shake Nathan's hand.

At the pool the manager came over to inquire about how Nathan was doing. "This used to be the place, Mr.

Briggs, for the pleasures of single people, to meet someone, to have a good time with someone new. I come from Trieste, and I used to enjoy those adventures, to work for Club Med. But I guess everyone gets older, more conservative, we slow down. Even myself, so I enjoy now the warm weather anyway, but things have changed at Club Med. Now they still come from all over Europe, and America too, but with their husbands and wives. They bring children, maybe because of the AIDS, other sickness. Sexy is not so free. When I first worked there were never children. This was once a so great a place for the single crowd, and people were very sexier. Times have changed, and now we have to accommodate with daycare and nursery, so the parents can relax. You are maybe fifteen years too late, but I hope we offer something here to make you happy."

It was relaxing, at any rate, a place to forget your bad dreams, forget your work, forget Saffron, forget Miriam, forget the tech, the clients, the market—these glitz-wells of oblivion, the same tropical fantasy everywhere on the planet. Bali, The Barbados, Cancun, Dominica, places middle-class could go to get out of the great cities to forget the pressures of the great cities. Without the ability to forget a human is heavy as a saturated sponge, unable to move. Forget Sicily, forget Messina, forget the Antonello whoever, his father's dreary obsession, everything dreary in Messina, where his mind suddenly lit with the obvious truth, that this was where his father's painter came from. It hadn't been real to him before. Da Messina, from Messina! Then the gorgeous blue he saw around the virgin in Palermo, her shawl. Who had ever painted blue that calm and startling? And the recognition that Antonello was from Messina, which was a real place where he stayed in a real hotel, that made him somewhat more real for Nathan, therefore more possible to forget. And totally forget Messina, that dreary, sad city, wasted by earthquakes. Antonello not even from Palermo. Forget Palermo, but it was at least a city of some hidden charms, cautious attractions, embedded in a long tradition of murder, and with that painting of the young Mary…forget Mary in her powerful ambivalence…but he couldn't forget blue blue cloth draping her as she was posed, maybe warning Gabriel off with her extended hand, or reluctantly offering her heavy assignment to the world; Mary who didn't look like Saffron, but made him think of her, (imagine Saffron getting the news from the archangel, Gabriel; like that's dope but let's like wait a second, like first we have to revirginize), and not like Miriam either, but something about them reminded him, her thoughts were thoughts he imagined…forget about it. How did a painter paint some thoughts. Forget about this.

"Beginner's wind this afternoon, Mr. Briggs," Moss knocked on his door, perhaps hoping he would open up, though not pushy, his caution suggesting bad experiences. Cautious as himself dodging rejection by Saffron. Forget about it.

"Thanks. I'm doing the scuba class at two."

He emerged from his room in the afternoon, and put himself in the hands of Jackie from the Canary Islands, a dark, masculine woman, competent with the equipment, who started to teach him to breathe through a snorkel, which he'd never done before, and he loved this immediately, watching the flow of creatures along the cliffs, shining schools that wound through the sunken boats and heaps of scrap that served as an artificial reef, all the bright fish, the eels hidden in their niches, the rays and sand sharks, the squid fleeing in clouds of ink, strange bottom feeders burrowing into the sand; under water and weightless, he easily could forget. Forget what? He couldn't remember. Himself!

At the next lesson, in a couple of days, she told him, she would introduce him to the scuba equipment. But tomorrow was her day off, and she was going to visit Corleone with her friend, Silvio, who came from there. She was excited because Corleone was where, for a long time, the guts of the Mafia was settled, the home of Tito Riina. Jackie was a photographer, an admirer of the great Letizia Battaglia, she explained, who had taken the photograph of Andreotti and Riina together that had destroyed Andreotti and the government. She had tried many times to meet the Palmeritana photographer and councilwoman who was her hero, but no success.

The woman understandably guarded her privacy. Jackie had her own agenda for being in Sicily, to photograph poverty. To help keep the world from forgetting these people, she explained. Forget about that, thought Nathan. Photographs were a license to forget. He would learn the equipment first in the pool, she said. He would enjoy it, staying down for twenty minutes at a time. Forget the pool, Nathan thought. Forget down.

In this way his first days at the Club Med moved slowly—minute, minute, minute, hour, hour. It was total luxury, this empty time. He hardly knew where he was any more, and didn't care. The town of Cefalù seemed far away in a distant place called Sicily. Its cliff, its houses, its cathedral, its public beach stippled with tiny people, the lungomare flanked by restaurants lit at night, some dim music carried on the wind; the whole place seemed cut out of cardboard against the sky, a fantasy of Sicily, dreamed up as a show for the clients of Club Med, whose money paid to keep them luxuriating in a South Pacific fantasy residence no matter where they really were.

This day was mild, the sea calm. He loved to swim in the ocean, something he and Miriam did together at Brighton Beach, at Robert Moses Park off Fire Island, his stroke a little stronger than hers, though she was a better athlete. He guessed it was about a mile and a half to the town, not far, particularly if he borrowed some fins and a snorkel and explored his way over. The water felt good, as if he was swimming downhill, the clean wake he made cleaving the taut surface of the swell. Weightlessness felt good, because this trip so far had been weighted maybe too much with emotions and confusion. Maybe it had been a mistake to decide to do this at all. Forget about it anyway. He was like flying. He wished Miriam could be flying beside him.

When he reached the esplanade he pulled himself out of the water, and walked towards town, jumping from shadow to shadow, to keep his feet off the hot pavement. He'd brought no money, couldn't sit at a caffé with the other tourists before he swam back, so he settled on a hot stone bench and watched the bathers on the public beach—a salt and pepper of fair-haired northerners, darker Sicilians. From here the Club Med was curiously inconspicuous, not even its thatched cottages identifiable. A huge warship, aircraft carrier probably, with its complement of cruisers and destroyers, was passing to the west through the straits of Messina, a reminder of the grim world outside Club Med, grey USA ghosts in the afternoon sun. Destroyer, Nathan thought, what a word for a beautiful floating world. I am the Destroyer. I am the Cruiser, okay! I am the Carrier. Watch your back.

That evening he asked Elsa if she wanted to go to town with him for dinner, to get away from the precious isolation of the club, but her own Baldassare was supposed to come for her after seven. She told Nathan that her Baldy was a load of jealousy and potentially dangerous, and smiled as if she enjoyed that about him. Moss would always be glad to go, she jabbed him with her elbow. Or maybe Jackie, if she got back from Corleone with her rolls of exposed film, or she'd told Kate, the older Australian woman in charge of daycare, about Nathan, and she'd jump at the chance to have a meal with a grown-up. In just these few days, Nathan mused, he'd penetrated the social structure of these Club Med employees; not so strange, since it was their job to make him comfortable. He was alone, and they too were temporary on this island of dark people, reserved and courteous, not so welcoming, a people made cautious by too many years under the heel of the mafia, who had known for too long how easily the murderer steps from behind the politest mask—a knife in the ribs, a pistol at the nape of the neck, a spray of lead from an automatic rifle, into your crowd.

Alone he strolled the esplanade with the rest of the people, local youth, tourists, a pack of sailors in their ribboned hats, all taking their passegiata in the balmy air of the straits. This was nice. It was sweet and melancholy to be alone here. Ships in the distance strung with lights passed silently under a crescent moon, and closer to shore the lanterns of some small boats nightfishing bobbed on the waves. He hummed to himself, "Suzanne takes you down…" Leonard Cohen understood the heart of the solitary man.

The restaurant he chose was a golden room, well lit, spacious, with yellow chairs and tablecloths. It was noisy, packed with people. Large round tables in the center held a festive group, people jumping seats and visiting around the tables. They leaned out over the table to pour wine and lifted glasses to celebrate—a toast a toast. Nathan hadn't seen people this loose since he arrived in Sicily. Women dressed like schoolteachers strutted and teased. Men stood up as if to dance with them, then reeled around, red-faced and drunk. Whoaa! A woman jumped onto the table. Whoaa! They lifted her off to peals of laughter. The host seated Nathan at a small table against the wall. In Italy a man alone was often to be pitied. Solitude was rarely a preference. So the owner spent a good deal of time explaining how good the tagliatelle with ricci was, sea urchins and pasta, but an antipasto first of Sicilian sausage, and roasted peppers with marinated vongole and datteri (delicious), still in their shells, and then they had the spigola, caught that morning, and would sauté lightly in oil, with a bit of butter, rosemary, dry Marsala, that he served with cous-cous, because he was from a small village near Trapani, where cous-cous, not pasta, was the specialty, made with pine nuts, white pepper, and garlic. You don't have to go to Libya for cous-cous, he told Nathan, patting his cheeks. It was better in Sicily. This was the friendliest anyone had been since he'd come to the island. Perhaps it was the general festivity, the good humor in the room, this happy crowd.

The host excused himself to greet a group of young women milling in the doorway, their backpacks clutched to their bellies. One of these was Saffron. Her hair had become pink suddenly. Saffron. He slumped in his chair to hide. What he wanted really to do was to jump up and greet her. He didn't dare. He'd be shot down. He'd almost forgotten that he'd come here, all the way to Sicily, just to intercept her, just to tell her. What? He couldn't make any sense of it now. Why had he followed her? What did he have to say to her? And what was her bunch doing in this obscure little town? Not here to visit the Club Med, surely. The host seated them at the opposite corner of the great room, so he had to look through the tumult to see her, a flash of pink in the ruckus. He changed seats to allow himself to watch more comfortably. This was unmistakably Saffron through the clamor of faces and gestures and hair, of friendly shouts and lifted wine-glasses.

Nathan sipped from his *quarto* of red. The house wine came from one of the local Corvo vineyards, a wine he had frequently drunk with Miriam in New York, a decent cheap bottle, white or red. As he sucked up some tagliatelle with with the orange sea urchin tangled into it, he watched across the room for flashes of pink. Maybe at the end of the meal he would present himself to Saffron and her classmates. If she wasn't happy to see him it might be weird, but that would be okay.

Why wouldn't she be flattered? It seemed like centuries, but it had been little more than a week since they'd been together in Manfredonia. So close together then, so separated now. She probably needed more time before she would be happy to see him. He wasn't even clear about how he felt. How would he handle it if she was indifferent, or worse, embarrassed to see him? She could be totally pissed off. So what? Fuck her. This obsessing to guess her reaction made him giggle nervously over the cous-cous, which was delicious, and the spigola, that looked and tasted like sea bass, and the bitter greens. All these tastes, and the flashes of pink. He tried to listen to himself swallow and breathe in order to drown out the clamor of this bunch that decibeled the room with its conviviality. And he thought that on top of this he could smell the lime and gypsum that he knew was Saffronski.

"*Che umanità,*" said the host, coming by his table again, to check his food. "*Che piacere, che festa, che fortuna ch'abbiamo noi d'essere qui in questi momenti.* A party. A party." He placed a basket of sweet flaky crusts on the table. "*Crespelle. Fatto casalinga. Assagiare, godere, senza problemi. Stasera, non ce ne sono, problemi. Vero, signore?*"

Before Nathan could answer, the tone of a fork against a glass reverberated in the room like a cathedral gong. Everyone fell into silence. Then, as if they were one person, everyone at the large tables stood up. This silence was louder than the noise that had preceded it.

At the next strike of fork on glass, they all began to sing. It was as if some catalyst had dropped into the clamor to crystallize a sound so clear and pure, orderly harmonies so one would think that perfect bells were struck. The sound resonated deep into Nathan's breathing, and he felt tears well up. This clarity so sudden and spontaneous was baffling, the harmonies heart-rending. They lifted a boy in red socks up onto a table to solo, and he sent his voice, like a flyline out over a stream, high and vibratoless, whipping a story across the room. From what Nathan could make out, it was about a girl who goes down to the water to wash her clothes and meet her lover, and there was an embrace and a kiss, and there was someone else, jealousy, violence, blood, and then a melancholy resolution, with the chorus in tragic harmony. He would go over, no matter what, and present himself to Saffron. His heart was full, overflowed with this gift of clarity. He wanted to share with her the sudden crystallization into song of a place filled with nearly intolerable noise. How could this happen, Saffron? This was so great, an occasion for them both to be happy, together. The chorus filed out of the restaurant, singing another song onto the lungomare, a few paces down the esplanade, around the corner, heading for their bus. Now the restaurant was empty, and quiet. Nathan looked across the room, and the girls weren't there.

"They come from Como," the host explained as

Nathan paid the bill. "The Como in Sicily, not from up there." He waved his arm towards the North. "A very great chorus, world famous."

Had Saffron Denes and her friends really been there, or had he just imagined them? Would they leave in the middle of a famous chorus? Nathan rushed out onto the esplanade, and didn't see them in either direction. Remnants of the tourist crowd strolled into the hot wind, but no Saffron. A storm had begun to roll across from Africa, the sirocco, large drops of rain full of sand, that hit and stung like wasps. It drove the remaining people into their hotels. Nathan stopped at discos on the way back to the hotel, hoping to find Saffron at one. They were dismal scenes, each with its few local lotharios, looking out from the back of the bar as he entered, to see if this time it was fresh female meat. Maybe he'd hallucinated Saffron. Until the restaurant he'd almost put her out of his mind. Perhaps she'd come through as a waking dream, to remind him of why he had come to Sicily.

People had moved into the other half of his duplex cottage, and he heard them arguing, perhaps in Dutch, as they tried to settle a screaming child, frightened by the thunder and lightning, and the strange bed. Nathan bucked the wind to find the bar, out near the pool. The surface of the pool frothed in the bar lights as if someone was shaking shampoo in a pan.

A few couples danced inside to the odd quartet of concertina, trumpet, clarinet, and bass, and a mechanical beat played by the drum feature on an unmanned keyboard.

"Will you dance with me, mister?"

Elsa surprised him, coming from behind. He turned, and her arms were spread to receive his lead. She was exactly his size. "Where's your jealous man? Bor…? Bell…?"

"Baldassare. Baldassare is with his mamma."

They turned onto the dance floor, and she pressed very close to him, though the beat was Latin. He felt all of her body through her thin dress. The lightning threw their shadows over the musicians and up the walls. This felt like some noir movie, his own Casablanca of shadowy fate.

"Have you met his mamma?"

"No. Of course not. He has a *fidanzata*. His mother doesn't want to meet me. In her mind I am the *putana* at the Club Med, if she knows about me."

"And still, he is jealous?"

"Yes. He is very jealous."

She pressed even tighter against him as they danced into the shadows, and she tugged his hand up so his knuckles pushed into her breast. Lightning lit the corner they had entered.

"So, what will he do? Am I in danger?"

She pulled back, and looked at him. "Are you afraid? Danger? Such a little Baldassare?"

She leaned forward to kiss his cheek, and he looked around, spooked slightly. "I don't want…"

"Trouble, yes? Why did you come here, to Sicily?"

"I'm looking for a woman."

"If you look for a woman you should go to Denmark, not to Sicily. No trouble there." She pulled him close again. He liked the way their bodies fit together in the dance. He could feel the shape of her mound, rubbing on his thigh. Slow dancing, it was good.

"Then, have you found a woman?" She laughed in his ear, her breath warm. The concertina was playing solo, some melancholy tune. He'd heard it before.

"A girl, really. I followed her here, to Sicily, because she…I…."

"So you are a romantic man." She kissed him again, awkwardly catching his nose.

"I thought I saw her tonight, in a restaurant." Nathan remembered now, the tune on the concertina was the same as the one the chorus had sung.

"Well, where is she?"

"Then I lost her again. Maybe I just imagined it."

"Poor man, lost his girl." This time her kiss caught him full on the mouth. Her tongue flicked in for an instant, then she pressed her full open mouth against his lips. A roll of thunder drowned the music. Nathan pulled back.

"What?" She poked his chest with her fingertips. "You are frightened?"

"No…not. I don't want trouble."

"You are American?"

"Yes."

"Americans always make the trouble."

Nathan turned out of her arms, and then turned back to look at her. This was a few too many grappa. What she was doing confused him. The next lightning illuminated Moss, watching them from the bar. Everything was false in this melodrama of the Club Med.

"I don't like Americans," she said, wrinkling her nose, and snorting. "They are pigs."

"But you told me you like your pigs."

"Yes. My pigs. I love my pigs." She kissed him on the cheek again, and lightly stroked his crotch.

Yes, too many drinks, Nathan thought. Affections of the bottle. They were separated now. The moment had passed. The music stopped. They stopped dancing.

"After this storm, tomorrow the wind will be good," said Moss, in passing. "I'll see you for a lesson."

When Nathan turned, Elsa was gone. He slugged down a grappa and went back to his cottage. The storm had passed, some thunderheads riding over the mainland, occasional distant thunder. His room was quiet now, and he crawled between his sheets, hoping that perhaps he'd have some luck, and Elsa would knock on his door.

On the next morning he was up early, and he left for town before the Club Med activities began. He parked by the beach and strolled into the town, up the hill to the Piazza Duomo, dominated by broad-shouldered Norman cathedral. The place was attractive, not what he'd anticipated. Its strength made his faux South Pacific accommodations seem silly. He settled for the morning at a caffe with some coffee, and pastries, and watched the few shopkeepers raise their shutters, and the light traffic of people going to work. Shades of light nuanced pastels across the white stones of the cathedral. When the cathedral opened, he went in and was astounded by the powerful mosaic that glowed in the apse, as if it had been put there yesterday. He had no idea this was here. He was a tourist only accidentally. From a pew he watched as other tourists payed ten thousand lire for a young man to turn on some incandescent lights. Nathan preferred this image of the saviour of the world to glow itself in the dimmer natural light.

He followed other tourists down a narrow street opposite the cathedral, and into a small museum set up in an old palace, The Mandralisco Museum. He'd had no idea either that this was here. Because the Count Mandralisco had been an oceanographer and an early ocean ecologist, several rooms of the small museum were taken up by his seashell collection. In the other rooms were

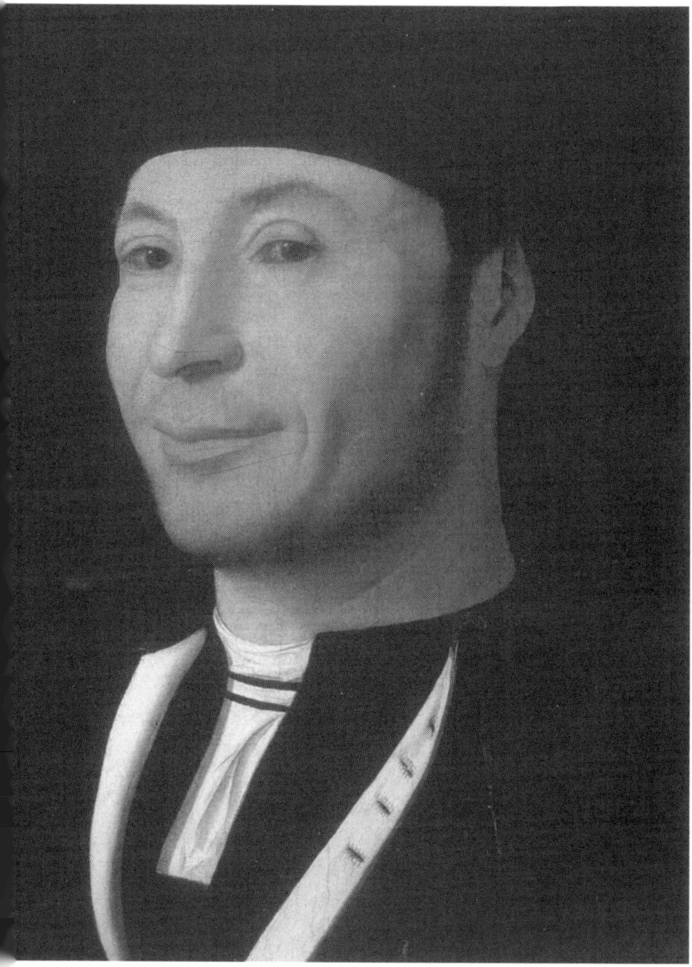

some paintings, and at the very last, backlit in its own room, in its own glass case, protected by electronic warning devices to prevent people from approaching too closely, was one small portrait, surrounded, when Nathan arrived at it, by a group of young women, one of them definitely Saffron of the pink hair.

He turned once, as if to escape, but then turned again. She surprised him totally by exclaiming when she saw him, "Mr. Briggs!" She jumped out from among her friends, and came towards him, holding out her hand for him to shake. Her classmates stayed back in a tight group, and watched them. "I'm so glad you got here. Isn't he just like the best? This is so totally excellent, one little portrait like the whole world. Is he sinister, or what?" She touched his elbow to urge him closer to the portrait. "He's definitely the man I love."

"Who is he?" Nathan asked, meaning the man in the portrait.

"He's such a great painter. It's Antonello, silly. He's the most sublime of all of them, Raffaello, anybody, Fra Angelico. They call this his portrait of the unknown sailor, but we're clueless who the dude is."

"Remember me," said a voice Nathan dimly heard.

"Your father was a most mental dude, to like pick out Antonello," she said. "Look how friendly and fierce this one is. Does he trust anyone? What's he got figured out about me? Does he trust you? It's so genius, Mr.

Briggs."

"Remember me," again.

"Come on, Saffron. We're going." Her friends had started out the door.

"Got to go, Briggs." She kissed her fingers and touched his face. "Tomorrow we fly to Frankfurt, and then home. I'll see you next time, Briggs. Watch out for bats. Watch out for goats."

She had been not embarrassed at all, even nice to him, though her classmates must have known who he was, and what had gone on. He turned automatically, and almost started after her.

"Remember me," he heard again, louder. He turned back to the painting. Had the painting said something? No one else was in the room now. It looked like someone he knew, or had seen before, perhaps just the other day.

"Remember!"

"What?"

There was a silence, and then, "Remember!"

Was it a voice, or his own mind he was hearing? Yes, that face was someone he had recently seen. Elsa's jealous friend, maybe. Yes, Elsa's Baldassare. Everything took its own place eventually.

"Remember me."

Shut up! Yes, he recognized that face, but even more unnerving was the way the face looked at him, had scoped all his weaknesses, could anticipate all his petty moves. This was a portrait that knew more about the observer, than he could surmise about the subject portrayed. Yes.

"Remember," whispered again.

"Yes. Okay I'm ready now. I'm back on my way now."

CHURCH MOTHER

CHURCH MOTHER

From Lecce Solomon phoned Isabel at the Mestre studio. She was happy to hear his voice. So excited to have missed her second period, and so sure she was pregnant now. Her work was going well, even with morning sickness, for which she had absolutely no time. She wanted to see him soon, said she needed him with her as the child grew in her womb. Her voice was ebullient, and almost innocent. He hardly ever heard that from her, not even when she talked about her new work. She wanted him there to feel it start to move, to kick inside her belly. This enthusiasm was disorienting. He was conditioned to her cynicism, and her patent indifference to himself, and he missed it, in a way. The name of Iera flashed on and off in his mind as she spoke. Isabel definitely wanted him to see the new work. She told him Mario had heard from his family that Iera, his sister, had fallen in love with him. Isabel loved him too, she told him. He never remembered her saying that before, and she joked that she'd be willing to surrender him to Mario's sister, as long as he'd vow to behave as father to their child. It was a girl, she insisted. That was what it felt like, and she wanted to call their daughter Isabel, Jr.

The merry mood of Isabel Brightwatch lightened his own spirit. Now she liked him better, now she wanted him more, now that he'd been gone. The dance of absence making the heart grow? He thought of Iera. He didn't expect Isabel's delight to last, but enjoyed the glow; in fact, the idea that she might actually need him now sent some tiny moths of ambivalence fluttering through his heart. Did he really want this? Yes, he absolutely loved the idea of being a father. No, he wasn't sure he wanted to go into this parent assignment coupled with Isabel. Yes, he did have feelings about Isabel. Iera kissed his mind. No, he didn't trust Isabel's feelings about himself. As much as you love the art, you should never trust the artist.

Nonetheless, the prospect of fatherhood put him into a great mood about the world, and the future of everything. The idea that Isabel thought about him as her man was like some vitamins, a nourishment that gave him a sense of freedom, and he saw a whole new array of options open in front of himself. It was strange. They were the same options, really; but freshly polished to his advantage. You'd think he would feel trapped, he told himself; but even now Iera was added to the possibilities, and without conflict. He was ready to bet now that at his next stop something clear about Antonello would illuminate, a bright gift; that somewhere in Galatina, a tiny, unheralded town in the heel of the boot, somewhere in the archives something would be there, though the name of his painter was never associated with this place. But Iera had told him of Galatina, and the festival of Peter and Paul, and the mysterious *tarantati* receiving grace and relief. Aldo, the coach driver, had mentioned it too, the bite of the tarantula, the source of the tarantella. The history of the town went at least back to the Greeks, and the sublimity of Antonello's portraits and his figures was something ancient Greek, with a difference, however; that the beauty wasn't just to be admired for its sublimity, but to be engaged as a path to your own.

It took him all day to get there, though Galatina was only twenty kilometers south of Lecce. He couldn't muscle his way onto the first bus, through many determined women in black, with children on their hips, and the small, wiry men with skin like leather stretched on bone, hauling sacks of greens, and zucchini flowers, and live chickens, ducks, guinea hens, and boxes of dry goods they loaded on top of the bus, a pair of peacocks in a straw basket, and casks of oil, and wine, and vinegar, ready to sell on the market day for the festival of Peter and Paul. He loved the mix of festivities and business, but for the second bus everyone else was more festive and more businesslike than he, and more determined to get on, and it was almost a dance, when he got a leg up on the first step, got a whiff of the interior of the bus, like a poultry yard, then felt himself yanked back, a tiny man setting him down on the pavement, and apologizing and pushing him away, and jumping aboard himself, pointing at his goods on the roof as an excuse for manhandling him, and others drove him back in the line, though he was bigger, a head taller than most of them; but they were poor people, and setting themselves up for this bit of income figured big in their survival.

A heavy-set man, in a dark, grease-stained suit, standing behind a large refrigerator carton, waved at Solomon to come over. His eyes were narrow, and mistrustful, hands pudgy and strong. He had sunglasses for sale, arranged neatly in rows on a tray on the carton. "Don't worry," he told Solomon, as he shifted a black rope of a cigar between his stained lips. He placed a pair of the glasses on Solomon's face. "Makes you look like La Dolce Vita," he said. He explained that he too had missed the bus, and that Solomon should follow him and take the bus to Otranto, which wouldn't be crowded, and from there they could catch another that took a roundabout route through Calimera, Gallipoli, and Galatone, and finally ended up in Galatina. He sold Solomon the sunglasses, and some cream for sunburn, and as the bus pulled out Solomon noted the man with his cartons still standing by the curb.

The wait was five hours in Otranto, a small harbor with buildings of white stone, quiet as a ruin, that seemed devoid of population despite its gorgeous waterfront, and the fine Norman cathedral behind a wall on the cliff. Solomon had a lunch of spaghetti with mussels, and a fry of tiny fish sprinkled with lemon, at an empty trattoria near the wharf, then he strolled along the seawall, and sat for several hours to gaze out over the green Adriatic. Poor Albania was listing just beyond the horizon.

He often tried to see everything through Antonello's eyes. That was how he benefited from being close to these paintings. The face of the one who sold him sunglasses, who sent him to Otranto, was from the family of faces of the portrait he had visited in Torino, slightly mistrustful, unassailable, ready to thwart your next gambit, ready to seize his opportunity, slightly unshaven, jowly, irascible. But the man of the Torino portrait must have had great social standing, a judge, a notary, a big merchant, owner of a fleet of swift sailing ships, ready to defend himself against any stupidity. He wasn't so oily as his brother at the bus stop in Lecce, certainly didn't sell sunglasses off a cardboard box. The portrait perhaps was some rich ancient uncle of Mr. Sunglasses. Gulls lifted desultorily from the stones near the seawall, and settled back down. A man rose from where he had been squatting to take a crap, near the ancient watchtower, and he waved at Solomon.

Each portrait he ever saw by Antonello was a rush, a sudden stab of clarity. The paintings offered themselves as confrontation and negotiation. They were the opposite of stereotype and caricature, and their function wasn't to tell a story about the subjects, but to encourage a negotiaton between the viewer and subject. There was a florescence in them of all the richness and ambiguities of character. It could be so complex, and yet absolutely clear. That clarity kept Solomon loyal to Antonello, a crystalline humanity, as in no other painter he knew of. Maybe Vermeer, in his own place. After going through everything you have to do to see some of the paintings—get to the city, find hotel, find transportation, find museum, find curator to get permission if the work isn't hanging, passing tons of mediocre works in miles of galleries—you were always rewarded in the end by this experience of absolute clarity, you got to see the painting itself, the product of an undistracted, transcendant mind. Not even Giovanni Bellini, not even Rembrandt painted this way. Piero, Massaccio, Botticelli, Beato Angelico, Raffaello, all were telling stories, however beautifully; they were interpreting character for you. No one but Antonello actually flat out presented the total human being, with whom you were drawn irresistibly into a dialogue, and had to be perfectly yourself. In other words, he thought, every other painter gave you an interpretation of the "other," but Antonello took it further, and if you truly engaged with his portraits, you had to admit that you, yourself were the "other," as the portrait gazed out at you, estimating you in all your ambivalence and weakness. This was a great step out into the knowledge of what was human, acknowledgement of the self as the "other." It felt like a secular spirituality.

For him this was the epitome of the humane, the best of the experiment that was western culture. In no other art that he knew of, from no other culture, did artists attempt to, have the freedom to, define the human being so completely in his, in her space, physical, psychological, spiritual. Here it is, the human being, at its highest, at its lowest, with all its potential, its successes, its failure. He looked South. Somewhere in the mists south on the Adriatic, was Greece. Not so far, when you think of it. And below that, the orient. In every other culture, and even in early Christianity, art was used to illustrate doctrine, and lessons of mystery and dogma, and lives of saints, all through narrative, in which the figures are cyphers, like pieces on a game board. But here, somehow despite the influence of the church, (or maybe inadvertently because of the influence of the church) humanity had sidled itself into the foreground, like a secular upsurge, and Antonello was at the apex of that manifestation. There was so little of his work left, ruined by weather, crumbled, buried by earthquakes. That was why he had to find the St. Francis. To retrieve some lost works, to raise Antonello into the light again, would be to raise the spirit, to polish the soul of all humanity. Islam and his own Jewish heritage prohibited these graven images. But this was a human, not a religious quest, a post holocaust retrieval of the humane. On the other hand, maybe the focus on the human story in itself had never been a good thing? It might have been a mistake from the start, misunderstanding of what really are human capacities; perhaps sowing the seeds of cruelty, brutality, bestiality, even genocide. Perhaps populations are better off locked in doctrine, ruled by those who claim to know, who warrant only tradition and dogma. But not so! Look at Antonello's portraits, look even at his religious scenarios, and figure it out for yourself, Solomon Briggs reassured himself.

Dusk lay on Galatina by the time he finally arrived, everything behind a veil of dim radiance, a residue the sun had left in the stone. The bus emptied at one end of an oval park, neglected, full of litter, with a few sickly umbrellone pines, some benches splintered, the sandy garden spaces overgrown with weeds. A market was set to open in the morning. Under awnings stretched from their donkey carts, their three-wheeled scooter trucks, their bicycle carts, and hand wagons, merchants were camped in anticipation. Small fires lit around the park cooked the evening meals—a little pasta, a few greens. Solomon strolled the length of the park, to where it fed into the Piazza San Pietro. There the baroque facade of the Chiesa Matrice, elevated by the few steps up to its vestibule, spread its legs, dark doors closed. A few last photons of the dusk glowed on the stone. He climbed the few steps, as if something had invited him in. From there the park seemed a gathering of gypsies. Across the piazzetta was a small chapel, and the street beyond funneled into darkness. He knocked at the door on the left, expecting no response, and was surprised when on the right a door opened, and a robed figure gestured for him to come over. That he was bent by some deformation of the spine made him look older than his face showed him to be up close. With a quick, sideways jab of his chin the young sacristan asked Solomon what he wanted. Solomon looked behind him, into the church, a vast space of arches and domes, sparsely furnished naves and a few rows of pews, the whole confusing orderly layout of a big cathedral.

"*Ma, che vuoi, signore?*" The sacristan's voice was a surprisingly deep growl. He looked barely five feet tall, but was so bent so that if he could straighten up he might be a foot taller. To talk he had to twist his neck painfully, and look up, and even then he could address only to Solomon's chest. "*Allora, dimmi, signore, che vuoi?* What you want?" The English was a surprise.

Solomon explained as best he could that he had come to look for the painting of St. Francis, by Antonello, and was exploring as many archives as he could enter, wherever he went. The sacristan punctuated Solomon's explanation with "*Si, si, si,*" as if he understood, and had frequent visitors on such a quest.

"*Domani, venire, signore.* Tomorrow," he growled. "*Domani, presto la mattina, gli tarantolati ballano, ballano,*

ballano, gridare. Dance, scream. You be in the church, signore. Better for you. Safe in the church. *Tarantati, maladetti. E di la, signore."* He pushed on Solomon's hip to turn him to look across the piazza, pointing diagonally across the piazza at the small chapel. *"Cappela San Paolo. Sconsecrato. Sconsecrato, signore.* Deconsecrated. *Fuori chiesa.* Outside church. Not for God."

"Not for God," Solomon repeated. How did he know even a little English? Maybe he'd learned it from G.I.'s. During the war, American troops were billeted in all these towns. That was a war he might have fought in willingly. He would have left some American language behind, in these towns.

"These Tarantati, what are they?"

"Vieni domani, signore. You come. Better to come this church, consecrated San Pietro. And then I will show you the picture."

"Which picture?"

"You want the picture, no? The St. Francis picture. We have this one. Come tomorrow."

"What do you mean you have this?"

"On the wall of the chapel, yes."

"By Antonello?"

"Si. Yes, *signore.* San Francesco. Big painting. *Domani.* You will see what it is. Tomorrow. Come tomorrow."

The young sacristan slid back into the darkness, like

a moray eel pulling back into its reef. He shut the church.

Solomon sat on the steps and stared into the evening. Stranger things had happened than the discovery of some masterpiece hanging in plain view, for years unacknowledged; in fact, Antonello's annunciation was just such a painting, for centuries hanging against a damp wall in the church in Pallazuolo, until some scholar, going through papers of the period discovered that such a painting had been commissioned once for the church, and then they found it there, two-thirds ruined, but there nonetheless, and obviously a great masterpiece. This could easily be such a find; well, not easily, but there was a chance this could be one. Who before himself would ever have come to this unlikely place to look, to ask about such a painting? No one else, not yet, obviously.

Two feeble street lamps lit the Piazza San Pietro. It was too late to return to Lecce. He would have to find a room for the night. Cooking fires still glowed in the park. Some music from portable radios. Kids ran around, squealing in the darkness. A few people of the town were out on a stroll before supper. It was usually close to midnight before you ate, in this part of Italy. He set out through the quiet streets, to find a hotel. The people he asked all shrugged, as if they had never heard of such a thing as an hotel in Galatina. They told him there were hotels in Lecce. This was a dark and quiet place. A tobacconist finally suggested a place he thought was a pensione, although maybe, he said solemnly, it was a whorehouse. At any rate, beds. He got there to find the rooms rented on a weekly basis, and for the festival of Pietro & Paolo everything was occupied. The couple that owned it had given up their own room, and were sleeping with relatives, and even the extra beds in the hallway were filled.

Solomon returned to the park to spend the night outside, with the merchants and their families. Some slept beneath their awnings or under their carts or on the benches. He found an empty bench with some slats missing, swept a circle clean of trash, rolled his jacket into a pillow, and lay down beside the bench. A mild wind brushed the tops of the umbrellone, and a radio squawked softly into silence from somewhere on the other side of the park. A few stars blurred through the humidity. He listened to a family arguing over there. They stopped. A bird sang into the night. What was it? He wished he knew his birds, by their songs. Was it a nightingale? What were the birds he knew? Of course, the robin, robin redbreast, the bluejay, the chickadee, the bald eagle, the golden eagle. Turkey vulture. He'd seen them. And the red-tailed hawk. He knew some birds. The tufted titmouse. English sparrow. Common tern. Ring-necked pheasant. Penguin is a bird. The emperor penguin. The ostrich, emu too. Gulls and cormorants and gannets and kittiwakes, all birds he knew. Many warblers many finches he'd seen. Baltimore oriole. Cardinal. How were they different, warblers and finches? Kingfisher, house wren, marsh hawk, pigeon, mourning dove, mockingbird. How many did he know? Chickens were birds, and ducks, mallards, muscovy, turkeys, swan. He was too excited to sleep. Junco. On the next day he might see the St. Francis; unlikely, but maybe. As close as he's gotten yet. Bluebird, kingfisher…he'd said that already. Woodpeckers, downy, hairy, red-headed, the flicker, nuthatch, all those birds. More birds than he knew he knew, each with its own language. The wicked small house wren, nasty hummingbirds, minute. What did St. Francis say to speak to all of them? Catbird and grouse and loon…

In the morning first a low vibration came, then it was as if an enormous bell dimly clanged above and was about to plunge down like a trap on him, and he was awake. A fanfare sounded somewhere in his mind, or on the piazza, a brass chorus took him to his feet. Here was dawn, a rosy light smeared the sky. Some of the vendors already were moving around their carts, lighting the fires again for chicory coffee. One woman pulled back the cover of her tray of religious artifacts, kitschy virgins in the shadows of dawn. She dusted them off, as her little girl squatted to piss under the table.

He walked slowly towards the church, towards the

squawk of a crudely bowed fiddle. In the brightening morning, it played for what looked like a great cauldron of bubbling tar. Women all in black stirred around the door of the deconsecrated chapel of Saint Paul. They rose like bubbles swelling, then collapsed into the arms of their companions. They jumped in an ecstasy of pain and delight, arms flung into the air. They spun and twisted, wracked by energies they couldn't control. The sounds, screams, and ululations, could have come out of North Africa. Solomon sat down to watch from the steps of the cathedral. A trap drum, a guitar, a squeezebox, joined to form a quartet with the fiddle, all grey-haired men. They played next to the door of the chapel, the music slowing, the pulse intensifying as the movement of the women intensifed, all abandoned to the rhythms, heaving and collapsing like one thing. Solomon felt very outside these mysteries, a cheat even to observe them. This was more ancient than the church itself, its sophistication and mystery beyond any ritual he knew. There were only a few other people like himself, dressed in ordinary clothes, looked like they'd been caught here by surprise, who remained watching from the perimeter. The music repeated and repeated like some sufi trance music, pulsing the women out of themselves, and into an ecstasy, a confusion of pain and joy. They screamed, ranted in tongues, sang over and over the same syllables. Solomon couldn't sit still in the pulsing. He closed his eyes, and swayed to his feet. One woman broke from the mass and ran screaming at the wall of the chapel as if she could penetrate stone with her voice. She clawed at the stones, climbing part way up the wall. Vendors in the park had all uncovered their wares, ready for commerce. The smoke from their cigarettes lay above their displays like gauze. How could anyone ignore this, to sell cheap cups? Some of the women threw themselves to the ground, and crawled towards the chapel door. Why only women? Except for the musicians, and a few companions who tried to keep them from hurting themselves, these were all women.

Iera had told him something about this, the Tarantati purging themselves of the consequences of the *"tristo evento,"* the sad event, the bite of the tarantula, imaginary, probably, rather than real. Here, at the festival of San Pietro & Paolo, they could cure themselves of lethargy, incoherence, uncontrollable movement, the symptoms of their affliction. Iera had said she never, never wanted this to happen to her, but it was not by choice, she told him. It was the bite of the tarantula.

The doors of the chapel slowly opened inward, and the musicians entered. Women threw themselves to the ground, and crawled on their backs, pulling themselves towards the chapel with their elbows, pushing with their heels, chanting in high-pitched gasps, but clear enough for Solomon to hear, *"L'amor è bello / e dio lo fa."* Others ran into the dark interior, yelping after the musicians, who never stopped playing, and now filled the small chapel with the pulse of the music. It wasn't his business. Whatever was there might tear him apart. But he couldn't keep from moving towards it. A woman moved to block his way.

"Signore, go away. There is nothing here for you. Go back. It is not good for you to watch these afflicted ones. This is no circus to perform for you."

It was difficult to break away, as if some suction had been dragging on his spirit, and he turned back toward Chiesa Matrice, and then he felt bereft, as if the loss was much greater than merely the frustrating of his curiousity. The air he tried to breathe felt too thick to take in.

The sacristan beckoned him from the vestibule. Solomon gestured back, asking him to wait. Something had milked down these tears. Was it in the music? The incessant minor keys? The pulse like a drum underground? Maybe it was just seeing these women, these *contadine*, who flaunted their pain, ceded their bodies to this ritual, to the belief that it could help them take control of their lives, to reverse the *"tristo evento"* that had made them fall into lethargy and madness. But everything about it wasn't bad. It allowed them to stop, actually released them for a while from a life that was little more than unrewarded labor, relentless work in the fields all day, then in the kitchen and laundry, to stifle the soul. The so-called affliction perhaps let them at least rest for its duration. So was it the bite of the tarantula that was the "sad event," or was it this rite that cured them of the spell that had at least given them a breather? Maybe the thrall of this ambiguity had drawn all these emotions out of him? The sacristan's beckoning became more insistent. The doors of the chapel had been closed, but the music still pulsed at his back, and pushed him to cross, to join the church man, bent as a shepherd's crook, standing in front of his church.

"*Che diavoli, signore.* Devils we see across from the holy church." He grabbed Solomon's forearm. "Never, never, never, you. You come into church. Chapel San Paolo, sconsecrato. Sconsecrato, povero signore." His hand gripped like a vise. "Deconsecrated," he roared, as if he would shrivel all the participants with his voice.

Solomon yanked his arm out of the grip in a gesture that seemed to threaten the little man, because he leaped back into a corner of the doorway, and looked out at Solomon like a cur that has too often been whipped. The fingers had bruised Solomon's arm. He turned back to the chapel where the rest of the women in black had formed a scab over the chapel door.

"No, signore. Please. In the church. Go in the church."

The urgency of what was happening outside dissipated when he reminded himself of why he was there. "The Antonello." Even evoking the name of the painter in the silence of his own mind could overwhelm anything else. It had become his purpose for everything, justification of anything. The sacristan held the door open for him, and urged Solomon into the church. A mass was in progress, and the pews were almost full. Solomon felt a thrill of anticipation, as if he was a child waking on Christmas morning. The man led Solomon to a seat far from the altar.

"You are American?" the sacristan whispered.

"Yes. American."

The sacristan scrutinized Solomon more closely, reached out and lightly touched his face. "My father, American."

"Really? American? From America?"

"During the war, my mamma, to feed her brothers, her sister…"

"Do you know your father?"

"John Kennedy," he laughed. "The Hemingway. The Bernard Berenson." That he even knew these names, especially Berenson's, surprised Solomon.

"And your name?" he asked.

Solomon told him, then asked for his. The man pulled a little notebook and pencil from under his robe, and printed GIAI GIAO. "How you say?"

"Ja Jow?" Solomon tried to pronounce it.

"No. GI Joe, you say."

"GI Joe. Okay, GI Joe," Solomon patted the humped

shoulder. An appropriate name, maybe. "Where is your mother, then?"

"No mother, just father American. Mother, tarantata."

"Where is she now?"

GI Joe motioned for Solomon to sit down. "Here you are safe. I come back after mass." The man shuffled quickly past the altar, and down some steps behind it. Solomon listened for a while to the liturgy, and watched the congregation, still as a pond under the nave. Sounds of the tarantati drifted from behind himself, and was dispersed by music of the organ and choir. This was an official high mass for the festival of Peter and Paul. But out there, he thought, were the people exercising the differences of their own understanding, people trying to heal themselves. Who can help the people? Those outside tried to take control of their lives, rather than give it up to the control of the church, rather than accept the helplessness, the mysteries the church dealt them. He rose from the bench, and not seeing GI Joe anywhere, went back to peek through the door across the piazzetta at the deconsecrated chapel. It all seemed arbitrary, faith on this side, or faith over there.

Some of the women had formed a line at its side that extended into an entryway to a courtyard. The doors to the chapel remained closed, but music still pulsed onto the pavement that widened into the piazza. He looked back in to the church, and saw no GI Joe, so he slipped out to check what the women were doing at the side of the chapel. On their knees they approached a small fountain there, an open pipe coming out through the hands of a faded fresco of St. Paul. Some had little cups in hand. Others sipped directly from the pipe. Some splashed water on their faces, on their feet. When they stood up and backed away they were smiling, and they gathered into small groups in quiet conversation. Solomon wondered where the water came from, how clean it was, as a woman approached him with a cup of what he was afraid she would insist he drink, which was exactly what she did. He felt too weak, out of his element; too much of when in Rome motivated him. Do what the Romans do.

"Bene, signore. Assiagi. Bevi." She extended the cup towards him. *"Ha sete, lo spirito tuo. Ci ne vediamo noi."* She pointed at her own eyes with thumb and forefinger, to indicate she saw his soul was thirsty. *"Si, si. Niente male. Il Santo beato, San Paolo, ci da quest'acqua benedetta per il guarigione. Buona, buonissima. Pulita. Grazia, signore. La grazia il santo beato ci da. Bevi, signore. Niente male. Fa male mai."* She put the grey ceramic cup to his lips so he felt its chips at the rim, and as she tilted it he couldn't but swallow some, slimy as eggwhite, a taste slightly alkaline. What saints had he swallowed? What devils were there in it?

He returned to the church, and sat in the pew, and

looked up into the vaulted ceiling at the frescoed angels and saints fading there. He tried to keep it down, but the taste of the water kept rising to coat his tongue. GI Joe watched him from the shadows. His body stood almost erect against a column. As soon as Solomon caught his eye he warped into his gargoyle shape, as if suddenly some fervor twisted him. The mass had ended and the church quickly emptied. Joe slowly approached. From his position sitting on the edge of the pew, Solomon had to look up at the little man, who reached over to run fingertips along Solomon's lips. He sniffed at his finger.

"You tasted, yes?"

"What?"

"The waters? Deconsecrated waters. Devil waters. Yes!" His eyes were narrowed.

"I, uhhh…" The taste lingered in his mouth.

"Ahh, *signore, hai fatto male.*" He shook his hand at Solomon. "Bad. Bad, you did. *Ma, niente paura.* Don't worry. Here you are in the church. All here is well." He swayed back and forth like a worshipper at the wailing wall.

"Now will you show me the paintings?" Solomon asked, uneasily. For some reason, everything seemed now less urgent.

"I will show you, yes. You will see everything."

He pulled on Solomon's arm to get him to rise, and then led him back outside. The sun had risen above the roofs to a startling brightness. They turned to look at the facade, and GI Joe began his explanations. *"Chiesa Matrice, or Chiesa Madre, come vuole.* Whichever you wish to call her. The facade late baroque, Leccese baroque, but church is much older. In architrave, central doorway San Pietro, San Giuseppe, statues. Left doorway, San Sebastiano.

Saint Sebastian caught Solomon's attention because of the astounding Antonello painting in the Gemaldliche museum, in Dresden, where he visited, just to have a taste of that one masterpiece, saved from the firestorm caused by the pounding smother of allied bombs, the destruction still evident, and he felt like he had to push through vestiges of that barbaric war, through his discomfort at being in someplace German, to savor this vision of the martyr tied to a column, body pierced by arrows, cylinders of architecture and columns, figure of a fallen man, foreshortened, as in Mantegna, women on the parapet indifferent to the suffering, one broken column foreshortened, yes.

"And on the right, San Marco. The church built of Leccese stone, very soft."

Across the square the door of the chapel had opened, and the women were leaving slowly, everyone quiet now. The fiddler was at the doorway, with his instrument under his arm, bending over to tie his shoe. When he straightened up a woman embraced and kissed him. Solomon watched them as they disappeared like ravens hopping then taking flight down the narrowing street, or dispersed among the vendors in the park. It was a very harsh sun, a very blue sky. Later he would close his eyes to remember how blue the sky was above easy commerce of this field of folks.

Joe pulled on his arm. *"Dentro, adesso, signore. La Chiesa Madre.* Come."

He followed Joe inside again, and stood at the doorway to let his eyes adjust to the dark interior. Joe gestured that he should dip and genuflect. Solomon had to fake it. He had never done it before, was sure he screwed it up, started at the bottom.

Joe pointed up at the frescoes. "By Vincenzo Paliotti, Neapolitan, settecento; and now, over there, we go to the Capellone del Sacramento, built 1664 - 1675, by the archbishop of Otranto, in the time of Monsignore Adarzo de Santander. Look on the right, is an altar and statue of the Immaculata in white marble, by Giuseppe Sammartini." Joe led Solomon around, jumping at random from place to place, rushing across the floor as if inspired to show the next thing. "Here is the washing of the feet. Magdalen. Jesu. A canvas by Serafino Elmo, Napoletano him too, 1756."

How boring these were, these endless competent, uninspired pictures of saints and religious narrative. He agreed with La Piumina about the saints. "Joe, the Antonello, the Saint Francis, take me to that, please."

"Just a second. Patience, *compagno mio.* Let me ask

you this. Who painted the frescoes above in the vault. Who was it, *signore Americano?*"

"I don't know. You said, but I don't remember. Why should I know that?"

"You must know everything, *comandante.* Otherwise I tell you these things, and it's like putting water into a *colino.* How you say? Colander. Now the left nave is La Madonna del Rosario…"

Solomon was going through his familiar premonitions of disappointment. He knew it was absurd to think the church would have such an important Antonello hanging somewhere, and not know of it, even with the Palazzuollo Annunciation to the contrary. It was true that since Antonello was a Sicilian, his work could more likely be ignored. From Solomon's perspective its importance had surely been passed over, history hanging the tag on him of being responsible for bringing Flemish techniques into Italy, as if after saying that you could ignore his real accomplishment, the more resonant implications of his vision. Even so, it would be hidden somewhere, buried in an archive, but not in the nave of a church, even an obscure church.

"…and there is the Crucifixion of San Pietro, second half of settecento, by Pietro Picca of Galatina, from here, this little town, although he was also active in Galatone. And look into there, on the walls of the choir, there on the left is the Holy Family, and on the right, the keys-giving to San Pietro, Neapolitan school, yes."

Solomon felt strange, his eyelids heavy, almost asleep on his feet. The taste of that water was still in his mouth, and he heard the music in the back of his brain, and it made him sway and shift his feet.

"So who, signore, please, painted the Crucifixion of San Pietro?"

"Picca, Picca, Lorenzo Picca…" Solomon answered, as if he was a student looking for a gold star.

"Pietro, signore. Pietro Picca. But you are doing better to learn. Now look." He turned Solomon to the opposite wall.

"What?"

"San Francesco, signore. Here is St. Francis."

Solomon opened his eyes to a huge, dark painting of Saint Francis on his knees, palms out, receiving stigmata. It was vulgar and melodramatic, and it made Solomon shudder to look at it. He walked away.

"Signore…"

Down a few steps behind the altar, Solomon noticed a small door. The sacristan came up beside him, and took his elbow. "What?"

"Where does this go?"

"It goes down, signore."

"Down where? Is it a crypt? Does it go to the archive?"

"Si, signore. To the archive. You go?" He rattled the ring of keys tied to his rope belt.

"Tomorrow. Maybe tomorrow. Thank you so much

for showing me. I am very tired now. Is this all right, if I come tomorrow?"

"As you wish, signore. It will be here tomorrow. It was always here. After the church is gone, it will be here."

"What do you mean?"

"I mean it is fine you come tomorrow."

"I can go through the archives?"

"Why not, signore."

GI Joe escorted Solomon to the door past the few lit candles, the few worshippers whose furtive glances from their prayers followed him outside. He plunged into the light. Midday heat landed on him like a steamy towel. He had thought to browse the market, but felt so strange and slightly sick, that he immediately went back to the pensione he had visited the night before, found that a room had come free, so he rented it for the whole week and spent the rest of the morning vomiting into the bidet, and then dry heaves, and then was afraid to be more than thirty seconds away from the toilet for the rest of the day, as he felt like the whole heel of the boot ran through his bowels.

By midday next he felt well enough to go out again. The market was gone, streetsweepers desultorily moving the trash with coarse brooms of twigs tied together. A few people crossed the piazza on foot, or moved about on bicycles and scooters, like ghosts of a world long gone. Everything was bleached to whiteness by the sun, the facade of the Chiesa Matrice, the statues in the architrave, their shadows dissolved by the brightness back into the porous stone. The chapel of St. Paul was quiet now, small and undistinguished. He pulled on the church door, and it slowly came open. It felt heavier than on the day before, when it almost flew out as soon as he touched it. The battle with his stomach had weakened him, and caused him to sweat so the coolness inside was welcome. The vault and nave now seemed vast, a spaciousness he didn't register the day before, perhaps crowded by the presence of GI Joe. He looked around at everything he had been shown yesterday. Compared to churches in the north, this one seemed empty, just a few poor sculptures, and dark, undistinguished paintings, the once gilded chapels peeled and faded.

He found again the awful painting of St. Francis. This was such a mockery, the hands huge, with dull orange rays radiating from the wounds. Antonello's painting would not be so stupid. He would lead us to apprehend the transition from the rational to the miraculous. That manifestation he would show to be sudden in its effect, though only gradually absorbed into the humanity of the good saint. The expression of the figure would present a whole array of ambivalences and wonder, human questions in the thrall of this holy, and supernatural event. The expression on the face here made Francis of Assisi look like a man trying to decide which was worse, his constipation, or his upset stomach. A halo of winged brats circled his head like an affliction.

"Ah, good, signore. I thought you would not return. Good." GI Joe was standing behind him. "What can we do today?"

Solomon looked towards the altar, remembering the door behind it. "I came…you mentioned the archive. I would very much like to spend some time just looking through it, maybe some…"

"Great archive. Many treasures there." He motioned for Solomon to follow him. "Many caves, many rooms, many doors you can open. You will spend all of your time."

The sexton opened the gate to the choir, and they descended six steps where with a long, double-bitted key that turned seven times in the lock, he opened a heavy iron door. Solomon counted twenty-nine steps they descended to a door below, which opened with another seven turns of a different key. They both had to push on this door, so heavy and creaking on its hinges as if it hadn't been swung for many years. They then descended a sloping corridor cut out of the stone the church sat on, and at the bottom there was a wooden door closed with two hasps and locks. This opened with some difficulty into a great room, like a cave, carved out of the stone. A switch turned on three dim light bulbs hung from the ceiling on an old lamp holder. The room was furnished with great wooden cabinets from floor to ceiling, and the niches carved out of the stone concealed other mysteries under grey drapes. Here and there a mummy covered with a grey sheet leaned against the wall, or sat up high in a niche. He was glad he'd gotten used to these in Palermo. There was a large table, and a desk, some long benches, a large armadio, doors open, with clothing hung inside, a narrow wooden bed, covered with a straw tick. Everything looked ancient, made of dark wood, joined and carved with ancient skills, a fortune of antiques. Yet with all this stuff spread throughout it, the room still seemed almost empty. This was very great, Solomon felt in his heart. How great that he will be able to tell his son, or his daughter, about this adventure, about finding this great painting. How his intuition had told him there was something here.

GI Joe opened a drawer at the base of one of the cabinets. "Here you have paper, pigments, brushes. Here are some pencils, some pastels. Over there are some tablets of wood. You make a painting. You make pictures."

"No." Perhaps it was futile to explain. He wouldn't get it, if he hadn't got it by now. "I am not a painter. I am not an artist. I am looking for a painting, not to paint one. This painting I look for I think was lost maybe, painted by Antonello da Messina. Everywhere I can, I look for this painting."

"Si. Si. You look."

"Or I look for a clue. Everywhere there's an archive, or storage."

"Everything open to you, signore. The light is here. And you have also these lamps." He opened a closet that had in it several oil lamps and a supply of oil.

Excitement started to build in Solomon. He had never been given this much freedom to explore. "It will take time. There are other rooms, aren't there?"

"Many rooms. You have all the time you need, signore. And here mamma will see to your needs." He pulled the covering off one of the mummies seated in a niche, on a wooden stool, and adjusted her black dress. "You will take care of him, won't you mamma?" He patted her hand, shriveled like a chicken's foot.

Later, when he thought of all this, he questioned why he hadn't found it very spooky and frightening. Maybe because he'd seen it in Palermo, and he was only grateful that it wasn't so ostentatious and celebratory. "Is this your mother?" he asked.

"Tarantata," the sacristan replied, straightening almost to his full height. *"L'acqua n'assegiata voi."* The sexton was almost shaking. He glared fervently at Solomon. "Now you are in the church, signore. *Niente paura.* No fear."

Solomon turned away, and later thought he should have acted on the discomfort he felt, but he was anxious to start searching. He felt like a little kid turned loose in a toy store after closing. Another closet held leather portfolios of documents, hung carefully on racks, and deep inside the closet underneath were some votary paintings, crudely done on wood. Something was here. There would be clues. He had this strong feeling in his gut.

He wasn't aware that GI Joe had left until he heard the lock turn seven times at the end of the corridor. He tried the wooden door. Locked. "Joe," he shouted. He pounded on the door, but the boards were so thick his fists made only a dull thud. Had he forgotten? But he would be back. "Joe," he shouted again. He had left only to allow Solomon some privacy to look through these archives. It would take time. And he had locked so no one else would bother him. It would take time, days. He would come back. He'd locked the doors out of habit, of course. Solomon turned back to work, and started to rummage through the stuff. So much stuff. He would need more light. "More light," he said aloud, as if there was someone to hear.

LION

LION

The city of Lecce had been wrapped in heavy veils of burlap. This was the fruits of prosperity and new wealth in the South that had arrived in Lecce with its particular problems. Most families now had at least one or maybe two cars or more to drive around the narrow streets of the old city, or to race down the new autostradas incised on the heel of the boot. Increased smog blanketed the city and slowly ate into the buildings, crumbling the soft tufa, and threatening to erase the sixteenth century baroque facades. The remedy was to defend the stone with burlap and canvas hung from scaffolds. The old city looked to be perhaps auditioning for a project by Christo, wrapper of monuments and islands, cross-country curtain king.

"This could be a pretty town, if they ever get it unwrapped," Nathan joked aloud to himself, as he crept through the central piazza of old Lecce, Piazza San Oronzo. He might have enjoyed saying that to Saffron. His best lines now were totally unappreciated. There's nothing more lonesome than telling jokes to yourself. Saffron was gone probably forever from his life, a college girl again, and then on to some serious vocation within her wealthy purview. He came away from Sicily at least acknowledging the real differences between them, put more or less into his own place by her reassumption of hers. He was comfortable with it. They had gone through something together, some weird revelations, a mutual hallucinatory reality sink. Though it was already fading in memory, he would never forget her, nor would she forget him, he imagined; still, he would have enjoyed her response here, how she unflaggingly topped his remarks with something off the wall, and brilliantly on target. She was young, but quick and smart and funny, and now she was behind him (was Miriam in front of him?), back into her own generation, and her future wealth, leaving him alone for now in his. He missed her.

Brightwatch had confessed that she'd gotten a call from this unlikely town just before his father had slipped into oblivion, and had further mentioned he was headed for somewhere else nearby, though she didn't remember the name of the place. Iera filled in that one. On Saffron's hunch, Nathan had returned to Peschici to speak to her, and she had confirmed that she had once known an American by the name of Solomon, who looked so much like Nathan, and he'd stayed with her for a while, then promised to come back after he went to Galatina to look for some painting.

"What sort of painting could there be in Galatina?" Iera asked.

"By Antonello da Messina," Nathan said.

"That's the name. Yes. Messina." Her eyes welled

with tears. "Far away from here." She went on with a passionate, indeed, operatic description of how he had struck her heart as if with a sword, and out of heart and mind and womb she had built a palace, of which he was the lord and master, and that edifice was her indestructible refuge in hope. When she saw that Nathan looked exactly like her Solomon, she could hardly breathe. She had to sit down in the restaurant.

"You returned, with the keys to the gate of my palace. Except you are still young, and I am old."

Saffron had been on target. For Iera it was as if Solomon had come through yesterday. Nathan told her he was probably the son, and mentioned his father's disappearance. He had to hold her as Iera spooled out an ancient sound, long wailing, and collapsed to the ground, as if the grief she repressed through every day of disappointment since her Solomon had left released itself at once, and the same fantasy she maintained of being wife caused her now to accept that she must forever be a widow.

Everything was sweetness, everything was sadness. He had thrown himself into an affair with a girl fifteen years younger than himself. He still felt full of that energy, and at the same time he felt himself emptying as if all his life was coming loose and rattling away. The curse of curiosity kept him moving. He would have to face something, alone in this city all burlaped against decay, like another attempt to bandage the wounds of the world. For the first time since he came to Italy he felt homesick. Homesick for what? Where was any home in this world? Not with Brightwatch, not with Miriam, not in her place. Why go to a place called Galatina? His phone conversations with Miriam had been tepid at best. Not once had she even hinted that she missed him. He would have occasionally enjoyed her company here, but he also would have had to deal with her impatience. About what home was he sick? Saffron had been the perfect companion for a while, and now she was gone. It was never a possibility to be at home with Saffron. And this place was not a place where he'd ever dreamed of finding his father. What the fuck did he care about finding his father, anyway? A stupid notion from the get-go. Miriam had been…No! It was just that he might have liked better to catch him wandering the hills around The Vatican, or babbling in the Boboli Gardens, or dedicating himself to Kabbalah on a kibbutz in the Negev, or chanting on an Ashram in Ganeshpuri, or meditating in a monastery near Kyoto, or holding discussions with himself in a lobsterman's shack in Meat Cove, or hoarding newspapers in a basement in Alphabet City. Or okay, he could be a family man haunting the strip-malls of Indianapolis. Not here, though. Not this strange bandaged city. He drove slowly through the streets. Lecce seemed to him a self-destroyed nowhere, and he didn't want to find his father in such a field of wounds.

The hotel, recommended to him at a filling station, was on the road leading out of town towards San Cataldo, the beach resort on the Adriatic some twelve kilometers away. This was a shiny, efficient, new hotel for businessmen, the rooms small, with low ceilings, with an internet connection and two telephone lines, easy email access, a well-stocked minibar, videos available, a hefty surcharge for porn. The hotel was full, because of an industrial exposition in Galatina. Galatina was where he was going, he told the clerk. Like everyone else, the clerk responded. A cancellation while he was standing there got him one of the smallest rooms. It seemed strange to come into this ancient place, and find the industrial world.

He relaxed onto the bed, and clicked on the TV. A local sports station was broadcasting a soccer game, switching occasionally to a cycling marathon, and peppering it all with a little basketball. The basketball, he thought, looked slow and clumsy. He dozed off, and when he woke there was a story on the news of a holdup on the lightly traveled autostrada to Santa Maria di Leuca. Several people were killed by young initiates of La Sacra Corona Unita, the local mafia. Organized crime was late getting to Puglia, the commentator explained, but the province was catching up, and now harbored the most vicious gangs in Italy. With the next item he sat up on the edge of the bed. It was about two men living on the outskirts of Lecce, who for years had resisted selling their land to developers, who had been killed and eaten by the lion they kept as a pet. It was a small lion, and very old, the reporter said. How could the municipality have allowed such a beast? He asked. Didn't the neighbors hear it roar? How did it get both of them?

He sat for a while in the crisp white light of the lobby, and eavesdropped to get a sense of what thoughts were in the air. Most conversation was about the *disgraziati* of the *Sacra Corona*. The mob was business, of course, and these were businessmen. How many times had Nathan himself recommended investments in the mob? He didn't want to remember. There was no one talking about the two men who were meat for the lion. That one interested Nathan.

He noticed a gentleman impeccably dressed, his moustache waxed to two fine points. The man leaned against the banister, a hand poised on the brass ball of the newel-post. His lips puckered and relaxed as if he was sipping through a straw. The greased back hair covered his pate like a shining salt and pepper helmet. He wore a perfectly pressed light summer suit of pale, beige silk, a blue-striped shirt, button-down, a lime green tie knotted with a four-in-hand, pulled tight to his throat. He moved closer to Nathan when he caught his eye, and sat down stiffly on the edge of the cushion of a metal easy chair. The man's manner made Nathan feel like prey, as if he was being watched by a used car salesman on a lot. Each time he caught Nathan looking his way he grinned mechanically, and twirled the right point of his moustache. Nathan felt uncomfortably underdressed in this traffic of elegant businessmen. His grey faux turtleneck, under a stained denim shirt, covered by a frayed sleeveless blue cardigan sweater, was not enough for his own comfort. His own moustache, he was sure, was in disarray. He had long ago given up trying to match the Italians in elegance, especially in the south where everything seemed so formal. While he was with Saffron it had made little difference, but by himself he wished he had the right clothes, to keep him from being noticed.

Nathan rose to step outside, and saw the man was no longer sitting there. He was relieved not to see him. Outside the sirocco blew a gritty mist from Africa that smelled both of the desert and the sea. Cars along the street were covered in a layer of fine sand. He looked up and down the thoroughfare to choose a direction to walk, and decided to go left.

"Pssst," he heard from behind himself. O no, he thought, always that same beckoning. He turned to see the man who had been watching him in the lobby. "You have made the mistake, signore." His puckering lowered the tips of his moustache. "Going that way there is nothing. Some garbage, the garbage center under those lights, but nothing for you. That way is to the…how you say it? To the dumping." There was a slight twitch in the man's pucker, that indicated some strain in the his otherwise impeccable presentation. He maintained his grin with some effort. "You are the American, is it not?" He had almost no accent, despite the peculiar turns of his syntax.

Nathan nodded affirmatively.

"Yes, I know American. You must know Mr. Fowler. Maybe not. I am so sorry to disturb, but you have come for the Galatina, for the festival of commerce and industry. Tonight you will go to the opening ceremony, is it not?"

"Yes." That was easier than an explanation.

"O, bene, bene. Good. Perfetto. I will help you. Tonight we will go together. Fireworks ceremony, and it begins."

"Why? What do you want? Why do you want to go with me?" He didn't intend that to sound as rude and mistrustful as it might have.

"Signore, there is nothing. I am a good man. I am to the industrial myself. I am translation for you. I am help with you to bargain."

"I haven't come to buy anything. I don't need to bargain."

"Signore, you are in the south here, *meridionale*. You need to bargain. For everything you bargain."

'It's very kind of you to offer, but…"

"*Si, signore.* Yes. *Perfetto.* I am Ghiaccione, Paolo Ghiaccione. *Piacere.* Big ice, my name. Yes.

"Nathan Briggs, but I don't think…"

"Perfetto. Piacere. Molto Piacere, Mister Briggs." He shook Nathan's hand.

Nathan wished the man would let go of that strained smile, relax his face, hide his teeth under the moustache.

"Thank you so much, but I don't want to impose. I'm not here…I don't need…"

"No. No, Mister Briggs. Not to impose. But look how you have already mistaken the way. *Perduta la strada justa.* You will turn around, and I will show it."

Nathan had mistaken the lights at the dump for a street of shops lit up before sundown, so the big ice was right. If he turned around at this suggestion, he knew this irritating man would be with him for the duration, but if just to avoid that he continued in this direction, he would get only to the garbage dump. The man placed his hand lightly on Nathan's shoulder. "You come my way, please."

Nathan suddenly had an idea. "Do you know about that lion, who ate the two men who kept him? Do you know where that is?"

"I know where that is. Of course, I know that, signore. I take you there." A slight pressure of the hand turned Solomon to walk back to the hotel. "Perfetto." With the man holding his elbow, Nathan felt somewhat busted, discreetly arrested.

"You picked me, from everyone in the hotel. Why

did you pick me?"

"You have nice face. You are a nice man. I come to you because…"

"But the hotel is full of people."

"Dear sir," the man said through his relentless grin. "I am not from here. Not me either from this place. Like you, I am alone here. I come here from the north, from Brescia. You know the city, Brescia? Every year I come here, to this show. I am companionship. Is good, the companionship. I sell here the agriculture machine. Big tractor. John Deere, Massey Ferguson, Claas. Fiat – LaVerda, big harvest machine. So for to harvest the *girasole*, how you say this? Turn sun…sun…sunflower, yes? Perfetto. Many sunflower grow now since EU. Sunflower, *si.* Olive, *nyet.*" He turned his thumb down. *"Girasole, jawohl."* His thumb turned up.

"Great." Nathan had noticed the damned sunflowers. You couldn't avoid them, endless sunflowers as you drive through Tuscany, Umbria, Emilia-Romagna, Abruzzo, Molise, everywhere sunflowers turning their endless ranks of dull golden heads to follow the sun. It wasn't that he found them bad, or ugly, but there were so damned many, such an endless army of them. He remembered driving around Italy before with Brightwatch, through these same regions full of small farms then, hay stacked around poles, livestock everywhere. He climbed a stack with a *contadino,* and watched him slice down feed for his stock with a large, two-handled blade. Near Siena he'd watched them slaughter a pig, catch the blood in a large pan, dip the carcass in a vat of boiling water. He'd touched the cool muzzle of a gentle ox. He got a ride on a donkey at farm near Spello. You didn't see those animals any more. Centuries of slow, sweet nurture had been given over to industrial agriculture, to sunflower oil, changing the face of Italy. Who would go back to the dawn to dusk backbreaking labor of that life? Nobody. But it was startling when he saw it at first, a golden mat of flowers stretching for kilometer after kilometer of tedium, expressing the new life and the drive to maximize production and profit, laying this new monotony on the world.

"Mr. Ghiaccione, I think I'll pass. I don't even want…"

"Ah, *caro signore*. I am your friend. I am companionship. Yes."

"I need to be alone, Mr. Ghiaccione. I have to…"

"And it is no problem, because I practice English this way, and you have good friend this way." He looked into Nathan's face, his grin like a crack in a rock. *"Perfetto.* Alone is not so very good. You want to buy something, I help you. Alone in the south, dangerous. Sacra Corona kills the people, you see him on television. I help you here. I speak for you."

"I don't know you, Mr. Ghiaccione. Maybe you are from the Sacra Corona." Nathan wanted to retract that as soon as it came out of his mouth.

The man spread his arms as if he was being crucified, and stepped in front of Nathan, losing his smile for the first time. "Mr. Nathan, no. I am not that. I am no mob, how you say it? No mafia me. I am senior executive officer. And I am your friend."

He stared at Nathan for some moments, till Nathan sighed with resignation, and then the new friend let down his arms, stepped around, and took Nathan's elbow again. "So for what have you come here to Galatina? What is your wish?"

"I have some reasons."

"Perfetto." His grin was on again. "And I am here to help you."

"And that lion. I want to see that lion."

"Lion?"

"Yes. The one that ate its keepers, its owners. It was on television."

"Ah, *il leone. Bestia. Gatto grande, si.* Yes. Not a problem. We go."

The way to the lion wound through a jungle of new development that seemed laid out in random tracts south of the city, among remnants of old stone wall and fig cactus. Ghiaccione explained that these developments had sprung up as prosperity took hold, after the workers, once exiled to Milan, Germany, Switzerland, England, Sweden, brought back the cash to improve their lives at home, and built these homes in rings of suburbs they called *Germania, Svizzera, Svezia, Inghiliter-*

ra. They drove to some abandoned projects at the edge of development, empty shells of tufa, ranked around a few square hectares of land, all dust and stone and cactus, but for a rough dirt driveway they approached. Parallel rows of dying umbrella pines led to a small house, windows smashed out, roof half open to the elements. The smell of coffee reassured that at least something was alive here.

A trio of local police, in faded green uniforms, relaxed on chairs next to the front door, dipping biscotti into bowls of coffee. Arched above the door of the old house a slogan was painted crudely in German – ARBEIT MACHT AUKEN. A swarthy *Carabinieri* approached, tall and menacing in his spiffy uniform, with white belts and trim, his pistol in a white holster that he unsnapped as he leaned towards Paolo on the driver's side of the car.

"Fifty thousand lire, quickly," Paolo whispered to Nathan. "Give me." Nathan pulled out a fifty thousand lire note.

"No. Five of ten thousand, give me."

Nathan had only four in his wallet. Paolo shrugged, and took them, and held on to the fifty grand. He handed the carabinieri thirty, and pocketed ten more. The officer pulled the bill of his hat to snug it down, sneered at Nathan, and waved the car on. They pulled up by the fence of cactus and rusting sheep wire that surrounded the compound. As they got out of the car, a creature on four legs stepped from its half collapsed shed and blinked against the sun. This was the lion, a queer beast, much smaller than Nathan had imagined when he first heard about the tragedy. With slender legs and sad face, it looked like a starved dog, a great dane with a ratty mane tangled around its face. Nathan felt he had seen this before.

"Will they let it live? It devoured two people." Paolo translated Nathan's question for the police, who had followed them.

One of them, a small, unshaven man, launched into an explanation that he enjoyed telling. "The poor beast," he said, and Paolo translated. "There was no nutrition on them, skin and bones. The miserable lion got almost nothing out of it." Nathan looked around the compound at some sculptures, all of them of the same wingless bird, made in concrete, glass, plaster, wood, polystyrene, Styrofoam, a whole flock of these.

"The lion never attacked the men," Paolo went on translating. "In the note they left they explained that they had offered themselves to the poor beast. It had been difficult to convince it to eat at all. At first it had turned up its nose altogether at the meat they proffered off their own bones. These weren't the most appetizing of old men. Towards the end of their lives all they had to eat themselves was the wild greens that still grew in their ruined fields, as they no longer had the strength to plant anything, nor to gather fuel to make even a pizza in their oven. Even in their abject poverty they protested the new housing going up all around them, and refused to sell their few hectares. They were courageous, maybe foolish. Their skin was like leather shrunk onto chalky bones. Maybe if the lion could cook for itself, maybe a thin minestrone would come of them, a minestrino, a light sauce for some pasta, some orrechiette characteristic of the region, if such a lion would eat some pasta, or a few scraps of leather baked onto a focacce, those old men. How could you blame the lion?"

"What kind of birds are these?" Nathan indicated the sculptures.

Both of the police shrugged when Paolo relayed the question.

The lion coughed several times as it tried to roar. The effort collapsed the poor creature to the ground, where it lay panting like a mongrel in the sun; its tongue flopped out onto the dirt. With some strain and shaking it rose again and staggered back into the shadows of its shed. Seeing it in the obscurity, Nathan realized where he had encountered such a skinny beast before. It was in a famous old painting in a book that Brightwatch had. He had looked at this many times, because this was by the artist with whom she told him his father was obsessed. This was of St. Jerome, he was told. The saint was seated in a raised alcove, at a desk, reading a book. There was a gallery of columns, as he remembered, on either side, receding to some windows through which you could see beautiful landscapes, birds in flight. In the shadows of the gallery that receded behind the back of St. Jerome, a skinny lion lurked, with one paw raised as if the starved beast was about to move or turn. This one resembled that lion, and none other he had ever seen. A domestic cat curled contentedly on a shelf near the reader's feet, and he remembered a bird there, a peacock, or perhaps a pheasant. Yes, it was by Antonello da Messina. He had studied that picture in the book so many times, as if that saint could have been his father. He often wondered what it might have been like to approach his father reading in his alcove. "Father?…Father?" He would have interrupted the busy saint. He looked around at this place, protected from encroaching development only by some stones, and a weakening lattice of prickly pear. He felt it so strongly now, that his father had been here. His presence was palpable. St. Jerome, Brightwatch had told him, was always shown with a lion. Like anything else, this lion could be a lead to his father. It was not so unlikely, though it was weird, how almost step by step he had been tugged down here. "Remember me!" He'd heard the voice in Cefalu say that, definitely a Hamlet moment. This place was on its last legs, as if it had waited for him to come before completely turning to dust. Was it too far-fetched to imagine that his father had been here once, in this very place? Could he have left prints? He might have shed some DNA. Everywhere anyone goes he sheds DNA.

"Mister Briggs, look at there. Over there."

A light had gone on inside the shed, a bare incandescent bulb. The lion shuffled back and forth inside, swinging its head. Scattered about on the floor were what looked like eggs, some big as whales' eyes, others small as pearls. Was this the natural world? The lion paced in a tightening spiral, closing in on a clutch of them heaped in a nest of straw. This behaved like the natural world. The lion settled on the small pyramid of eggs as if he were a hen determined to hatch a brood.

"The eggs," one of the policemen said through Paolo. "They are made of stone. The lion never lays an egg."

On the way back to the hotel Nathan spilled his whole mess for Paolo Ghiaccione, told him about his father, the jacket, the painting in the Borghese gallery, his search, his doubts, the futility he felt in what he was doing. He tried to explain the Antonello connection, and the lion in the painting, and what his father might have been up to in Lecce and Galatina, his search for a phantom painting. The self appointed guide and companion steered the car with one hand, twirled his moustache with the fingertips of the other, answered his cell phone, cradling it on his shoulder with his head. He sometimes nodded as if listening, and occasionally responded with *"niente da fare"* or *"magari"* or *"Cosi e la vita"* or *"hmmm."*

He finally said, *"Niente paura.* Not to worry, Mr. Briggs. You are very close. You will get what you need. Now you must rest."

As they entered the hotel, Paolo answered his cell phone, put it on hold, and gestured at Nathan. "We meet here in lobby at seven, more or less, have a little early *cena,* then go together to Galatina, be there in time for the fireworks. You like some fireworks?" He turned away to speak into his cell.

"Yes. Yes." Nathan said, to no one. Whenever he "confessed" to a stranger like this, he felt he was digging a deep pit, his voice getting dimmer and dimmer, the despair he expressed way out of proportion to his situation, as he unloaded so much personal stuff on someone who didn't get it, and didn't care.

Paolo covered his phone. "You will love there. You will buy whatever you want, and I will help. The Americans, magnificent consumers you are. The best. *Perfetto.*"

Nathan switched on his TV and flopped across the bed. He set the phone on his belly, and dialed his mother's number in Venice, expecting the voice mail, or a busy signal. It was answered on the second ring.

"Brightwatch studio." It wasn't his mother's voice.

"Hello. This is Nathan. Can I speak to Brightwatch?"

"You're Nathan? Her son? Hi. I'm Lolly. I'm so sorry

I missed you when you were here." Her voice had a bright, feminine, singing quality. "I've wanted to meet you, especially when she took so long even to tell me she had a son."

"I wanted to meet you too."

"So she went to Milano, to be a famous international figure. Do you have a message? She said she'd call this evening."

He thought for a moment. "Yeah. You can tell her I found the lion."

"You found the lion?"

"Yes."

"And she knows what that means?"

"I think she'll know. Maybe."

Lolly laughed, a friendly laugh. "I like that message. I'll tell her. Nathan found the lion. That's cool."

They agreed that the next time they would definitely have to meet, and have a drink together, and share Brightwatch stories. They hung up. Nathan laughed out loud, pumping his arm as if he'd won some contest. He felt really good; felt that Lolly could actually be an ally in his endless skirmishes with Brightwatch.

He dozed off, and was soon awakened by a call from Paolo Ghiaccione at the desk downstairs. As he washed his face, he stared in the mirror at the grin that stretched across it. This wasn't his grin, and it wasn't a voluntary grin. This was some grin virus he'd caught from Paolo Ghiaccione. He couldn't relax it away. He couldn't stop it. His face was like paralyzed into this grin. This could be the grin to end the world. Not with a bang, but a grin. Once it infects every face – all kaput. It pulled up the corners of his mouth as he watched the ads pass on TV, one by one, proclaiming the latest improvements on the previous improvements, selling even smaller cell phones, quicker food processors, more organized personal organizers, quick shampoos, cheeses processed, reprocessed, and packaged in tubes, the window covers, the speedy computers the software the scooters the quicker internet the soaps the pasta. Digestive drinks for sale. Cynar. Punt e Mes. Gucci. Olivetti. Fiat Fiat Fiat. Barilla Barilla.

A toasted mortadella and pecorino sandwich, and then they set out for the exposition. The road from Lecce to Galatina had recently been widened to accommodate the semis hauling all the stuff on display at the exposition. Banners announcing the exposition flapped from a line of poles down both sides of highway. Fireworks sizzled in the dusk above the exposition grounds on the outskirts of Galatina. A complex of hangar-like structures covered the exhibition; the whole shebang lit by mercury lamps, surrounded by hurricane fence topped with razor wire. It was a secure operation. They parked in a space reserved for participants. Paolo led him through the exhibitor's entrance, saving him the eight thousand lire admission. They stepped into the enormous atmosphere of the first pavilion, and froze there a moment, Nathan dazzled by the space, the rippled steel sheeting bolted to curved girders arcing high above them. The place felt bigger than a domed stadium. Huge company banners hung from the girders. Lights flashed in the booths below. Electronic tunes scribbled through the air, like a cell-phone jubilee. If Max had been there, and maybe he was, he would be pushing his dildonics, his virtual voyages, his grown-up video games. This was hard to resist, as much as something in Nathan resented his attraction to it. He usually found the shopping imperative creepy and avoided it whenever he could. Here he was like a kid in a stroller, first trip to Disney world, pushed through the attractions by Paolo Ghiaccione, the grin tugging them along; that grin like a family birthmark stretched across both their faces.

Nathan wasn't even aware of when he pulled out his credit cards, and started to buy the stuff. Perhaps it was the massage chair that Paolo sat him in to demonstrate what was available in a booth of gadgets that promote your wellbeing. A deep massage ensued, an assault of steel knuckles and thumbs. Paolo negotiated the price, discounted from several *millioni*, down to one *millione e mezzo*. And for less than another *millione* the salesperson threw in a body inversion table, because after the massage you want to hang upside down.

How exhilarating, Nathan thought, to be able to spend millions, and millions. The freshly massaged man always needs new gear, so they hit the big booths where the Aumantis, the Bulloneys, the Kaaka Kliins, the Farfoolis, and etc. and etc. all plied their heights of fashion. He bought a bale of elegant sweaters, of the latest socks and ties, though he rarely wore a tie, but now, under his grin…And Paolo introduced him to an army of tailors, all of them *bravi, in gamba,* who showed him samples of their work, and swatches of fine fabric in sharkskin and tweed, polished woolens light as cotton, linens to beat the band, cottons that felt like silk, and silk weighted as canvas. They measured his inseams, his shoulders, his sleeve lengths, one arm just slightly longer than the other, his hang to the right, his various girths, so he ordered several of these, single and double breasted, sport jackets, cardigans, dozens of pairs of slacks, in every fabric. If he lived forever, he would never wear all this. How will he get this stuff home? No problem with Paolo there for him. He negotiated with a shipping company for half a container going to New York, insurance included.

Nathan was a helpless, happy consumer fiend in ecstasy. He felt the pain in all his credit cards – the Visa, the Mastercard, the Diner's Club, the Amex. They all whistled their encrypted tunes through the card machines. Magnetism was known to fail sometimes, but not here, not yet, not for the smile, not before he bought barrels of dinnerware, hand painted ceramic, two sets because who could decide between the lush flower design, and the gorgeous roosters? A touch of nouveau nouveau in some couches and ottomans. Where would he put all this? That was not the concern of the super consumer. It would land on Miriam in a couple of months, and she would feel the love in each item of the heap. There was space, always space in America. A dining room set, table to seat twelve, twelve chairs, all a wood and Plexiglas miracle of transparencies and contemporary design. He charged side tables for the sides of everything, and end tables for the ends, and coffee tables to set in the middle. Entertainment centers, one to wheel into each room in his imagination. America the beautiful. Fill it up.

They called Visa, Mastercard. They got American Express to answer, and Diner's Club. His credit lines spun out into the ether. They expanded to a whole shipping container, and maybe even another would be appropriate. Paolo Ghiaccione applauded, sounded like a whole audience of approbation. And he sang, with a complete chorus contained in his one voice, folk songs from Brescia, his home town. And he sang with this voice of a multitude, songs of the Beatles, the Kinks, the Rolling Stones; songs from way before yesterday. Just for a thrill. All you need is love. You can't get no…Nathan rolled on. Where were the lamps? Paolo took him to the table lamps, the halogens inset and floor models, the track lights, buy them here and get the discounts, Italian designs made in Bulgaria, tiny spotlights, new fluorescents wavy as dreams in colorful glass. Fill that container, out of Bari shipped to New York, New York, a toddling town. No, not. Nathan wept, he laughed. He was disconnected from himself, but connected to all the possible stuff of the world. He looked for his life. It was over there. The grin was intact, laughing or crying, the grin was there. "I want it," he told his guide, when he pointed at the flat screen LCD's, the plasmas. Paolo embraced him, almost swallowing his head with a kiss. He wanted the miniaturizations, many many to the container. Top of the line camcorders, DVD players, editing decks. Get a dozen people movers, to move a dozen people. Get Lamborghini to build the Humvee for me, and a trailer for the ultralights. We need to fly. We need to sail. That boat, charge it. Someone paid, someone profited. You bet they did. That's how the world goes round. When he got back to America he'd settle into the money. He wasn't afraid of prosperity now, not anymore. Not Nathan Briggs over there. He'd put his fatherless back to the wheel. Money was his game. Nathan Briggs was his name.

Paolo looked at his American friend, his eyes moistened with love. "Now I show you my baby, my love, my piece of resistance," Paolo said, leading Nathan into another space, through some huge drapes hung from the rafters. This separated the agricultural from the rest of the exposition. Tractors, cultivators, combines, balers, rakes, plows, everything that spins, whirrs, chops across the land, tetters, harvesters, discs, and milking parlors operating with plastic cows, the milking machines capable of squinching milk out of three thousand teats in an hour extend across the broad concrete floor, unto the vanishing point, and beyond the edge of discernment, laid out like the bivouac of an army that has won a great battle, somewhat wounded, but relaxed and confident.

"Here it is," said Paolo. "Libby-Lou (Libby for liberty)." They stood in the shadow of the most enormous machine Nathan had ever seen, so large he had ignored it. It was over four stories tall, as wide as three buses are long. Down what roads could this Libby-Lou move on its forty-three wheels?

"My dear friend. This is my everything, my baby, absolutely my baby. You get inside my baby, and you love my baby. She will harvest the girasole. It will be your flower of the sun harvest, no. She can go to the pumpkin, and the canola will not stop her. Everything she will harvest. She is not shy. You love her, no? Mr. Briggs." Paolo started up the ladder built into the side. "She waits for you. *Perfetto*, Mr. Briggs." He looked down at Nathan. "Come. Come up now into Libby-Lou. Experience the advantage of ultimate harvest. Yes, Nathan Briggs."

Nathan followed Paolo up the ladder. Printed next to it were some lines of poetry. "Ah sunflower," it said. "weary of time/Who countest the steps of the sun…"

etcetera. Great lines of sympathy for the sunflower, he thought. Poetry made the day. Who wrote those? Allen Ginsberg maybe, but probably not. Someone older.

"Get in, and look at it from up here."

There was a long, narrow room, like the bridge of an oil tanker. From the windows you could survey the expanse of lesser farm machinery.

"Do you love it?"

Nathan didn't know about the category of love, but he felt helpless to redefine his feelings, so he went along with it. "I do," he said. "I do love."

"And here is the Bopps-Nikamicci music system, so every sound for you can be in heaven while you work the sunflowers; and air-conditioned climate control everything perfect and filtration, so healthy for as never before you worked the land. And from inside here you don't feel a machine, nothing. You pick the sunflowers, you strip it, you husk the seeds, and you choose to roast them or not, or press into oil and bottle, even print labels, and you make sunflower butter, or meal, very good for you, all from this control panel automatic, and if you want bags, barrels, plastic, even cellophane. Remember cellophane? Or if you want this you can employment, if times are bad for the people outside there, up to twelve people, all down inside the machine, instead of the automatic, but every step controlled in here, and digital. My baby."

"It's automated?"

"Better. My baby is so smart. She will tell you if you have made too much oil, and should try butter, or roasted seeds. She knows the markets. She monitors, and tells you." Paolo kissed the LCD screen. "And you switch to canola to pumpkin to maize to gourd. Even tomatoes soon."

"Olives?"

"Haha, Mr. Briggs. You joke with me. See here how she moves, with these controls. Fast as you need. How many acres an hour you want? Like hovercraft she whispers forward and back. She tells you, only move me at night, only early morning, so not to disrupt the traffic. At night she lopes, she cruises, she ambles, she shambles, she pokes. You say pokes?" Paolo opened a drawer in the console and pulled out some papers. He waved them in front of Nathan. "These are contracts." Nathan was salivating around his grin. "And we will ship you her for free. Yes, is free. When you come back to America she will be there for you." He handed Nathan the contract and a pen.

"I live in New York City," Nathan protested weakly. Though he had examined and evaluated many contracts, and rejected or altered quite a few, now the lust of acquisition was on him, and he had already acquired so much stuff so easily, and now there was little hope of stopping. He looked out over the vast encampment of tractors with their brightly painted implements. He took a deep breath, sucking the bubbles of saliva back off his lips. This was definitely the king of all items. *"Perfetto,* Mr. Briggs. Yes. You buy here. No?"

He felt the grin ripping through his cheeks, and flattened the contract over the LCD screen. This could be his sunflower ship enterprise in New York to go where no other goes which he was buying with the scratch of this pen. Refusal was futile.

"For eight hundred thousand bucks she is our bargain. You come just at the right time the floor model available never used before. In German more than a million dollars for you buys this piece of equipment. More than that. You will be first in North America. And look at her. You can live inside the Libby-Lou. Look, is so good." Paolo pulled a cord above his head, and behind them a door slid open to reveal the cozy bedroom, the kitchen, the living space, nicely appointed in teals, eggshell, rosy pinks, and silver grays.

"Yes. I see. Of course." Nathan touched the pen to the space Paolo indicated with his pinky. It was marked with a red X, as were other spaces requiring his initials.

"Anywhere if you break down, Mister Briggs, our technicians will be there within twenty-four hours. The harvest must never stop, Mister Briggs. *Perfetto."*

Nathan tried to sign quickly, but was holding the pen upside down. Paolo righted it in his hand. "Haha, Mr. Briggs. You joke with me like a good American man." He slapped Nathan across the back. "You are in North America the first." He took the signed contract, and Nathan's credit cards in hand. "Twenty-four hours we are on the place to solve problem. Of course there is not problems." Paolo Ghiaccione climbed out of the machine. *"Perfetto, perfetto, perfetto, perfetto,"* he sang on the way down the ladder. Nathan watched him stagger off into the shadows, and through a door to some offices behind a wall of frosted glass. Those offices were lit by flames.

    Nathan felt all the ambivalence that attends a purchase of this magnitude. The questions of how will he pay for it, and the rationalization that this is on credit and will slowly evaporate assailed him at first. Then he thought, "Now this is mine," and he felt safe in this world of gain. He wanted to weep. He started to laugh. The warm tide of joy that rises with ownership lifted him on its flood. "I know what I can do with this," he said to no one. He slipped out of the driver's seat and into the living space. A small fridge was stocked with beer, ginger ale, salty snacks, with the Limonata and Chinotto San Pellegrino. There was Vodka in the freezer. All of this was included in the purchase. The two burner hot-plate was no extra charge, and the convection oven, same as the two he'd bought to ship to Miriam, made in Torino by DeLonghi. This was a definite plus. Everything reassured him that he'd made a score. It would arrive in the port of New York, and he would claim it. If nothing else, it would be a nice place to live. Rents in New York were way out of hand, anyway. Anything to beat the housing crunch. How great he'd feel to drive it off the pier into Brooklyn. Or into Jersey. Or take it to Brighton Beach. He could drive it up Broadway, which was one way downtown. He would drive it uptown, changing the direction of the world with his harvester, letting her sniff for sunflowers in a city bereft, to satisfy her sunflower appetite. Some must be growing somewhere in a metropolis so great; but if not, so what? She could find other stuff that needed processing in a New York, so diverse and imponderable a city, with all its wealth and poverty and diversity and artistic talent and intellectual power, and its restaurants. She would suck all the hemp from under the grow-lights throughout the boroughs, and squeeze forth their value in oil, and turn the pulp into hempen condoms. So many people guided their huge vehicles, their great SUV's and vans, their powerful, mountain-flattening four wheel drives, through the Manhattan streets, piloting those back-road specialists into the heart of the great city. His enormous hound could easily outrun those puppies.

Nathan woke before dawn on the narrow cot of the harvester. He had dreamed of the lions, the mangy one in Lecce, and the one in the painting. Brightwatch and he looked at that painting a lot when he was a kid, and asked about his father. He had told her once that Saint Jerome reading a book was not his father. His father was the lion. Though she told him that the lion symbolized the suppression of the baser instincts by the good saint, Nathan had insisted it was different. The lion was his father retreating into the shadows, away from his duty; or he was the lion that might step from shadows to protect Nathan, when he was needed. He awoke, at any rate, with those lions coughing in his ear.

Then the birds nesting in the rafters bounced their songs off the steel. He remembered hearing in the night Ghiaccione climb back up the ladder. He had pretended to be asleep, like a little kid, head covered by blankets. Then he fell asleep. He woke up to see his copy of the contract, and a stem of yellow tea roses in a bud vase. Sweet touch. The contract looked official, and insistent on the night before as anyone's hangover. He would have to get to a phone, call in his credit cards. What would he say? Lost! Stolen! Maybe it would work, maybe not. It was a long ride back into his own life. He had overindulged a grin, and now the consequences.

RELAXIN' AT ANTONELLO

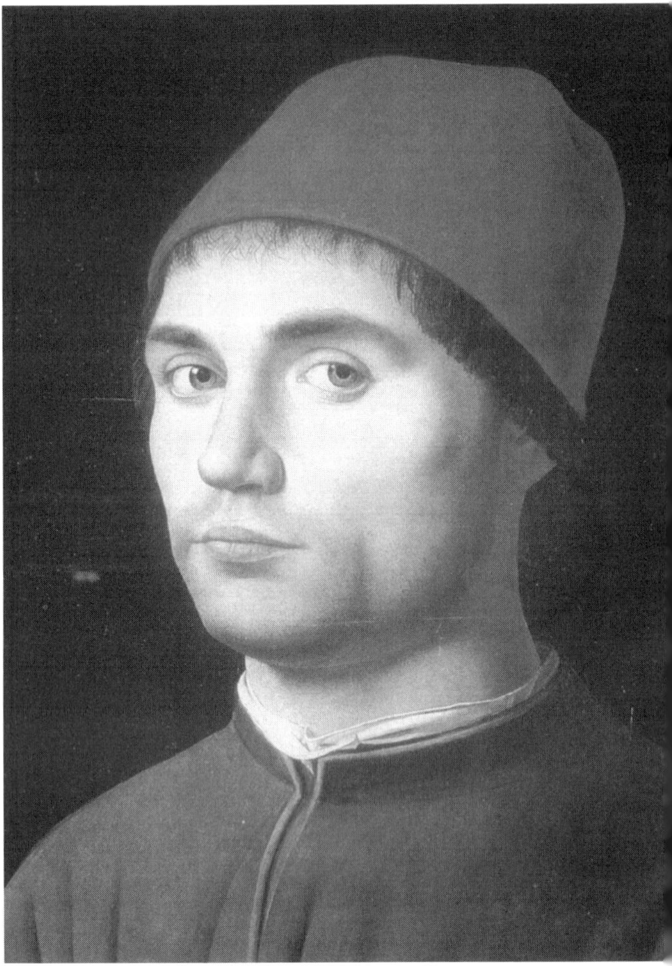

RELAXIN' AT ANTONELLO

"Okay, joke's on myself," Solomon spoke loudly, just to hear a voice in the isolation. "I made a mistake. I was an idiot to look for some lost painting, on such a dumb clue." He moved around the dimly lit vaulted room, slapping the walls as if he hoped they would turn insubstantial at some point, just as this experience felt like some dim nightmare realm he had entered. "So arrogant. Me. To hope that I could do something, some bit to save humanity from its own brute. As if the art can be a correction. I'll say it again. I was arrogant and presumptuous. Something I got from too much time with Isabel. This bestial, this ridiculous, my century. I'll admit I've added my own stupidity," he laughed. "Just stop. Let me out of here." He looked up as if he could talk through to the sky. "Okay, I'll concede it. I never saw that scrap of paper—Antonello Pinxit. An hallucination, I'll say it now. The woman in Sicily, what was her name, Violeta, Violeta—violet, she had it right. No one just finds such an important painting. Everything is a joke, my whole life a joke, and this is supposed to be the punch line. **ENTOMBED.**" The sound rolled as if off a kettle drum, his own life some melodramatic gag. Just the sound—entombed…entombed…entombed.

Trapped. In his tomb. This was a tease. Surely nothing but a joke. This wasn't part of the tour. Something had slipped the mind of GI Joe, that was all. He would remember. He would come back. Solomon practiced his Italian, dismissing expected apologies—"...*no, non fa niente. E molto tranquillo quiggiu. Un bel riposo, facevo. Figurati, GI Joe.*"

How much time had passed? He had left his watch in the hotel room on purpose, to be free of schedules, free of time. How long had it been? Was it a week? He heard scraping, then saw the tray slide under the door, boiled pasta spread across the tray, sprinkled with some bitter greens, and then a shallow tray of water followed, the precious stuff spilling over the rim. He was a prisoner, no doubt about it, eating weeds on cold noodles. The water smelled like it had been dipped from some stagnant puddle. This wasn't the first time he'd been fed. How many times? He made a mark on the wall. How long had he been there? He was helpless, like soft in the bones. *LETMEOUTOFHERE*, he screamed into futility, his voice dead against the door, just as his shoulder thunked when he tried to smash through. He lay down to shout through the crack below the door. With a wooden spoon he grabbed from the table, he banged on cabinets and doors, enfolding only himself in the noise. Everything faded into silence. In the dim light he thought he could see what was left of himself sink into the hush. His companions here, how had they dried so easily to their bones? Here he was intitiating one himself, his own mummy.

But what this felt like wasn't his own, but it was some other's life, and that was the real joke—the dim light, the sticky air, the weird companions. He was a witness. Entombment here for even another minute was the ridiculous fate of someone in a stupid story. Something like this would happen to his brother, Harry, not to himself. He had kept Harry Briggs out of his mind for so many years, whose life was always like an adventure movie scenario. He'd last seen him some ten years back, when his brother had returned sickly from a three year expedition exploring the estuaries, and tributaries of the Amazon. He had been stricken with a strange fever, and lesions that left a ring of scars around his forehead and temples, as if he'd been forced to wear a crown of thorns; in fact, he had been given up for lost then, until he suddenly reappeared, to everyone's delight but Solomon's.

He lifted the tray and spilled some water across his mouth, couldn't waste it, careful not to waste it.

Solomon lit a candle he had found in a drawer, and started to explore all the rooms. The one adjacent had a long narrow slot to what looked like some daylight. Like a channel in a pyramid. That was one route of escape, to work a hinge off a cabinet door, and scrape his way out; two lifetimes of work, probably. The last room partially excavated and abandoned, narrowed like a mine to a two foot face. Mining despair. No way out of there, just that long slot, long shot, maybe 300 feet, to daylight.

When the water and food came again, he carefully lifted the water tray and poured the liquid into a chipped earthenware jar he had found in a closet. Otherwise, die of thirst. Occasionally on top of the pasta came a thin slice or two of gelatinous *"muzzo,"* cut from the nose of a boiled cow's head. Mario and Angelica ate this, and it had always made him queasy, but now he did. It might taste great with some beloved wine, maybe some pecorino. He lay down once by the door, to stretch his fingers out through the crack, hoping to remind GI Joe that he was human in here, change his heart. The tray was shoved against his fingers, not a word. The next time there was a printed prayer next to the pasta.

Soon the food stopped coming altogether, though for a while there was still water, and then the water stopped; as if GI Joe just lost interest. Or was trying to quicken Solomon into his mummy. Solomon remembered, in the furthest room, some dampness against the narrow face of the excavation. He ripped a brass hinge off a cabinet and scraped the wall till it produced a slow consistent drip. That seemed like a victory, water somewhat alkaline, but drinkable, and with the same tool he managed a bit of nourishment, scraping with this sharpened hinge at the skin left on some of the mummifieds. Okay world, call this cannibalism, but his only other choice was to die. If he ever got back into the world he might regret having done this, though he also could imagine some pleasure in telling of it, to Isabel, for instance, to say "I was a cannibal" in the redness of her studio. There was little flavor in the leathery stuff, but a slight change in texture from one to the next. Sometimes crisp, sometimes tough. What could be learned about anybody from that, he wondered? Is taste related to personality? A bitter person, for instance? *O, hello, good evening, buona sera, mmmm, pity but you taste like yourself this evening. Or to gender? Have you tasted the woman tonight?* A cup of wine occasionally might have made this entombment more civilized, more… *gemütlich.*

Harry, maybe he had been cannibal. He bragged about visiting some cannibal tribes in South America. Solomon remembered the description of the strict etiquette of these peoples. Who got the tastiest knuckles. They could trade stories on this. For a white man all it took was money to become a cannibal, money to travel to the cannibal islands.

Harry had been the brother favored by his parents, and they had left almost three fourths of the value of their estate to him. This wasn't all because of Harry's charm, but because he was more suited to running the small sporting goods empire that had made them rich. Harry was definitely the more athletic and more knowledgeable about the business, though he sold it out as soon as possible to support his personal adventures, all the stores in New England and the profitable work-out gear stitcheries throughout Maine and Northern New York, and the sneaker factories in Rhode Island and Maryland, though they'd been scheduled to restructure in the Philippines anyway. Solomon realized he would never see those states again, and never meet anyone again from Providence, or Maryland, or from Washington, D.C.; not unless he got out of this. He had to get out of this. He would do something. Keep his equilibrium. If fate twists, twist it back. Go up right in the face of the son of a bitch. He threw himself at the door and screamed, "I'm in here, goddamit. I'm in here." He pried with a hinge he had torn loose from a cabinet, scraped at the stone floor by the door. Every effort was exhausting. No energy without fuel. A dream-like level-headedness came to prevail over him. He felt afloat and alone, but the only one still wet, after all, among these other absences dried and hanging from the walls. He thinks, "There's a reason I am here. Yes, this is happening to me. If I can just figure out what I have to do, I can turn this into an opportunity. I'm an American. Haha! I'm here for something. To change disaster into opportunity is the American way. Ha!"

Portsmouth came to mind. That was where their trophy factory had been. He thought, "I'll never see Portsmouth again." The first time he'd gone there was with his father, to the red brick factory building, a small one they had built, where there was a team of workers, contented they seemed, who liked his father, never organized against him, though he reigned there like a stern but honest despot. He'd gone back again with Harry, to help prepare the place for sale, one of the few assets that in the will was clearly half Solomon's, and Harry had tried to take even that away from him with his fancy accounting. He had thought many times, in Portsmouth, about killing Harry; except that was something he couldn't do, kill anyone, not even his own brother. Ha! Harry was expert enough at nearly killing himself, anyway, as in the Amazon, as he did climbing alone in the Andes, as he did misreading a downdraft when hang-gliding near the cliffs in Banff. He never quite died from any of this, but never fully recovered, either, from those shattered bones and rare blinding diseases. Solomon wondered, though, if in all his adventures Harry had ever faced something like this. Had Harry ever been entombed? The chill pressed into the bone. Had Harry ever been with no hope for escape? There was always hope for escape. After all, someone had to have carved that slot up into the light in the first place. I need to get back to the world, Solomon thought. I'll track Harry down, tell him about this.

In his family, Solomon carried the weight of his father's sensitivity, the intellectual bent; the father who always expressed regret for not being able to follow a literary predilection, his love for Thomas Hardy, for Walt Whitman; regret for not having the time to write about literature, or perhaps create literature himself, because the success of his business required so much attention, all the detail to manage—management, he always said, was the opposite of creativity. Management was the death of the soul. When his father pronounced the word "literature," it was as if he said the name of God. In his library, which Solomon was allowed to enter only later in life, every book his father had read was covered in plain brown paper, though his father always knew which book was where. But for Solomon opening any of those books yielded a surprise. Thomas Mann, Plutarch, Anatole France, Albert Camus, Benedetto Croce, in plain brown wrappers. The real entrepeneurial drive in their family came from his mother, and the sense of adventure and risk-taking, the need to expand investment horizons. His mother's nature was Harry's heritage that he corrupted on the extreme playgrounds of the world.

Harry Briggs in this situation would probably exhaust himself scraping at the stone slowly to eke an impossible passageway, or try to dig a tunnel through the rock under the door. Or he would pound all day at the door, till he collapsed. Solomon gave up too easily, he'd say. Harry Briggs would spend all his energy screaming for help. But Solomon Briggs' philosophy was to hang on, conserve the energy. Don't waste it in futile attempts at escape. Consider the restraints of sparse diet, lack of water, the heavy air that made just moving from chair to wall a serious expense of energy. Wait it out. If GI Joe remembered, or had a change of heart, he might let Solomon out, but escape was a vain hope. If this entombment was discovered during some random general inspection of diocesan catacombs, or maybe an earthquake would come and crack the shell of rock that cased him, then he had a chance. At any rate, Solomon Briggs was trapped here, really trapped here was what he finally had to admit, and Harry Briggs was only a passing thought.

For exercise he toured the rooms several times a day, investigating each cabinet. He ran through them occasionally, to keep his circulation going, but that took too much out of him, and he'd start to sweat and his own sweat stank for him like death. The dessicated bodies hanging from their hooks were not like humans, not like they once had been alive, but as if they were nothing more than some tools hanging in a shed, waiting on their racks to be used, and except when he enlisted one into his diet, he had little idea what that use could be.

He could almost smell Isabel in Venice, could almost taste her fingers in his mouth, how he'd like now a visit to her studio, to see her body move, share her enthusiasm for her work, field her attitude towards himself, just a walk with her and a conversation along the canals, to discuss Antonello again, or just a day at the Lido, a trip to Trieste, or maybe Dubrovnik, and a night of great fucking like he had only with her, followed by a pillow conference about the child on the way, his hand on her belly, waiting for a kick. And Iera, that lovely unexplored passion that he could only imagine. That was such a lovely potential, lost. He didn't weep, pity himself for anything he'd lost. Pity sucked too much energy, especially self pity. It would waste him and move him away from his faith, this faith, that at some point the purpose would be revealed what he had been put there to do.

After the trays stopped arriving, time dissipated into the windlessness of the rooms; duration, a measure of intervals, was irrelevant—a month maybe, a week, five hours, twelve years, really some days of a number he couldn't grasp. At some point he started to devote himself to the scraping, grinding at the stone with the brass hinge. Decided once the pressure pushed him that way, to gouge, widen the slot that led to the light. It was a long way, but better than to try to get under the door. He would be detected doing that. And then there was the next door, once he got under the first. As long as he felt strong enough, he ground at it. Heaps of talc-like dust gathered at his feet. He learned he didn't need to press so hard as he did at first. Just allow the friction of the brass hinge to skim layer after layer. Use less strength, just the weight of his hand. It opened slowly, so slowly. His beard lengthened. The veins on his hands stood out like the ribs of a glove. Day after day he scraped. Months. Years of scraping. And when he looked up the shaft, it seemed he had gotten nowhere, the light still way out of reach, way beyond what a man could accomplish in a lifetime. He lost track. How much time had he spent? How much time did he have? There was no time for him. No time left, no apparent progress, no time passed.

Once the hegemony of time relaxes its grip, then distance, space, become also irrelevant, and travel is an exercise of clarity, the purified mind. So each of the rooms could evolve instantaneously into any place he chose to be. Like a cool visit to Oslo, the quiet boat trip into some fjords, the melancholy iceberg trapped in one of them, and platters of smoked fish, great platters of translucent slices of salmon, of sturgeon, of halibut and mackerel marinated in elderberry vinegar, sprinkled with capers and dill, oysters glistening in a pool of aquavit, so they assumed the stiff tang of caraway. Addis Abbaba just next door, its air of peppery dust, excrement, and coffee. People beautiful, poor, reach for Solomon with their rough hands and offer him gabis woven in Axum and Kozaga. Prices next to nothing. And through the arched corridor, he arrives in Bombay, Calcutta next, Delhi after that, Bangalore, Madras, Cochin, Trivandrum, all nicely located, a long, relaxing train ride one place to the next, Solomon riding air-conditioned for comfort, riding the luggage rack for experience. Here were the curries for him. Here was basmati rice. Portugal—Oporto, Nazare, Lisboa where at the bars the great singers of Fados make him appreciate his sadness. Not to mention cheese. Not to mention the green soup. Not to mention wine. And in one room he found Fiji, and in that same room again a kayak through a great flotilla of icebergs now off Greenland coast, in conference with the blue whale. No place inaccessible. Lhasa, and its great monastery, and the narrow streets redolent of musk, of sounds, of gongs and chanting monks. Tibetan laughter was his favorite human noise. And suddenly in Cuzco, on the train backing up the cliff, on the way to Macchu Picchu. And Belo Horizonte, its mining curiosities, and then to Marrakech, and from there to Timbuctoo, where he never expected to find a cucumber sandwich, and then to Bhutan of the butterflies, to Vladivostok, all the geography he would cover, just to scrape a little meat from a bone. No one missed the meat. No one saw the tourist passing through.

When he got back to his studio he was thrilled to find he had a visitor; though when she turned around, swinging her blonde hair across her shoulders, he wasn't surprised that this was Kristin, even more radiant in her maturity than when he'd known her before, as a girl in her grandfather's studio.

"Antonello." In her voice his name sounded pure as notes struck from tuned crystal. She kissed his cheeks, and they embraced. He pressed against her, knowing that no one, not even his wife, not Jacobello either, would disturb him in his studio. How had she found the way in?

"Kristin, where did you come from? How did you get in here?"

"There were great difficulties, Antonello. First to find a ship from Bruges, carrying lace to Genova, but first they loaded barrels of salt fish in Bilbao. Months of waiting. Then after Genova, to Naples, and they stopped at Reggio just for me, and an oarsman took me across the straits, and from Reggio it was no problem. On road on the back of a cart, though I had to keep my hair tied up, and covered, because the men down here…" She swung her hair back across her shoulders.

He touched her face, and combed his fingers through her hair. "This makes me very happy. I never thought…I mean I always think of you, but that was long ago, in a different lifetime. I never expected to see you again."

From under her cape she pulled a portfolio that she laid on the table. "I want to work in your studio. That's why I came. I want you to be my teacher. I am ready to be your apprentice, because I believe no one is greater." Her eyes were wet with tears. As she untied the leather thongs of the portfolio and spread her work in front of him, he remembered his visit to her grandfather, when he had done the same thing for John of Bruges, to be accepted as apprentice.

Her studies were perfect in anatomy, rendered with

absolute clarity, with grace of line and gesture, and with a forward elegance that one would expect of a descendant in the Van Eyck family. She had worked from models, made discoveries of her own. Where did she find them? How did she get permission to work with them? Her studies were precise observations, elegant inventions, limbs twisted and bent to the limits of possibility, connections of sinew and skin, definition of muscle and ligament almost beyond credibility, yet natural; smooth sweeps of fascia across the skinned and slightly twisted torsoes of her male subjects, their organs, penises, also skin peeled back, often playfully erect, as if tugging the figures off the paper into the room; and lightly rendered asymmetries in the faces, keen observations of subtle discrepancies in the eyes, one attentive, the other distracted; one observing the parade, the other looking inwards towards the soul, towards regret or grace. Antonello observed that she manifested not just a fine hand for pencil and brush, but a true visual intelligence that could translate her observations of psychological nuance into renderings of the most humane ambivalences and discretions. A pity, he muttered, that she was a woman, because no one paid attention to these talents in a woman. She had a more potent grasp of the art than his own son, Jacobello. He would surely work with her, do his best for Kristin.

She moved into the small room adjacent to his studio, where only a few others rested beneath a curtain, and those were discrete, made only slight clicking sounds when disturbed. Her requirements were minimal, taking from him just the smallest portion of his own meagre rations, himself not wanting to increase his demand for fear his wife would get curious and find her and would see her just as a beautiful young woman, not as an apprentice in his studio. Everyone out there would have the same idea, that he was supporting a courtesan, while they knew he could hardly support his family. Antonello Gagini, his great sculptor friend and colleague, would understand because he too was an artist, though he was more bound by conventional church moralities. They each had so much work they hardly met any more. There was no physical involvement with Kristin now; they both had little energy for anything but their art; and the memory of the fervor of their passion in Bruges was enough to relax them out of the physical, and into a transcendant collaboration. There was plenty of heat while they worked together, always touching as they passed, a light brush of the hand, charged with affection. They were closer than master and apprentice, because she was already a painter on her own. This was an artistic coupling, a mutual unfolding of genius.

She was excited to complete the St. Francis altarpiece that he had long since abandoned because of all his other commitments; but with Kristin as his assistant he was willing to work on it without commission, for his own, for both their satisfactons. Her enthusiasm stoked his own, even though her interest in the figures of the story had nothing to do with the church. Sainthood celebrated what for her was a suspect mode of human disposition, which she occasionally found comical. Saints and their asceticism were a contradiction, she told him, because their denial of the body was voluptuous by reversal. "The material world is a gift, not a restriction. We're here to experience and enjoy, not reject it. Plenty of time to deny pleasures of the senses after we're dead," she said. "Then it will be obvious and easy." The characters in the Saint Francis story, she told him, unfold a rich variety of human paradox, hypocrisy, even virtue, she granted. Plenty to explore.

The church still had its grip on Antonello; after all, he was raised in it, and lived in it still with his family, but he sympathised with her understanding of things. More than that, he felt a great warmth, a harmony of heart and mind in her presence. She had come to visit him at the right time. "We aren't interested in the sweetness of Francis as he is given to us in the legend," he told Kristin, who was at first irritated that he used "we" without first asking if she agreed. But then she thought it was more of a regal "We," and he was speaking as head of state for the kingdom of art that he ruled. Who deserved more, after all, to be a king, than this great painter, clarifier, revealer of the enigmas of the soul? It bothered her less, once she found he listened to her respectfully when she voiced disagreement about choice of gesture, color, or background, and would defer to her when he agreed, never defending his opinion out of petty pride. There was nothing petty about Antonello. "We" was tolerable. "We are more interested in the witty Francis, the troubador, the warrior, the man who loved to dress in fine clothes, his father's son. We want to know the Francis that gave everything up. That's the one we need to know. We want to explore whatever it is within him, that understanding of himself. We want to see in that man of privilege and self-indulgence the seed of the St. Francis who followed his inclinations into his legendary mildness. Because every young man hides his future in his face, just as a green worm nourishes the flight of the moth in the slow cylinder of its body. All the contradictions interest us. We have to be able to lock those oppositions into a harmony that becomes stronger and more revealing and more provocative through its delicious dissonance. We can never resolve, and don't want to resolve that dissonance, but maintain it as the core of beauty."

"Antonello," Kristin said. "You sound like a pompous old professor."

He laughed. "I've earned the right to be pompous, and boring."

"Never boring, Antonello." She touched his hand, and he drew it back. He didn't like anyone to touch his hands any more.

"We'll start with Francis' father, Pietro Bernardone, a portrait of him. We'll use one of these rich ones here." He pointed at a figure hanging by the cabinet, grabbed its sleeve and rattled the bones. "Even in the disposition of the body, all his wealth and influence shows itself, the luxury of the fabrics he sold, one of the wealthiest men in Assisi, that's clear in his face; and as he looks at you, you know you can't resist, that you will buy something, want it or not. So to look at the portrait you have to acknowledge that you are there. My portraits don't tell stories about people. I don't make judgments or come to conclusions, but always create a transaction with the viewer. Do you understand what I am saying, Kristin?"

Kristin laughed. "That's why I've come to apprentice here with you. Only you do that, only Antonello has reached this insight. Otherwise I would have stayed in Bruges, with the dozens of painters of bourgeois drama. Why do you think I'm here? I know how to mix the pigments. I have the formulas for the varnishes. Antonello, what snared me from the beginning, besides your beautiful Sicilian body, was how you found the new way to enter human spirit, a way in to the soul. Only you know how to create this arch between the viewer and the subject, this bridge of recognition. Your paintings engage us when we look at them, like no one else's. Looking at them you have to admit that these others exist, and that for them, you are the other. *I am that* is what you make me recognize. I am the other. It's an example that can bond everyone in the world, and lead to a new connection through the most humane passages. It's a secular and individual transcendance. Totally outside religion." She had embarrassed herself to be so presumptuous to say all this. She felt she understood so little of it herself. She changed the subject. "But who can pose for these portraits?"

Antonello circled his hand, to indicate the audience in their quiet positions against the walls. "We have all these choices."

She looked at him, her eyes moist. He had these feelings he needed to express. She would listen. "Kristin, painting is a language. Any language itself is nothing, just an invitation to dance with the material world, with things, and also with all the ideas running free in the world, yes. Language gives us only itself. No language gives us what is there." He made a large gesture with his arms, as if to embrace everything. "Always disjunction, always. All we can do is refine the dance, to get at what is, to get at what we see, to brush as close as we can. Sometimes the closer we think we are, the further we are away from it. Poets taste these disjunctions most, in their exalted sadnesses, their melancholic joys. The lesson that the artists teach the people is that you can't have the world, you can't hold it, it's not property; it disappears the moment it is grasped; but maybe you can be here fully present with it, and enlist in the dance.

My paintings are to invite that. I want them to look at these portraits and not see themselves, or recognize anyone else, but to acknowledge that someone looks at them, they are present in the negotiation, that there is some deal struck."

"What kind of deal, Antonello?"

"A confrontation with mortality. That's in everyone's contract." He touched her cheek. "Not so serious. We all have to die, Kristin. Look at so many rich people, Kristin, rigid, nasty from trying to protect what they think they have, as if with wealth you buy more life than you are allotted. Look how they die into their possessions. You can get very fat, but you can't put on even one minute more. And they commisson my paintings. Thank you, rich ones. Then what do they have with my paintings?" He too was embarrassed as the meaning of what he was saying slowly slipped away from himself. They smiled, and understood the silence, and turned back to their work table.

In one of the studies for the Pietro Bernardone panels, the angry father confronts his son at the door of his shack of mud and wattles; then St. Francis crosses the Umbrian plain on horseback, from Spello to Orvieto; the face of the leper as it tilts up to receive St. Francis' kiss, like an annunciation, the tinge of fear and disgust as Francis offers it. Francis gives his clothes to a beggar. Francis naked among the birds, among the animals he loved. The marriage of Francis and Lady Poverty. Portraits of John of Capella and Philip the Long, of Bernardo of Quintavalle.

"I want to work on the story of Lady Clare, of St. Clare," Kristin told him.

"Ahhhh," Antonello worked quickly, surely, with a stick of charcoal.

"But I have no church, Antonello. I am so much a skeptic, it makes me sick sometimes. Don't you think I could be happier if I believed," she laughed. "But I don't want to believe, just to make myself happy. That would be stupid. Happiness is nothing. It wouldn't be true. And I really don't understand these saints. They all seem to have been rich, first…Do you believe, Antonello? Do you have faith?"

He didn't answer the latter, but to the former he said, "Of course they are rich. You have to be rich before you can give it all away. If you are a beggar, what can you give up? Your bowl, a few rags…" He crumpled the paper. "Can you cut off your hand?"

"I don't trust them."

"Good. That's the right beginning. Don't trust the saints. A saint steals your dreams. Sainthood is for the cunning. Saints are God's weasels. And they are all crazy. And their job is to make you crazy."

"But St. Clare is so different from me. How do I paint that difference?"

Antonello laughed. "She makes trouble. You make paintings, my dear Kristin. The difference is there, but really, it makes no difference. You make trouble too."

She loved these contradictions. They were like fresh weather. They made her feel more alive in Sicily than she ever felt in Bruges.

For many months they worked as if both were possessed by the same happy demon. The St. Francis project was turning into something that might serve as a large altarpiece. Antonello had never done something this extensive without first being commissioned and paid. It could become the altar of an important cathedral. Great joy filled the studio, a radiance that Antonello carried into his home, that made his whole family happy. Even Jacobello, now in his own studio, doing a commission for the cathedral in Spoleto, was painting with new passion.

Once, after Antonello had been away for a few weeks to see to the site for the annunciation that had been commissioned for the church of the Annunziata, in Pallazolo Acreide, he returned to find Kristin still hard at work, but she looked a little pale. After greeting him weakly, she had to sit down. She rested her head in her hands.

"Is something wrong, Kristin?" He touched her shoulder, and her shoulder seemed to swell into his palm, as if hungry for his touch.

"Nothing. No. Nothing is wrong." She looked at him, her eyes moist.

"Then what is this about?" He wiped a tear off her cheek.

"I'm going to have your child," she said.

Solomon was startled. "But that's impossible," he said.

"I am very happy for us."

"Impossible." He looked at a candle guttering in its niche by one of the mummies. "We never even…"

"Shhhh!" She came forward and silenced him, a bony finger to his lips. "Nothing impossible, my husband."

Suddenly, Solomon had trouble finding his breath. How long had it been since he'd eaten anything? No food had come since long ago. He had no urge even to get the water, so much work to scrape for a few drops. "Ohhh." He fell to the ground as if he'd been struck a blow. "I'm going to be a father," he thought, an almost reassuring thought. "A father," he said, as the bells of the cathedral sounded dimly down through the narrow slot of light.

GIFTS

THE GIFT

The exposition was dark in the wee hours, quiet as a cork in a bottle. Nathan slipped his way out of the exposition grounds. He skirted wide a night watchman asleep on his feet against a steel column. With most of the exposition lights dimmed, Nathan could see the last of the stars before dawn. Good old heavenly bodies, Venus, morning star. He walked towards it, in a direction that he guessed was Galatina. A feeling of well-being, of joy welled up. Where did this come from, and from where this confidence suddenly that he would find his father? Here was the fresh air of an inevitably beautiful dawn, the bats return to their caverns, to their snugs beneath the chimneycaps, the doves coo and rise in flocks on the new light under their wings, the smaller birds conference in the trees, the arabesques of squirrels through the branches, everyone freely cavorts in the grace of the small hour before humans made their gross appearance again in the world. Morning may be what goosed him into hope and belief. No one was on the streets, but as he walked towards the center a music that at first he listened to as if it had invented itself in his own head became more distinct, a rusty pulse coming from the Cathedral end of the park central to the town.

Before it rose the sun first pinkened the stones of the buildings bordering the park, and the itinerant merchants slipped out of their trucks, and pulled back the plastic tarps from their tables for a day of selling their bargain wares, a modest imitation of the big exposition. Though it was still early, a crowd had gathered near a small chapel across from the cathedral. Two old musicians, dressed in threadbare old suits, neatly pressed, were pushing a sour, pulsing rhythm and music into the morning , one with a large tambourine, the other with an old fiddle. Spectators gathered in small groups, strange so early in the morning to see a crowd of people so sporty and prosperous, equipped with camcorders and telephotos, their clothes from Benetton, stylish Calvin Klein sweats and Birkenstocks or Nikes and shorts from Gap. "Last year no one came, not one tarantata," he overheard someone say. "It might be over, extinct," another said. "But if the musicians are here," someone offered. A team of students, intent on capturing whatever was about to happen, had set up a camcorder on a tripod, and another of them wielded one with a long lens, cradled on his shoulder. They passed the time posing for each other as they sipped coffee, yawned, exchanged hugs and kisses.

This he guessed was what Iera had mentioned to him, an ancient ritual, tarantella…tarantismo. A superstition, an affliction of the contadine, poor women, caused by the bite of an imaginary tarantula. Or maybe the tarantula was real once, but now with the pesticides there are no more tarantulas…and with such prosperity, Iera had said, not so much of the same superstition. But if he was lucky, she had told him, he'd find something.

"Where are you from?" asked a woman who approached him out of a small group, who except for one portly older gentleman seemed close to his age, a casual though immaculately dressed bunch, more leisure than sportive. Even among these easy-going ones, Nathan was conscious of his clothes, felt dressed wrong. This woman, small and dark as a crow, with what he'd call Spanish looks, black eyes, sharp nose, pointed chin, wore a loose, batiqued smock of a see-through fabric over thong sandals, henna in her hair, her eyelids darkened. "Come stand with us." She hooked a finger into his belt and tugged him over to her crowd. "This is mister, mister…" She looked to him for help.

"Briggs. Nathan Briggs."

"And he is from,…from…"

"I am from the United States."

"I told you so," said the older man. "Annella said you were probably from Great Britain. I said no."

"I said Great Britain, or Canada. Canada is close," said a heavy woman in a white crepe pants suit, who stepped forward to shake his hand. "Murphy here is from Australia, and his wife Katerina, she is from Torino, but she didn't come today."

"You could say I am from Lecce, already. I have

lived here so many years." said Murphy, who looked like he'd be more comfortable puffing on a meerschaum.

"Does everyone here speak English?"

"We are all Murphy's students. He teaches at the University, and we take his class to learn English. That's Maurizio, he comes from Malta. And Kenshi, he is over there, comes to University from Okinawa."

"And I am Ilaria," offered the woman who first approached him. "So you have come for this, from America, to see the Tarantati?"

Nathan shrugged.

"How ever did you hear of it?" Annela asked. "Did you read *La Terra Del Rimorso?* By Professor Ernesto DeMartino? I don't think…It was never translated." She looked over at Murphy, who concurred. "Or maybe *Sud e Magia*. He is a great ethnographer. I studied all his books. I am ethnographer too, but in Cape Verde, not here."

"We all thought this year we'd better come this year, before it's too late. Next year, who knows if there will be anything, probably not, so this could be the last," said Ilaria. "All of us live in Lecce, and we have never come to see this. Between us we have been all over the world, most of us, but have not seen this in, how you say, in our own back yard."

"It's over," said Maurizio. "Once the ethnographers have worked on it, that tells you it comes to an end."

"I don't think so," said Annela, slapping Maurizio's hand. "I have written about Cape Verde, and I am writing a book, but still there is great music comes from there. Typical music. Have you heard Cesaria Evora?" She asked Nathan. He said he hadn't.

"Maybe not in America yet, but here in Europe she is famous. Before you go, I will give you a tape. Tonight you come, Murphy is having a party, and I will bring a tape. She is very great, a great singer, like your Ella Fitzgerald."

I'm the only one here who has his own sunflower harvester, Nathan almost said.

Kenshi, halfway up a lightpole, was playing lookout. He whistled through his fingers, and pointed over the crowd that was parting slightly to let through two old women, clad in black, escorted by some younger women, also in black, black scarves around their heads, black dresses, black shoes on the women, Nikes on their young companions. Ilaria grabbed Nathan's arm in her excitement, and pressed against him. "Look. Look at them. Listen." The drumming on the tambourine, and the fiddle's repeated motifs became more focused and insistent. The expressions of the older women went from suffering to ecstasy and back again to suffering. The younger women tried to push the crowd of voyeurs and thrill-suckers back away from the women, shouting at them not to laugh, this was no joke.

"Such a pity, what this has come to," said Annela.

One of the young women took a swing with her umbrella at the camcorder tripod, knocking it over, berating the students as jackdaws, vultures, hyenas.

Annela shook her fists with enthusiasm. "Ohhh. Such great. You understand what she said? Did you hear her? These are not stupid people. She said, do you want us to pause to make commercials? That's what she said. She said, do you want us to show our breasts? Did you hear that, Maurizio?"

"This is super. I thought the Tarantati were finished, no more." Murphy said. "Catherine was sure none would come. That's why she stayed at home. She'll be so disappointed."

The old women, their expressions twisted in pain, shook and chattered in tongues. They threw their aged bodies around with manic energy. Their young protectors pushed and pushed the crowd away.

"Look. Look what they're doing," Annela exclaimed. One of the women fell onto her back, and crawled towards the door of the small chapel, chanting as her protector fended people off. "No joke. This is not a joke," she said in English, in Italian, in dialect, as she poked people back with the point of the umbrella.

"You hear what she's chanting?" Ilaria asked. "She chants, 'L'amor e bello / e Dio lo fa.' That means, love is beautiful, and God makes love. That's perfect. That's wonderful." The crowd continued to press on them. "What I've never understood, though, is the bird. I understand the spider, the bite. But there's always a bird. Can we ask them?"

"It's fragility," Murphy said. "A bird is freedom, hope. The bite of the spider captures them. Maybe the bird is escape. No. You can ask them. Maybe they won't answer."

The crowd, some sixty people, pushed forward to look in through the chapel door.

"This is not a performance. This is not for your benefit. Get your own lives." The young women at the open door of the chapel said, bravely holding back the press of the crowd, tears mingling with sweat on their faces. The musicians entered and all of them had to force the door shut against the crowd.

"O wonderful, wonderful. What a treat," said Murphy.

"You liked that?" Ilaria asked Nathan. Nathan couldn't answer. It didn't seem to him like something you liked or disliked. They could still hear the pulse from inside the chapel.

Kenshi rejoined his crowd, tapped Nathan on the shoulder, and pointed towards the steps of the cathedral. There an old bent monk looked down on everyone, but seemed to be focused on their group, and particularly on Nathan, whose movements he followed with a twitch of his head. "He looks you," Kenshi said. "I watch him look you. Every when you move he look."

"He's crazy, that monk," Ilaria said. "He is famous

for he's crazy. They keep him in the church. He has worked in the church forever. His father was an American soldier. Look how he stares."

When Nathan looked at him, the old monk started down the steps, and approached.

"Don't look at him. Don't say anything to him," Ilaria moved away.

The old monk came right up to Nathan, his back bent so the body looked like a question mark holding up his brown cassock. When he got close, he grabbed Nathan's arm, his grip like a clamp. Nathan's new friends gasped in unison to see this. The old fellow twisted his head sideways to look into Nathan's face. Nathan saw the puzzlement wrinkling his old face, confusion in his blue eyes.

"*Sconsecrato*," he said. "Eet…deconsecrated. *Come ho detto l'altro, l'altro, l'altro ieri..* I say before. I warn." He said the English words slowly, as if he had to go a long way to fetch them. A tear slipped down the monk's wrinkled cheek. Nathan brushed it away with his forefinger. The monk tightened his grip.

Murphy stepped in. "That's all right, old fellow. *Lasciate, lasciatelo.*" He pulled the hand off Nathan's forearm, and Ilaria hooked his belt again, and pulled him away, as Murphy pushed the old monk back. "Go back in the church. Everything is fine."

As he retreated, the monk wouldn't take his eye off Nathan. "I warned," he said. "I warned," he repeated, as he backed up the steps, and into the church.

"He's crazy as a goose," Ilaria said. "We apologize, Mr. Briggs."

"Come on," said Maurizio. "He's harmless. If you spent your whole life in that church you would look crazy yourself."

"It's one superstition or another, the tarantula or the church, that makes you crazy one way or the other," Annela said.

"The church, my dear, is not a superstition. It's a belief system," said Murphy.

"Were you raised Catholic, Murphy?"

"Of course."

"Then you went through communion. The Eucharist? How is the wafer, and the wine, not a superstition?"

"Tarantismo is a belief system too," said Maurizio. "It just doesn't have the money behind it."

Ilaria laughed. "Money is a belief system, kids. Possessions are a belief system."

"Yes, money, and a long history of literacy reserved only for the privileged, but those are irrational beliefs, the so called sacraments, justified because of the power of the church, because an elaborate literature has built up to explain, to justify blind faith."

"But this one is a good pope," said Ilaria.

"Good shmope, bad shmope, makes no difference," said the ethnologist. "It's still superstition, all these catholic mysteries. The tarantati are illiterate, have no elaborated written liturgy, no written history, except for what Professor De Martino has given them. The big difference is, superstition in the church is designated as miracle, and designed to control the people; whereas, most of the folk superstitions are instruments the people use to help them believe they can take a little control of their own lives. They work so hard, these women. Poverty is relentless. And they feel powerless to improve their lives. The bite of the tarantula, the 'miserable event,' gives them a chance to stop this work that steals their souls, and to turn inwards, be in themselves. You understand?"

"It's like the major superstition of our time," said Ilaria, seeming to speak out of a daydream. "We think that having this computer, or that car, will make us happy. A nice expensive vacation will make us happy. That's our superstition."

Nathan suddenly remembered that he'd better get somewhere and cancel his credit cards, even though his spree of the night before was fading out of mind, like the titillation of an orgy in yesterday's porn film.

The conversation about belief systems continued, he guessed, all day, because they were still at it when he found them at the party that evening. Through most of the day he had entered and left the hotel by a back door, so as to avoid Paolo Ghiaccione, who now was probably back at the exposition, perhaps with another American in tow. He felt somewhat comfortable with this bunch, in Murphy's apartment, furnished with bargain deco second hand and budget wicker in a crumbling building in the historic center of town. It seemed very familiar, like friends from college, though perhaps these people were more intellectual, more academic. One uncomfortable moment came up when Annela asked him was he raised Catholic, and what did he think about religion and superstition. He told them he thought his father had been Jewish, though he didn't know much about it, and he didn't know much about his mother, either. She never expressed belief. She was an artist. "Artists can have belief," Annela said. Nathan shrugged. This was like a skip in a record; a moment of uncomfortable silence as everyone looked away from him to deal with Jewish, but then they started conversations again. It became very congenial again, and very smart, and even raucous, as they moved several more grappas into the night. "Grappa improves the mind," Murphy insisted. "Or is it the brain?"

Although he didn't want to mention it, Nathan couldn't get the old monk's face out of his mind. Why had he stared so at Nathan? He'd seen something in Nathan's face, maybe the same thing Iera had seen. He would definitely return to Galatina to talk to him. He would have liked to bring it up for conversation, but thought he'd better not tell anyone at the party that he was going. One of them would insist on accompanying him. Maurizio, Murphy, Ilaria, Annela, Kenshi. Murphy's wife might volunteer, as she seemed drawn to Nathan. Katerina was much younger than her husband, a nervous northern Italian woman, whose greenish eyes flitted around the room, as if she expected something somewhere to leap out and suprise her. She complained about always missing the interesting fun, and pressed against Nathan, pouting. He couldn't go with any one of them because he knew it would change the experience. Alone, he thought, he might find something out; but not with one of them, especially not with Murphy's wife.

He drove into Galatina mid morning of the following day. The scirocco had intensified over night, a dense, sandy mist blowing through the streets. The atmosphere felt close, warm, malarial. The tangerine blot of the sun, hung over the cathedral as if fixed in aspic. Nathan broke a sweat just sitting in the car. The streets were quiet, the exposition pulling out that morning, the market vanished from the park. He tried the doors to the cathedral, but they were locked, so he sat down at the one caffe in the piazzetta for a cappucino. A couple of street sweepers cleaned around the steps, and in front of the small chapel. Only one worker alone down the street adjusted a ladder against a facade. To Nathan it looked as if the scene was a wrap, and they were ready to strike the set. The barrista paid no attention to him at the table, as he was talking with a man in a shiny grey summer suit, sunglasses wrapped around his temples.

Nathan went into the bar to order, and the barrista smiled, a familiar smile, and said, "Si, signore. Subito," and went on with his conversation, which was about the sand that would bury everything. Nobody wanted to go out in the scirocco. It was best to cover your car, because the sand would eat into the paint. Africa, grain by grain, the barrista said, was being settled onto the Salento. The whole desert would be lifted across the sea, and then what would they have? A Sahara Salento. Nathan went back to his table to wait. As the barrista finally turned to make Nathan's drink, the man in the suit bent over with a napkin to wipe the sand from his shoes. Nathan's hand when he pulled it back from the table was covered with damp sand that couldn't be brushed off. The wind worked it through his t-shirt. It was in his nostrils, in his ears. He licked it off his lips, and wiped his tongue on the sandy back of his hand.

The barrista brought him the cappucino, covered with a saucer to protect it from the sand. "How do I get into the cathedral?" Nathan asked.

The barrista looked at his watch. "This cathedral? Why do you want to go in this cathedral? You want to make a confession? There are other churches open. Go to Chiesa di San Rocco, or Santa Maria della Grazia. I think they have the Monday mass. Ninno, come here." He signaled to his friend in the grey suit. "I will never go into a church again," he said. "I get sick when I go in, from the hypocrites." The barrista crossed himself. "When you are in this profession, signore, you see a lot of things, and at this location…" He shook his head, then signaled for his friend again.

"No, no. Si sporca. No." The man in the suit didn't want to come outside because of the sand.

"Look at him. You'd think he was going to meet Monica Lewinsky. You know Monica Lewinsky?"

"I don't want confession. I need to go into this church. I am a student of the…"

"Of the architecture? Of the Leccese barocco?"

"Yes."

"Ahhh!" He went in to talk with his friend, then came back out. "Ninno will help you. Finish your cappucino, then Ninno helps."

While Nathan drank his coffee, Ninno disappeared in back of the bar and came out in coveralls and a pointed hat folded out of newspaper. Down the street another workman appeared who held the ladder while his partner applied some stucco to patch a hole on the facade.

Ninno led Nathan around the block to the back of the church, cursing the wind, *"scirocco, manniagia la sabbia putana."* He knocked on a narrow wooden door, underneath what looked like living quarters. A woman leaned out of a window above them, and Ninno explained to her what they wanted. It was the bent one, the monk, who finally opened the door. He cocked his head one way, to look at Ninno, and then the other way to look at Nathan and seemed to stagger back into the building.

Ninno gestured for Nathan to go in after the monk. *"Niente paura, niente. E un uomo semplice, nient'altro.* Simple man." He pointed to his own temple. *"Poveretto. É tutto…"* He shook his hand. *"…capisce?"* Ninno shrugged, and pulled the door shut, leaving Nathan inside with the monk.

"Giai Giao," the old one said, tapping his chest. "Giai Giao." He circled Nathan, inspecting him closely, and repeating "Giai Giao." It took Nathan some uncomfortable moments to realize the fellow was telling him his name.

"Nathan. Nathan Briggs." Nathan offered his name. Could the monk's name really be GI Joe, like a World War Two cartoon?

"You…wit…wit .. come," The monk gestured strenuously, as if trying muscle up some words in English. He led Nathan down a series of corridors, into the church, and then, practically at a trot, he led him around the church, pointing at random at paintings and sculptures. "Yes, good. Yes, good." Nathan forgot what he was doing there. What was the point of his coming out here? The monk suddenly stopped and turned. He reached out to touch Nathan's cheek with his fingertips.

"More," he said, the word propelled at Nathan like a missile. "More, you want." It was as if he had finally retrieved those words from a distant repository of English. "Come." He grabbed Nathan's hand and led him around the altar and down some steps, and through descending corridors, into the caverns beneath the church. The dry smell of the stone, and shifting shadows of their descent made Nathan fear something terrible was happening. Why did he follow this strange acolyte of this obscure church? His breath got shallow. The monk was leading him to a place where he would suffocate. When he opened the last door and stepped aside, Nathan hesitated. There was nothing to breathe in there. He didn't want to know whatever it was he would find out. The stifling air in the cavern never meant for humans.

"Inside. Go inside." Joe pushed on him.

Nathan stepped in.

A few photons of light squeezed through a slit at the far end. "More light," Nathan requested. He felt embalmed in the dimness.

"Ahhh." The monk threw a switch near the entrance and an incandescent bulb dangling from the vault on a worn wire crackled and flickered dimly. "You see now."

Nathan looked around the room at the shadows carved out of the foundation stone, a wall of cabinets, (he didn't want to know what was in them), and from hooks in the niches hung the mummified remains of people, monks in crumbling robes. He hit an object with his foot, and it slid across the floor, something of fur dried out that might once have been a cat. Joe tapped his back, and pointed to two figures, one seated straight up at a table, the other leaning on its elbows. Joe motioned for Nathan to go look. He didn't want to. He wanted out of that place. Nonetheless he approached. The hair on the skull of the seated figure was long and white, a long white beard. In its bony fingers it held, had been holding for who knows how long, a drawing pencil. Nathan looked at the face, all dessicate, skin leathery, clinging to the bone. Who was this? He pulled the head back by the hair and something cracked, a sound like ice snapping. He looked into the face, eyes dried shut.

"Who is this?" he finally asked. He tried to take a deep breath. "Is this…no…?"

"Eh. Eh. Eh." Joe made a little noise, stepping closer. "Breegess. Breeg…ess."

The one leaning had probably been a woman, since it had long hair, but no beard. "Mamma," said G.I. Joe. How had these two got here in the darkness? "Salomone," said Joe. "And mamma. Condannato. Sconsecrato…condem .. ned."

Nathan wanted to cancel this. He never wanted to know this. Joe sensed he might leave, so he grabbed Nathan's shirt, and held him. He pointed at the table, covered with dust, and brushed some of it clean from around the pencil that the poor bearded figure held. Nathan could see only some random lines there, a meaningless scrawl on paper, the paper sitting on top of others similarly marked. Joe brushed away a little more of the dust, where he uncovered some carefully printed letters, most of them obscured— NCESC_ ___ONELL_S ME ___XIT.

"I'm not breathing. I'm out of here," Nathan said, and turned to head for the door. He didn't want to inhale once more, not one more breath down there. Successful or not, this search was not successful. This was no father he was ever prepared to know. He wanted out of there, to get back into the daylight, to the place where forgetting begins. Somehow he found his way back up into the church. Joe was already there to meet him. He held out two large leather portfolios, tied with thongs. Nathan refused them, and ran for the front door of the church. It was locked. He wanted this over with, now.

"For you," said Joe.

Nathan refused to take them. "Let me out of here, please."

"Yours. For you," Joe insisted, and pushed them up against Nathan's chest. They were too heavy. Nathan wrapped his arms around them, and burst into tears. There were many many papers. He knew that now that he had touched this, he could never let it go. He wrapped his arms around them, pressed them to his chest.

"Bye bye," said the monk, as he opened the door, and let Nathan out, as if he was relieving himself of his own of burden. It was early afternoon. The wind had died. The town was blank. The streets, and his rented car, were covered with a layer of pale Sahara.

PSST
───────────────────────────

PSSST!
an epilogue

Nathan was split, as if the Boeings that had pierced the World Trade, exploded, smashed it down, had split his spirit from his spirit, his mind from his mind, his body even from his body. He felt all the time like his own double, one who lived the life he always lived, the other constantly crippled by grief, drowned in the weeping flood. Everyday things were unbearable, like getting out of bed, distasteful even taking the first usually wonderful sip of coffee, intolerable talking with his first client of the day, o no, where did all the money go? And through the months after the disaster the air of his world smelled like iodine, like rotting meat, and every taste was a mouthful of wet plaster. He had, he couldn't but recall almost with guilt, moved his offices from the forty-third floor of the second tower, the one that came down first, only a few months earlier, and but for that he and Erica and Satjay and Ross, who worked for him, not to forget Sandy, would have been ground with everything, everyone else into that smoking mountain of steel and ash that so many weeks afterwards still looked like the festering hillside of some coal deposit smoldering beneath the ground. The cranes and excavators and trucks creeped around in it like some slowly nesting insects, and the poor mournful rescuers, cloaked in grief and courage, looked like their unprotected larvae.

They'd watched downtown from the big windows in his own office—o no, omigod, help those poor, o shit—as the second plane flew at the building and then the explosion, themselves exploded, so many people pumped into his office, fused as if their common incredulity were some heat applied to blunge them into one creature, one common sob, and then the towers collapse and then great upsurge billows of black smoke they watched also now on television as well as out the window, all of it unreal now, even their own cries and mutterings, and all of life in front of them, around them, had become a sprawl of special effects, everything hyper real, and phony too, even the screams of Sandy seemed synthesized, whose brother and boyfriend worked in the towers, who looked at each of them in Nathan's office, and screamed one by one into each of their faces, as if sheer volume could obliterate this horror, and then she cried as she fled their office, "I have to go down there. I have to go there." And they thought they saw her later on television, but never heard from her again until they got a note from her after some weeks, from somewhere that seemed nowhere, from Ft. Davis, Texas, where she went to stay with her cousins, and she wrote to say she was giving up her job, and would probably never come back to New York. It was after her example, perhaps, that Nathan folded up his business, left its residue of clients in the hands of his three remaining employees who had nowhere to go away from New York, and took Max up on his invitation to the *housewarming* in Colorado, the irony of that word even somewhat chilling. Aside from a few clothes to take, the only thing he couldn't let go of was the gift he had been given, the portfolios he'd carried back from the South of Italy. And even as he toted them there to Max, half of him could not stop his weeping, while the other half presented himself normal in the world.

Nathan lugged the portfolios to the library upstairs. He had been carrying them for so long, it felt like their weight was grafted to his body. The couples sunk into the conversation pit of the great living room watched him ascend the curved staircase near the fireplace as if he was doing it for their amusement. In the walk-in hearth a bright gas fire hissed. He thought he heard someone call his name, but continued upwards and into the book-lined library, relieved finally to drop the weight he had carried all the way from Southern Italy onto the desktop. He'd been hauling these leather folders around everywhere since Italy, even into his sleep, through his dreams. He'd hung onto them through the catatrophe, as if they anchored him to something, maybe to a life long before suicide glamour cults. The scuffed calfskin with its rawhide ties lay against the polished cordovan inlay of the desk, like rough sandstone on a sunburned belly. This den was walled with the spines of books, all richly bound in leather, like books never read, classics that just by virtue of acquisition, lend the owner an aura of literacy, the gilt edges of their pages shining with genius. Actually in Max's library some of the spines were bogus, joined together to swing out on hinges, doors to little cubbies where Max's porn collection was concealed. The spines of the Bronte Sisters' complete works sheltered, for instance, "Tickle Me Suzy," "Big Toe Dipping," "Ripe and Wet," and Elizabeth and Robert Browning hid under double lock a rare series of Paraguayan snuff films, not that Max was proud of them, but he felt someone should archive these.

He undid the top portfolio, and fanned some of the drawings across the desktop. The puff of air they released into the room made him shudder, the mummified breath of their origin. This was the first time he'd done more than glimpse them. Even though carrying them everywhere was a struggle, and he resented the weight sometimes, he hung on because losing them, he felt, before they revealed their secrets to him would be horrible. Or maybe they had no secrets to reveal, really, but he just had to allow himself to accept what they were. That strange old churchman who had given them to him knew something. He had thrust them into Nathan's arms as if releasing himself from their spell, and Nathan had carried them away blindly, never asking what they were. What were they? To lose them would feel like a sacrilege, would mock his inheritance. Could he accept that this was his payoff for the hunt he had been on, these hints of his father in Italy? He never admitted anything, however, never said the words of what they probably were, and never said the name of the one whose leathery remains he had seen beneath the church in Galatina. That strange town, where he had become…become what? Something weirder. Silence ruled.

Meaningless stuff. The one on top was scrawls of pencil, and blots of ink, vaguely organized densities, some dubious Pollocky thingy, he could hear Brightwatch say, but somehow different, yes, and most of them labeled in a studied calligraphy in the lower right hand corner, strange because so specific, titles like "Lady Clare Kisses The Hem Of St. Francis' Robe." The portfolios must hold several hundred of these drawings. It was a discouragement not to have Miriam any more to look at them with him. She had dropped him for her new squeeze before he got back from his trip, without even a discussion. Just like that, he had come back and it was over. A breathless disjunct. He expected it somewhat, just from her tone of voice the last he talked with her, so cold; but he never could have anticipated how much he'd miss the intimacy. She had been at least someone with whom he didn't have to start from step A, to explain it all, to justify his obsessions. So maybe that was why he brought these for Max to look at. At least Max had known him for a long time, and had been there from the beginning of his Italian conversion; though intimacy wasn't usually the kind of thing you could do with Max.

Through the small fireplace in the den that connected to the same chimney as the walk-in one by the conversation pit, he thought he heard Miriam's laughter. It blew into the room like backdraft. He stepped through a door onto the narrow balcony that with part of the den was cantilevered over the living room and saw Miriam leaving with her nattily dressed new man, in a white suit, (he knew that guy), she in a bathrobe, her tanksuit underneath. Neither Max nor Holly had warned him she would be there. They were heading for the huge heated bubble, where most of the party was going on, an inflatable structure made of a waterproofed canvas that Max had painted after September eleventh so it was a great Stars and Stripes, that sheltered the pool, the bar, the live music. He didn't see Max in the living room. He was probably out under the bubble, with the rest of the party. Nathan took the narrow corridor to a door that connected with the balcony in front of the bedrooms. The chill folded Nathan's arms across his chest for warmth. A light snow fell onto the inflated shell. Shadows of the guests played in shifting grotesques across the luminous surface of red white and blue. Intermittent snow sparked onto the guest cabins below, and icicles had started to form on the lights strung between the masts of the catamaran. Despite the snowfall, he still could see the dark bulk of the mountains pressed against a fading green and vermilion twilight. The evening was strange. Without Miriam to test his thoughts then, he preferred to have none. He headed for the stairway, down to enter the light of the party.

"Pssst," came from a bedroom door that was cracked open. "Uncle Nate, here. Come over here." It was Max's son peeking out.

"O, hi Kevin. I was just on my way down to look for…"

"Come here. Just a little minute."

Nathan didn't want to join the boy, who was always ready to include him in a conspiracy.

"Just come in for a second. I need to show you something."

"You should be at the party. I'm sure there are plenty of other kids there, good looking babes in the pool too."

Kevin scrunched his face, and contemptuously mouthed the word, babes. "I don't feel like, you know, getting dressed, wearing clothes. I don't want to be my dad's kid." He held up his thumb and shook his fist. "Just for a second, come in. I want to show you something cool."

Kevin swung the door open for him. He was wearing only some briefs and sandals. The room was lit with three old oil lamps that he must have restored out of the debris of the original line shelter on the original ranch.

Nathan was startled to see the doll, naked and spread across the bedclothes. She looked real enough to make him avert his eyes.

"Don't worry. We remember you. Esther doesn't mind," Kevin said.

The corpselike figure lay there not exactly like a corpse, but like something about to come to life, lacking only a certain aura that might be backordered in eternity, or maybe some elixir, or the touch of one of Yahweh's teaching assistants. It had been a while since he'd been with Saffron, and so latex Esther twanged him where he was horny. For a piece of rubber, she looked good, as real as any porn bimbo. She had a smell, a confusion of perfumes. Between her legs the silkiest hair that he wanted to touch, and her slit parted slightly to reveal a moist nibble of the pink insides medium rare.

"What do you think of this?" Kevin tapped on his shoulder with something metal. Nathan turned to see the gun.

"It's a 'shorty.' Isn't it cool? AKS74U Kalashnikov, uncle Nate. It's so neat. Takes a 30 round magazine."

Kevin held it out for Nathan to take, but Nathan didn't want even to touch it. "This is real? Is it real?"

"It weighs about seven pounds. I took it to school inside my jacket. I took it to an Avalanche game. No one even knew I had it."

"Does your dad know?"

The boy winked at Nathan. "You're the first one."

He lay the gun down in the crook of Esther's arm, making the doll look softer, more vulnerable, more flesh.

"Ebay is so rad, uncle Nate. I found a Unitech 202 supersmall for less than two grand. That is totally beyond phat, dude. They say it's in perfect condition."

"What is it?"

"A night vision scope. It's going to be so cool, to be able to see everything at night. Pow pow pow. I bought it, but first they're checking to see if it will fit my model shorty. They're really honest."

"These are not times to be playing terrorist, Kevin, or whatever you're doing."

"I'm not playing, dude. It's just because exactly what you said that it's important."

"What did I say?"

"That it's not the times to be playing."

"You have to tell your dad you're bringing this stuff into the house."

"Mikhail Timofeevich Kalashnikov," he said, with dreamy reverence. "He was a genius, you know. A great genius. He should be my father. And he came from nothing but a peasant family. And when he was just 30 years old his design was adopted by the whole Russian army. He was given the Stalin Prize First Class…"

"Do you know who Stalin was?"

"Then he was honored twice as a hero of socialist labor, and was given a Lenin prize, whatever a Lenin is. And three more orders of Lenin, and the order of the

Red Banner of Labor, and the Order of the Great Patriotic War of the First Class, and the Order of the Red Star, all those orders…"

"How many innocent people, Kevin, how many have his guns killed?"

"Yeah. That's just what I mean. He's got so many medals, and he was made a citizen of honor in his native village, Kurya, a big bronze statue of him there."

Nathan backed out of the room. Since they brought him to Colorado, Kevin had become a really creepy teenager, something other than the bright kid he knew back East. Maybe it was the isolation of being thrown into a strange school. He didn't even want to think of…this was where it happened, wasn't it? The concubine disaster? porcupine? Some flower, though. Columbine, yes. "So many people, Kevin. So many have already died."

"And Yeltsin gave him the Order For Distinguished Service to the Motherland, Second Class." Kevin followed Nathan out the door.

"It's cold out here, Kevin."

"It's okay. I'm never cold. And he promoted him to Major General on his Seventy-Fifth anniversary."

Nathan turned away from the boy, and started down the stairs. He was going to panic. He just had to close his eyes, to see the World Trade Center collapse again. It happened over and over. He wished it would stop. The snow was heavier now, still melting off the inflated shell that glowed warmly, the whine of the blowers mixing with the sounds of jazz from within. Kevin kept shouting down at him as Nathan looked for the entrance.

"He lives in a city called Izhvesk. I want to go there so bad. You should come with me, Uncle Nate. They're building a museum. We can shoot all the…"

The heavier snowfall like a shroud closed on the vista of foothills, mountain, sky; so as Nathan entered the inflated dome, the inside space bloomed immense, and the people partying looked very small under the illuminated stretches of flag. This was Max's private astrodome. Huge fans that kept the bubble inflated swept moisture and chlorine into the air off the two pools, one a diving tank, the other almost twice Olympic size. In the humidity, Nathan started to sweat. The band at the other end was amped into the upper decibels to be heard above the fan roar.

"Hey, get out of your tie and jacket, Nate." Max had spotted him, and approached. His paunch hung over a black and yellow striped bikini, beach towel across his shoulders. He had to shout to be heard. "Gets like a steambath in here with all the people; hard to believe, the way it's really snowing in the world."

Nathan removed some clothes, down to the silk t-shirt that Saffron had bought him in Paestum, a picture of the temples and the name of the ruin embroidered tastefully over the right breast. Through the mists rising around the diving tank he saw someone doing disciplined spins, flips, and curls off a high board. He grabbed Max's arm. "That's not…it can't…"

"It's Miriam, yeah, and my neighbor, Reg Rogers. You know she has a fresh squeeze?"

"I didn't know who it was. Yeah, I knew. She met him here, right?"

"I guess so. Anyway, he tells her she's got a big talent, and he's determined to get her ready for the next Olympics. He's hired her a coach. She looks great."

"She'll be pushing on forty by the next Olympics." Nathan now thought it was insensitive of Max, to say the least, not to have alerted him that Miriam was going to be starring at this party. He suspected it was intentional. "She was never that good anyway."

"I don't know. That backwards gainer looked pretty good."

"That guy? He's the arms dealer, isn't he?"

"He's our neighbor. He publishes the "Shoot First" magazine, for mercenaries; yeah, I think he was a mercenary, and he made a lot of his money selling hardware. He's my neighbor down the road, and he convinced me to do the flag across the cover of the bubble. It's a great idea. I wasn't there, I mean in New York, you were, but that whole thing of September Eleventh made me feel patriotic again. That's maybe a good thing about it. How about you? I never was one for waving the flag, but now…"

Nathan couldn't get his eyes and thoughts off Miriam climbing the ladder again. "This is like I moved into that novel we read in college, remember, in that class we took from that weird teacher who stuttered, remember? You always had to sit a few rows back if you didn't want him to spit on you."

"I don't remember anything about college, except wasting my time."

"It wasn't Great Gatsby, but it was by the same writer, Fitzgerald; you know, she's been molested by her father, and she ends up leaving the guy, the narrator, for this mercenary, this soldier of fortune type. I've always remembered that."

"I've got no memory for books," Max said.

"Now it turns out to be prophetic."

"Yeah, well, Nate, I'm not the one to ask about books; but I wouldn't get your boxers in a bunch over it." He slapped Nathan on the shoulder. "Listen, I think I'm wanted back at the house. We're about to open the room for the Ellis celebration. Holly's dad, wow. He's a trip." He pointed down to the other end of the pool. "Why don't you go down to the bathhouse, grab a swimsuit and towel."

"I need a drink."

"You know where the bar is. Just follow your nose. Single malts galore. Go get yourself a drink, get to the bathhouse, get yourself wet. Tons of babes in the pool. Get yourself laid."

That Max had said something about patriotism finally hit him. Yes, he had thought about it when he went down to the site, and volunteered for several days in the sad and bootless rescue effort; and he mingled there with all the curious and the grieving, and had wept with everyone, young, old, people of every color, every race, many of whom had been through their own private hells to get into this country, all the religions, all together in mournful attitude, speaking all the languages of the world, in the greatest experiment in pluralism ever known to the world, an experiment called New York City, called the United States of America. Yes, he loved it. Not love of the flag so much as love of these people from everywhere, and the privilege of living with all of them, and he felt this fury against those self-righteous maniacs who could see only one narrow path to the dogma they call truth, only their way, and felt justified to kill as many people as they could for the stupid sake of it. Yes, he was patriotic. Alas for the poor victims. For them the flag was not enough. But here, to ward off the snow, it was a nice conceit.

From the other side of the pool, a young woman suddenly recognized Nathan as the older dude her friend Saffron had run with in Italy. It was a smallish world, to see him here. She had stayed in Italy because she wanted to ski, and brought home to Colorado the Albanian ski instructor she had met at the lodge in the

Abbruzzo, outside Sulmona. She stayed there to ski more after Marco, who had brought her into those weird mountains, had to return to work in Rome. It was like a kind of Vail with sheepherders, and donkeys running around. She and Agrom had been eyeing each other anyway, and they hooked up immediately. He was hunky, and a devil on skis. Agrom had left his friends in Barletta, on the coast near where they had come ashore, because he thought they had a better chance if they split up, and he learned they were hiring for some new ski resorts above Sulmona. He was good on skis, but never thought of it previously as a source of money. He would send for Zenepe, he thought, once he had enough. Then he met Deborah, who looked like a plump Zenepe, with a silver stud on her tongue. He never knew a woman like her, an American girl, so rich, and so much without any thoughts. He could work as a ski instructor in Colorado, she told him, and she offered to teach him American and bring him back with her. There was so much here, he realized. So much stuff. No one in Albania, not even Enver Hoxha, the devil, ever had so much. So he now was in America. His first time on an airplane, and he was in Colorado. He could take away a truckload from each house, and no one would notice a loss. He could take Deborah away, and take her money. She had her own money. He could sell her. Why not? Deborah thought for a moment of going over to introduce herself to Nathan, but then felt a little shy. It seemed weird. He might be one of the kind of guy who wouldn't even remember Saffron.

Nathan remembered Kevin just as he saw Max pick up his fur-collared bathrobe off one of the loungers. He had forgot to mention Kevin and the gun, which he had put first on his agenda. Max headed out into the snow. Miriam's diving had distracted him. He skirted the pool and headed for the bar, his path taking him close to the diving tank. Reg Rogers, dressed in white linen, stood by the ladder to the high board. Nathan remembered the first time he saw him, when Miriam had said. "That guy in white is into evil shit."

He looked older than Nathan remembered, maybe in his early sixties, but still well put together under his whites. "I enjoy your magazine," Nathan paused next to him. *Shoot First*, one of my favorites." The guy looked at him and grinned very slightly, the cliche of a steely stare from his greyblue eyes. "Thanks." Then he thrust his face back into his wrap-around shades, and tilted his head up to watch the dive. A thick scar ran halfway around his throat; surely his neck had once been slit. His grey ponytail swung in the breeze. Perhaps Miriam had heard Nathan's voice, or seen him, but she muffed her dive, landing almost on her back. "What in hell was that?" Reg Rogers reprimanded her, as she pushed up out of the tank.

Nathan passed the bandstand and headed for the

bar. A stoop-shouldered tenorman with a wispy beard and a long black braid paced close to the edge of the stage, holding his horn horizontally. He whispered into the pick-up mike clamped to the bell, as if talking to himself. "Ahhh…yes…people…wash-te…Indian jazz tenor saxophone player, Christopher Damian Half-hawk, full-blooded Cree jazz musician." He ran his fingers along the keys, without blowing into the horn, just for the percussive sounds. "I let my fingers do the walking," he laughed. He took the mouthpiece between his lips, and produced a light squawk. "Here where we are, here in the overworld." He swung his horn in an arc above his head. "I play for love. I play for you. I play for wampum…wampum…wampum." He danced to that repetitiion, setting down a tempo, as behind him the drummer laid out some brushwork, and the acoustic bass created the pulse, and a progression of chords from the piano, and the saxophone rose through some minor changes, modulating surprisingly into a lightly swinging rendition of "Wichee Ty To."

Nathan took a dram of single malt with a splash of water, then noticed someone had lost under the table a thin-strapped gold and transparent fuck-me sandal. He recognized this as Miriam's because he had bought them for her that spring, had really scored with them because they were very sexy, and they fit. He picked it up by a strap and, holding it in front of himself, moseyed over to a crowd near the pool, their circle formed around one man. Nathan approached to catch the lecture.

"…are so courageous, the Milsteins, and I have been very very lucky to meet them, and to convince them to allow me to build this. Sometimes I have to pinch myself to believe that god has helped me to find people who believe in me and support my vision, my sense of the history of American architecture. It is American! I can't emphasize that enough in these times, when all of us feel we need to celebrate what America means to all of us. I am a fuckin' American architect and builder. I say that with pride and in all humility in these sad times."

Pallad, Nathan thought. He had expected a taller architect. This one looked like an excellent lush, and he wouldn't have guessed the greying red hair, with a flash of bald spot when he bent his head, like the eye of a storm. His serious brow arched over his eyes that blinked too often; and as he talked he had the habit of flaring his nostrils, the nose pocked and veined from long lubrications at gatherings like this.

"Isn't it strange that I should be the only one in America to fuckin' defend the motel as architecture, and to continue the fight to transform it into a single family habitation." He grabbed a Gibson on the rocks offered by a bikinied girl carrying a tray, downed it swiftly, left the little onions on their silver spear, and grabbed another before she left. "But so be it. When we look at those motels built post World War II, into the eighties…" His moist lips puckered between phrases, to alert anyone listening that everything he said was in earnest. Even the expletives that he released lightly into his sentences, like decorative swirls, seemed sanctified by this kiss. "They are fuckin' genuine, an American architectural art form, a naive art form related to the mid twentieth century expansion of the the highway network, the interstates, the development, the demography of American mobility—like our heritage of corporate folk art, determined by the evolution of American life style—proliferation of motorcars, enormous swift growth of a paved highway system, etcetera etcetera. You know the story, nothing else like it in the world." He paused, worked his pucker, stared in the general direction of his creation, as if he could see it through the stars and stripes of the inflated bubble. His bald spot reflected shifting tints of light, from the slowly turning spotlights that went on automatically as the evening darkened. Music filled the hesitations of his talk like a sound track. "The need to escape, getting to somewhere different and better—better job, better life, better people, better romance, better exotic places—all the fantasies the road promises to fulfill, erotic fuck and suck fantasies, kinky fantasies." The architect directed his attentions mostly at a woman almost a head taller than himself, her stately naked body silhouetted by light diffused through her sheer robe.

"I think sometimes of our dear Chekov." She spoke with a slight accent. "If only he was here with the motel for his characters to play in. How much we need Chekov now to brighten up these sad times."

Pallad slipped in close to look up at her. "Well," he puckered. "Actually it's interesting that Nabokov, who loved Chekov so much, you know, and despised Dostoevsky, you could say he was Chekov's proxy in our time, and he fuckin' opens that Lolita with an homage to motels, and the whole trip is a bittersweet tribute to the American highway, and especially to motels, one after the other. He understood how the lovely blandness of design was like an enticement, an open notebook for anyone to scribble his or her desires. Be they straight, be they kinky. We all remember our dear J. Edgar Hoover, the lovable FBI closet queen, himself a fuckin' American original. He warned an unwary public that motels were…I quote him verbatim, '…dens of vice and corruption…behind many alluring roadsigns.'

Pallad turned to Nathan, and narrowed his eyes, as if trying to figure out if he knew him. "Indeed, when I build these homes I take advantage of the truth that underlies Hoover's assessment. You come back after work, and worry for a moment that there could be a "no vacancy" sign, no rest for you; then the relief of remembering that it's all your own place, always a room for you at this inn, and all the erotic resonances kick in, enough to make J. Edgar lick his lips, and I'm sure were he still with us, I'd build his goddam house, so he could suck a different cock in each unit; and then we've got all the references to being on a real road trip—of reckless pleasure with someone new, of showering with some treat you'd never seen naked before. You speculate on the history of the bed. You do things you wouldn't dare in real life. You move on in the morning, leaving the spills and rumpled bedclothes behind, anticipating pancakes at the Village Inn. It's a home that will never get stale. The space and the structures encourage everyone to play. You can continually refurbish your marriage, or whatever stale fuckin' arrangement your life has become." He winked at the tall woman, who bowed her head and turned away, as if trying to blush. "That's why I've designed and furnished even the bedrooms to echo the geography of the Travelodge room—two double beds in each, beautyrest mattresses, TV on a shelf with the remote bolted to the nightstand between the beds, desk and dressing table along the mirrored wall in each unit, shower and toilet separated by a door from sink and vanity mirror. No Gideon bibles yet." He smiled impishly. "But I'm considering that effect." Pallad leaned towards Nathan and whispered, "Are you looking for Cinderella?"

Until the architect reached for it, Nathan had forgotten Miriam's sandal that he held out in front of himself, like an offering cup.

"Here, let me." The architect took the sandal from

his hand, and turned with it to kneel at the tall woman's feet. She palmed his head for support, as he lifted her foot to try the sandal. The inside of her thigh brushed against his temple, and she uttered a low giggle.

"Too big for this princess." He handed the sandal back to Nathan, who slid it inside his shirt.

"So," the architect turned back to his admirers. "The Whiteleys have engaged me to do theirs, up the road here, in the style of the old Alamo Courts, and the Thurstons are looking at a Knight's Inn kind of a thing, a kind of Tudorama in the canyon, or a Motel Six Bauhausiness. Soon enough, mountain biking or four wheeling into the foothills here will have the soupçon of a road trip from Cheyenne to Salt Lake, or Louisville to Pittsburgh…"

Nathan looked back to the diving tank for Miriam, but she was gone. The band played "A Night In Tunisia," with the drummer tom-tomming it into ritual. As Max had promised, the pool was full of babes, but Nathan was too wounded to go fishing. He left the bubble, went back to the house. The snow continued, late October snow, great for skiers and snowboarders, allaying their fears for the time being that global warming might make their rivalry moot. A few people he didn't know indulged in the conversation pit, their faces like embers in the fireglow. He went back upstairs to the library, surprised to find that someone had spread the sheets from his portfolioes across the floor, and people were actually examining them.

"This is astounding," he heard someone say, a tall slim man dressed in a blue silk Armani, his grey hair neatly combed back. Another short round bearded one, affecting some expensive fashionable baggy youthgear, and followed by a youngish primped androgyne hair dyed lemon yellow, looked from one to another, mumbling, "What a find. Radical stuff! It's like the grinch stole Pollock, gave him to Keith Haring, and Haring punted, may he rest in peace"

Nathan backed out a door, into another room, where several people, including Max, were gathered. This was the map room, the one being dedicated to Ellis Prefontaine, Holly's father. Hung on the walls here was a history of the man's career, from his World War II battlefield maps, contoured and detailed, with every potential obstacle highlighted, to the maps he did for his kids, of fantasy landscapes that eventually turned into his series of Spanky Planet Prefontaine children's books, and then the uncanny polar projections of the earth seen as if from beyond, and through an accurately drawn veil of all the stars visible with the naked eye, and in the center of the room, the great Prefontaine cyberglobe, endless modes available with the touch of a remote stylus, so it could feature cities and roads, both day and nightscape; or a contour projection, with the capacity of magnifying down to a quarter-section; an hydrologist's projection of water resources, adjustable for consumption over time; demographic and economic projections; a projection of the distribution of world religions; an historical sequence of territories, city states, sheikdoms, principalities, nations; the migrations of tribes, so you could watch the armies of Saracens, Visigoths, Mongols sweep through. Alexander's map of the world. Hitler's. Bill Gates'. With the same stylus you could have it print out any of these maps, city maps, road maps, or print details down to specific neighborhoods. It was a total cartographer's tour de force, the ultimate globe, huge and inconceivable. The whole world glowed in the center of this one room in his daughter's posh new Travelodgy home.

"This is something, huh?" Max appeared from behind the globe, to put an arm around his shoulder.

"Yeah, impressive. What a life. I always heard he was great, but I never saw it like this before. You did a good thing for him, Max."

"Holly is really happy. I think she got the natural history museum to take one of the globes. He made three. One's in Paris. This is the most elaborate and complete, but it's quirky. Anyway, she's happy. All his greatest work in one…You could almost call this his museum."

"Where is he?"

"Who?"

"Her dad."

"Ellis? I've got a crew out looking for him. If he wasn't such a genius, he'd be a pain in the ass; in fact, he is a pain. Don't tell Holly. Someone hangs with him day and night, and still he manages to wander away. He gets lost. Who's going to stop him when he wants to get lost? He's the world's greatest map guy. Please don't tell Holly." Max swallowed her name, and looked around the room. "His mind is good. He doesn't even have the Alzheimer's. He's still productive and everything. I guess he just loses his sense of direction."

"Where is Holly?"

"She's below, I think, in the virtual rooms, with Miriam, playing with the dildonics. Before we stopped working on it, Holly put her foot down, and insisted we make some men. After World Trade we stopped working on it at all. Too, I don't know, frivolous. Not appropriate. But we'll start again. But not yet."

Nathan touched the sandal, still inside his shirt. "Where do you keep this stuff?"

"I'll take you there. I want you to try your program, anyway. I think Toni is doing a great thing for you. You'll see." He took Nathan's elbow, and led him out of the room. "By the way, I'm sorry about you and Miriam. I didn't know he was going to bring her. It's awkward for us, you understand. We don't want to take sides."

"Shoot First." Nathan didn't know why he said that, but Max seemed to understand.

"Yeah. That too. But Holly says he's really a sweet guy; you know, a kind of alpha male take charge kind of a guy."

"But sweet."

"Yeah, that's what Holly says. Sweet. You know, she had a…"

"Yeah, I know about it. Is he the one who found Kevin the Kalashnikov?"

They stopped by one of the rooms off the basement corridor. Max pushed a door open and there was Miriam sitting in a recliner wearing some bulky goggles. Next to her a small console on wheels blinked and whirred. Holly watched from a nearby couch. The room was institutional, with cinderblock walls painted beige, and fluorescents covered with purple Balinese batiks, as the only touch of fun.

"Looks like a dentist's office," Nathan whispered. "Like she's sitting for a root canal."

Holly hushed them with a finger to her lips, and motioned them in. "Done in a sec," she whispered. Except for a dim Mona Lisa smile, and an occasional soft exclamation or twitch, Miriam registered little response from beneath the goggles.

"We didn't put much into decoration of the real," Max whispered. "Everything goes into the virtual. And to answer your question. No. Kevin managed that one for himself."

Holly stood up to help Miriam remove the goggles

and the sensor patches. "That was different," Miriam said, her eyes closed against the light. "But he was such a Schwarzneggery thing, a little too much for me. I'd like something more Brad Pittish, or a little Cary Grant type thing."

"Eventually you'll be able to make a request, and adjust phenotype graphics with that little wheel by the left thumb."

"If it were…" Miriam stopped talking when she opened her eyes and saw Nathan.

"Hi, Mims." He pulled the sandal from his pocket and held it out to her.

"O, I'd given it up for lost. Thanks," she said, taking it, but not meeting his eyes. He held onto it for a moment, as if trying to draw some feeling from her through the transparent golden straps.

"It's good to see you." A virtual grin stretched across her face when she saw her arms merchant look into the room. She jumped immediately into the curl his arm made to gather her against his side.

"Nathan, this is Reg," she said. "Reg Rogers."

The man leaned forward to shake Nathan's hand, and Nathan obliged. "Good to meet you, chum. Of course, you know, I've heard all about you. I take it with a grain of salt," Reg Rogers grinned. "I come with a grain of salt, myself. Ha."

Nathan looked at Miriam's face. She cast her glance downward.

"So how was the thing, kiddo?" Reg asked Miriam. "Enough porn for ya?"

"It's not porn," Max said firmly. Holly looked at Nathan and rolled her eyes.

"Well, whatever it is. How much do I owe you?"

"It's not for money, Reg. That's not it."

"I'm really sorry about this," Holly whispered to Nathan, taking his hand.

"Okay, then. A pleasure to experience your nifty new technology." He slapped Nathan on the back. "And I'm glad we met. Some day we've gotta talk, just to compare notes between guys," he winked, and with his arm around her, hustled Miriam out of the room. Nathan felt ready to kill anyone.

"He's really a really nice guy," Holly said. "You made him a little nervous."

"I made him nervous? We'll compare notes? What is that about? What does Miriam see in that? It's like she's a totally different person."

"We'll make it up to you in the virtual," Max said, guiding Nathan to the recliner. "You need to forget about him. Forget about her. Your philosophy should be—woman leaves you, get another woman."

"What the fuck do you know about it, Max?" He threw himself down into the chair. Anger lay on his heart like a shroud. "You know, maestro, you'd better take that gun away from Kevin." He was glad finally to have said that, but didn't intend it to sound so nasty.

Max stared at him, took a deep breath, then rubbed the conductive cream onto Nathan's temples and wrists, and started to attach the sensors.

"Did you hear me, Max? I said, you better take that Kalashnikov away from Kevin, before something horrible…"

"He'll get tired of it on his own."

"It's no toy, Max. Wasn't it right around the corner from here, that thing at wherever that high school was? Those two kids who…"

"Wait, I've got a better idea." Max pulled all the sensors off in one yank, and pulled a spandex suit from a closet built into the wall. "We've been working on these prototypes, produces a more generalized sensation, a little less specific to the zones, but the feelings are there. You're a grown-up, right. Get into this."

Nathan shook his head, stripped down to his skivvies, and pulled it on, snug as a wetsuit, but an okay fit. You could feel the grid of wires woven into the fabric.

"With a teenager you can't force him, you have to use finesse, Nate. He'll give me the gun eventually. We've started to talk to each other again. I've stated my objection to the gun…"

"Be a fucking father, Max. For chrissake. It's a goddam Kalashnikov. Take it away from him. Don't be an idiot. He can hurt a lot of people, not to mention himself. Be a father."

Max breathed deeply, and closed his eyes. Discussion over. He opened them again. "Okay. Are you ready now?"

Nathan knew he couldn't take it further then. He let Max snap the goggles onto a helmet, and slip it over his head, and then button some leads from the spandex onto the ear piece. "Relax. One…two…three…" He pushed Nathan back against the chair. "Enter."

There was a tickling rush of small shocks as the suit fired up, and then his eyes opened on a field of blue, which soon filled with an enormous blonde, like a double Pamela Anderson claymation figure, leaning towards him with a massive pucker. She didn't look as real as Kevin's doll.

"Max, she's huge." As she approached to sit on his lap, he felt a terrifying sensation of weight. "Max…"

"Whoops. Must have switched boxes. I thought this was your father program. Sorry. Try this one for a while. I'll find the other." Max took one of Nathan's gloved hands and guided his thumb to a small wheel on a joystick. "You can adjust the size." Max's voice came through the external auditory feed like muffled static from another world. "Default is always great big woman, but with the wheel at your thumb you can find a percentage menu, and drop it down. Her movements are randomized, a limited repertoire so far, until you feed her back some pleasure vibes, then she'll repeat that cycle until you click her out of it. There's also a kind of potluck option, where she just goes through some playfuk stuff, and messes with you. We haven't got her voice matrix set up yet. But she will fuck you if you figure her out."

"There's no smell, Max."

"That's a project."

A wash of mild tingling followed her great lips mopping down his belly. He clicked a button that dropped a stack of percentages into the space in front of him, like ducks on the toilet paper. As he reduced her by steps to twenty percent, he felt some surprisingly pleasant pops throughout his spandex.

"We haven't got the virtual furnishings in place yet, either; just a choice of beds and a chair, on the far right drop-down. Everything else is just sketched in to the default. Works for me though, as long as the cyberflesh shows up."

The twenty percent version kept flying at him, like a forward pass, swifter than her bulkier sister, and he played matador to let her go by. The palpability of her flesh when she touched was a surprise, though somewhat peculiar, like a feel of cool pudding. As soon as it brushed him, it flew back into its default dimensions, and he enjoyed the peculiar popping as he pixeled her down again. Occasionally she hove to for a penetration simulation, on her own initiative it seemed, without any signal from him. And it did feel vaguely like penetration, though he couldn't really locate the sensation in a specific organ. Her image disintegrated somewhat in the act, and then there was an uncomfortable sensation of wetness spread throughout the spandex grid.

He found a menu that allowed him to stabilize her size, speed, and position. He liked her best when she perched on his knee, at about the dimensions of a large macaw.

"I'm going to call you Hilda?" He watched her small doll face for a response as she went through a preset routine of plasticized expressions—come hither smiles, winks, puckers, lowered eyelids, panting. "Hilda was my alcoholic aunt, Brightwatch's sister. I wont try to explain Brightwatch to you. Hilda pickled herself in Key West, Palm Beach, Boca Raton, and Panama City. She took me to the Everglades once, when I was really little. She told me my father was an alligator, and for years I believed her.

In New York she'd visit, take me to the Met. Once she got tickets to Barnum and Bailey, for me and my friend Arnie. Arnie had fear of clowns, and these seats were close enough so the clowns would come right up to us, and I had to hide his head under my jacket. And she left us there with twenty dollars, and actually forgot about us, so then we had to find our way back downtown ourselves. She turned up three days later. It was the first time I'd ever seen anyone come off a bender, and I vowed never to get that way myself ever. She looked like she'd been dragged out of the East River, filthy, her clothes torn, her face scraped up. She smelled like the Gowanus canal. She was missing some teeth. Her watch was gone. Her jewelry. She thought it was funny to lose the valuables. "They're worth more to him than they are to me," she said to Brightwatch, who was cleaning her up, and I thought she might have meant whoever stole them from her, but she could have meant her ex-husband too, or both. All men, maybe. She never took me to Yankee Stadium, though, or Meadowlands, even though she knew at that time my passion for baseball, the total ache of my Yankee fandom. That was something the alligator would have done with me, I always thought, had I ever had Solomon Briggs in my life."

He had to lift the goggles to wipe his eyes. Max was still shuffling through the discs in the cabinet. "She was my buddy, my confidante. She understood me, and she understood Brightwatch in her way. She would listen to me. We talked way into the morning like brother and sister insomniacs. Yeah, but ten years ago she checked out. She liked the high octane rum, and that makes cheese of your liver, and then cancer grabbed her. So life since has been without Hilda, Hilda."

"You are a good listener." He grinned at the cybercritter. How ridiculous. He shifted her from his right to his left knee, but the weight sensation persisted on the right. He lifted that leg, and stomped on the floor, until Hilda came loose and drifted back into the bright blue cybermist, then came at him again in her default dimensions, her mouth so great it seemed she could swallow him. He clicked her down just before her pucker hit his mouth, diminished to a moist ping on his lower lip, her breasts jouncing tiny just below his chin. He grabbed her, and she wriggled like a dachshund in his hands, then he settled her back onto his knee, for some more talk.

"Found it," Max's voice sounded off somewhere in the void of reality.

"So then I went to Italy to look for my dad, Hilda;" Nathan whispered. "but what I got, I can't even say what I got; I wanted a trace of him maybe through his obsession with this Italian painter…" As soon as he said the word, "Italian," there he was, sitting as if at a cafe at the edge of the "campo" in what he recognized as a virtual Siena. Hilda flew from his knee, twisting into the greenish sky above the Palazzo Ducale like a deflating balloon. Siena pulsed, as if under a swell of the Adriatic. Then seamlessly, as if it was his own dream, he stood at the entrance to a spacious gallery, a long palace corridor. As he started down this corridor some paintings pushed out at him, suspended weightless in front of the walls. His mood had shifted to a forlorn sweetness that stirred in him nostalgia for something that had never been, as if there was a ritual of his father and family that existed only in a dreamlife he never been invited to enter before.

One after another the portraits that he recognized as those painted by his father's Antonello confronted him. At least his father had an overwhelming enthusiasm, an obsession. At least his father hadn't been some bland anybody. He'd had this passion. They weren't just paintings, they were presences. There again was the guy from Cefàlu, and the one who had summoned him (pssst!) in the Borghese museum. Nathan took them one by one into his consciousness as if each was a member of his family. Even the saints, on their gilded backgrounds, entered him as people, and Saint Sebastian exposed in glorious martyrdom, tied to his pillar in some ancient geometric cityscape, pierced by arrows, face gazing heavenwards, clear as October wind, a fragment of a pillar, broken, on the ground nearby, indifferent women gossiping on the parapets, distracted citizens conducting business by the wall, the body of a guard or companion lying in Mantegnesque foreshortening to his right; and further there were the several amazing faces of Christ bound to the pillar, rope around his neck, an expression that transcended all emotion; and Mary came forward hooded in such blue that only Mary Marvel from his memory of comic books ever wore, this Mary drafted into childbirth, carrying the son of her belief, held her hand extended into the world, after she's been told she'd been chosen; and there she was again in blue, seated on the throne with her astounding child, and even fragments of another ruined annunciation, and St. Jerome there, in his cubicle, reading passionately, long perspectives down the arched galleries and out the windows on either side of him, onto landscapes extending away out there, birds tilted in the sky. And the cat curled on the sill at his feet, and the pheasant there, and back in the shadows to the right, the lanky beast he recognized as the woeful lion he had seen on his journey to find more of his own father.

This was too much. How could he go on? He had to go on. He wanted more. He had to stop. He ripped the helmet off, and gasped as if surfacing from a deep dive. Max was right there to greet him in the real space.

"Man, you look so…unbelievable. I bet that was a trip for you." He pulled a disk from the player and held it up. A wave of revulsion overcame Nathan

"I wanted this to be a surprise," Max said. "I previewed it myself, and thought it was excellent. I was so happy for you. Toni is some kind of genius. She is Ms. Creativity. I can't wait to see what she does with the father, himself." He hugged Nathan, and leaned back to look into his eyes. "You see, it's the least we can do for you, to show some gratitude…I mean, you know how we…"

That Nathan had thought for some moments that this had been a vision of his own, and not some trick on himself turned his stomach. Everywhere trivial magic.

"…we appreciate you and…"

"It's okay, Max. Everything's cool. I don't need anything." It was true that he'd learned something from this.

Max handed him the cd all mirrory and prismatic, its plastic reflex of coloring tricky in the light, a mirror in which he couldn't even see himself. Would every great thing in the world be cheapened now by this trivial magic? Did he have to feel humiliated by this thrill that he had passed through his father's world?

"See. Now you have something to look at, and it doesn't ever wear out."

"Yes." Nathan needed to change the subject. His disappointment was too vague. He didn't want to seem ungrateful. Max had meant well. It was probably just his own mind that was intolerable, and if that's the case he had to change the subject. "Listen, Max," he said. "I've been thinking." He hadn't actually been thinking at all, but he hoped a shift of focus could be a relief. "If your offer of that piece of land below is still on the table, I'd like to look at it again. I think I might take you up on that."

"Of course it is. Why wouldn't…?"

"Well, I thought Miriam, maybe…"

"Worry not about Mimsy," Max dismissed it with a wave of his hand. "Her new gunner guy bought twelve lots, over five hundred acres. He's got his own firing range. I'll bet he's already given her a piece of her own, as part of the bargain."

"What bargain?"

"You know, a piece of pussy for a piece of property. Isn't that the way it works in the man's later years.""

"Not, I hope, with Miriam. You know her, but maybe not." What was most troubling was to be so wrong about the woman he thought he knew best.

"He tells us she's going to raise horses."

"That she'd love. That would definitely tempt her. She always wanted to keep one to ride in Central Park, but we never had that kind of money. This arrangement will be better. She never would have got that out of me."

"Got what?"

"Horses." He needed to stop talking about Miriam too, just as painful. "I'll go down there in the morning to have a look. I will own it, won't I, I mean…?" Everything felt uncomfortable and unreal to him now, even accepting this gift. The only property he had ever owned was a co-op apartment in Murray Hill. His financial wizardry never included real estate.

"Yeah. Nate. What do you think? We'll have to finesse the zoning, though. Whatever you build on it we'll have to build in my name, before I turn it over to you. I've got some good lawyers working on it; but I mean, it'll be under your control, your design, everything. Whatever restrictions apply, like zoning for a secondary building, all that."

"I can do a Stuckeys kind of a place, to keep up with the neighborhood," Nathan said, but didn't push his sarcasm any further.

Back in the living room, the gas fire burned merrily, without a crackle, but everyone was in too sober a mood to echo the merriment. Darkness had come, and with it heavier snow. Holly's father, Ellis Prefontaine, still hadn't reappeared. People surrounded her in the conversation pit, reassuring her that everything was okay. He couldn't be lost, they assured her. He was, after all, Ellis Prefontaine. His maps were definitive all over the world. Holly seemed to enjoy the attention. She didn't worry any more. In recent years her father had been lost plenty.

Nathan volunteered with a crew of other guests to snowshoe out, as part of a search grid, and all of them worked non-stop, flashlight beams batting futiley into the gauze of snow until three in the morning. When they got back they found the big bubble of a flag had collapsed under the weight of snow, and Max along with some of the guests was giddily slicing through the heavy stars and stripes with some kitchen knives, calling names of people who might have been trapped—"Brian" "Link" "Heather" "Rudy" "Grover" "Stacy"

"Sisko" "Starr." Everyone seemed to be taking this as another party game. Survivors popped laughing out of the wrinkled wilderness of cloth, no injuries yet. One of the musicians came running from the kitchen, brandishing poultry shears. He started cutting their equipment loose from the field of stars. Nathan saw Kevin in front of his room on the balcony, in a heavy trench coat, digging the chaos, the muzzle of his Kalashnikov lifted to point towards the source of the falling snow. He looked much older from this distance. Nathan was too tired to join this other frenzy. Maybe a disaster, but no tragedy here. He found his room, and his bed, and stripped to slide between the chilly sheets. He lay there thinking he'd tell Max to buy flannel. Under the polyester blankets he couldn't get the chill out of his bones, so he got up again to put on his pants and his down jacket and crawled back into bed as if he was setting off on an expedition, and didn't stop shivering till he fell into some genuine, incoherent dreams.

The next afternoon was already underway by the time Nathan arrived at the catered brunch. The dining room was nice, both spacious and cozy. A great brushed steel table accommodated over twenty people. One wall of the room was covered with a mural done by the ECCO group, the cooperative of artists from D.C. committed to individual anonymity, and collective success. The whole wall was done as a hyper-realistic portrayal of a lunchroom on some kind of illuminated liquid crystal screen, booths and a counter, the customers sitting around in Hopperesque lonely studies; and occasionally, by some other technological magic, these figures moved flatly to lift a spoon of pea soup, or turn the page of a newspaper. Entering the dining room was like a step into a diner, perhaps across the street from a Travelodge, even to a low murmur of background noise that decreased as the real guests increased, even to a sign near the door—Please Seat Yourself. The mural dimmed automatically as more people came to table.

Max and Holly had the brunch catered by what they called the "miraculous" Front Range Deli. It was run by Russian Jewish immigrants, profits skimmed by the local Russian mafia, bringing to the culture of the New West a welcome addition of flavored vodka, smoked fish, hot borscht, blinis, kasha, stuffed cabbage, and a handful of performers from the Don Rostov Cossack dancers, all torn loose into poverty by end of the millenium Russian chaos. They had defected and drifted down to Denver like the snow still accumulating out there.

Holly and Miriam were deep into a conversation at one corner of the table. Miriam gave him a quick glance as he grazed the buffet. Her Reg Rogers was not present. "I take it your dad is okay," Nathan asked Holly as he passed to find himself a seat at the table.

"O, he'll turn up. I'm sure. Since his accident he does this all the time, and he always survives. He's had tons of wilderness experience. Of course, maybe one time he won't," she said, almost blithely. "Whoops. Here's Tanya and her friend." She grabbed her plate, and stood up. "Sit down here. I need to tend to the girls. When Tiffany is here it's like mischief central." Thus Nathan got to sit down next to Miriam. He felt as if a hatch had opened to suck him out into a cold orbit.

They watched Holly intercept the girls, who had donned the oversize grey spandex dildonics suits and were tripping over them and giggling.

"Where did you find those suits?" Holly asked Tanya, who was very proud of herself, her expression pure self-righteous mischief. Nathan had forgotten how beautiful she was. He was almost embarrassed to look at her as much as he was drawn to her. Holly grabbed her arm and shook her slightly. "Did you go into the Off Limits?"

"A little bit," Tanya said. Even when being scolded she had a kind of natural dignity. "It wasn't an actual transgression type transgression. We just reached into the room and took the suits. We didn't step. We're sorry." She looked at her little friend, and they erupted into giggles. Tiffany then ran over to her parents, a couple dressed in matching powder blue/lemon yellow sweatsuits.

"You know you shouldn't go there, Tanya. That's a place for grown-ups only."

"I'm going to be a grownup. I'm in double figures,

and eleven is almost teenage." She waved at Nathan, and he felt a little thrill.

"You're still ten, and you're not a grown-up yet," her mother said.

"That is a matter for the courts to decide, and my birthday is next month, anyway," she said, with a great show of haughtiness

Holly looked at Nathan and Miriam. "She's not used to the house yet. No one really is." She sat Tanya down at the table, and Tiffany joined her again. "Just don't get any juice or cheese on those suits. Your daddy will have a fit." Holly left through the swinging doors into the kitchen.

Nathan turned to Miriam, whom he'd felt staring into his cheek. "Eat, " she said, her lips pulled tight against her teeth. "Don't worry about me."

"Wasn't," Nathan said, flipping a slice of sable with his knife. "Where's your man?" He could feel her eyes drilling through him.

"All I want to know is one thing." Her anger had a ferocity he'd never heard from her before. "I want to know, when I talked to you the last time on the phone, when you were in that town, wherever."

"Manfredonia."

"Manfredonia. That's the last time we talked. Was there someone with you in the room? Were you with a woman?"

"Why do you want to know now? What difference

does this make now?"

"I think I have a right to know."

"What right? Are you trying to justify dumping me for that…that…Poor Mims is feeling guilty?"

"You're such a prick. No. I don't need to justify anything."

He'd never heard her use the word, "prick" before, and it made him laugh. "So have you quit Loosenuts.com?"

"Loose**knit.** No. I still…I work from here, and I go to New York once a month for meetings. So, answer me."

"I don't see why I should."

"Shit. A simple question. Why can't you say yes or no?"

"Yes or no."

Miriam stood up, whipping her hair across her neck in exasperation, but she sat back down as Max approached, stood behind them and placed a hand on each of their shoulders. "Wait till you see these dancers. And, by the way, have you met our neighbors, the Elliot's. They're the parents of Tiffany over there, cute as a burrito. They get to play with the dildonics this afternoon." The mention of dildonics got the Elliots' attention. "Nate and Mims did it last night."

"Did you love it?" Mrs. Elliot asked, grinning just like her daughter.

"They made some new friends." Max reached between them to the center of the table and grabbed a fresh bagel to slice. "Virtual friends are the best kind. No splashback. Spotless fondling. They never stray. They never betray. After what happened 9/11 it's just what you need."

"I don't know what you two need, but everyone's been so tense since that. I hope this will relax us."

Nathan and Miriam both grimaced, uneasy to be taken for a couple again by the blue and yellow Elliot pair.

"I don't need no virtual." Max's dad made his entrance at the other end of the table, his scantily dressed girlfriend on his arm. "Viagra always does the trick." He slipped a hand under the girl's pink satin skating pants.

"I thought it was worthwhile," Nathan said to the Elliots. "It helps you confront your loneliness. It helps…"

"What loneliness?" Max interrupted. "It's all cyberbabes and virtual beefcake. You leave loneliness, all that bullshit, as soon as you put on the goggles."

"Well," said the Elliots, in blue and yellow unison. "We won't be lonely. We're doing it together."

"Okay. Here they are. Watch this," Max said, as a trio of men in Cossack costume strolled by the table, strumming balalaikas, and struck poses in their baggy black pants, belted with red sashes. Then two couples, the men in their cossack drag and the women fully petticoated, in flowered blouses, red ribbons in their hair, taps on their shoes, came out dancing.

"Isn't this great. It comes with the catering. Russia's loss, is Colorado's…"

Nathan spotted Kevin, half hidden behind the door, his baby Kalashnikov hung from his shoulder by a strap, as if he was thinking a Russian gun might give him some comraderie with the Russian people.

"Listen," Max sat down with Nathan in the seat Miriam had vacated, sneaking away. Nathan hadn't noticed her leaving. "Adriane Porcospina asked me if you were approachable about showing those drawings, those paintings, that you brought in the portfolios. None of us knew you did anything like that. Of course, you are the son of Brightwatch. She wants to show them in Scottsville, and then in Aspen too. She has a share of a gallery there. And she's affiliated in Paris. I mean, it's not small. It could be big. Expressionists of the new abstraction, or Sacred Abstract Expressionism, something like that she thinks is going to be really big." He slapped Nathan on the shoulder. "And we thought you were all about money."

"It's not…my father." But he stopped. He couldn't begin to sort out, to explain what he'd learned. Not for Max. He hadn't even sorted it out for himself yet.

"I'll tell you, she's got the eye. She's going to set the trends for the next decade, mark my words. A return to the spiritual, is what she says. Talk to her. What can it hurt?"

Nathan caught another chilling glimpse of Kevin and turned to face Max squarely. "Take the gun away from Kevin, Max."

"Kevin?"

Nathan saw the dancers' jolly, flirtacious moves, over Max's shoulder. "Look." Nathan thrust his chin to indicate where Kevin stood, half hidden behind a drape, holding the weapon as if it were a saxophone. "Take it away from him."

"Kevin? Shit…I can't."

"Take the gun away. Be a father."

"It's not…Not that simple. I can't…He has to…"

"Be a fucking father to your son, Max."

Someone leaned on a carhorn in the back of the house, and Max stood up. "Shit. I know who that is. I'll be right back." Max left, passing Holly, who came over to sit in the seat vacated. The dancers and balalaikists followed Max out the door.

"Miriam is crying. She's really upset. She went down to the sauna…"

"Why are you telling me this, Holly?"

"Well, you still have an affect on her, you see."

"That's reassuring. How's your father situation? Is he back?"

"Everyone's still looking, but it's best if I don't worry about it, so I don't. Like I said, too many times it's happened. And so far so good. Little map angels look after him."

"I think Max ought to do something about Kevin."

"That's not my son."

"I know, but you've seen his gun. He could kill someone. Himself."

"Look what Halfhawk gave me," Max said, returning, his cheeks pinked from the cold wind outdoors. He threw a string of shells onto the table. On the wall the mural characters lifted spoons to their mouths, and turned the pages of newspapers. The walls of the diner shifted from pale blue to lemon yellow. Everyone's silence staring down at the string of shells allowed an increase in the background noise programmed into the mural, and the room filled with clatter and din.

The girls began to giggle, for no reason, or just because grown-ups were silly.

Holly picked up the string, and let some of the shells lie on her palm. "Could these actually be the real thing?"

Nathan thought it was time now to do something himself. Pushing Max never worked. "I'm going to go over to him and take the gun away from that kid."

"Good luck, Natesy." Max laughed. "Don't let him shoot you."

Nathan took a long breath, and left the room. Max's flip attitude filled him with dread and nausea. The kid had gone out the door with the Russian dancers. Nathan stepped into white paradise. Wind had drifted billows of snow against the house.

"Hi, uncle Nate," he heard from the balcony. Kevin in commando drag was back upstairs, balanced on the balcony rail, using the gun to stabilize himself. "Watch this." Nathan darted for cover behind a decorative pillar as the boy leaped into a snowdrift, holding the Kalashnikov above his head as he sank into the snow. Nathan's courage sank with the boy into the snow. He was not so good with kids anyway, he rationalized; and it would be better for the family if Max stood up to his own son, and took control of the situation. It was getting late, anyway, and he had promised himself to go down to the acres he might be taking over. Maybe he could deal with Kevin later. Maybe the gun wasn't so bad, after all. Yes it was. But not a responsibility he should shoulder.

He picked up the snowshoes he'd worn the night before on the hunt for Ellis Prefontaine, got into the ski pants and down parka, and shushed around the collapsed tent, the brightly painted catamaran now half buried in snow, past the three lower bungalows, and headed towards the boxcar on the land that soon would be his. He knew vaguely where it was, down there behind the falling curtains, snow filling what he could start to think of as his own small piece of the American West. He said that aloud, and it sounded strange, "Small Piece Of The West." "Small West," an oxymoron for the twenty-first century.

It was already pretty late. His day had got off to a

late start, and the dark was setting in earlier now. He might have trouble seeing things now. Except for a diffuse reddish glow around some shadows in the air behind himself, when he looked back he could hardly make out the house through the snow. Without the frigid gusts occasionally pushing through, the air felt almost warm.

"Uncle Nate, Uncle Nate." It was Tanya, running after him from the house, tripping over her small snowshoes. "Can I go with you?"

"I'm taking a walk down to look at the land your dad wants me to have."

"You'll be our neighbor. I know. It's a happy thing. Can I come?"

"Where's your friend?"

"Tiffany had to go home with her mom and dad."

"Okay, but first go back to the house and tell your mom and dad you're with me, and tie up your snowshoes better, and get a warmer jacket."

She ran back to the house and he waited for her in the pelleting snow that dropped straight into the woods. Not since he'd been a kid, he reckoned, had he seen real snowflakes. What was it? The greasy air? It seemed a punishment to settle for this powder, these pellets. He missed the small intricacies settling onto the back of a glove.

"Hi," Tanya grabbed his hand when she got back, and they started walking down.

"I think Kevin is going to shoot his gun," Tanya said.

"Why do you say that?" He was surprised, for some reason, that she was aware of the gun.

"He's got bullets now. He bought some bullets."

Tanya let go of his hand, and pulled off her mitten, and let it hang by its safety pin from her parka sleeve. She tugged on his glove so he removed it, and she snuggled her small hand into his palm. He closed his fist around the nugget of warmth. She smiled up at him, not a little girl smile, but a smile that to him looked like a prediction of the woman she would become, a beautiful, dark, green-eyed woman. It made him feel goosey and proud.

She had a smile that stretched so far, he felt it stretch across his face too. He hardly noticed when, but his mood had changed. His happiness grew perhaps just from being outdoors. Or just from the girl's hand in his. The weather was big. He had crossed with her from the zone of anxiety into the zone of joy. The good world hustled at them through the dusk, and Tanya started to giggle and this joy penetrated his down jacket, his flannel shirt and insulated pants, his lycra longjohns. Her giggling embarrassed his loins, and he giggled with her. His skin felt effervescent, his heart open as a geyser. They were laughing at nothing, like kids at the threat of a tickle.

That was a light, he thought, flickering below

among the trees, and some slab dimly visible in the woods, the rectangle he took to be the boxcar. Someone still must inhabit that. Max hadn't yet got rid of whoever that was.

"Someone's down there," he said.

"I know," said Tanya, in her most apprehensive tones. "He's got thick strong teeth, and big big toes. He's a misanthroat, and he always tells the truth. He's the abominalable snowperson, and I don't think he's a very gregarious one." She sounded like she'd talked about this with her friends before. "He could be a terrorist."

Nathan pulled her close. "I don't think so."

In the light snowfall the boxcar among the trees looked enormous now, and alien, a dark frosted window onto some indecipherable eternity. How did anyone come to live here, like this? Nathan knew what he would tell the person, if someone was there.

The light was from an old lantern, hung from a corner of the car. The closer he got, the more he could see how neatly everything had been fixed up, a couple of windows cut into the front, the sliding door on one side sealed and welded shut, a small door cut into one end. It had been a refrigerated car, so was well insulated, and heatable in the winter by a small wood stove. The chimney poked out the side and rose above the junipers.

"Hello," Nathan spoke into the doorway that was

rolled all the way open, half of it covered by a patchwork of old plastic sheeting and fragments of windows tacked onto a screen door, the open half hung with a curtain of heavy felt. "Hello," he said again. "Anyone home?" Tanya hid behind him, excited. She had never been down here before. She kept pinching his thigh, so he grabbed her hand.

"It smells like batsmoke. It peeuugh," she whispered.

It was the pungent lair of a recluse. He nudged the felt aside.

"I won't look," said Tanya.

A couple of candles guttered by the old washtub that served as a sink, drained with a piece of garden hose through the floor. It was intoxicating to look in, a window into the simple elegance of someone's survival, who had pieced a life together from scratch, out of absence, so to speak. It looked weird, and it looked familiar. A shelf full of stones and seashells. The sea? Some feathered artifacts. A raven's wing. A hand-carved paddle. Everything must have meant something. Behind the stove, a large circular sawmill blade, like a blank mandala. He could see no person inside, but when he turned around he saw something he had missed; almost disappeared into the snow was what could once have been an easy chair. In it a large felt hat, stetson in the Spanish style, sat upon a shape, everything covered in snow. Here was someone sitting in a chair, someone buried in winter.

He approached, lifting the snowshoes and setting them down slowly, lightly, to avoid any squeak. Tanya followed, hanging onto the hem of his jacket. The figure was almost obliterated into whiteness. He must have been sitting there at least from when the storm began. "Hello sir, hello mam." Nathan reached out tentatively to touch the shoulder, and brushed off some snow. The figure didn't budge. Perhaps frozen dead, Nathan thought. But the mouth released puffs of steam at regular intervals. He tried to shake the chair, but that was frozen to the ground. He carefully lifted the broad-brimmed hat, revealing a shaved head. A line of curious welts, like an intermittent scar, ringed the temple and forehead, mimicking a crown of thorns. This idea amused Nathan. He shook the snow off it and replaced the hat. The eyes opened.

For some long moments Nathan stared into those dark opacities, waiting for a sign that the eyes looked back at him. The illumination all around pushed from orange to red. Rusty shadows brushed across the figure. This was like some infernal scene, except that Nathan felt so good. Tanya stepped out from behind him, her face lit as if by a light from the netherworld. She started to laugh, and he tapped her on the head to signal her to stop, but then he started laughing too. Maybe the infernal is too amusing, and that's the problem. This old one was some laughable Beelzebub.

Nathan finally gathered himself. "My name is Nathan Briggs. I'll soon be owning this land, and I want you to know something first." He paused, and watched the dark eyes again for a response. Nothing. The eyes seemed to follow Tanya, who had moved back behind Nathan, and peeked out first from one side, then from the other. His tongue flicked like a serpent's, feeling for the heat. Nathan spaced out a moment, forgetting what else he wanted to say. Tanya was giggling again. Then Nathan retrieved his words. "You see, if everything goes right, where you live is going to be on my land. At least, I think. I feel like we can't really own land anyway." The idea sounded flat and old, not like any real thought he'd ever had. "But I don't want you to worry. I want you to know you can continue to live here."

At first the head nodded, totally hiding the face under the hat brim; then the covering of snow jumped slightly, as if some small jolt had undermined it. "I will hit you." The voice was slow and big, turning snow into thunder.

"You can stay as long as you need to. I don't expect…"

"Go away. I will hit you." The person stood up slowly. From under his layers of blankets he raised an old Louisville Slugger in his right hand. Tanya screamed.

"It's not…I won't…"

"I will hit you now. You go, or I will hit you. Yes."

By the voice, this must be a man. He scanned the surroundings as if homing in on Nathan's sound, and turned towards him with the bat poised above his head. Perhaps he was blind.

"Okay." Nathan stepped away. Tanya had already run to hide behind a tree. "I'm going now. Goodbye. I just wanted you to know."

"Thank you."

Nathan couldn't figure if the thanks were for his leaving, or for expressing his willingness to let the fellow stay.

Snow fell heavily again. Was the redness in his mind, or was this real red snow?

"Do you see all the redness?" he asked the girl.

Her hand was balled tightly, turned like a pestle in his palm. "It's the night," she said. "Sometimes it comes with bloodshot eyes."

The lights of distant Denver? He walked around the boxcar and started back up towards the house through the metallic silence of the trees. Should he have helped that guy back into his warm place? He'd obviously chosen to be outside. How can anyone help anyone? The man wanted to be in the storm. Let the man rest out in the storm.

"Psssst!"

"O no," said Tanya, and jumped behind him again.

Nathan turned. That pssst pssst pssst. He would never learn to ignore that. Someone motioned at him from the small door cut into the side of the boxcar.

"Just a moment of your time," he heard the man say. Nathan couldn't deal with his vulnerability to the pssst. When he got close to the door he saw there, backlit by a blackened kerosene lamp, a well dressed older man, although somewhat disheveled. He felt Tanya clinging to his thigh. "Could you tell me," he asked. "What are the exact coordinates of this place?" The old man reached out to take Nathan's hand, and he straightened up as if the younger man's grip gave him some strength. "I've taken shelter here, provided generously by an anonymous party, until I can determine again my exact position on the graticule, the azimuth of return, I should say, you know, the attitude, mine, that is, along this isopectic linearity."

With some relief, Nathan realized who this was. "You're Holly's father, aren't you? Mr. Prefontaine?"

He pulled Nathan into the boxcar, where the warmth felt peculiar. Tanya let go of him, remained at the door. "Still peeeeughy in there."

The old man whispered conspiratorially. "Who I am is of no consequence. Where I am is at issue, from my perspective, and I'm sure from that of the others."

"You're very right, Mr. Prefontaine. Holly is so worried. Your daughter." Nathan knew that wasn't true.

She was totally casual about this disappearance. So was Ellis Prefontaine. "And this is your granddaughter." Nathan turned to look for Tanya, but she had hidden herself.

"Correct, actually. I am the father. And the grandfather. Indeed, that's who I am, and all my life I have been making maps, some of them drawn by hand." He leaned forward to whisper. "Even freehand." He laughed as if that was a joke. "But incorrect about the daughter. She would prefer me dead, and in that way always she could locate me."

"I know about you, Mr. Prefontaine. I've wanted to meet you, and Holly promised, and here you are. And she esteems you, and loves you. Your room in that house is so beautiful."

"Bullshit, Mr.…Mr.…?"

"Briggs."

"Bullshit, Mr. Briggs. You're talking about my tomb in that hideous house. I have made maps all my life, and now it is my pleasure to be lost. So then, Mr. Briggs, if you could just find out for me what the numbers are. A few seconds off of latitude or longitude is of little consequence to me; eventually I'll draw my way back, hopefully after most of the weasels are gone."

"You should come back with me, sir."

"Please, Mr. Briggs, just bring the numbers, and if you do, I will show you something you never could have dreamed."

Nathan stepped back into the more comfortable cold outside. He felt Tanya grab his jacket from behind. Perhaps he would tell them at the house that he had found Ellis Prefontaine. Perhaps not. "I'm going back, Mr. Prefontaine. You should come."

"Good. Go. You are a tiresome person, which doesn't mean I haven't taken a liking to you."

Nathan grabbed Tanya's arm, and held her by her shoulders in front of himself. "And this is your granddaughter, Tanya."

"I know my granddaughter. Baybilbuk, Tankokokookooroo."

"Bilbukbay Granbubbles."

It occured to Nathan that Tanya probably knew where her grandfather was all along.

"Is this your fiancé?" The old man asked her.

"Yes, Granbubbs. But I must tell you we have been married for many years," she posed melodramatically, "and I've grown so tired of him." She lifted the back of her hand to her forehead. "He will never grant me my freedom."

"Then you have to take it for yourself, Kokookooroo." She jumped into his arms and kissed him, then dropped back down to take Nathan's hand. Nathan had paid most attention to Kevin in this family and had seen Tanya only for her beauty, never before for her precocity.

"You should come with us."

"No way, as they say. You see, I am a boring one too. I've earned the right to be boring, and that's what I like about you. And I've earned the right to be lost. I hope you have listened to me."

"Arrivederci," Nathan said. "Ciao." He turned and stepped away.

"Yes," the old man leaned out the door and shouted after him. "Remember the earth is an oblate spheroid. Had it been prolate, that would have made all the difference."

Nathan doubted that anything could have made a difference. The shape of the world was not the world. They started back towards the house, their track down already obliterated by this new snow. For all that had happened he still felt good. He was glad to have found Mr. Prefontaine, and recognized in his face one of the faces from his father's Antonello. He had seen it first in a book, and then in the virtual of the night before, the face of San Nicola da Bari. This was in a work from the museum in Vienna. It amazed him that he remembered out here in the snow. There was the same tender sadness in the eyes and mouth. Finding Prefontaine, he had found another scrap of his father. By bits and clips he was cobbling together a someone, a father of his own.

Tanya ran off to a tree that was clear of snow at the roots on one side. She dropped her pants and squatted. When she came back, Nathan said, "Wasn't that cold?"

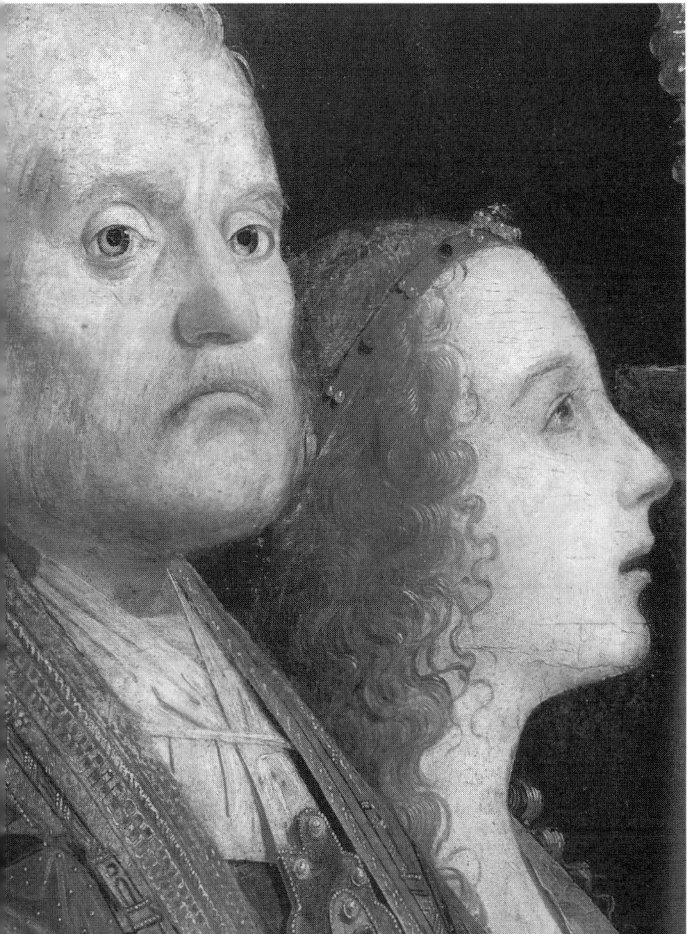

She held her arms up for him to lift and carry her. "I had to pee." She covered her face with her hand to hide her blushing, and then laid her head on his shoulder.

He felt good, walking slowly on the red tinged snow, carrying the little girl in his arms. Really good. Was the light of every city a different color in the snow? Denver, red; Pittsburgh, yellow? He would, he suddenly realized, sell whatever that was in those portfolios, as much as he could. It was his inheritance. Who could ever predict what a father gives his son? It might save him from ever having to look at the market again. That would be a relief, to be outside the vortex of those essential trivialities. People wrapped like mummies in the market's spiritless winding. Once it had been exhilarating, but now… And if all the paintings, all the drawings sold, he could do more, on his own. Why not? He was the son of Brightwatch. He understood what they were, and could do more of them. This was his heritage.

He looked around, himself in the midst of this darkening woods, branches all heavy with their rosy encumbrance of snow. He put Tanya by the roots of a tree blown free of snow, then pulled up a piece of metal half buried against a stump. It was an old tractor seat, welded to a bar of steel, for some lost purpose. He didn't know why it made him smile. He felt good. This was something he'd always wanted to do. He scooped the snow out from under some branches laden and drooped into a drift. This would be a little shelter for themselves. He felt good about this. They would go back to the house eventually, but not yet. He snapped some dead branches from trees around, and gathered them into a heap inside the snow shelter. He'd read about this a long time ago, in a book in high school. Inside the shelter the snow was white, though it fell outside still with its reddish tinge. He thought about Saffronski. It felt good to think about her. He knew he would see her again. Maybe she would be married. Maybe by then she would have two kids. Maybe she'd have a girl friend, instead. The red snow falls on Saffronski and her two kids. The red snow falls on her girl friend too. It falls into the galleries that keep the paintings of Antonello. It falls through the stone, into the room where he had been with his father's bones. He knew now he would never tell about that, not to anyone. He felt so good, about his friends, and even his losses. Red snow falls on Miriam as she dives into the Olympics.

Back at the house party, Deborah and Agrom broke away from dinner with her parents and their friends to go outside in the snow. Agrom was the first guy she'd brought home, Deborah mused, that her parents actually liked. A far cry from Simit, her Rastafarian dude she'd brought last time from MoBay. Her father called him Mr. Spliff, and actually banned him from the house.

That they liked Agrom was hopeful. They were amazed, as was she, at how fast he'd learned English.

Outside they started throwing snow at each other and laughing in the cold, and kissing, and then they began to build a snowman. He felt like a kid with her, and she loved his forceful energy.

"Shush," he said, suddenly, when he heard a sound immediately familiar, totally unexpected, that he knew to be a Kalashnikov. Loud, but like potatoes hitting a wall. He'd hoped never to hear that sound again.

"Look," she said, and pointed at a young kid on the balcony, firing a gun into the air.

"Shit, Zenepe," said Agrom, not noticing his mistake, as he pushed Deborah out of harm's way under the balcony, and ran up the staircase.

"Be careful, Agrom," Deborah said. *"Stai attento,"* she repeated in Italian, wishing she knew Albanian.

Agrom stepped onto the balcony and like a fool, as if he'd forgotten everything he knew about combat, he shouted at Kevin in Albanian, who turned the gun on him, and without thinking, or knowing what he was doing, squeezed off a measure of rounds, several of which found Agrom.

"Shit. Shit. Shit." Agrom grabbed his stomach. "Life is stupid," he thought. "Not even accident, no irony, no tragic…Life is stupid."

Tanya woke up under the tree, and looked startled.

"Mamma," she called, and then she saw Nathan bending over to pick her up. He carried her into the little cave he had made under the snow-laden branch of the tree. It was very cozy. They looked at each other when they heard the popping sounds from the direction of the house.

"That's not very reassuring," Tanya said.

Her vocabulary, her precocious ironies, made him laugh.

Rapid fire again. "Not to laugh, Uncle Nate. That's my brother, my half brother. I told you."

He suddenly understood what pleasure there could be in that, in Kevin's enjoying that. He was just a kid. Red snow falls through the thrill of a boy's bullets. Nathan felt really good, life was good just then, to crawl into the space under a dome of snow on his own land. He wanted to try this since he'd first read about it. He pulled a box of matches, that had "Fiera Nazionale 2001" printed on it. "Galatina" on the other side. If he remembered right, that huge machine he vaguely purchased then, it would fit nicely on this land. He lit the whole box of matches, and threw it into the branches. He was getting cold. Tanya crawled over to sit against his chest, between his legs, a bundle of warmth. And fire was always warm.

"I love you, Uncle Nate. How long do you think we can hold out here? Do you think we've got a chance?

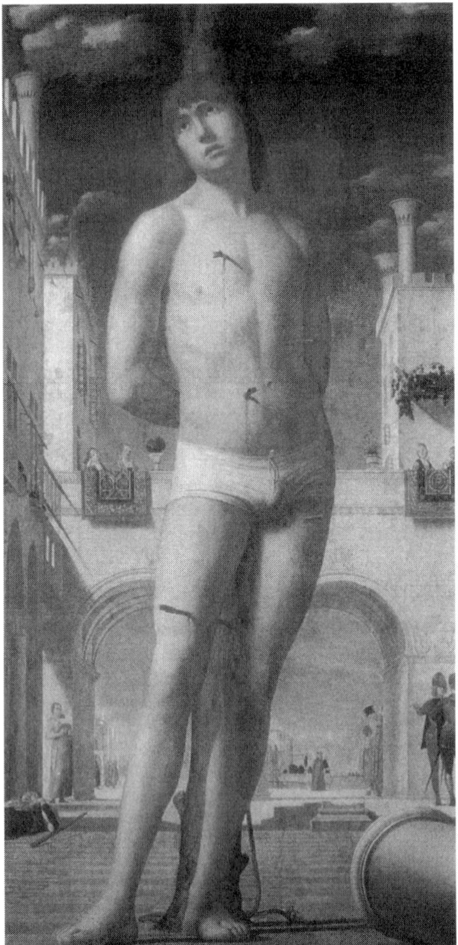

Maybe we can go get mom and dad down later. If we all pull together…" She looked into his face with an expression on hers of mock gravity.

Love rocked his bones, like a tremor in the earth.

She pressed harder into his chest. "Maybe not mom and dad. But definitely I am going to marry you, as soon as I am as big as you are, and mature too. And it won't be infestuous because…"

"Incestuous."

"It wont be incestuous because you're not my real uncle, but you're my favorite uncle."

"Tanya. Tell me the truth. Have you known all this time where your grandfather was?"

She grinned across her whole face. "I am Tankokokookooroo. And I have a question too."

"That's good," he said. "What's your question?"

"My question is," she snuggled against him. "What comes next?"

He squeezed her close. "Something else happens."

"Good." She wiggled against his belly.

This was something perfect, he thought. What had happened in the other story? The fire had melted the snow, and it slipped from a branch to snuff the flames. There were wolves involved too. There was freezing to death. That was then, and this is now. This fire was slow to catch. If something went wrong, there was always Max's house again, but maybe not. He didn't want to be numb any more. At least when he closed his eyes he didn't see the towers collapsing any more. "Fire will be nice," she said. He watched the branches, to see if there could be ignition. Ignition was always beautiful.

"And I have another question," Tanya said.

"Good," said Nathan, and kissed the top of her head.

GREEN INTEGER
Pataphysics and Pedantry

Douglas Messerli, *Publisher*

Essays, Manifestos, Statements, Speeches, Maxims,
Epistles, Diaristic Notes, Narratives, Natural Histories,
Poems, Plays, Performances, Ramblings, Revelations
and all such ephemera as may appear necessary
to bring society into a slight tremolo of confusion
and fright at least.

*

Green Integer Books

1 Gertrude Stein *History, or Messages from History*
ISBN: 1-55713-354-9 $5.95
2 Robert Bresson *Notes on the Cinematographer*
ISBN: 1-55713-365-4 $8.95
3 Oscar Wilde *The Critic As Artist* ISBN: 1-55713-368-9 $9.95
4 Henri Michaux *Tent Posts* ISBN: 1-55713-328-x $10.95
5 Edgar Allan Poe *Eureka: A Prose Poem*
ISBN: 1-55713-329-8 $10.95
6 Jean Renoir *An Interview* ISBN: 1-55713-330-1 $9.95
7 Marcel Cohen *Mirrors* ISBN: 1-55713-313-1 $12.95
8 Christopher Spranger *The Effort to Fall*
ISBN: 1-892295-00-8 $8.95
9 Arno Schmidt *Radio Dialogs I* ISBN: 1-892295-01-6 $12.95
10 Hans Christian Andersen *Travels* ISBN: 1-55713-344-1 $12.95
11 Christopher Middleton *In the Mirror of the Eighth King*
ISBN: 1-55713-331-x $9.95
12 James Joyce *On Ibsen* ISBN: 1-55713-372-7 $8.95
13 Knut Hamsun *A Wanderer Plays on Muted Strings*
ISBN: 1-892295-73-3 $10.95

14 Henri Bergson *Laughter: An Essay on the Meaning of the Comic*
ISBN: 1-892295-02-4 $11.95
15 Michel Leiris *Operratics* ISBN: 1-892295-03-2 $12.95
16 Sergei Paradjanov *Seven Visions* ISBN: 1-892295-04-0 $12.95
17 Hervé Guibert *Ghost Image* ISBN: 1-892295-05-9 $10.95
18 Louis-Ferdinand Céline *Ballets without Music, without Dancers, without Anything* ISBN: 1-892295-06-7 $10.95
19 Gellu Naum *My Tired Father* ISBN: 1-892295-07-5 $8.95
20 Vicente Huidobro *Manifest Manifestos*
ISBN: 1-892295-08-3 $12.95
21 Gérard de Nerval *Aurélia* ISBN: 1-892295-46-6 $11.95
22 Knut Hamsun *On Overgrown Paths* ISBN: 1-892295-10-5 $12.95
23 Martha Ronk *Displeasures of the Table*
ISBN: 1-892295-44-x $9.95
24 Mark Twain *What Is Man?* ISBN: 1-892295-15-6 $10.95
25 Antonio Porta *Metropolis* ISBN: 1-892295-12-1 $10.95
26 Sappho *Poems* ISBN: 1-892295-13-x $10.95
27 Alexei Kruchenykh *Suicide Circus: Selected Poems*
ISBN: 1-892295-27-x $12.95
28 José Donoso *Hell Has No Limits* ISBN: 1-892295-14-8 $10.95
29 Gertrude Stein *To Do: Alphabets and Birthdays*
ISBN: 1-892295-16-4 $9.95
30 Joshua Haigh [Douglas Messerli] *Letters from Hanusse*
ISBN: 1-892295-30-x $12.95
31 Federico García Lorca *Suites* ISBN: 1-892295-61-x $12.95
32 Tereza Albues *Pedra Canga* ISBN: 1-892295-70-9 $12.95
33 Rae Armantrout *The Pretext* ISBN: 1-892295-39-3 $9.95
34 Nick Piombino *Theoretical Objects* ISBN: 1-892295-23-7 $10.95
35 Yang Lian *Yi* ISBN: 1-892295-68-7 $14.95
36 Olivier Cadiot *Art Poetic'* ISBN: 1-892295-22-9 $12.95
37 Andrée Chedid *Fugitive Suns: Selected Poems*
ISBN: 1-892295-25-3 $11.95
38 Hsi Muren *Across the Darkness of the River*
ISBN: 1-931243-24-7 $9.95

39 Lyn Hejinian *My Life* ISBN: 1-931243-33-6 $10.95
40 Hsu Hui-cheh *Book of Reincarnation* ISBN: 1-931243-32-8 $9.95
41 Henry David Thoreau *Civil Disobedience*
ISBN: 1-892295-93-8 $6.95
42 Gertrude Stein *Mexico: A Play* ISBN: 1-892295-36-9 $5.95
43 Lee Breuer *La Divina Caricatura: A Fiction*
ISBN: 1-931243-39-5 $14.95
44 Régis Bonvicino *Sky Eclipse: Selected Poems*
ISBN: 1-892295-34-2 $9.95
45 Raymond Federman *The Twofold Vibration*
ISBN: 1-892295-29-6 $11.95
46 Tom La Farge *Zuntig* ISBN: 1-931243-06-9 $13.95
47 *The Song of Songs: Shir Hashirim* ISBN: 1-931243-05-0 $9.95
48 Rodrigo Toscano *The Disparities* ISBN: 1-931243-25-5 $9.95
49 Else Lasker-Schüler *Selected Poems* ISBN: 1-892295-86-5 $11.95
50 Gertrude Stein *Tender Buttons* ISBN: 1-931243-42-5 $10.95
51 Armand Gatti *Two Plays: The 7 Possibilities for Train 713
Departing from Auschwitz* and *Public Songs
Before Two Electric Chairs* ISBN: 1-931243-28-x $14.95
52 César Vallejo *Aphorisms* ISBN: 1-931243-00-x $9.95
53 Ascher/Straus *ABC Street* ISBN: 1-892295-85-7 $10.95
54 Djuna Barnes *The Antiphon* ISBN: 1-892295-56-3 $12.95
55 Tiziano Rossi *People on the Run* ISBN: 1-931243-37-9 $12.95
56 Michael Disend *Stomping the Goyim* ISBN: 1-931243-10-7 $11.95
57 Hagiwara Sakutarō *Howling at the Moon: Poems and Prose*
ISBN: 1-931243-01-8 $11.95
58 Rainer Maria Rilke *Duino Elegies* ISBN: 1-931243-07-7 $10.95
59 OyamO *The Resurrection of Lady Lester*
ISBN: 1-892295-51-2 $8.95
60 Charles Dickens *A Christmas Carol* ISBN: 1-931243-18-2 $8.95
61 Mac Wellman *Crowtet I: Murder of Crow* and *The Hyacinth Macaw*
ISBN: 1-892295-52-0 $11.95
62 Mac Wellman *Crowtet II: Second-hand Smoke* and
The Lesser Magoo ISBN: 1-931243-71-9 $11.95

63 Pedro Pietri *The Masses Are Asses* ISBN: 1-892295-62-8 $8.95
64 Luis Buñuel *The Exterminating Angel* ISBN: 1-931243-36-0 $11.95
65 Paul Snoek *Hercules, Richelieu,* and *Nostradamus*
ISBN: 1-892295-42-3 $10.95
66 Eleanor Antin *The Man without a World: A Screenplay*
ISBN: 1-892295-81-4 $10.95
67 Dennis Phillips *Sand* ISBN: 1-931243-43-3 $10.95
68 María Irene Fornes *Abingdon Square* ISBN: 1-892295-64-4 $9.95
69 Anthony Powell *O, How the Wheel Becomes It!*
ISBN: 1-931243-23-9 $10.95
70 Julio Matas, Carlos Felipe and Virgilio Piñera *Three Masterpieces of Cuban Drama* ISBN: 1-892295-66-0 $12.95
71 Kelly Stuart *Demonology* ISBN: 1-892295-58-x $9.95
72 Ole Sarvig *The Sea Below My Window*
ISBN: 1-892295-79-2 $13.95
73 Vítězslav Nezval *Antilyrik and Other Poems*
ISBN: 1-892295-75-x $10.95
74 Sam Eisenstein *Rectification of Eros* ISBN: 1-892295-37-7 $10.95
75 Arno Schmidt *Radio Dialogs II* ISBN: 1-892295-80-6 $13.95
76 Murat Nemat-Nejat *The Peripheral Space of Photography*
ISBN: 1-892295-90-3 $9.95
77 Adonis *If Only the Sea Could Sleep: Love Poems*
ISBN: 1-931243-29-8 $11.95
78 Stephen Ratcliffe *SOUND/(system)* ISBN: 1-931243-35-2 $12.95
79 Dominic Cheung *Drifting* ISBN: 1-892295-71-7 $9.95
80 Gilbert Sorrentino *Gold Fools* ISBN: 1-892295-67-9 $14.95
81 Paul Celan *Romanian Poems* ISBN: 1-892295-41-5 $10.95
82 Elana Greenfield *At the Damascus Gate: Short Hallucinations*
ISBN: 1-931243-49-2 $10.95
83 Anthony Powell *Venusberg* ISBN: 1-892295-24-5 $10.95
84 Jean Frémon *Island of the Dead* ISBN: 1-931243-31-x $12.95
85 Arthur Schnitzler *Lieutenant Gustl* ISBN: 1-931243-46-8 $9.95
86 Wilhelm Jensen *Gradiva* Sigmund Freud *Delusion and Dream in Wilhelm Jensen's Gradiva* ISBN: 1-892295-89-x $13.95

87 Andreas Embirikos *Amour, Amour* ISBN: 1-931243-26-3 $11.95
89 Kier Peters *A Dog Tries to Kiss The Sky 7 Short Plays*
ISBN: 1-931243-30-1 $12.95
90 Knut Hamsun *The Last Joy* ISBN: 1-931243-19-0 $12.95
91 Paul Verlaine *The Cursed Poets* ISBN: 1-931243-15-8 $11.95
92 Toby Olson *Utah* ISBN: 1-892295-35-0 $12.95
93 Sheila E. Murphy *Letters to Unfinished J.*
ISBN: 1-931243-59-x $10.95
94 Arthur Schnitzler *Dream Story* ISBN: 1-931243-48-4 $11.95
95 Henrik Nordbrandt *The Hangman's Lament: Poems* $10.95
96 André Breton *Arcanum 17* ISBN: 1-931243-27-1 $12.95
97 Joseph Conrad *Heart of Darkness* ISBN: 1-892295-49-0 $10.95
98 Mohammed Dib *L.A. Trip: A Novel in Verse*
ISBN: 1-931243-54-9 $11.95
99 Mario Luzi *Earthly and Heavenly Journey of Simone Martini*
ISBN: 1-931243-53-0 $12.95
101 Jiao Tung *Erotic Recipes: A Complete Menu for Male Potency Enhancement* ISBN: 1-892295-84-9 $8.95
102 André Breton *Earthlight* ISBN: 1-931243-27-1 $12.95
103 Chen I-chi *The Mysterious Hualien* ISBN: 1-931243-14-x $9.95
105 William Carlos Williams *The Great American Novel*
ISBN: 1-931243-52-2 $10.95
112 Paul Celan *Threadsuns* ISBN: 1-931243-75-1 $12.95
113 Paul Celan *Lightduress* ISBN: 1-931243-74-3 $12.95
114 Fiona Templeton *Delirium of Interpretations*
ISBN: 1-892295-55-5 $10.95
116 Oswald Egger *Room of Rumor: Tunings*
ISBN: 1-931243-66-2 $10.95
117 Deborah Meadows *Representing Absence*
ISBN: 1-931243-77-8 $9.95
119 Reina María Rodriquez *Violet Island and Other Poems*
ISBN: 1-892295-65-2 $12.95
120 Ford Madox Ford *The Good Soldier* ISBN: 1-931243-62-x $10.95
121 Amelia Rosselli *War Variations* ISBN: 1-931243-55-7 $14.95

122 Charles Bernstein *Shadowtime* ISBN: 1-933382-00-7 $11.95
123 Ko Un *Ten Thousand Lives* ISBN: 1-931243-55-7 $14.95
124 Émile Zola *The Belly of Paris* ISBN: 1-892295-99-7 $15.95
127 Harry Martinson *Views from a Tuft of Grass*
ISBN: 1-931243-78-6 $10.95
128 Joe Ross *EQUATIONS=equals* ISBN: 1-931243-61-1 $9.95
129 Norberto Luis Romero *The Arrival of Autumn in Constantinople*
ISBN: 1-892295-91-1 $12.95
131 Jean Grenier *Islands* ISBN: 1-892295-95-4 $12.95
140 Anton Chekhov *A Tragic Man Despite Himself: The Complete Short Plays* ISBN: 1-931243-17-4 $24.95
142 Steve Katz *Antonello's Lion* ISBN: 1-931243-82-4 $14.95
143 Gilbert Sorrentino *New and Selected Poems 1958-1998*
ISBN: 1-892295-82-2 $14.95
147 Douglas Messerli *First Words* ISBN: 1-931243-41-7 $10.95
163 Dieter M. Gräf *Tousled Beauty* ISBN: 1-933382-01-5 $11.95

Green Integer EL-E-PHANT Books (6 x 9 format)

EL-1 Douglas Messerli, ed. *The PIP Anthology of World Poetry of the 20th Century, Volume 1* ISBN: 1-892295-47-4 $15.95
EL-2 Douglas Messerli, ed. *The PIP Anthology of World Poetry of the 20th Century, Volume 2* ISBN: 1-892295-94-6 $15.95
EL-3 Régis Bonvicino, Michael Palmer, and Nelson Ascher, eds.; revised and reedited by Douglas Messerli
The PIP Anthology of World Poetry of the 20th Century, Volume 3: Nothing the Sun Could Not Explain—20 Contemporary Brazilian Poets ISBN: 1-931243-04-2 $15.95
EL-4 Douglas Messerli, ed. *The PIP Anthology of World Poetry of the 20th Century, Volume 4* ISBN: 1-892295-87-3 $15.95
EL-51 Larry Eigner *readiness / enough / depends / on*
ISBN: 1-892295-53-9 $12.95

EL-51 Larry Eigner *readiness / enough / depends / on*
ISBN: 1-892295-53-9 $12.95
EL-52 Martin Nakell *Two Fields That Face and Mirror Each Other*
ISBN: 1-892295-97-0 $16.95
EL-53 Arno Schmidt *The School for Atheists:
A Novella=Comedy in 6 Acts*
ISBN: 1-892295-96-2 $16.95
EL-54 Sigurd Hoel *Meeting at the Milestone*
ISBN: 1-892295-31-8 $15.95
EL-55 Leslie Scalapino *Defoe* ISBN: 1-931243-44-1 $14.95
EL-56 Sam Eisenstein *Cosmic Cow* ISBN: 1-931243-45-X $16.95